WHO NEEDS MISTLETOE?
BY
KATE HOFFMANN

AND

NO HOLDING BACK
BY
ISABEL SHARPE

GW00726150

MILLS
& BOON

Dear Reader,

If a girl is going to be lost for twenty-four hours, my choice would probably be a high-end department store or the food court at a local mall. But throw in a handsome companion and I might opt for a deserted tropical island. After all, where else would clothing be optional?

In *Who Needs Mistletoe?* I had a chance to combine a bit of *Survivor*, a dash of my last Caribbean vacation and a few other secret fantasies to pen my latest effort for Blaze®. Added to that was a little bit of Christmas, too. It's not the typical Christmas story—no twinkling tree or stacks of wrapped presents. But hopefully this book will give you more than a little holiday cheer.

So enjoy this escape to the South Pacific while you're drinking eggnog and sitting in front of the fire. And have a wonderful holiday season!

Happy reading,

Kate Hoffmann

WHO NEEDS MISTLETOE?

BY
KATE HOFFMANN

All the characters in this book have no existence outside the imagination of
the author, and have no relation whatsoever to anyone bearing the same name
or names. They are not even distantly inspired by any individual known or
unknown to the author, and all the incidents are pure invention.

First published in Great Britain 2010
Harlequin Mills & Boon Limited,
Eton House, 18-24 Paradise Road, Richmond, Surrey TW9 1SR

© Peggy A. Hoffmann 2008

ISBN: 978 0 263 88148 6

14-1110

Harlequin Mills & Boon policy is to use papers that are natural, renewable
and recyclable products and made from wood grown in sustainable forests.
The logging and manufacturing processes conform to the legal environmental
regulations of the country of origin.

Printed and bound in Spain
by Litografia Rosés S.A., Barcelona

Kate Hoffmann lives in a small town in south-eastern Wisconsin with her two cats and her computer. In her spare time she enjoys golf, genealogy and gardening. She is also involved in local musical theatre activities with school students.

1

THE ARTIFICIAL CHRISTMAS TREE looked even tackier than it had the previous year, the plastic pine needles worn thin in spots and the wire branches drooping. Sophie Madigan hung the last of the ornaments on a high bough, then stepped back, forcing a smile. "Doesn't that look festive, Papa?"

She glanced over her shoulder at her father, who sat at the huge desk in their parlor, his reading glasses perched on the end of his nose, aviation manuals and charts spread out in front of him. He nodded distractedly, then took another sip of his whiskey. It was barely noon and he had already poured himself a drink, Sophie mused.

"I should have bought some new lights," she continued. "Half of these are burned out."

"Looks fine, darlin'," he murmured, without even looking up.

Sophie sighed and began to gather the boxes and bags strewn over the plank floor. Why did she even bother? Trying to celebrate Christmas in the middle of the South Pacific was a lost cause. She remembered Christmases past, when she and her parents had traveled to places where entire towns had been decorated, places where it actually snowed.

Outside their small house on the tiny Polynesian island of Taratea, the trade winds kept the temperatures at a constant eighty-three degrees and the wet season made the air thick with humidity. The heady scent of tiare and hibiscus and frangipani seeped through the shutters that lined the lanai and she could hear the soft patter of raindrops on the tin roof. Sometimes it seemed as if it would never stop raining.

Sophie had hoped to spend this Christmas with her mother in Paris. But for the third year in a row, she'd reluctantly refused the invitation, choosing instead to stay with her father, Jack "Madman" Madigan. Christmas in Paris would have been a happy affair. Her uncles and aunts were all excellent cooks and there would have been food, followed by gifts, followed by more food.

When she broached the subject of spending the holidays in Paris, her father had told her to go. But as the time to leave got closer, Sophie saw him sink further and further into a deep depression. He had no one except her. No family, few friends. Since his eyesight had gone bad, he'd cut himself off from nearly everyone.

Sophie turned away from the tree and crossed the room, peering over her father's shoulder. "What are you working on?"

He had a map of the Society Islands spread out in front of him and he was studying a small archipelago through a magnifying glass, squinting to see the fine print. Her father's eyesight had been failing for nearly five years. It had become so bad, he'd been grounded, prohibited from doing what he did best.

Since then, Sophie had been forced to take over his air-charter operation, making almost daily flights between Tahiti and any one of the fourteen inhabited islands nearby. To make ends meet, they'd sold off four of the five planes to pay her father's debts. With one small plane left and only one pilot—Sophie herself— they made just enough to get by.

Sophie had tried to convince her father to sell the last plane and move back to the States where he could get medical care and she could get a better-paying job, but Jack held out hope that his eyesight would suddenly return and he'd be back in business. "Are we going on a trip?"

"I'm mapping out a flight plan for you for tomor- row," he murmured.

"I didn't know I had a charter," Sophie said, frown- ing. "Papa, tomorrow is Christmas Eve. Don't you think we could take the day off, maybe do a little celebrat- ing? The tree is up. I thought I might make a nice dinner and we could open our gifts and maybe even listen to some Christmas music."

"This guy is willing to pay ten thousand American for three days' worth of flying. I didn't think it was a job you'd want to refuse."

She gasped. *"Ten thousand* dollars? For three days' work?"

Jack nodded, then handed her a slip of paper. "His name is Peter Shelton. He's some bigwig for the Shelton Hotel chain. They're looking for a new location to build some fancy-schmancy new resort and they want to buy a whole island, make it real exclusive. You need to meet him at eight tomorrow morning at Faaa. At the hangar."

Sophie stared down at the name and phone number written on the scrap of paper. *"Quelle chance,"* she murmured. "Peter Shelton. Shelton Hotels." He sounded like a pretty important guy. Anyone who worked on Christmas Eve and paid more than three thousand dollars a day for a charter had to be important. "Why would he choose us?"

"Probably because no one else would take the job on Christmas Eve," Jack replied. "Here," he said, pointing to the map. "Fly him up here to this little atoll. There's a nice-size island with a decent lagoon."

"Suaneva? Didn't they try to build a resort there once?"

"About thirty years ago. But the developer ran out of money. The lagoon is a little tight for landing and taking off, but a good pilot should be able to get in and out. Hell, if he decides to build there, I can fly his workers in and out. We'll haul freight, and later the guests. We could work out an exclusive long-term contract and maybe buy a few new planes. I want you to really impress this guy, Sophie girl. Make him see that a partnership with Madigan Air would be good for both of us."

Sophie rested her hand on his shoulder. "Yes, Papa." She knew it was all just a pipe dream. Or maybe he did expect her to spend the rest of her life flying for him. She'd found a doctor in Sydney who'd promised a simple but expensive surgery for her father's sight problems, but when she'd mentioned this to him, Jack had completely discounted the option, preferring to stick to the herbal remedies a local *tahua* woman had prescribed.

Besides, it wasn't as if they had the money for the operation. Though ten thousand American dollars would go a long way toward paying for it, it still wasn't enough. Sooner or later, she'd have to accept the fact her life was here, caring for her father and eking out a living for them both as best she could.

She glanced around the small *fare* they called home. Built onto a hillside overlooking the water and perched on stilts, the interior of the cottage was small, just enough room for a few bedrooms and a parlor. But most of their living was done outside, on the wide lanai that circled the house.

Tourists would say she was living in paradise, but to Sophie, it often felt like a prison. Unable to enjoy the beauty that surrounded her, she longed for the excitement of living in a city, the noise and the people, never knowing what was around the next corner.

Slipping out of the house, she walked across the

small lawn to a point that overlooked the bay. People paid thousands of dollars to come and admire a view like this, she mused. The steeply raked crags covered with lush vegetation, the turquoise water and white sand, the little *fare,* surrounded with flowering vines and bushes.

Perhaps she might convince her father to sell and find a place in Pape'ete. Maybe then she could meet some people her own age, maybe even find a man to distract her from her troubles. She flopped down onto the lawn and stared up at the sky, the dampness from the rain soaking through her pareu.

Though she was emotionally exhausted, something inside her couldn't seem to rest. She felt as though she was ready to jump out of her skin. She smoothed her hands over her body and closed her eyes as the rain pelted her face. The sensations her hands evoked were enough to remind her how long it had been since she'd been touched by another.

It had been nearly a year since she'd enjoyed the pleasures a man's body offered. Though her Irish-American father would be more than happy if she decided to enter a convent, her French mother had given Sophie a very practical and healthy attitude about sex. One must accept that a woman has desires, her mother had told her, and they must be fulfilled. There is no sin in acting upon these feelings. As long as both parties agree there will be no promises the next morning.

After she finished flying Peter Shelton around the

islands, she'd take a little bit of the money, buy herself a new dress and find herself a man, Sophie decided. There were always tourists at the resorts on Tahiti and Bora Bora, handsome men who'd offer a temporary diversion.

She'd make it her goal to ring in the New Year in the bed of a sexy man. "I'll make it happen," Sophie muttered, stretching her arms above her head and arching her back. "A lover for New Year's Eve. And for New Year's Day."

But would a few nights in a man's bed really satisfy her? Or would she still have to make some more drastic changes in her life in order to be happy? "I'll start with the lover," she said, sitting up. "Then we'll see what happens."

TREY SHELTON GLANCED at his watch then cursed softly. He was already an hour late and the taxi he'd hired at the hotel had managed to get him to the airport but no farther. "Are you sure you don't know where Madigan Air is? It's a well-known charter company."

The native driver peered at him in the rearview mirror. "*Non.* Maybe this way?" he said in heavily accented English, pointing to a small cluster of hangars on the periphery of the Faaa airport.

"Let's try there," Trey suggested. "Someone should know." He'd hired the plane for three days, but he hoped to get his business settled early so he might enjoy a short vacation in paradise. He'd spent last night with an attractive Polynesian dancer from one of the local clubs and he'd promised to meet her that evening for dinner. Though she'd been interested in spending the night in his suite, Trey had begged off, explaining he had an early morning.

Since he'd begun working for his father a year ago, Trey had been forced to leave his jet-set Casanova lifestyle behind. Six months ago, he'd ended a relationship with a somewhat crazy, but sexy, English actress. Since then, he'd had a few one-night stands, but they'd left him more confused than satisfied.

He'd spent his adult life indulging in one whim after the other, all of it fueled by a seemingly bottomless trust fund. But now, at age twenty-nine, the money was almost gone and the lifestyle with it. His father's job offer was his only option.

"Ah!" the driver cried, pointing at a rusty sign dangling from above a hangar door. "*Nous sommes ici! Madigan Air. Voilà!*"

Trey paid the driver in colorful French Pacific franc notes, then grabbed his bag and slid out of the cab. He slowly walked through the huge overhead door into the interior of the hangar. The place was a wreck, parts strewn everywhere, a bent propeller dangling from the ceiling, an old girlie calendar hanging on an open office door. A small amphibious plane was parked inside. Either the guy on the phone had oversold the company, or Trey was in the wrong place.

"Hello?" he called. "Anybody home?"

"Bonjour!"

The female voice came from the direction of the plane.

"Is this Madigan Air?"

"Oui. This is. You're late," the voice said. "When you didn't come, I decided to do some maintenance. We'll be ready to go in about fifteen minutes. Just find a seat and relax. I won't be long."

Though she spoke flawless English, Trey could detect a French accent. He approached the plane, circling around the front until he came upon a slight figure standing on a small ladder, her head bent over an open engine compartment. He expected her to be cleaning the windows or polishing the mirrors, not wielding a wrench!

She wore a skirt made of fabric so thin he could see her bare legs through it, a tiny T-shirt didn't even cover her midriff and her dark hair hung well below her shoulders, held back by a colorful scarf. She'd tucked a flower behind her ear, the creamy-white color a stark contrast to her deeply tanned skin. "Are you sure you should be messing with that? Maybe you should wait for the pilot."

Her head snapped up and he met her gaze. Trey's breath caught in his throat as the most stunning pair of sapphire eyes fixed on his face. He watched as her expression quickly shifted from thinly veiled annoyance to embarrassment. A pretty blush colored her cheeks and she forced a smile. "I—I *am* the pilot, *monsieur,*" she murmured.

Trey couldn't help but laugh. "*You're* the pilot?"

She straightened her spine. "What? You don't think a woman might be capable of flying a plane?"

A smudge of grease marred her exquisite complexion. Even from this distance, he'd become lost in her eyes, rimmed by long, dark lashes. Her features were perfectly balanced, and even without a bit of makeup, her beauty stole the breath from his lungs. "No. Of course not. I was just…surprised, that's all."

She grabbed a rag, wiped her hands, then climbed down the ladder. "It seems I'm both. Pilot and mechanic. Sophie Madigan." She said her first name in the French way, with the accent on the last syllable.

"This is your plane?" he inquired.

"No, it belongs to my father. But I fly it. I am a licensed pilot," she said. "There is no need to worry, Mr. Shelton. I know what I'm doing."

He reached out and took her slender fingers in his, shaking her hand. God, she was stunning. This island was teeming with gorgeous women, but this woman put them all to shame. She was slender and delicate, with long legs and graceful arms. Her clothing clung to every curve of her body and if he had to guess, Trey would venture she wasn't wearing a whole lot underneath.

"You are younger than I expected," she said, a tiny smile curving the corners of her mouth. Her gaze was still fixed on his face, her eyes slowly taking in his features. For a moment, he thought she might say more.

She didn't seem to recognize him, even though his

name should have given him away. Trey's reputation as a celebrity playboy usually followed him wherever he went. The press had dubbed him the male equivalent of Paris Hilton. They'd documented his exploits with women and poked fun at the various careers he'd attempted.

Most women found his bad-boy reputation irresistible. But he found the thought of going unrecognized for once intriguing. What would it be like to be judged on his own merits rather than an image perpetrated by the press?

"My friends call me Trey," he said, turning on his most dazzling smile. She still showed no sign of recognition.

"*Très? Très* what?" Sophie asked, frowning.

He chuckled softly. "My name is actually Peter Shelton the Third. My grandfather was the first and my father was the second. I'm the third. Trey."

"Oh, like *un, deux, trois*. Well, that makes sense then," Sophie said, dragging her hand from his. "But I'll call you Mr. Shelton. Okay, just have a seat and let me finish and we'll be on our way." She climbed back up the ladder, then gave him an odd look.

"I'm good right here," he said. "I'd be happy to give you a hand."

She shrugged and went back to work. His gaze slowly drifted along the length of her body, lingering on her backside. Hell, he'd flown in a lot of planes, but he'd never had a pilot like this. The thought of going up with her made him a little uneasy. Was it because she was a beautiful woman? He couldn't deny his immediate attraction to her, so why even bother? Or was it because she seemed so young?

"Do you mind if I ask you a question?" he ventured.

"It depends upon the question," she said.

"How old are you?"

"This is not a proper question for a man to ask a woman," she said, sending him a coy smile.

"But I think it's highly proper for a passenger to ask his pilot."

"I'm twenty-six," she said.

"Are you French?" he asked.

"Half," Sophie said, glancing up and bracing her arms on the edge of the engine compartment. "And the other half, American. Why? Is that a problem, too?"

He shook his head. "I was just curious. The accent. It's a little confusing."

"I can talk American," Sophie said, her accent shifting with lightning speed. "If that would suit your ears better."

He shook his head, grinning. "No, I like the way you talk," he said. "It's…exotic."

His words seemed to take her aback for a moment. She gave him an uneasy look, then returned to her work. "My father has chosen some spots he thought you'd like to see. Is there anywhere specific you want to go?"

"Three islands," Trey said, pulling a crumpled sheet of paper from his leather messenger bag. "Waruhatu, Pareaa and Suaneva."

"Those are all on my list," she said. She glanced over at him, then reached up to close the cowling over the engine. "All done. I'll just do the preflight and we'll be ready to leave in about ten minutes. There are some cold drinks in the cooler over there if you want to grab one. You can stow the cooler behind the front seat, if you'd care to help."

She brushed by him as she returned the wrench to the tool cart and Trey caught the scent of her perfume, or maybe it was the flower in her hair. Whatever it was, he found the smell incredibly intoxicating. What was this beautiful girl doing in such a place? he wondered.

True to her word, they were rolling down the runway ten minutes later, Trey strapped into the passenger seat and Sophie Madigan behind the controls. Though Trey had never been afraid of flying, something about this situation made him nervous. For the first time in his life, he'd placed himself in the hands of a beautiful woman. The most he'd ever surrendered to a woman in the past was his body and even then, it had never been complete surrender.

The plane smoothly lifted off the runway and soared into a steeply banked turn over the water. As they continued to climb, Trey closed his eyes and drew a deep breath. She seemed to be a very competent pilot, at least so far.

"Are you all right?" she asked.

He opened his eyes to find her staring at him, her brow furrowed. "Yeah."

"If you're going to be sick, there's a bag under the seat."

"I'm not going to be sick," he said. "I'm just not a big fan of small planes."

She shrugged again. "Don't worry. I can put this plane down anywhere. That's the benefit of an amphibious plane. Water or land."

"How about on the side of that mountain over there?" he said.

"Why would I want to put it down there?" she asked.

He'd never met a woman quite so unimpressed with him. Trey knew he was a handsome guy, and charming, quite the catch according to everything he'd read in the tabloids. Although he wasn't sure how much of the attraction had to do with him, and how much with his money. But now that the trust fund he'd inherited from his grandfather's estate was virtually gone, he'd had to make some changes.

In less than a year, when he turned thirty, his father would decide whether to give him his share of the larger Shelton family trust, millions set aside for each Shelton heir, controlled by a man who thought Peter Shelton III had nothing substantial to offer the world.

To prove himself, Trey had gone to work for Shelton Hotels, focusing on a new division that developed smaller, more exclusive resorts, the kind of properties that appealed to his celebrity friends.

To Trey's surprise, he enjoyed the work. He'd found himself building resorts in his head—from the basic architecture to the linens in the rooms. After living in hotels nearly his entire adult life, Trey knew what worked and what didn't. And he was beginning to wonder if he might have something to offer the family business.

It was still a rather revolutionary concept—Trey Shelton, giving up the fast life for a real job. He figured he'd decide what to do with his future once he convinced his father to release his share of the Shelton family trust. If he still found the job appealing, then maybe he'd stick around.

He looked over at Sophie. She seemed quite relaxed behind the controls, as if she'd been a pilot for a long time. "Where did you learn how to fly?" he asked.

"I just picked it up. I flew all the time with my father, and one day we were doing preflight together and he put me in the pilot's seat and we took off. He taught me what I needed to know and I got my license."

"How old were you?" Trip asked.

She smiled as she remembered. "I was twelve when I first got behind the controls." Sophie laughed softly. "I think my dad always wanted a son. So, for a while, I was happy to become that son."

"I think you make a much better girl than a boy," he teased.

Trey watched her face as another smile curled the corners of her pretty mouth. Maybe she wasn't immune to his charms, after all. He certainly found Sophie intriguing. He didn't see a wedding band, so she probably wasn't married, but beyond that, his radar wasn't working. He couldn't seem to read her reactions to him. Had she been flattered by the compliment or just amused at the attempt?

He reached out, curious to push the issue a bit further. His movement startled her, causing her to draw away. "Sorry," he said, pointing to her cheek. "You have a smudge of grease there and it's been bothering me."

"Really?" She reached up and rubbed her cheek, missing it entirely. "There?"

Trey shook his head. "Do you mind?"

Sophie hesitated, then shook her head. "Not at all."

He gently rubbed a spot just above her jaw, the grease wiping away easily. Yet he didn't stop. Instead, Trey continued to smooth his thumb over her soft skin, fascinated by the silken feel of it. "There," he finally said. "Perfect."

She seemed to be as affected by his touch as he was, shifting uneasily in her seat and trying to focus her attention on the instruments in front of her. If she'd been driving a car, he might have asked her to pull over so they could explore his attraction in a little greater detail. But unfortunately, there weren't any curbs in the sky and one couldn't just park a plane in the middle of a flight.

Trey slowly pulled his hand away. "When will we see our first island?" he asked.

"I'm heading out to Suaneva first and then we'll work our way back to Tahiti."

They flew for a long time in silence, Trey studying

a report on power-generating windmills he'd brought with him in between watching her. He'd been right to call her exotic. Though she spoke like an American, she acted more like the French women he'd known—haughty, aloof, indifferent at times. And then there was a bit of Polynesian in her, as well, in her dress, in the careless addition of a flower behind her ear, in the sexy little tattoo above her ankle.

She glanced over at him and caught him staring. Trey quickly turned his gaze back to the report.

"What are you reading?" she asked.

He held it up, showing her the cover. "Just researching an idea I had. It's nothing."

"Windmills?"

"They're ecologically friendly," he said.

He'd been turning the idea over in his head ever since his father had put him on the payroll. Why not build an eco-friendly resort in the South Pacific? He'd have to deal with the problems of providing power and water to a small island anyway and there were now methods to do it without impacting the environment.

"This is not really a good season to be seeing our islands," Sophie said.

"I've noticed it rains a lot."

"It's the rainy season," she said with a smile. "Sometimes, it rains for days." She looked out the window of the plane. "Today is a good day. I can't promise you that tomorrow you'll even be able to see anything below us."

Trey grabbed his messenger bag from between his feet and pulled out a pad of paper and a pen. "Tell me everything you know about Suaneva," he demanded, anxious to keep her engaged in conversation.

He listened, silently taking notes as she explained the physical topography of a Polynesian atoll in comparison with an island. But he was less interested in the facts than he was in the sound of her voice.

"Suaneva is an atoll. An atoll begins with a volcano sticking out of the water," she explained. She let go of the controls and turned to him to gesture with her hands. But when she saw the startled look on his face, she sent him an apologetic smile. "I set the autopilot."

Trey exhaled the breath he'd sucked in. "Oh. Well, fine then."

"Coral builds up around the base beneath the water's surface," she continued, "and over the years, the volcano top falls away until all that is left is the coral ring and a huge lagoon in the center. Vegetation grows on the ring and beaches form and you have an atoll. They look like little rings in the sea." She pointed out his window. "There. You see? This atoll is part of the *Archipel des Tuamotu*. The Tuamotu Archipelago. We are about 150 miles from Pape'ete. Tahiti is part of *les Îles du Vent*. The Windward Islands. Mostly mountaintops that haven't erupted or disintegrated. Although there are many atolls, too. *Vous comprenez?*"

He stared at her hands, wondering what it might be like if she actually reached out and touched him. Trey wanted to capture her fingers and pull them to his lips, to kiss each neatly manicured tip until he got a reaction from her. How could such a simple gesture intrigue him so? "Yes," he murmured.

"In an atoll, there are often separate islands in the ring and these are called *motu*. A *motu* can be very large or quite small, but they are…lower. Flatter than an island like Bora Bora."

What he wanted right now didn't have anything to do with islands or resorts or trust funds. Listening to her voice, watching her beautiful mouth, was pushing his thoughts in a very different direction. If he had his way, he'd demand she land the damn plane so he could drag her into his arms and kiss her. And once he sensed her surrender, he'd strip off all their clothes, lie in the warm sand and make love to her. It wasn't just a fantasy. There was definitely an attraction between them. He could see it every time their eyes met.

But as long as they were in the air, nothing could happen. Trey wondered how long it might take to make their tour before heading back to Pape'ete. He could always just cut the trip short once he saw Suaneva. Hell, maybe it would suit his purposes perfectly and there would be no reason to continue. Or maybe they could simply continue tomorrow, after they'd spent the night together in his bed.

"How long before we reach Suaneva?" he asked.

SOPHIE GLANCED DOWN AT HER hands clutching the steering yoke of the plane. They were white-knuckled, frozen in place, the only part of her body that looked the way she felt.

It all happened so quickly Sophie hadn't found time to think. From the moment her gaze had focused on this gorgeous man, she hadn't been able to breathe. And the instant Trey Shelton took her hand in his, she'd felt a current race through her body, setting every sense on edge.

She couldn't remember a man ever affecting her in such an intense and immediate way. Had she possessed any common sense at all, she would have refused to take him up. Flying with Trey was like flying drunk! Every nerve in her body had shifted into overdrive. The scent of his cologne filled her head and the feel of his warm hand still tingled on the tips of her fingers. His voice sent a shiver down her spine and she could barely stand to look at him without moaning.

Of all the times for her to fall apart, this was the worst possible moment. A man as sexy as Trey didn't just walk into her life every day. And if she had any intentions of seducing him, she couldn't make it seem easy. Her mother had taught her a lot of valuable lessons about the opposite sex, and one of the most important was to let the man take up the chase. She wanted to be elusive and mysterious, but right now she just felt breathless, giddy—*desperate.* She'd vowed to have a man by New Year's and she was a week ahead of schedule.

Thank goodness they were flying over Suaneva, she

mused. At least she had conversation to distract her from studying his handsome face and incredible body. Yes, she'd imagined him undressed more than once and as they'd flown northwest from Pape'ete, she'd managed to catalog each perfect feature.

He had an attitude that many American men possessed, an easy confidence that made his masculinity even more powerful. His smile was stunning, his features rugged yet refined, and his hazel eyes were so penetrating she thought he could see right through her flimsy facade.

"Suaneva is one of the smaller atolls," she said in a shaky voice. "Though the lagoon is small, there's a fair amount of land to build on."

Trey peered out the window. "I was told someone already tried building a resort there."

"Yes, but I don't know what's left of it. Can you see anything down there?" She banked the plane steeply to the right to give him a better view, but the moment she eased into the turn, Sophie felt the engine hesitate.

A few seconds later, it sputtered. *"Merde,"* she murmured. Maybe it was just moisture in the fuel line. That sometimes happened during the rainy season. The engine cut out and Sophie's instincts immediately kicked in. She switched to the auxiliary tank and tried the ignition, but to her surprise, it wouldn't turn over. The battery was dead and without it, there'd be no way to restart the engine.

"What's wrong?" Trey asked.

She and her father had practiced dead-stick landings on several occasions and his words came back to her now. Keep the nose up, maintain airspeed and find a smooth place to land.

"The engine cut out," Sophie replied, attempting another start.

"I can see that," he said, his voice laced with concern. "Don't you think you ought to start it up again?"

"I'm trying. But I need to pull us out of this turn first." She lined herself up with the tiny lagoon below, then pushed the ignition for the engine again. There was no response.

"I'm going to have to put us down," she said.

"What?"

She heard the panic in his tone. "Don't worry. We'll land, and I'll radio for help. We'll be fine. I've done this before."

"Run out of gas in midair?"

Sophie shook her head. "We didn't run out of gas. I think there's moisture in the fuel. I drained the sumps, but sometimes this happens."

"Sometimes you crash?" he asked.

"No. Usually, the engine will start up again. But the battery seems to be dead. Don't worry. I can put us safely down on the lagoon." She glanced over at him to see a dubious expression on his face. "You're not going to die, Mr. Shelton. It might be a bumpy landing, so make sure you're strapped in. If the plane flips in the water, kick open the window and get out as fast as you can."

"I knew I should have trusted my instincts," he muttered. "The moment I saw the inside of that hangar, the moment I saw you fixing that engine, I should have just turned around and walked out. But no, I brushed my doubts aside. You were beautiful and I figured, why not spend the afternoon trying to seduce you? This is exactly what I deserve. I put my need to get laid in front of my need to keep breathing, and now I'm about to die."

"You're not going to die," Sophie repeated, a warm blush rising on her cheeks. He had wanted to seduce her? The thought made her dizzy with desire. She drew a shaky breath and pointed to the instrument panel. "I want you to watch this gauge. This is my airspeed. I need you to call it out to me." She could keep an eye on the gauge herself, but this would give him something to do.

She ran through the checklist in her head, her father's voice speaking to her. *Maintain your composure, fly the airplane, watch your glide speed.* Sophie adjusted the flaps and lined the plane up with the near end of the lagoon. Landing the plane without power would be tricky, but she was more worried about coral heads in the lagoon tearing apart the plane's floats or stopping their forward motion once they hit the water. If they hit coral, it might flip the plane. If they hit the beach too fast, they'd flip, as well. She banked slightly, determined to give herself as much water to work with as possible.

She drew another deep breath, said a silent prayer and began her descent to the lagoon. If they died, she'd never get to enjoy sex again, much less sex with a man as beautiful as Trey Shelton. So, she'd just have to make sure she landed the damn plane safely.

Trey called out her airspeed, but Sophie could feel the plane respond. Outside, the air rushed by and she was amazed by the silence that surrounded them. For a moment, she worried she might be coming in too fast and may overshoot her landing zone, but then the headwind picked up and the plane drifted lower.

And then, to her relief, they touched down on the water. The plane skimmed toward the water's edge and she held her breath, ready to use the rudder to spin them around if it looked like they might be in trouble. But in the end, the plane gently slid to a stop twenty feet from the shore of the lagoon.

With trembling hands, Sophie unhooked her seat belt and shoved her shoulder against the door of the plane. The door gave way and she tumbled out, falling into waist-deep water. Floundering, she struggled to the shore, her heart slamming in her chest.

The adrenaline was pumping so fast she felt as if she could run a mile in ten seconds flat. When she reached the beach, she braced her hands on her knees and gulped in a deep breath, trying to slow her pounding heart.

"Shit, that was incredible," Trey shouted as he followed her to the shore. "You'd think that was the way we were supposed to land. I mean, you just set us down perfectly." He stood in front of her, his khakis soaked, his hands braced on his hips. "How did you do that?"

She looked up at him, taking in his awestruck expression, still gasping for breath. Then, with a burst of energy, Sophie lurched forward, threw her arms around his neck and kissed him.

Trey stumbled back, grasping onto her waist to balance them both since Sophie's knees had gone boneless beneath her. He wrapped his arm around her waist and pushed his other hand through her hair, tossing her scarf aside. Sophie was aware of every detail of the kiss, the way his mouth opened beneath hers, the sweet taste of his tongue, the immediate rush of desire that seemed to propel them forward.

Slowly, he pulled her down into the sand, never breaking contact. He stretched out beside her, his hand smoothing along her thigh until it reached her backside. Sophie moaned softly, rolling over on top of him, pressing her hips against his.

His reaction to the kiss was immediate, his erection hard against her belly evidence of that fact. Sophie reached between them and touched him, slowly rubbing her palm against his desire. This was crazy, but yet, it seemed so right. Had they been over the ocean, they might be slowly sinking to the bottom right now, both of them drowned, never to be found.

But they'd been lucky and they were alive and she wanted to celebrate that fact. Sophie fumbled with the buttons of his shirt, damp from his trip through the lagoon. When she became frustrated, Trey grabbed his collar and yanked, the buttons popping open all at once.

His chest was smooth and finely muscled, exactly what Sophie expected to find beneath the cotton shirt. It had been so long since she'd touched a man intimately, that she wanted to take her time, enjoying the feel of his body beneath her hands.

He didn't appear to object to what she was doing. She risked a glance up and saw his eyes were closed. Why not take advantage of the situation? she wondered. If she radioed for help, they'd have an hour, maybe two, alone on this island. Right now, she wasn't in any hurry to be rescued.

Sophie pressed her lips to the center of his chest, then traced a trail of kisses to his collarbone. If she was going to take a lover, then this man was as good as any. Unless he already had a woman in his life.

Sophie paused, knowing the only way she could proceed was to know for sure. Though she had an open attitude about sexual desire, she'd experienced, firsthand, what an affair could do to a marriage. Her father's infidelities had been the cause of her parents' divorce. She certainly didn't want to be the other woman in any man's marriage, even a man as sexy and geographically available as Trey was.

His hand skimmed up her belly, slipping beneath her shirt to cup her bare breast. Drawing a deep breath, Sophie placed her hand over his. "Wait," she murmured.

He froze, his own breath catching in his throat. "Sorry. I thought—"

"No, it's all right. I just have a quick question."

"Yes, I do," he said, chuckling softly.

Sophie frowned. It was an answer, but to what, she wasn't sure. "You do? Do what?"

"I have…protection." He reached around and pulled his wallet from his pants pocket. "I have two. And I might even have a few more in my bag."

Though she was glad he'd come prepared, it didn't really soothe her doubts. "I wanted to ask if you were involved. Married, engaged, otherwise spoken for."

"Would it make a difference?" he asked.

"Yes," Sophie replied. "I'm not a home-wrecker."

He bent closer and pressed a kiss to a spot just below her ear. "No," he whispered. "Not married, not engaged, not even dating. Completely free to do whatever it is you want me to do."

Sophie stared into his eyes. She didn't know this man and couldn't tell if he spoke the truth. If he didn't, she'd deal with the consequences later. Sitting up, she pulled her top over her head and tossed it into the sand. Slowly, his gaze drifted from her face to her breasts and back up again.

Following her lead, he shrugged out of his shirt. Neither one of them was dressed in much, owing to the humid weather. Her pareu came off next, leaving her in just a skimpy thong. Sophie had always been comfortable with her body and was used to sunbathing naked. But the way he looked at her, with such desire, she wondered if she should have taken things a bit slower.

She reached for her pareu, ready to cover up again,

but Trey caught her hand. He slowly got up, his body
casting a shadow over her, and unzipped his khakis,
then skimmed them down over his hips. He stood there,
wearing only cotton boxers, tented out in the front
where his erection pressed against the damp fabric.

There was no going back, Sophie mused as she
stared up at him. She held out her hand and he lay down
beside her in the sand, drawing her into another kiss.
This time, it was slow and sensual, his mouth possessing hers, his hands skimming over her nearly naked
body.

She didn't want to go back. She didn't want to be
rescued. For now, Sophie was exactly where she needed
to be—alone, on a deserted South Pacific island, with
a man who was about to make delicious love to her.

2

WHEN HE'D CRAWLED OUT OF BED that morning, Trey had assumed he'd be in for a rather ordinary day, spent cooped up in a small plane with a competent male pilot. As he teased at Sophie's tongue with his, he couldn't help but wonder at this odd turn of luck. The scene was straight out of the encyclopedia of male fantasies.

Stuck on a deserted tropical island, with a beautiful, naked woman who'd ripped off her clothes right in front of his eyes. Maybe he'd actually died when the plane crashed and this was his version of heaven. "Touch me," he murmured as he dragged his lips from hers.

She skimmed her fingers over his belly and wrapped them around his cock, the fabric of his boxers creating an enticing friction. Trey bit back a moan. It sure felt real, his heart pounding in his chest, his body aching with need. But how could he prove it to himself?

He slowly drew back, cupping her face in his palm and looking into her eyes. Did it really matter? After all the debauchery in his life, he'd ended up in heaven, with a sexy companion. He'd done pretty well for himself. If he was really dead, then dead wasn't so bad.

Trey kissed her again, smoothing his palm over her shoulder and arm until his fingers were laced through hers.

Drawing her hand over her head, Trey gently pushed her back into the sand, his body stretched alongside hers. He buried his face in the curve of her neck, inhaling her exotic scent as he kissed her. Slowly, he moved lower until his lips fixed on her nipple. He teased and Sophie arched toward him, twisting her body until a tiny moan slipped from her lips.

The sun, filtered through a thin cover of clouds, was hot on their bodies, but it felt good to be free of clothes. When she slipped her hand beneath the waistband of his boxers, Trey quickly stripped them off. A moment later, her thong was gone and there was nothing left between them but the salty ocean breeze and the sand clinging to their skin.

Though the seduction began in a rush of desire, the pace had grown almost lazy. There was time, and Trey wanted to take advantage of every moment. But when Sophie touched him again, without his boxers as a barrier, he wondered if he was already too far gone.

He pulled her body against his, their hips meeting, his shaft hot and hard between them. Seduction had always come so easily to him, the clever balancing act between pleasure and complete surrender. But this meeting was different. As she drew her leg up along his hip, he knew he was just an instant away from burying himself deep inside her.

He wanted it now, needed it to happen, as if it would provide proof he was still among the living. Breaking contact for just a moment, Trey grabbed his khakis and pulled out his wallet, retrieving the condoms he kept there for "emergencies." Though the little packages wouldn't fix the plane, they'd certainly come in handy.

The moment she saw the condoms, Sophie grabbed one from his hand and tore open the plastic. He held his breath as she smoothed it over his cock, her touch causing a groan to rumble in his chest. It was obvious she wasn't into long, slow seductions. She preferred to skip the preliminaries and head right to the main event.

Pulling her beneath him, Trey drew her legs up alongside his hips and slowly entered her. A sigh slipped from her body and he watched as a smile played across her damp mouth.

"Oh," she murmured, as he withdrew. Her hands clutched at his ass, as he buried himself again.

Trey had always been able to control his desires, but this felt far too good. Maybe it was the leftover adrenaline from his near-death experience. Maybe it was the exotic setting. But most likely, it was this woman writhing beneath him, so incredibly beautiful and uninhibited.

"We are alive, aren't we?" he murmured, his hands braced beside her shoulders.

"We are alive," she replied, meeting his gaze.

He slowly began to move, but every sensation seemed heightened by what they'd experienced. When she touched him, it was as if an electric current passed between them. The taste of her mouth was like the sweetest fruit he'd ever eaten. And the sound of her voice wove a silken web around him, until he felt as if he were born to do her bidding.

Her fingers dug into his hips as his rhythm increased. Pleasure pushed aside rational thought and Trey found himself lost in the feel of her body beneath his. He was so close, yet he stopped himself from surrender, knowing she was almost there herself.

A moment later, Sophie cried out, arching against him, her body trembling. It was only then that Trey allowed himself to give in, to feel her body convulsing around him. He teetered on the edge, the sensation of exquisite anticipation lasting far longer than it ever had before. And then, his orgasm blindsided him, coming from deep in his core.

He'd never felt such an incredible surge of pleasure, his body shuddering, driving deeper, until he was completely spent. Trey's arms grew weak and he lowered himself to lie beside her, pulling her along with him, still intimately connected.

She winced and he smoothed the hair from her eyes. "Are you all right?"

"Something bit me, I think," she said, reaching back to rub her hand over her backside. "There are little crabs in the sand."

Trey grinned, then gently rolled her over, holding his breath as he slipped from her body. He brushed the sand from her skin and examined the spot she pointed to. "It looks a little red," he said. Bending close, he kissed her backside. "Better?"

"Much," she murmured. She reached down to caress him, removing the condom as she smoothed her hand over his still-rigid shaft.

He was ready to go again, but condoms were in limited supply. If they were going to spend any time on the island, he might need to conserve his resources.

When they'd both caught their breath, Trey levered to his feet and reached down to help her up. Lacing his fingers through hers, he led her to the lagoon. Silently, they waded in, washing the sand from their naked bodies as the warm water enveloped them.

Sophie submerged, then swam underwater until she was a fair distance away. When she broke the surface, she smoothed her hair back and tipped her face up to the sky. "When did you first decide you wanted to seduce me?" she asked.

Trey frowned.

"You said in the plane, when we were going down, that you intended to seduce me. When did you decide?"

Trey swam over to her, then stood, his feet barely touching the bottom of the lagoon. "A man will say a lot of crazy things when he's about to die."

She sighed softly. "I knew the moment I saw you," she said.

"Knew I'd seduce you?" Trey asked.

She shook her head. "No. That I'd seduce you," she said in a matter-of-fact tone. She submerged and then swam underwater toward the plane. Trey watched her naked body move through the water of the sun-dappled lagoon. When she popped back up, she smoothed her hair back from her face, her arm draped over the pontoon. "We should pull the plane in," she called.

It had drifted farther out into the lagoon, though it was still in shallow water. Trey swam out to where she stood, her words still drifting through his mind. Had she seduced him or had it been the other way around? Though it shouldn't be important, it was. "Can you fix it?" he asked.

"I don't know," she said. "If it's the battery, there's no way to charge it. It might be something electrical."

Trey wanted to reach out and grab her waist, to pull her into another kiss, to test the limits of her desire for him. Hell, as far as he was concerned, they could stay out here for the week, as long as he had Sophie with him. But he held his impulses in check.

Sophie unhooked a line from beneath the plane and swam to a spot where she could touch the sandy bottom of the lagoon. He grabbed the line and helped her pull. To his surprise, the heavy plane easily glided through the water.

He stood in the waist-deep water as he watched her walk across the beach to a nearby palm, where she tied up the plane. She was magnificent, her naked limbs slender and supple, her skin tanned all over and gleaming in the sun. She was obviously comfortable with nudity, making no attempt to cover up. Or was she deliberately trying to provoke his passion again? He felt himself growing hard and cursed softly.

He'd never been in this situation before. Usually when he had sex with a woman, it had come after a short but amusing chase. Once the flirtations and silly games had been completed, mutual desire led to the bedroom. But this time, there had been no games. The sex had come from a primal need to reassure themselves they were both alive. What was the etiquette in this situation? Was he supposed to act as though nothing had happened?

"Now what?" he asked.

"I'm going to radio for help," she said. Sophie had waded back into the water and crawled up into the plane, providing him with a lovely view of her backside as she pulled herself up. She was oblivious to her nudity, but he certainly wasn't. The sight of her was doing all sorts of things to his desire.

Taking the opportunity to hide his reaction, Trey walked back to the beach and retrieved his boxers and khakis. He tugged them on, then sat down in the sand to wait. Though he couldn't see what she was doing inside the plane, Trey trusted they weren't in any immediate danger. The weather was good, they had a cooler full of drinks and rescue was only a few hours away.

As he stared out at the lagoon, Trey mentally began to plan his next move. No doubt, they'd be back in Pape'ete before dinner. He'd insist she accompany him, perhaps in gratitude for saving his life. Or maybe he wouldn't need an excuse. Maybe she'd be just as anxious as he was to continue what they'd begun on the beach.

Fifteen minutes later, she emerged from the plane, making a shallow dive off the float before she swam to shore. Muttering to herself in French, Sophie grabbed her pareu and wrapped it around her waist, tying it in a knot. "The radio's not working," she said. "I'm pretty sure the battery is dead."

In any other situation, Trey might have been angry. After all, bad fuel, a dead battery and a useless radio didn't speak well of Madigan Air. But he'd been looking for an excuse to spend more time with Sophie and now he had it.

"What are we going to do?"

"There's not much we can do. There's a small dry cell battery in the back of the plane. If there's any charge left, I may be able to wire the radio to it and we can call for help. But I'm not sure the voltage is compatible." She shrugged, then forced a smile. "I'm sorry, you must think—"

"No," Trey said. "I'm happy to be alive. Besides, won't they come looking for us?"

"Of course. They know where we went and they'll easily be able to see the plane from the air." She paused. "But they won't know to search for us until after sundown. They might send out a plane then or wait until morning. Either way, we're probably going to be here all night."

"It's not so bad," he said, looking around. "There are worse places to be stuck." He paused. "And far worse companions to be stuck with."

She smiled, as if pleased by the compliment. "Of course, I will refund your charter fee. It wouldn't be proper to—"

Trey reached up and grabbed her arm, pulling her down beside him. "You don't have to do that," he murmured, cupping her face in his hands.

She stared at him, wide-eyed, as she waited for him to make the first move this time. Gently, he ran his thumb over her lower lip and kissed her, his mouth lingering over hers as he traced the outline with his tongue. "Let's just call this a side trip," he said. "An adventure. We can continue our survey once we get off this island."

"You may not say that when the rain is pouring down and you're wet and miserable," she teased.

He pulled her closer, his hand splayed against the small of her back. Her breasts brushed against his chest and Trey bit back a moan. "I'm a pretty tough guy," he said. "I think I can handle a little rain."

SOPHIE SAT WITH HER BACK against the trunk of a coconut palm, a seat cushion providing extra comfort. She'd retrieved an old blanket from the plane and spread it out in the sand and settled in to wait for someone to realize they were missing.

Though she should have been trying to get the radio to work, she'd decided to hold off. If she got it working too soon, they might be rescued before sunset. If she got it working later, she could call in their location and reassure her father that everything was all right. Then, she and Trey would have an entire night together.

Still, if she couldn't get the radio fixed, her father would be in for a very long night. Sometime after sunset, he'd come to the realization she might have been forced to ditch in the open ocean. Though the plane had floats, landing on open water was always risky. One wrong move, one swell, and they could have rolled end over end and sunk too quickly for anyone to get out. They'd been lucky to be where they were when the problems occurred.

In truth, after what had happened between them on the beach, she had to wonder if maybe this was more wish fulfillment than sheer luck. She'd been determined to find a lover and now she had one, complete with a deserted tropical island. They were probably going to be stuck on Suaneva until at least tomorrow morning. And she had every intention of taking advantage of her good fortune.

When Sophie had thought about finding a man, the individual had been just a vague image in her mind, someone with the physical prowess to satisfy her desire and to make her feel like a woman again. But Trey was much more than that. There was a powerful physical attraction between them, an attraction that wouldn't be quelled by just one passionate encounter on the beach.

She recalled the conversation she'd had with her father

about this trip. He'd wanted her to—what was the word—
impress? Perhaps the gods had stepped in and given her
the solution to all their problems. She'd get what she
wanted and her father would get what he wanted.

Sophie pulled her legs up and rested her chin on her
knees, silently observing her fellow castaway. She
couldn't help but feel a little guilty. Once her father
realized they were missing, he'd be beside himself with
worry. She, on the other hand, would be enjoying a host
of carnal pleasures with her sexy passenger.

Trey had decided to raid the tail of the plane for
anything that might improve their comfort while they
waited and had come away with a wide variety of items
he'd arranged on the beach. He was now focused on a
canvas tarp and a length of nylon rope, the small toolbox
she kept stowed beneath the pilot's seat open at his feet.

"What are you doing?" she asked.

He squatted down and picked through the toolbox,
then pulled out a large pocketknife. "I'm making us a
shelter, in case it starts to rain."

"Give me that knife," she said, wriggling her fingers.

He walked over to her and placed it in her hand.
Sophie reached out for the leg of his khakis and cut the
fabric at midthigh. She tore off one leg and then the
other. "There. You'll be more comfortable now."

"I'm not sure I'll ever be comfortable with you lying
around topless like that," he said wryly, staring down at
her, the soft light outlining his gorgeous body.

Sophie glanced down at her chest. "Americans are

far too obsessed with breasts," she muttered. "It's too hot for a shirt. You're not wearing one. Why should I?" Sophie paused. "You know, we could always sit in the plane if it rained."

"It's kind of hot and stuffy in there," he said. "It's nicer outdoors. And I don't want to sleep in the plane. It's too cramped. I need space."

He hesitated, then looked her way. Considering what they'd done on the beach an hour before, Sophie could attest to that fact. Making love in the plane would be more than uncomfortable. When they did it again, she wanted comfort, not privacy.

Trey straightened, turning in a slow circle, then looked over at her. "Which way is the wind coming from?"

She pointed to the northeast and he grinned. "Thanks." He took a small length of rope and ran it through the grommet in the tarp, then tied it onto a tree. "When I was fifteen, my parents sent me on an Outward Bound trip. They thought it would make a man of me."

"What is this? This Outward Bound?" Sophie asked, curious to learn a little more about her lover.

"It's a program where they drop kids in the middle of the wilderness and they have to learn how to survive by working together. You learn all these skills—how to make a fire and how to build a shelter. How to find drinkable water."

"These are good things to know," Sophie said.

"This is the first time I've ever needed to use them,"

he said ruefully. Trey paused, staring down at the knot he'd tied. "You know, that was the last time I remember ever feeling a sense of accomplishment. I was happy that summer. Happy with myself."

"So it made a man out of you?"

Silly question, she mused. The answer was right in front of her eyes. In all her life, she'd never met anyone who was more "man" than Trey. He exuded masculine sexuality, from his careless stance to his easy athletic grace, from his boyish smile to his unchecked desire.

He glanced over her shoulder, chuckling softly. "Yeah, in more ways than one. I lost my virginity on that trip. To a red-haired girl from Burlington, Vermont. Her name was Elizabeth and she could portage a canoe all by herself."

Sophie giggled. "Sounds like the right kind of girl to be stuck in the wilderness with. Tell me more."

"About the girl?"

"No, about losing your virginity. Was it all you thought it would be?"

He considered her question for a long moment and Sophie was afraid that she'd offended him with her bold inquiry. They'd just shared the most intimate experience between a man and a woman. Why shouldn't they speak about sex as easily as they'd shared it?

"It was over pretty quickly," he admitted. "And it was out in the woods. We'd been sent to gather firewood. And neither one of us had had a bath for days. The mosquitos nearly ate us alive. But I liked it." He nodded. "I really liked it. And I've liked it ever since."

"And did it happen again?"

Trey shook his head. "No, she moved on to an older boy. What about you?"

"I was sixteen," Sophie said. "I was spending the holidays in Paris with my mother's family. I met a boy. He was an art student and he was sketching along the Seine. He took me back to his parents' apartment and we did it. It was pretty much the same as your experience."

"It's a wonder we survived," he said. "And that we managed to get so good at it."

"So what attracted you to this girl?" Sophie asked, wondering just what kind of women he usually chose to bed.

"She had very large…"

"Breasts?"

"Shoulders," Trey said. "Like I said, she could haul a canoe down a muddy path for miles. And carry two backpacks at once."

"So you admire capable women?" Sophie asked. "Some men find them…intimidating."

"I admire you," he said. "When the plane was going down, you acted like it was just another day at the office." He looked over at her. "Just how close were we to dying?"

She smiled. "If I told you all the things that could have gone wrong, you might not want to fly again. We were lucky," she said.

He tipped his head, a grin quirking at the corners of his mouth. "I guess we were."

There was more than one meaning to his words, Sophie mused. They were lucky to be alive. But they were also lucky to be stuck alone on this island. Had they met any other place, they might have enjoyed a quick afternoon in bed and then gone their separate ways. But here, they were able to take their time, to test their passion.

Sophie pushed to her feet and strolled over to where he worked, grabbing the edge of the tarp and pulling it tight. She caught him staring, then looked down at her bare breasts. It was obvious that her nudity was causing him a great deal of unease. He was growing hard, his erection bulging out the front of his khakis. Was it just her, or was he always so aroused around women?

She sighed, then tossed her hair back over her shoulders, exposing herself completely. "There," she said. "Go ahead. You can look. I don't mind."

He focused on tying a knot around the trunk of a coconut palm. "I'm not obsessed," he murmured.

"*Mais non!* It doesn't bother me. I just don't understand this American fascination with naked breasts. There is nothing special here. One, two. Now, if I had three, there might be something to stare at. But, sadly, I only have two. Like every other woman on the planet. And every man, for that matter."

Trey grabbed the edge of the tarp, covering her hand with his. The moment they made contact, Sophie's breath caught in her throat. She wanted him to touch her again, to pull her into his arms and run his hands over her naked skin.

Slowly, Sophie stepped closer, until her breasts brushed against his chest. It was a subtle challenge, a dare for him to touch her more intimately. She saw the desire in his eyes and his reaction was unmistakable. Trey drew in a sharp breath and held it.

A heartbeat later, his hand found her shoulder, then slowly drifted down to her breast. "I beg to differ," Trey said softly, as he rubbed his thumb over her nipple. "Yours aren't quite as ordinary as you claim. Besides, how can you be upset that men find that part of your body so distracting?"

"I didn't say I was upset," Sophie protested, placing her fingertips on his chest. "Just curious. And perhaps a bit amused. Would you rather I put my top back on? So you wouldn't be distracted?"

He bent close and brushed a kiss across her lips, his hand still cupping her breast. "When you look at a naked male body, you don't see anything sexual?"

"I didn't say that."

"All right, let's limit our discussion to my male body." Trey stepped back and held out his arms. "Be honest. Take your time. I'll wait."

Rising to his challenge, Sophie stared at him, taking in every detail of his form between his chin and his belly. Her gaze skimmed over his wide shoulders to the well-defined muscles of his abdomen. She reached out and ran her finger along the trail of dark hair that went from his navel to a spot beneath the waistband of his khakis. She'd followed that trail before and knew what was waiting at the end.

Her mind skipped back to their encounter on the beach. It had happened so quickly, she hadn't taken the time to think. In truth, everything was a bit hazy. But, there were some small details that kept teasing at her memory, tempting her to try it all over again. It had felt good. *He* had felt good moving inside her.

She returned to the little valley in the center of his chest, following it down to his muscled abdomen. Her eyes focused on a bead of sweat that traced its way through the ridges and contours. Her fingers twitched and she fought the urge to taste it.

Unable to resist, she reached out and ran a lazy finger from his collarbone to his khakis, tracing the trail of hair before stopping where his waistband began. "This," she murmured. "I like this."

Sophie pushed up on her toes and gave him a kiss, letting her tongue slip between his lips for just a second. Though she was tempted to pull him back down on the blanket and have her way with him, Sophie fought her need for instant gratification. If he wanted her, he'd have to wait, at least until they found something more than sex to sustain them.

"Are you hungry?" she whispered, her lips still touching his.

"For you? Always."

"No, for something to eat." Sophie stepped back. "When we were circling the island, I think I saw some old rainwater tanks over on the other side of the lagoon. I'm going to see what there is. Meanwhile, you can build a fire and then we'll try to catch some fish."

"Do we have a fishing pole?"

"There are hooks and line in the bottom of the toolbox."

"Do we have matches?"

"Yes, but using them wouldn't be much of an accomplishment for a man so well trained in wilderness survival, would it?"

She found his shirt and slipped into it, then tied the tails at her waist and rolled up the sleeves. Sophie grabbed the plastic water jug he'd pulled from the tail of the plane. Despite having shared an incredibly passionate encounter, they were still virtual strangers. She didn't know how he took his coffee, whether he preferred showers to a bath, or whether he slept on the left or the right side of the bed. But she was learning what made him hard with desire. And for now, that was enough.

Though he was ready and willing to have her again, Sophie thought it might be a good idea to take things a bit slower. He only had one condom left and they had the whole night ahead of them. She intended to make the next seduction last a lot longer than the first. Their gazes met and it was as if there was a silent understanding there. They would touch each other again, but next time would be much more powerful than the first.

"Maybe I should come with you," he said, his hands

braced on his hips. "I wouldn't want you to get eaten by alligators."

Sophie laughed. "There are no alligators on this island."

"Well, there are probably all kinds of poisonous snakes and spiders."

"In the water. There are sea snakes."

"Poisonous?" he asked.

"Yes, but very rare. You have more to fear from the centipedes. They have a nasty bite. And there may be *taramea* and jellyfish and *rori* and *nohu* in the lagoon. And sea urchins. Although, if we find any sea urchins, we should eat them. They're a delicacy."

"I'll come and protect you from sea urchins then."

"I'll be fine," she insisted. "Why don't you finish the shelter and get a fire started. We'll probably need to boil any water we want to drink. The old fronds from the coconut palms burn really well. And you can probably find some driftwood if you walk over to the ocean side of the atoll."

"Are you sure you'll be all right?" he asked.

"If I get in trouble, I'll scream and you can rescue me." Sophie pointed to the other side of the lagoon. "Over there. I'm just going to follow the beach around. You'll be able to see me most of the way."

He crossed over to her, wrapped his arms around her waist and brought his mouth down on hers. It was a sudden, almost possessive, gesture, followed by a long, deep kiss. "Don't get lost," he murmured when he finally drew back.

"I—I won't," Sophie stuttered, stunned by the fierce tone of his words.

She started off down the beach, her knees wobbling from the power of his kiss. Sophie glanced over her shoulder to find him staring at her, his head cocked to the side as he watched.

In truth, she needed to put a bit of distance between them. Given time alone, she'd be able to reexamine all the details of what had happened—the way his lips felt on her breasts, the scent of his skin, the sound of his moans as he buried himself deep inside her. Even now, she got goose bumps at the thought of the two of them, naked, limbs entwined.

"Be careful, Sophie," she muttered to herself. It would be silly to get all wrapped up in this man. Yes, they'd enjoy each other again before they got off the island. But that was where it would have to end, with a physical need that begged to be satisfied. Any type of emotional attachment to Trey would be foolish at best.

THE HEAT HAD SETTLED OVER the island as the noonday sun rose behind the thin cover of clouds. Sophie shaded her eyes as she peered across the beach toward her destination. Even though she was alone, she still felt an overwhelming connection to Trey.

They'd already shared the most intimate of acts, but it was more than just sexual attraction that had brought them together. There was a bond now, a shared experience, forged when they'd both come face-to-face with death, a thing that made the sex they'd shared even more intimate.

As she waded through a shallow channel that fed seawater into the lagoon, Sophie wondered if she ought to just set up camp on the opposite side of the lagoon from Trey. Yes, he was charming and handsome and unbearably sexy. Just the kind of man it would be impossible to forget. How easy would it be to walk away from him? Or to watch him walk away from her?

Her mind was still occupied with those thoughts when she reached the ruins of the abandoned resort. She stood on the sand and surveyed what was left—a collection of crumbling *fares* set back from the lagoon in a grove of coconut palms. Hidden behind the palms, she was surprised to find a small wooden cottage, once whitewashed, but now peeling with age. It had been built on stilts near the water tanks. Colorful flowering vines clung to the porch, nearly hiding the facade of the building. The metal roof still seemed to be intact, though rusty.

Sophie climbed the stairs and tried the door and to her surprise, it opened. She walked into a huge room, with sunlight filtering through the slats of the rotting shutters. It was nearly empty of furniture and the air inside was stuffy and stale.

Though Trey's shelter was admirable, this small house offered much better protection from the rain and dampness. She walked to the nearest window and unlatched the shutters, then pushed them open. Daylight splashed across the floor and as Sophie looked up, she noticed writing on the whitewashed walls.

She opened a few more shutters and began to read. The walls had become a logbook of sorts for passing sailboats. Over the past thirty years, people from all over the world had anchored inside Suaneva's reef and left messages on the walls.

She wandered over to a low counter against the far wall and picked through a meager assortment of canned food. She'd heard of the tradition, how sailors would trade something from their stocks, for something left behind on many of the deserted islands in the Pacific. She searched through the tins, examining a can of smoked oysters and another of beef stew. At least they'd have something for dinner if they didn't catch any fish.

The steel water tanks were set behind the cottage in a small meadow, about fifty yards from the back door. When Sophie reached the nearest tank, she searched for an outlet. She expected the faucet to be corroded and impossible to open, but to her surprise, it turned easily. Obviously, passing sailors had taken advantage of the water supply, as well.

When she'd filled the water jug, Sophie circled around the tank to find a makeshift shower hooked up to a second faucet. But then, something else caught her eye—a small grove of trees, distinctly different from the coconut palms that grew on the island. Someone had thought to plant fruit trees thirty years ago!

She found mangoes, bananas and papayas hanging

from the trees and scattered on the ground below, along with broken branches, blown off in storms. Sophie wondered how the fruit could grow in such poor soil, but as she approached, the answer was evident. The original resort owners had hauled in soil so that the trees might flourish. Squatting down, she gathered some of the fallen mangoes, using her pareu as an apron.

They had everything they needed to survive on this island for more than just a few days. With fish and fruit, firewood and shelter, not to mention drinkable water, they could survive on Suaneva quite easily for as long as they had to.

How long would be enough? Sophie wondered. Would a week with Trey dull this irresistible attraction? What about a month? Somehow, Sophie sensed it was better that they'd only have wait twenty-four hours to be rescued. Any longer and desire might turn into something much more serious.

3

TREY RUBBED HIS PALM, the skin nearly raw. As Sophie had suggested, he'd gathered wood from the beach on the other side of the atoll and had stacked it over a pile of dried palm fronds and old coconut husks. But building a fire was a lot easier than starting one.

He'd learned three methods during his time with Outward Bound. Without a flint, he was left with only two options. But then, a decent stick was also hard to come by on an island with nothing but palm trees, so he'd been forced to eliminate the bow-and-drill method. Left with the fire-plow method, he'd been optimistic about his chances to succeed. But for some reason, the castaway guy in the movie had a much easier time of it.

"That's Hollywood for you," he muttered. There was probably some expert there to make sure conditions were perfect. Maybe they even used matches.

Trey sat back on his heels. He should just admit defeat and use the matches. If he got the fire lit before Sophie returned, she'd never know that he cheated.

Besides, it was ridiculous to pin his manhood on his ability to start a fire. They were living in the modern world, so why not use the conveniences available.

He looked around the camp, now very quiet without Sophie's presence. A man alone would go crazy living on this island, he mused. Hell, a man living with Sophie would probably reach the edges of sanity on occasion, as well.

Just one look at her was all it took for the fantasies to start spinning in his head. Her body was enough to tempt the most devout monk to break a vow of celibacy. And then there were her very open-minded views on sex. She seemed quite at ease discussing her desires—and his, as well.

Naughty talk had always been a turn-on for him, but this was different. Sophie wasn't doing it to play games. She was simply being honest about her passions—and her curiosity. He'd never met a woman quite like her and Trey had to wonder how deep her curiosity ran. What limits would she be interested in testing now that they were alone on the island?

Trey knew it wouldn't take much to convince her to make love with him again, to let him strip off her clothes and possess her body. From what he could tell, she wanted him as much as he wanted her.

But in just a matter of hours, he'd become obsessed by thoughts of her...of her body...of the way she made him feel when she touched him. She'd changed the way he felt about sex. With other women, it had been all about release, a need to momentarily lose himself in a warm and willing body. But there was something else pulling him toward Sophie, something much more powerful that just physical desire.

"I have lunch!"

Trey looked over his shoulder to see Sophie approaching, the water jug in one hand and her pareu gathered in the other. Though she'd only been gone an hour, he realized he hadn't stopped thinking about her since she'd left.

He slowly stood and brushed the sand off his knees. "What did you find? The local mini-mart?"

Sophie frowned. "Mini-mart? What is that?"

"Convenience store? Gas-and-go?"

"Oh," she said with a smile, finally understanding. "No. No mini-mart. But I did find some fruit trees." She stepped beneath the tarp onto the blanket and dumped the load of fruit onto the ground. "Mango," she said. "Papaya. There were bananas, too, but I would have needed the knife to cut them down. We can go back later."

"Wow," Trey said, joining her beneath the shade of the tarp. "This is great. I can see you would have done well in Outward Bound."

"I would have definitely seduced you before the red-haired girl did," she teased.

His gaze fixed on her lush lips. "I meant with the foraging."

"There wasn't any foraging involved," Sophie replied. "Whoever decided to build the resort thirty years ago planted some fruit trees." She knelt down on the blanket and picked through the toolbox for the pocketknife. When she found it, Sophie used it to slice open a mango. "There's plenty of firewood over there, too. We might want to think about moving camp."

Trey shrugged. At least he wouldn't have to admit his failure in making a fire. It was probably just the wood on this side of the island. Wood from the other side would no doubt be easier to start. *Right*.

He sat down in front of Sophie and watched her score the juicy orange flesh and flip the skin inside out. She handed it to Trey and he bit into the fruit, the juice running down his chin. "Oh, God, this is good," he said. "I didn't realize how hungry I was. I don't remember mangoes tasting like this."

Sophie prepared a piece for herself and took a huge bite. "All natural, right off the tree." She took a bite and then licked the juice off her lips and fingers.

Trey found himself captivated by her mouth. He fought the urge to lean over and taste the mango on her lips. "Look at us," he murmured. "We've got shelter, food to eat. If I can get a fire going, we'll be warm." Trey dragged his gaze from her face and stared over her shoulder at the lagoon. "How long do you think we could survive here?"

Sophie licked her fingers, then shrugged. "For a pretty long time," she said. "There's enough to eat, decent shelter. Sooner or later a sailboat would come by and we'd be rescued."

"I wouldn't call this tarp a decent shelter," Trey said.

"Actually, there's a cottage on the other side of the lagoon—it looked like it might have been an office at one time—and a few *fares* that were probably built for the workers they were going to need. If the weather turns bad we can go over there."

"You don't like the house I built for us?" he asked.

She handed him another piece of fruit. "It's a lovely house. But the one on the other side of the lagoon has walls and a real roof."

Trey shrugged. "Sometimes, I wonder if I'd have been better off living a simple life like this," he said. "I think I might have been happier if my life hadn't involved so many temptations. Here, I'd eat, sleep, look for food. Give me an endless supply of books to read and music to listen to, and I could be happy."

"You wouldn't miss all the things the world has to offer?"

"You would?" he asked.

"I wish I had more temptations." Sophie laughed softly. "I'd give anything to be able to go out and see the world. To breathe in all the excitement of a big city. To go to a shopping mall. Or to see a movie whenever I wanted. To go to a club and dance the night away. I wish I had those choices."

"There are nightclubs in Pape'ete, aren't there?"

Sophie shook her head. "Of course. But they're in Pape'ete, not London or Paris or Rome. Besides, if I left, there would be no one to take care of my father. He needs me."

"He's an adult. Can't he take care of himself?"

She forced a smile, then picked up another mango and cut it open. "These are good, aren't they?" She handed him a piece, leaving Trey with the distinct impression that she didn't want to discuss the subject any further.

He reached out and grabbed her hand, examining her fingers distractedly. "You can talk to me, Sophie. I'm the last person to judge anyone when it comes to family loyalty and duty."

"Is that why you're not with your family on Christmas?" she asked.

"That's a long story." Trey paused and gathered his thoughts. He wanted Sophie to admire him, to see him as a good person. But some of the things he'd done in his life had been awfully silly and self-centered.

"Until recently, my father disapproved of my lifestyle," he admitted. "And my spending habits. I had a trust fund I got when I turned eighteen and I used it to move as far away from my family as possible. Going home always meant listening to my dad's lectures on personal responsibility. After a while, I'd been gone so long, nobody even expected me to show up on the holidays."

"But you're working for your father now."

"Out of necessity. I don't have any money left. And he figured it was about time I settled down and made something of myself. I didn't really have a choice."

He'd never really wanted his father's respect, at least that's what he'd told himself. And from the moment Trey was old enough to stand up to Peter Shelton II,

Trey's mother, Carolyn, had abdicated her role as mediator in their relationship.

But as Trey began to see his life for what it really was, he realized that his father had a point. Sooner or later, a man had to take responsibility for doing something of value in the world. Trey's first realization came when he found himself out of money, with nothing to show for it. But the second realization came just hours ago, as the plane was descending without power.

What would he be remembered for if he'd died? In a few years, no one would even miss him. He had never truly loved a woman, never had a family or permanent home. He'd be forever known as the wastrel son of a successful billionaire. It was time to change that, time to make his father see that he was worth the investment.

"When they realize we're missing, they're going to call your family, too," Sophie said.

Trey laughed. "My father will probably be relieved," he joked. "One less worry in his life." The joke just wasn't funny anymore, he mused.

"Don't say that," Sophie murmured, reaching up to press her finger to his lips. "Things couldn't be that bad."

"My life was planned out from the time I was born. I was the male heir to the Shelton Hotel empire. Even though my two older sisters have been devoted to the family business, my father wanted *me* to run it. That's a lot of pressure for a teenager and I guess I felt I should be the one to decide. So, from the time I was about thirteen, I started to rebel. And it felt good, to see him finally realize he wasn't in control of my future."

"And what do you want now?" she asked, leaning back on her elbows and stretching her feet out in front of her.

That was a loaded question, a question he'd been trying to answer his entire adult life. What did he want? Right now, he wanted to kiss Sophie, to lean over and pull her down onto the blanket with him. "I'd settle for more of that mango," he murmured.

She handed him the knife and a fresh mango and he cut off a piece, slicing it in the same way she had. He pulled a small square of flesh off the leathery skin and held it out to her. When she moved to take it into her mouth, he held it back. Slowly, he approached her lips, then ran the fruit along her lower lip before placing it on her tongue.

It was meant to be a playful gesture, but the moment their eyes met, Trey realized how easy it was to mistake the game for sexual foreplay.

His gaze dropped to her lips, damp with the fruit's nectar. Unable to stop himself, he leaned over her and drew his tongue along her bottom lip. They were both sticky with the juice and the sweet taste was like an aphrodisiac. She licked his chin before returning to his mouth.

Sophie kissed him, her tongue slipping between his lips to tease at his. Trey held back, wanting to see how far she might go to seduce him. When she pulled away, he noticed a tiny smile curling the corners of her mouth.

She took the slice of mango from his hand and squeezed it over his chest, the juice dripping down from his collarbone to his khakis.

Sophie pushed him back until he was braced on his elbows. Slowly, she began to lick the juice off his skin, her tongue tracing a tantalizing path over his chest and abdomen. When she'd licked up nearly all the juice, Trey grabbed the other half of the mango, tore at the flesh and squeezed it over his belly.

He closed his eyes, enjoying the feel of her lips against his skin. But Sophie didn't stop there. She worked open the button on his khakis and slowly drew the zipper down. Thinking she'd stop once she finished the last of the juice, Trey reached down to run his fingers through her hair.

But she didn't stop. Instead, she tugged at the waistband of his pants until she'd pulled them and his boxers over his hips, exposing his desire to her touch. Then she picked up another mango and sliced it open, before rubbing the fruit over his belly and his cock.

The juice felt cool against his hot shaft and he moaned as her lips brushed the swollen tip. Trey knew what was coming and he waited, the anticipation of it almost too much to bear.

A moment later, a jolt of pleasure coursed through his body as she took him into her mouth. It was like nothing he'd ever felt before, the sensations so intense that it made rational thought nearly impossible.

She took her time, using her tongue to bring him closer to the edge before allowing a gradual retreat. He'd enjoyed this same act with other women, but his reactions had never been quite so powerful. Every movement sent a flood of sensation racing through his body.

Trey felt the breeze on his skin, her silky hair sliding across his abdomen as she moved above him. He heard the palms rustling and the tarp snapping. Every nerve had become more attuned, until he was alive with desire.

This was paradise, he thought as he gave himself over to the rush of surrender. He reached for her, knowing he was close but she continued making love to him with her lips and tongue. And when he finally allowed himself, he found exquisite release in the warmth of her mouth.

He lay back, his body tingling and his thoughts hazy. Nothing had prepared him for this. Her touch was so arousing, he was barely able to control himself. And the feeling of surrender that she evoked was becoming dangerously addictive.

Trey pushed up on his elbows and looked down at Sophie. He reached out and tipped her chin up until her gaze met his. A satisfied smile touched her beautiful lips and she reached for another mango and bit into the tough skin before sucking on the fruit.

"Are you still hungry?" she asked, holding out the mango.

Trey shook his head. For the first time in his life, he felt completely satisfied. And that scared him.

"I DON'T THINK THE FISH are hungry."

Sophie leaned out of the plane. Trey sat on the float,

his back braced against the wheel strut, his feet dangling
in the water. "Your feet are probably scaring them away.
Haven't you ever fished before?"

"No," Trey said. "Maybe you should do this and I'll
try to fix the radio. I built a ham radio for a science
project once."

Sophie had pulled the radio out of its bracket and
exposed the wires, but no matter how she attached them
to the battery, nothing seemed to work. With a frustrated
groan, she reached for the pocketknife that had fallen
beneath the pilot's seat. As she searched, Sophie noticed
a small plastic case shoved almost out of reach. To her
surprise, she found a flare gun and an EPIRB transponder inside, part of an old life-raft kit that had once
been stored in the tail of the plane.

All the tools they'd need for a quick rescue, she
mused. But did she want to be rescued? If the batteries
were still good on the transponder, she'd merely have
to flip a switch and an emergency radio beacon would
go out from their little island to any passing planes or
ships. They could be back in Tahiti by dinnertime.

Already, she was coming dangerously close to
feeling something for this man. When he touched her,
she became alive and aware. He made her believe she
was the most desirable woman in the world. And though
this was a fantasy world they were living in, she didn't
want to leave it. Not yet.

Still, she had a responsibility to her father. A night
filled with worry for him was not worth a night filled with

pleasure for her, was it? Once Jack Madigan realized she wasn't coming home, he might do something stupid, like borrow a plane and come looking for her.

"Have you figured out what's wrong with the radio?" Trey called.

"No," she replied. "I think this battery is dead, too." She stared at the emergency radio beacon, turning it over in her hands and rubbing her thumb over the activation switch.

"Why don't you just leave it? You said they'd find us."

"It's Christmas Eve," she said. "It would be nice if my father didn't have to spend Christmas Eve wondering if I was dead or alive."

A moment later, Trey opened the passenger-side door and slid into the seat. His hair was dripping and his khakis were wet. "I guess I shouldn't have asked you to take this trip," he said. "Not on Christmas Eve."

Sophie shook her head. "We needed the money. I could have turned the job down, but I didn't. Besides, who could have predicted we'd end up here?"

Trey took her hand and drew it to his lips, pressing a kiss in the center of her palm. "Still, I'm sorry. I guess I'll have to find a way to make it up to you. Once we get off this island."

His words sent a shiver skittering over her body. Did that mean there would be something between them after they were rescued? Or was she just reading meaning into words that had none? Drawing a deep breath,

Sophie held up the EPIRB. "Do you want to get off the island?"

"What is that?" he asked.

"An emergency radio beacon. It will send out a signal. Passing planes will pick it up, ships, too. Maybe even some of the nearby airports."

He took it out of her hand and examined it carefully, then glanced over at her. "Do you have to turn it on for it to work?"

Sophie nodded. "There's a switch right there."

"Why haven't you turned it on?" he asked.

What was she supposed to say? That she was contemplating putting it back in its case and forgetting she'd ever seen it? "I—I just found it," she said. "You turn it on."

"Do you want me to turn it on?"

"Why wouldn't I?" Sophie asked, frustrated with the back-and-forth debate.

He handed it back to her. "Then you turn it on."

"You don't want to be rescued?"

"Of course I do. Don't you?"

She bit her bottom lip as she fingered the switch. "I have to do this," she murmured. "My father will be worried. I can't do that to him." Closing her eyes, she gathered her resolve and flipped the switch. But when she opened her eyes, she noticed the little light above the switch wasn't blinking.

"How long?" he asked.

Her fingers trembled as she moved the switch back

and forth. "It—it's not working. The battery must be dead." A flood of relief washed over her, followed quickly by guilt. Was she really so desperate for a man that she'd put her father through the worst worry of his life? At least the decision was out of her hands now.

"Sorry," she murmured. "I seem to be having bad luck with batteries today."

"I'm not sorry," Trey replied. "I'm not going to lie to you, Sophie. I don't mind spending the night on this island. With you."

She handed him the plastic case, then crawled out of the door to balance on the float.

"What is this?" he asked.

"Flare gun," she said. "In case we see any passing boats or planes." Drawing a deep breath, she jumped off the float into the lagoon, sinking down to the bottom before bobbing back to the surface. She swam toward the beach, then turned and floated on her back, staring up at the sky.

Was it wrong to want this time with Trey to last a little longer? Was she being selfish? Or was she simply taking pleasure where she might find it? She'd already given up her life for her father. Would he really begrudge her just one day of happiness before returning to her ordinary existence?

The sun broke through the clouds and the ocean breeze cooled her wet skin. She felt weightless, as if all her concerns had sunk to the bottom of the lagoon and only pleasure had risen to the surface. She'd never wanted a man the way she wanted Trey. It wasn't just about his body, or about him satisfying her desire. There was more there.

Sophie heard a splash and a moment later, she felt his arms around her waist, pulling her beneath the water. They surfaced together, wrapped in each other's arms, their limbs tangling.

He kissed her, his mouth molding to hers, his hands tangled in her wet hair. She wasn't sure what he meant by it, but she knew there was a reason. He demanded a response and Sophie returned the kiss in full measure, her tongue savoring the taste of him.

When he finally drew back, Trey looked down into her eyes. "There are moments when I don't want to go back," he murmured. "Ever."

Sophie nodded, knowing exactly how he felt. The more time they spent together, the more it felt as if they could live a lifetime on Suaneva. But they couldn't survive on passion alone. And though their desire might feed the soul, it didn't go very far to feed the body.

"Aren't you uncomfortable in those?" Sophie asked.

Trey glanced down at his shorts, the khakis still wet from their swim in the lagoon. "Yeah. I guess. I suppose I could wear my boxers."

Sophie shook her head. "Take them off," she ordered, levering to her feet from her spot beneath the shelter. "Go ahead. As long as we're staying here for a while, you might as well dress like a native."

Regarding her suspiciously, Trey stripped out of his

shorts. She pointed to his boxers dismissively and he skimmed them over his hips and kicked them aside, too. Though they'd already been intimate more than once, he felt a bit exposed running around the island naked.

"I'm not sure I like this," he said.

"It doesn't feel good?" she asked.

"Well, yeah. It feels really good. But I'm not used to running around with all my bits and pieces showing. Something might bite me."

"I promise I won't," Sophie teased. "Besides, you don't have to be embarrassed."

"Well, you're dressed and I'm not."

She glanced down at her outfit, his shirt tied beneath her breasts, and the flowered pareu knotted around her waist. "I think you need to get rid of your inhibitions," she suggested. "No one is going to see you…or your bits and pieces, except me. And I've already seen you naked."

"There are times when I'd prefer to hide my reactions, if you don't mind."

She let her gaze drift down below his waist and then back up again. "It's a perfectly natural thing," she said. "It doesn't bother me at all. In fact, I find it flattering."

"It kind of takes all the mystery out of things, don't you think?" He paused. "I mean, I might as well have a big neon sign on my forehead that blinks *Horny* every time I get aroused."

"I don't need a neon sign to know when you're

aroused," she said. She unknotted the pareu from her waist and wrapped it around his, fastening it low on his hips. "How is that?"

Trey wriggled, enjoying the feel of the thin fabric on his skin. It felt much better than the damp khakis or his boxer shorts. "The breeze just blows right up beneath it and makes everything very…pleasant," he said.

Sophie giggled. "You look nice in a skirt. Not many men can carry it off, but you can."

"And what are you going to wear now?" he asked.

She was dressed in just the shirt and her thong. Sophie picked up his boxers and held them up. "We are a little short on clothing. I could wear these."

Trey shook his head. "No, I think I like you just the way you are." The thong was sexy as hell, showing off the sweet curves of her backside. And the shirt was thin enough that he could see her breasts through the fabric. Any fewer clothes and he'd be walking around with a perpetual hard-on all day. Any more and he'd be depriving himself of his one true pleasure—looking at Sophie's delicious body.

Sophie wrapped her arms around his neck and kissed him, arching against him as he held her close. "See, already you're starting to adapt to the ways of the island."

"I'm wearing a skirt," Trey said, looking down at the brightly flowered fabric.

"I know. But it's practical. When you want to swim, you just untie the knot. And if it gets wet, it dries very quickly. It's the perfect thing. You'll want to buy five or six of them for yourself when we get back to Pape'ete."

Trey chuckled. It was a fair swap, but still, he liked the way she looked dressed in his shirt. It made him feel as if she were his and his alone—at least until they got off the island.

She grabbed her bag from beneath the shelter and rummaged through it until she found a brown plastic bottle. "You should put some of this on."

She handed it to him and he screwed off the top and sniffed. He recognized the scent from her skin. "What is it? Your perfume? First a skirt and now perfume?"

"It's called *monoi*. It's for the sun, to keep you from burning. It has coconut and sandalwood and jasmine in it. And citronella for the mosquitoes. They can get bad at night." She glanced around. "Although, they shouldn't be too bad on an atoll like this."

"Why?"

"There's not a lot of standing water. And it's always pretty windy. But it is the rainy season and they're at their worst when it's damp."

Trey sniffed it again. He liked the way she smelled, but he wasn't sure he wanted to smell the same. "I think I'm all right."

Sighing impatiently, Sophie grabbed the bottle and squeezed some of the oil into her hand. As she began to rub it into his chest, Trey started to believe in the benefits of the oil. Her touch was like a narcotic, relaxing him, yet exciting him all at once. The scent of the oil filled the air and he pressed his hand to the small of her back, pulling her closer.

"That feels good," he murmured.

She smoothed her palms over his shoulders, then circled around behind him to rub the *monoi* on his back. Did she have any idea what her touch did to him, how deeply it stirred his desires?

With Sophie, even the most benign things became seductive. She could wiggle her toes in the sand and he got turned on. Or she could lick her bottom lip and he'd lose himself in a fantasy about how those lips might feel on certain parts of his body.

When she was finished with his back, she put the cap on the bottle and tossed it on the blanket. "There. You're ready to go," she said.

"Where are we going?"

"You'll see," she replied. "Since we didn't have any luck at fishing, we'll have to find dinner. And I know the perfect place."

"Are you asking me on a date?"

"A date?"

He slipped his arm around her waist as they began to walk. "I think you just asked me to dinner. Before we go, I want to make something perfectly clear. I don't kiss on the first date."

"I see," Sophie said, giggling. "That's good. Because neither do I."

As they walked along the lagoon to the south end of the atoll, Trey wondered what other delights he and

Sophie would share before the night was over. Once they settled in for the evening, there was nothing else to do but amuse themselves with sexual activities.

But then, there was always conversation. With Sophie, Trey enjoyed that almost as much as sex. This time together had proven one thing—they enjoyed each other's company. For Trey, that was saying a lot.

There were very few women he'd met that he'd wanted to spend an extended period of time with. Mostly, he enjoyed their company in bed, and that was about it. The women he'd known had usually been silly and shallow and interested in only one thing—his money.

But Sophie didn't seem to be aware of who he was, or of the life he'd led. Their acquaintance began in the hangar at the airport and she didn't care at all about what had come before.

"Tell me more about this resort you want to build," Sophie said, wrapping her arm around his waist as they walked. "What would it be like?"

"Luxurious," he said. "But primitive."

Sophie frowned. "How is that possible?"

He'd been turning the idea around and around in his head for such a long time that Trey was almost afraid to talk about it, afraid that if he did, the idea might not hold up to scrutiny. "There's a segment of the population, a very wealthy segment, that's looking for a completely unique vacation. I want to find a location so secluded that they can feel safe enough to relax and enjoy themselves."

She didn't say anything for a long time, but he could see she was thinking about what he'd said. "It will be very expensive to build on an island," Sophie warned.

He shrugged. "Money really isn't a problem."

"What about the other things? You'll need electricity and fresh water. A way to get materials on and off the island. A way to get guests back and forth to a major airport."

"You've thought about these things?"

"Well, haven't you?"

"Yes," he said. "Of course."

"I live in these islands, Trey. I know what it's like. It's not like living in a big city with all the conveniences. Everything is simpler there, yet it's much more difficult, as well. Here, everything comes in by boat or plane and it's expensive."

"Well, if we build it right, then it will sustain itself," Trey said, pulling her to a stop. "We'll power everything with windmills. We'll collect rainwater. We'll sail our guests to the island. We'll prepare simple meals with all-natural foods, grown on the island. We'll serve the kind of meals that islanders have eaten for centuries." He paused. "What do you think?"

"What does your father think?" Sophie asked.

"I haven't told him about that part of the plan yet. He's kind of a traditional hotel developer. He really doesn't have any imagination. Do you think it's a good idea?"

"Yes!" she said with a smile. "I think it's a marvelous idea."

They continued to walk, Trey suddenly more excited about the project than he'd ever been. It *was* a good idea, but he'd been afraid to talk about it, afraid that his father would immediately find fault or discount it completely because he'd been the one to come up with the idea. But Sophie lived in these islands and she knew them well. If she thought the concept would work, then maybe it wasn't so crazy.

"If you're bringing people by boat, your location needs to be closer to an island with an airport," Sophie suggested.

"I'm kind of flexible on that," he said. "We could bring people in by plane."

"Then an atoll is a better idea," she said. "You can land in the lagoon or you can build a landing strip on a larger *motu*. And if there's a deep enough channel, you could bring boats right into the lagoon."

As they continued their walk, they discussed more of the details, Sophie listening quietly as he explained everything he wanted to accomplish. In the end, Trey felt as if the project were suddenly real. This wasn't just a pipe dream anymore. He could make this work.

But he could use Sophie's help. Why not hire her? After all, she'd be in on it from the very beginning. They could work together on the project. She certainly knew enough to coordinate all their transportation needs. And Madigan Air could use the business.

"I should hire you," Trey said. "I'll need someone here to be my liaison if the project goes through.

Someone who knows the islands. Someone who can cut through the red tape."

Once the offer was out there, Trey realized just how stupid it sounded. Though they might get along quite well as lovers, stuck on a deserted island, what made him think they could have a working relationship once they went back to the real world?

"I-I'm not sure how much longer I'm going to be in the islands," Sophie said. "The business isn't doing real well and—"

"But don't you see? This would be an answer to all your problems. I could hire you to fly me back and forth. I'd pay you well. And—"

"We'll see," she said, cutting him off.

They continued the rest of their walk in silence, their fingers laced together as they waded through a narrow channel that fed the lagoon.

After five minutes of silence, Trey was certain he'd made a mistake. Perhaps this was all they were supposed to have, just twenty-four hours on this island. She didn't seem interested in anything more than that. But he didn't want to believe it would end so soon. He was beginning to care about Sophie, and he wanted to know her much better.

He silently chastised himself. Hell, he'd never in his life felt so vulnerable. And it was his fault, letting himself believe what they were sharing was more than just a temporary passion. From now on, he'd accept the fact that their affair would end the moment they got off the island.

That didn't mean he couldn't enjoy the pleasure her body offered. He just wouldn't attach any expectations to their relationship. It would be purely sexual.

4

THE CLOUDS HAD BROKEN and sunlight filtered through the grove of coconut palms, illuminating the remains of the old resort. Trey stood at the edge of the beach, staring at the rotting *fares,* an odd expression on his face. He seemed almost perplexed by the ruins of the village, the scene putting a damper on his good mood.

Was he having doubts about his plan? Sophie wondered. The person who had tried to develop Suaneva thirty years ago had had big dreams, but this was all that was left of them. "Maybe he just didn't know what he was getting himself into."

"Maybe," Trey said. He shook his head. "At least he tried."

"Just because he failed doesn't mean you will. With enough money, you can do almost anything."

"My father is the one with money," Trey said. "I was thinking if he doesn't approve of my plan, then I might strike out on my own. You know, build the resort anyway. I could find investors or take out a loan against my trust-fund money." He drew a deep breath. "Then again, maybe I don't know what the hell I'm doing."

She reached out and grabbed his hand. It seemed to help, for as soon as she touched him, he glanced over at her and smiled. "I think it's a great idea," Sophie said. She pulled him along toward the cottage. "Come on. Let's go find something for dinner."

They walked past the *fares* into the grove of trees and she led him up the steps of the weather-beaten cottage. The flowers on the vines created a thick scent in the air. Trey stopped to pick one and tucked it behind her left ear.

"There," he murmured. "I like that. It's perfect."

She reached up and plucked it out, then drew a deep breath of the scent. "You have to learn the meaning of the flower," she said softly as she ran it along his bottom lip. "When you wear it behind your left ear, it means you're taken. When it's behind your right ear, you're available."

He reached to take it from her, but she shook her head and held it back. "There's more. If you wear flowers behind both ears, it means you're taken, but available for the right person. And when you wear the flower backward, it means follow me and you'll have a good time."

With a playful smile, Sophie turned the flower around and put it behind her right ear, the bloom facing backward. Then Trey pulled another flower off the vine and did the same. "Now we know where we stand," he said with a rakish grin.

Sophie opened the door to the cottage and stepped inside and he followed her into the dark interior. Light filtered through the slats of the shutters, creating an odd pattern on the floors and walls. Trey pulled her into his arms and kissed her, his hands running freely over her body. "Alone in a dark room. Is this what you mean by a good time?"

They'd gone past the point of denying themselves pleasure, Sophie mused. Now, it was possible to act on their urges without a second thought. If she wanted to touch him, she could. If he wanted to kiss her, he'd do just that.

The kiss was slow and delicious, his hands making her body come alive with wonderful sensations. He cupped her bare backside and pulled her against him, the evidence of his arousal growing hot and hard between them. Sophie sighed, desire aching deep inside her. Though they were still new to this passion, it didn't make it any less powerful. Instinctively, she reached down and ran her fingertips along the length of his shaft, the thin fabric of the pareu providing little protection from her touch.

Slowly, they explored each other, using touch instead of sight to guide them. Sophie wondered if she should be playing harder to get. But why deny themselves the pleasures? They were both consenting adults and they only had a limited time on the island. Besides, she had every intention of keeping her emotions in check. This was about sexual gratification and nothing more.

If she had learned anything from her parents' relationship, it was that love couldn't be trusted to last. As a small child, Sophie had looked at her mother and father as a fairy-tale king and queen. But her innocence was slowly stripped away by her father's infidelities and her mother's abandonment.

She'd never be able to trust a man with her heart and soul. But she could give him temporary custody of her body. Passion and desire didn't need to transform into an emotional connection.

"Do you have any idea how beautiful you are?" Trey whispered.

"You can't even see me," she said, his touch sending a rush of sensation through her body.

"But I can feel you. And you feel beautiful."

He kissed her again, Sophie melting into his arms. She'd grown so familiar with this, the way his tongue invaded her mouth, the way he tasted. It felt good to know a man again. But then, she didn't really want to know him. Sex with a stranger was so much less complicated.

Sophie drew back. "This is kind of silly, don't you think?"

"Kissing you?"

"No, hiding in a dark room while you kiss me. There's no one here to see us. We don't have to sneak around."

He chuckled softly. "You're right. Old habits, I guess."

Sophie wanted to ask what he'd meant by that, but she bit her tongue and stepped out of his embrace. Light poured into the room as she threw open a set of shutters. When Sophie turned back around, she found Trey survey-ing the interior of the cottage with a look of amazement.

"What the hell is this?" he asked. Crossing to stand

next to one of the windows, he frowned as he read. "This is really weird. Who wrote all of this?"

"Passing sailors," Sophie said. "From all over the world. It's like a diary of this island. Thirty years' worth of visits. And look what they left." She crossed the room to the small counter and picked through the assortment of canned goods. "Spam," she said, holding up a square tin. "It's some kind of canned meat, I think."

"Ah, no thanks."

"Artichoke hearts?"

Trey shook his head, wrinkling his nose. "Only in a nice parmesan sauce over pasta."

"Baked beans. Men always love baked beans." She grabbed another tin. "And smoked oysters."

"I've heard those are an aphrodisiac," Trey said, sending her a playful leer. "I don't think we need any more help in that area, do you?"

"Probably not," Sophie said, pleased that he found no fault with their sex life. She bent down and opened the cabinet beneath the counter, curious to see what there was in the way of cooking utensils. She gasped in surprise. "Oh, my! Look at this. I think I've found something we can both agree on." She grabbed one of the bottles lying on the shelf and held it up. "Wine."

"Really?" Trey strode across the room and knelt down beside her. There were five or six bottles lying inside the cabinet including a couple of French vintages and a Merlot from the Napa Valley. "Nice. Although in this heat, the bottles might have gone bad. We'll need a corkscrew."

"I think there might be one in the pocketknife you were using from the plane," Sophie said.

Trey sat back on his heels. "Instead of carting this stuff over to the other side of the lagoon, maybe we should just move camp, like you suggested. This cottage seems pretty weather tight. And the food and water are here."

"But what about your shelter?"

"I think my ego will give way to comfort," Trey admitted. "It did the trick for a while, but this seems to be a much better place to spend the night, don't you agree?" He slowly stood and glanced around the room. "So this isn't really a deserted tropical island. And we could have company at any minute."

"I suppose we could," Sophie said. "But it's not likely. There aren't many sailors who'd brave the typhoon season in the South Pacific. It would make for miserable sailing."

"Good," he murmured. "I don't want any company. I'm enjoying the relaxed dress code."

Sophie rearranged the cans on the counter. "After we move over here, I'll make us a Christmas dinner and we'll settle in and wait to get rescued."

Just the word *rescue* brought a flood of regret. As much as Sophie wanted it to last, this time on the island would come to a very quick end. It would be over before she knew it, and all she'd be left with was memories. She let her gaze drift slowly down Trey's body, then back up again. She had grown so used to having him near, and in such a short time.

They'd tossed aside the last of their inhibitions when they'd discarded their clothes. Now, there was nothing but a bit of fabric between her touch and his body, between his hands and her bare skin. If she wanted him, all she had to do was reach out and untie the knot in the pareu.

Temptation was always there, just within her reach. She could be naked in a matter of seconds and so could he. Both of them knew they wouldn't be able to keep their hands off each other for very long. But it was an arousing game to try.

Sophie stepped toward him, tempted to pick up where they'd left off. But she twisted her fingers together in front of her. They had a lot of work to do and the sooner they got it done, the sooner they could relax. "If you could go gather our things from the other camp, I'll get wood for the fire," she said.

"I can help you with the wood," he countered, grabbing her hand and placing it on his chest.

Just a simple touch sent a shiver of desire through her, strong enough for Sophie to realize that, from now on, working together was impossible. No doubt they'd find some excuse to touch each other again and then work would be forgotten in favor of sex.

"I'll be fine," she said. "The sooner we get this done, the sooner we can…relax."

He gave her a look, as if he knew exactly what she implied with the word *relax*. "All right," he said.

They strolled out of the cottage and stood on the porch. "Go on," she said. "I'll be here when you get back."

He took her hand and pressed a kiss to the middle of her palm, drawing his tongue along her index finger, before putting her fingertip in his mouth. It was a provocative gesture and one that made her heart skip a beat. "You promise?"

"Where am I going to go?" Sophie teased. "It's an island."

Trey nodded reluctantly. "Yeah, I guess you're right." He kissed her hand again, then stepped off the porch. "So, I'll see you in a little while."

"Yes, you will."

They made a good team, Sophie mused as she watched Trey walk away. He was so even-tempered, so unselfish, that she couldn't imagine them ever disagreeing. And even though they didn't know each other at all, she couldn't imagine having a better companion on a deserted tropical island.

Maybe working for him wouldn't be such a crazy idea. If he really was going to build his resort, then she could be a valuable help to him. And it would add a lot more excitement to her life. Plus, there was the benefit of spending more time with Trey once they got off this island. And more time meant…well, more sex, didn't it?

Still, Sophie had already decided her future wasn't here on the islands, but in some exciting city. Was she willing to give up on that dream for good sex? A tiny smile quirked at the corners of her mouth. Maybe. If the sex was really good.

As for a real relationship, one that included love and commitment, Trey had a life of his own back in the States. And she wasn't about to follow him around, begging for his attention whenever he might want to give it. This was a twenty-four-hour fling, nothing more. Once the twenty-four hours were over, they would be, too. And then, she'd find a way to start her new life away from these islands—on her own.

IT DIDN'T TAKE VERY LONG for Trey to gather their meager belongings. He put everything he could carry onto the canvas tarp and then tied it up with the ropes. He thought it might be easy to drag it along the sand, but in the end, he waded out into knee-deep water and floated the bundle as he walked.

The plane and his attempt at a campfire were the only things he left behind in their first camp. In truth, he was a bit sad to leave, even though they'd only lived at the location for the morning. They'd made love on the sand there and she'd pleasured him beneath the small clump of coconut palms. Once they moved, would things suddenly change?

When they'd first tumbled onto the beach, wrapped in each other's arms, he hadn't even thought about the consequences of what they were about to do. He'd been so glad to be alive, he hadn't thought of anything else.

But with each touch, each kiss, his feelings for Sophie were growing. Was it simply because they were here alone, without anyone to interfere? In the past ten years, the press had hounded him unmercifully. Every relationship he'd gone into had been splashed across the pages of some magazine. He hadn't been able to enjoy anything close to a normal romance with a woman.

Being here with Sophie was the nearest he'd come. And to his surprise, he was falling fast. He could barely stand to be away from her, so addicted was he to her presence. He had to fight to keep from touching her and kissing her. And there were times when he honestly felt he could be content simply listening to her voice for the next fifty years.

Was this what it was like to fall in love? Trey shook his head, pushing the thought from his brain. He'd met Sophie seven hours ago! Besides, he didn't have a clue about what it was like to be in love. Lust, now that was another thing. But love wasn't something Trey had ever experienced for himself.

As he approached the ruins of the old village, Trey called for Sophie. When she didn't respond, he dragged their belongings onto the shore and went in search of her. After ten minutes, he came to the conclusion that she was either too far away to hear him or something was wrong.

Raking his fingers through his hair, Trey tried to calm the fear that coursed through his body. If something had happened, there was nothing he could do. They were alone on this island with no help available. Drawing a deep breath, he tried to think of where she might have gone.

He would have seen her had she walked along the

shoreline. "Wood," he muttered, spinning around to find a small pile of palm fronds near the front steps of the cottage. She'd probably walked across to the ocean side to search for wood.

He ran back through the grove of palms, past the water tanks, toward the ocean side of the *motu*. Sophie wouldn't have been stupid enough to go swimming on her own. Hell, even he knew better than that.

Trey ran until his lungs burned, weaving through the tangled underbrush and dodging palm trees. When he burst out of the trees onto the beach, he bent over and gulped a deep breath of the humid ocean air. Sweat dripped down his chest and his legs were cut and bleeding from the sharp edges of old palm fronds.

He scanned the beach, then caught sight of her sitting on the sand a hundred yards away. Cursing softly, Trey kicked off his shoes and jogged toward her. She didn't see him approach and when he called her name, Sophie jumped as if startled. Shading her eyes from the sun, she stared up at him.

"Jesus, Sophie, didn't you hear me calling you?" He squatted down in front of her and peered into her face. "When I got back to camp and couldn't find you, I was worried."

"Where am I going to go?" Sophie asked.

"I don't know. I thought you might have taken a swim in the lagoon and drowned. Or been bitten by some poisonous spider and were now lying under a tree, dying. Don't scare me like that."

"There are no poisonous spiders on this island," she said. "Or in all of French Polynesia. I told you, the only thing that might kill me would be a centipede bite. Or a shark attack."

"Well, there you go. I did have good reason to be worried."

"There's more chance I'd be killed by a falling coconut than a shark," she said with a shrug.

He plopped down in front of her. "Really?"

Sophie nodded. "There are a lot of people killed by coconuts," she said.

Trey reached out and grabbed her hands. "What are you doing out here?"

"Just sitting. I was curious what the beach was like on this side of the *motu*. This is nicer than the lagoon side, don't you think? I mean for your resort."

"Yeah, I guess." Was that really what she was thinking about? He tried to calm his anger at her, knowing that he ought to be happy she was fine. But as he stared at her beautiful face, Trey realized he wasn't really angry at her at all. She was a grown woman and could take responsibility for her own safety. He was angry at himself, for caring so much, for being frightened at the possibility of losing her.

"We're going to get some bad weather," she murmured. "There's a squall coming in."

Trey glanced back over his shoulder to see a wall of slate-gray clouds building on the southern horizon. "How long?"

"A few hours at least. We may have to secure the plane."

"Why?"

"If the wind is high it will pick it up and flip it over. I saw some old pilings on the west side of the lagoon. We can pull it over to that spot and tie it down properly."

"How high would the wind need to get to flip it over?"

"High. At Faaa, we just put it in the hangar." She looked at him, a frown wrinkling her brow. "If the plane gets wrecked on this island, Madigan Air is out of business."

Trey reached out and took her hand. "If it gets wrecked on this island, I'll buy you a new plane," he promised. He straightened, then pulled Sophie to her feet. She bent down and picked up her sandals and then wandered over to the water's edge. Trey watched her, wondering at her subdued mood. Was she having regrets about what had happened between them? Just an hour ago, he'd never felt closer to a woman, but now, she seemed a million miles away.

"Come on, let's go," he said, holding out his hand.

She turned to face him, and took a step. An instant later, he saw a look of pain cross her face. "Oww!" she cried, as she hopped on one foot.

"What is it?"

Sophie looked down at the sand, then groaned. "Jellyfish."

"They can be poisonous, can't they?" he asked, a current of fear shooting through him.

"Just box jellyfish," she replied, wincing as she hopped on one foot.

Trey stepped to her side and she wrapped her arm around his for balance. "How do we know what kind that is?" He pointed to the nearly transparent corpse lying in the sand.

"Help me rinse off my foot," she said.

He scooped her up and carried her into deeper water, wading in up to his thighs so she could dip her foot in. "How do you know if it was a box jellyfish?"

She sighed impatiently. "Well, if I die, then we'll know," Sophie said in a wry tone.

"Don't kid about that," Trey warned.

She winced. "I think I can stand. You can put me down."

"I'm going to carry you back to camp." He set her on her feet and then turned his back to her. "Hop up."

"You don't have to do this," she said.

"Don't argue, Sophie. Just do as I say."

He waited. He didn't want to care so much, but Trey couldn't help himself. What if something went wrong? What if the jellyfish *was* poisonous and there was nothing he could do to help her? They were stuck in the middle of nowhere, helpless and completely vulnerable. What had seemed like a fun time could turn deadly serious in a heartbeat.

She barely weighed more than the backpack he'd carried during his Outward Bound trip. Driven by adrenaline, they made it back to the cottage in less than fifteen minutes. He set Sophie down on the front steps, then bent to examine her foot. An angry red welt ran the length of it, from her ankle to her little toe.

"What should we do?" he asked.

"There's not much you can do," Sophie replied. "There's a gel that I have at home that stops the sting… but that's at home." She leaned back, bracing her hands behind her. "You could always pee on it," she suggested. "That's supposed to work when you don't have anything to relieve the sting."

"You want me to pee on your foot?" Trey shook his head. "No, I'm not going to do that. I can't."

"Why not?"

"There's a limit to how kinky I go and that's beyond my limit. There has to be something else."

"This isn't sexual," Sophie said. "It's medical. I need something acidic and that's all we have."

"No, it isn't," Trey said. He took the steps two at a time and returned a few moments later with a bottle of red wine. "We have this."

Trey made quick work of the cork, then dumped the wine over her foot, the liquid running down the steps and into the sandy ground. He took a quick swig for himself, then handed her the bottle and she did the same. "Is it feeling better?"

Sophie wrinkled her nose. "I think so."

"How about you? Do you feel all right?"

She nodded. "I don't think it was poisonous. Really, you don't have to worry."

He sat down on the steps and stared at her foot, trying to control his frustration. Why was she taking this so lightly? Didn't she realize how serious it could have been? It would kill him if anything had happened to her and he wasn't able to help. Trey took another gulp of the wine, hoping that it would calm his nerves. "From now on, we stick together. You don't go anywhere without me. Understand?"

"I'm not a child. You don't have to talk to me like I am." Her chin was set at a stubborn angle and she looked at him through narrowed eyes. The sweet, funny Sophie he'd known was suddenly replaced by a obstinate, dismissive, fiercely independent woman.

He wanted to lash out at her, to scold her for her part in this all. She'd made him care about her, made him want to protect her. And now he'd been forced to face the fact that he did care—more than he wanted to.

He leaned closer and pressed a kiss to the soft skin above her knee. "You have to be more careful," he murmured, hoping to defuse the situation.

Sophie ran her fingers through his hair, brushing it away from his eyes, her lips pressed into a pout. "Don't order me around. You have no right."

"I'm sorry. So, what can I do to make you feel better?"

"Can I have more wine?" she asked.

He held the bottle out over her foot, but she grabbed it before he could pour and took a long swig. Sophie pointed to her sole. "Can you see any stingers? If you take the blade of the knife, you should be able to scrape them off."

Trey held her foot up to the light and shook his head. "I don't think so. But you probably shouldn't walk on it for a while. I'm going to get a fire going and then we'll figure out what to do about the plane."

THE RAIN BEGAN SHORTLY AFTER they returned from the beach. Within seconds, a few droplets had turned into a deluge, with water running off the tin roof in sheets. Trey had jogged to the other side of the lagoon and pulled the plane over to the submerged pilings. Relieved, Sophie had thought her worries were over.

But when Trey returned to the cottage, he'd informed her that the wood pilings were so rotted, it was impossible to tie it down securely. In the end, he had done what he could, but wasn't confident that the plane would stay where it was.

Sophie rested her back against the weather wall of the cottage, freshly picked flowers from the vines scattered around her as she wove them into a wreath. They'd finished the first bottle of wine and Trey had opened a second. He occupied himself with tearing the canvas tarp into strips, intent on fashioning a hammock by weaving and knotting the canvas together.

She watched him surreptitiously, wondering at the argument they'd had earlier. She thought she knew him, enough to assume that he didn't have a quick temper. But his anger over her trip to the beach and the jellyfish seemed completely out of character. After all, what right did he have to chastise her like that? She wasn't a child. And it wasn't her fault the jellyfish had picked that place to die.

Perhaps this was a character flaw coming to the surface, she mused. Though Trey might appear to be easygoing, he showed a possessive streak that she didn't care for at all. Had she even been considering him as boyfriend material, that characteristic alone would have disqualified him in an instant.

Sophie grabbed the wine bottle and took another sip. Either she was getting drunk or her foot was feeling much better. Or maybe it was both. A tiny hiccup slipped out and she covered her mouth with her fingertips.

She glanced over at Trey. His back was braced against the porch railing, his long legs crossed in front of him. The pareu barely hid his assets and Sophie allowed her gaze to drift.

She wondered what he was thinking. Was he only pretending to concentrate on the hammock? Or was his mind caught up in some sexual fantasy? If he was thinking about sex, then he was doing a pretty good job of hiding it. Perhaps she'd have to give him a little nudge. Sophie stood and stretched her arms over her head, then began to unknot the shirt.

"Where are you going?" he asked, his attention suddenly sparked.

"To take a shower," she said, letting the shirt fall to the floor of the porch. She skimmed out of her thong and dropped it on top of his shirt. "The rain will wash off the salt on my skin."

She wandered down the stairs, then stopped and

tipped her face up, letting the downpour soak her thoroughly. The rain was warm, the water fresh, and Sophie closed her eyes and opened her mouth, letting the drops fall on her tongue.

She didn't want to look to see if he had followed her. But a few seconds later, she felt his hands on her shoulders, the heat of his body against her back. Trey's palms smoothed over her skin, but she didn't turn around. Instead, she sighed softly and arched back against him, an invitation for him to go further.

His fingers tangled in her hair as he held it out, letting the rain fall through it. Everywhere he touched, Sophie's nerves tingled, her body came alive, her senses aware. His path wasn't deliberate, moving from her breasts to her feet and then back up to the nape of her neck, as if he couldn't decide which spot he liked best.

When she turned in his arms and looked up into his eyes, she saw the desire there. In a heartbeat, he captured her face with his hands and pulled her into a deep, mind-numbing kiss. He seemed desperate to possess her mouth, demanding that she meet his need. But there was something else there—a need to set things right between them again.

Sophie opened beneath the assault and let the kiss consume her. Nothing in her life had prepared her for the power of his touch over her body. In the past, men had come and gone from her life without a sense of loss. But already, Sophie had to wonder how she'd deal without this chaos he'd created in her body. Every cell of her being seemed to surrender to him, to ache for what they shared. She thought nothing of resisting his charms the first time, but now Sophie knew she'd completely lost that capacity.

Breathless and dizzy with desire, Sophie pressed her hands against his chest. He pulled back and smiled, the droplets of rain clinging to his dark lashes. She smoothed her fingertips along his torso, then untied the knot in the pareu.

She slowly circled around him, washing the salt off his body with the damp fabric, running it over his muscled back and arms. It felt good to be clean again, to be able to press her lips to his flesh without tasting the ocean.

Sophie pushed up on her tiptoes and kissed the nape of his neck, then trailed her lips and tongue down to the small of his back. She heard him moan softly, pleased that he wasn't immune to her touch, either.

They stood in the rain for a long time, letting the water wash over them, exploring the curves and angles of each other's bodies. Though it was a practical choice, Sophie had no doubt about where their "shower" was leading.

He took the lead as he ran his hand down her belly to find the warm spot between her legs. His caress was soft and slow, but almost immediately, she felt an overwhelming surge of desire building inside her.

Determined to share the exquisite pleasure that raced through her body, Sophie wrapped her fingers around his erection and began to stroke him, the warm rain causing him to be slick and smooth.

She drew a deep breath as she nuzzled her face into the curve of Trey's neck. He smelled like the rain and the last traces of the *monoi* left on his skin. Sophie didn't hesitate to tantalize him, to touch him in a way that was meant to make him ache for release.

There were no walls between them that hadn't already been breached, no part of his body that she wasn't allowed to touch. Here, on this island, they were free to explore their desire without any outside interference. For now, time stood still, no one else existed, the real world was just a clouded memory.

Her fingers slid over the tip of his shaft and then back down again. This man who had such control over her desires was completely at her mercy. She looked up at his handsome face, his eyes closed and his lips parted.

She continued to watch him as she placed a kiss in the center of his chest. When she moved to his nipple, Trey sucked in a sharp breath and when she delved lower, he tangled his fingers in her wet hair and groaned. But this time, he wouldn't allow her to go further.

He pulled her back up along his chest and then took her hand and led her over to the front steps of the cottage. Gently, Trey sat her down on the top step, while he knelt below her. His hand slid down her belly and his fingers found the soft folds between her legs, now slick with her desire.

Sophie had been with enough men to know exactly what he wanted. She leaned back, turning her face up into the rain that poured off the porch roof onto them both. And when his tongue continued what his fingers had begun, Sophie moaned out loud.

She knew he was watching her, knew that everything he did to her was designed to end in absolute pleasure and shattering release. He teased and tempted her, learning by her reactions what she liked best. And when she seemed to move close to the edge, he slowed his seduction.

Minute by minute, he brought her ever nearer before dragging her back, until her eyes were hazy with desire and her breath was quick and shallow.

"Oh God, what are you doing to me?" she whispered. She tangled her fingers in his wet hair, pulling him along her body until their mouths met. He was still hard and his shaft teased at the spot between her legs, rubbing back and forth until she was desperate to have him inside her.

Sophie was stunned at how quickly it came upon her. One moment, she was running her hands over his back, and the next, she was writhing beneath him. The spasm came hard and fast and she pulled his hips against hers as she dissolved into her orgasm. A moment later, he joined her, his essence warm and sticky between them both.

When they'd both floated back down to reality, Sophie reached between their bodies and touched him again. Trey sucked in a sharp breath. "Stop," he begged. "Sophie, stop."

She did as he asked, tossing her hair back from her

face to look up at him. She waited for a long moment, watching him regain control over his senses. He shifted his weight and sat down beside her on the steps, stretching his arms over his head and moaning softly.

The rain had begun to subside and the air was fresh and cool for the moment. His fingers ran through her hair and Trey pulled her into a deep kiss, his mouth possessing hers, leaving her breathless. The kiss spun out into one long, delicious ending. A few moments later, Trey opened his eyes. A grin curled the corners of his mouth. "That was…incredible."

Sophie reached down to touch him again. "It was?"

He moaned, grabbing her hand to stop her teasing. "You know those questions they ask, about the three things you'd want on a deserted island?"

"Yes," Sophie replied.

"I could never decide what I'd take. There were too many things that I thought were necessary. But now that I'm here, I know exactly what I'd need."

"Food and water?"

He shook his head. "We have that here."

"What then?"

"You. You'd be on the top of my list."

"Any woman? Or me specifically?"

"I'm pretty sure it would have to be you."

"What else?" she asked, now curious about his answers.

"Condoms," he said. "An unlimited supply. So we'd never have to keep ourselves from doing anything."

"What, are you going to have them air-dropped? How many would you need?"

"Oh, I don't know. Maybe three a day. About a thousand a year. Taking into account the average life span, I'd say we'd need fifty thousand, just to be safe."

"And what else?" Sophie asked. "Besides a warehouse to store them in?"

"A good fishing pole," he said after a few moments of thought. "With all that sex, I think I'd need some protein every now and then." Trey reached up and tucked her hair behind her ear. "And what would you take?"

"I don't know. I never thought about it. Probably an airplane, so I could get off the island when I wanted."

Trey frowned. "But that's not following the rules."

"I've lived on a little island, not much different than this one, for my entire life," Sophie said. "Sooner or later, it will make you crazy."

Trey sat up and raked his hands through his damp hair, a frown wrinkling his brow. "It can't be that bad."

"It's easy for you to romanticize all of this," she said, pushing up beside him. "The warm breezes and the blue ocean, the white sand and the beautiful flowers. The naked women. And it will be interesting for a week or two. But then, like all the tourists, you'll grow bored and go home. I can't go home. This *is* my home. I'm stuck here."

"Is it that bad?" Trey asked.

She shrugged. "I just wish I had a choice, to stay or go."

"I'll help you, Sophie," he offered. "When we get off this island, I'll buy you a ticket. You can go anywhere you want, just name it."

Sophie shook her head. "My father won't leave. And I can't leave him alone, with his eyesight so bad. He doesn't have anyone else to take care of him or the business."

"Then we'll make sure he can take care of himself. I'll find him a good doctor. I don't care how much it costs. I owe you something for this mess I've put you in. If it weren't for me, you wouldn't be here."

"Maybe. But the plane might have gone down somewhere else, somewhere a lot less fortunate than this place. Somewhere without a nice big lagoon to land in." Sophie smiled at him then dropped a grateful kiss on his lips. "It's a nice fantasy," she said. "But fantasies don't always come true."

Sophie pushed to her feet and walked out toward the lagoon. She picked up the discarded pareu, shook it out and wrapped it around her body, knotting it beneath her arm. Funny how every time they were intimate, it left her feeling more vulnerable.

Though it was just a silly answer to a silly question, Sophie couldn't help but wonder if island life might be tolerable with Trey at her side. Was she really looking for an adventure of her own? She'd always believed the empty spot inside her would be filled by an exciting career in a glamorous city. She'd never even considered it might be filled by a man.

"Now that the rain has stopped, we should try to get the fire started," she suggested, turning back to him.

Trey watched her, his expression inscrutable. "Just give me a few minutes to recover."

Sophie turned and wandered to the edge of the lagoon. She stared into the water, watching a small school of fish dart back and forth. She pressed her palm to her heart, feeling the ache of emotion there.

After her mother had left, Sophie's dreams about love and happiness had been put aside. How could she possibly let a man into her heart if there was a chance he might break it into a thousand pieces? She had a big empty spot that love could have filled. But if she wasn't willing to allow herself that emotion, she'd have to fill that spot with something else. But what?

5

THE HUMIDITY HUNG IN the late-afternoon air and the breeze had disappeared, leaving a strange stillness over Suaneva.

Trey sat on the top step of the porch, his gaze fixed on the plane on the far side of the lagoon. Just minutes before, he'd thought he heard the sound of an engine overhead. It was strange to be so close to rescue, yet so incredibly far away.

He and Sophie were alone on this island until someone came looking for them. And though it had proved to be an interesting adventure so far, Trey had to wonder what would happen when it was over. If it was *ever* over.

There was always a small chance that they wouldn't be found, that her father might have forgotten where she went. Or that a search party might miss them. It was a remote possibility, but a possibility nevertheless. The more likely scenario would be the opposite—that they'd be found in the morning and that a rescue plane would land in the lagoon, pick them up and take them back to the real world.

But what then? Would they just walk away from each other as if they'd never met? Or would they make hasty plans to have dinner together? If Trey had anything to say about it, he'd take her hand, drag her off to his hotel suite and let nature take its course.

They'd enjoy a long, hot shower together, then wrap themselves in thick robes. After that, they'd have a huge dinner with dessert and champagne. And then they'd go to bed for the next three or four days. Only after that would they be ready to make plans for the future.

Their rescue wouldn't be the end of their affair, it would be the beginning. When the sex was this good, you didn't just walk away. He and Sophie shared incredible intimacy in a relationship unencumbered by inhibition. But would they have to begin all over again once they got back? Or could they continue on as they had?

He turned to look at Sophie, sound asleep in the hammock he'd made. The effects of the wine and sex and incessant heat and rain had been enough to make her drowsy. The moment he'd finished hanging the hammock, she'd crawled in and fallen asleep.

He glanced down at his wrist, then remembered that his expensive waterproof watch had stopped running when he'd first jumped into the water. From what he could tell by the intermittent sun, it was probably getting close to five in the evening. He'd already spent eight hours with Sophie and he felt as if his life had completely changed. What would happen in the next sixteen? When he left Suaneva tomorrow, would he be a different man?

Trey found it difficult to believe that he could change so much in twenty-four hours. He hadn't really cared about anything in his life, so what made him think he felt something deeper for Sophie? But then, the things he'd tossed aside so quickly had always been things he'd bought and paid for.

No matter how much he spent, he never seemed to find any satisfaction, any comfort. He'd gone through millions and had nothing to show for it. He wasn't any richer, any smarter or any happier. But he couldn't buy Sophie's affection. Maybe that's why Trey found it so valuable—and maybe that's why he wanted it more than anything he'd ever wanted in his life.

He slowly stood, then walked across the porch and bent down to look at her face. Her dark lashes were thick and feathery, her lips parted slightly as she slept. Trey reached out and brushed a strand of hair from her forehead, his fingers instinctively needing to touch her. This was crazy, he mused. If he couldn't resist touching her now, how would he ever get along without her?

Women had always occupied a specific place in Trey's life, as social accessories. The more beautiful, the better. He'd never really thought much about compatibility since he'd never intended to stay with one woman long enough for that to be an issue. But he liked Sophie. He admired her strength and her determination. He thought she was, by all accounts, the most beautiful woman he'd ever met. And when he was with her, he felt good about himself.

But would his feelings last? Or were they so intense only because she was the one thing he might not be able to possess? Trey sat back on his heels, his gaze still fixed on her face. This was the woman who had saved his life. Perhaps that was the reason for the attraction and nothing more.

As long as they were here on this island, he didn't need to think about the future. He'd take each hour as it came and deal with the difficult stuff later. Trey drew a ragged breath. Yeah, he could keep telling himself that, but he was far from convinced that he'd ever be able to let Sophie Madigan go.

Trey picked through their belongings, which he'd tossed into a corner of the porch. He found his khakis, then tugged them on. Though it felt good to walk around naked, he felt vulnerable without clothes. How the hell was he supposed to fight his attraction to Sophie, when the proof of it was there for all to see?

Trey walked back to the grove of fruit trees and collected enough wood to get a fire started, making four trips back and forth before he was satisfied it would last through the evening. Sophie had been right about this side of the lagoon. Things were a lot easier when they had shelter, food, water and a supply of firewood.

Trey arranged the wood in a pile on top of the damp palm fronds, then searched for some kindling to start the fire. In the end, he grabbed his messenger bag and pulled out the notebook he kept inside, crumbling up sheets of paper and stuffing them beneath the firewood.

Ten minutes later, to Trey's great satisfaction, they had fire. Though the matches were damp, it had only taken three tries to get a flame going. The wet wood popped and sparked and sent a cloud of smoke drifting straight up into the still air.

"You're a man now," he muttered to himself. He flexed his biceps and grunted, sure that he must have a caveman gene left inside him somewhere.

It was strange how self-reliant he had become when needed. In the past, money had always solved his problems. If he wanted something, he just paid for it. But here on the island, it didn't matter that he had money…or privilege…or fame. He was just a regular guy who'd made a very respectable fire.

"Nice fire."

Trey turned around to see Sophie standing on the porch, her hip braced against the railing, her hair tumbled around her sleepy face. He slowly let his arms fall to his sides.

"Hey," he said. "How was your nap?"

"Good," she murmured, rubbing her eyes. "I think I drank a little too much wine."

"Headache?"

She nodded, smiling winsomely. "But my foot feels much better."

"That's good," he said. "I thought I'd make us some dinner. Maybe heat up those beans. And I found a tin of crackers. They might be pretty tasty with the oysters."

"I am hungry," she said.

"Good. Why don't you sit and I'll get things ready."

Sophie plopped down on the top step and watched him as he gathered up the collection of canned goods for their meal, her elbows braced on her knees, her chin cupped in her palm.

"You know, if we didn't have this pocketknife, we'd be in pretty big trouble." Trey held it out. "Corkscrew, can opener, knife, scissors, tweezers. If we just had a few more tools we could build a boat and get ourselves off this island. Kind of like MacGyver."

"Does he have a lot of tools?" she asked.

Trey chuckled softly. He kept forgetting that he and Sophie had grown up on opposite sides of the world. Her cultural references were completely different from his. Still, he was amazed at how easily she moved between cultures. Now that she'd spent the day with him, her accent had all but disappeared. "Yeah, he's got a lot of tools. He could make a luxury yacht out of a chewing-gum wrapper and a rubber band."

She stared at him, her head tilted. "How is that possible?"

"American television," he said. Trey set an open can of beans on the edge of the fire, then stood back to watch it. "I'm going to buy myself one of these knives when I get home."

"You can have that one," Sophie offered. "As a memento of our time together."

"Thanks," Trey said, staring down at the knife. "That's nice of you."

Though the knife was a thoughtful gesture, Trey wanted more than that. He at least wanted a promise that they'd see each other again. A chance to find out if there was anything between them once they were off the island.

"You are about to enjoy the full extent of my cooking skills," he said, when the beans began to bubble.

Sophie watched as he straightened and carried the can over to her, using a piece of canvas as a potholder. He set them down, shaking his hand, burned from the heat from the can.

Sophie took his fingers and licked his fingertips, then blew on them. The cooling effect sent a flood of desire racing through his body and Trey cursed inwardly. Would there ever come a time when she could touch him and he wouldn't automatically think about sex?

When she was satisfied that his fingers would be all right, Sophie sat back and waited while Trey laid out the rest of the feast between them. Sliced papaya, smoked oysters, another bottle of red wine. A tin filled with crackers that they could use to scoop up the beans. All in all, Trey thought it was a rather well-rounded meal.

"Five star," he said.

"Are you sure we should eat these oysters?" she asked.

He sat down opposite her. "I don't know. Do you think they might make us do something crazy later?" Trey asked.

Sophie giggled. "I hope so." She plopped one on top of a cracker and gobbled it down. "What's the craziest thing you've ever done in your life?"

This was not a game Trey wanted to be playing. He'd done far too many crazy—and stupid—things to recount. Things he was ashamed of now. "I don't know."

"Have you ever had sex in a public place?" Sophie asked.

"Oh, we're talking about crazy sex? I thought you meant like losing a hundred thousand on one spin at roulette in Monte Carlo or wrecking a vintage Ferrari sports car the day after I bought it or punching out a policeman in Paris."

Sophie gasped. "You did all that?"

Trey had almost forgotten that Sophie knew nothing of his life before she'd met him. "No," he lied. "I was just using those as examples."

She ate another oyster. "So. Tell me."

Hell, he didn't want to lie to her. But his sexual escapades were a lot worse than anything else he'd ever done. "Well, there was this one time. With this woman I barely knew. We met on an airplane and—well, you know the rest."

"I do?"

He nodded. "You were there."

"That was the craziest sex you ever had?"

"Yeah," Trey said. "That was pretty crazy. How about you?"

She drew a deep breath. "I've always wanted to do

something crazy. I guess attacking you on the beach was the high point for me."

It was a decent concession, he mused. Trey certainly didn't want to hear about her past lovers. And he didn't want to talk about his. They'd start fresh, without a romantic or sexual past for either one of them.

"Well, maybe we'll have to work on that," he said. "We could always aim for something higher, don't you think?"

She gave him a sexy smile, then popped another oyster in her mouth. "It's good," Sophie said, nodding at the meal.

"You know, this is the first time I've ever cooked for a woman. Until now my culinary skills stopped at ordering takeout and reading French menus."

"So what else are you good at?" she asked, her brow arching up. "I mean, besides…you know…"

"I do?"

"Sex," she said. "You're good at sex. But I'm sure you already know that."

"So are you," he said. He considered her question for a long moment, trying to come up with an answer. Most men his age had at least one thing they could do well. But all the things he could list didn't really make a whole lot of difference in the world. He could drive a race car really fast, he could ski better than anyone he knew. He was a daredevil when it came to motorcycles. He was good at blackjack and could speak six different languages. He could seduce a stranger in less than an hour. And he knew how to spend money.

"I'm good at taking care of you," he said. "And that's all that really matters." He picked a cracker out of the can and held it out to her.

"I guess life really isn't so bad on this island," she said.

"After we get back to civilization, I'm going to take you out for a really good meal. The best restaurant in Pape'ete. We'll drink champagne and order the most expensive entrée on the—"

"You don't have to say that," Sophie interrupted.

"Say what?"

"That we'll go out. I mean, I appreciate the gesture, but I think it would be best if we just went our separate ways once this is over."

"Why would you say that?" Trey asked, startled by her indifferent attitude. At the least, they ought to leave the island as friends.

Sophie shrugged. "Because it's silly to pretend. We're attracted to each other. We're the only two people on this island. Believe me, if there were another woman here, you'd be attracted to her, don't you think?"

"Not if she looked like my aunt Marjorie," he teased.

She smiled. "All right, any reasonably attractive women under the age of forty."

"Forty-five," Trey said. "I've always liked older women."

"See. It's just a matter of availability."

"So you don't think there's something…special to this attraction?"

She shrugged. "No. Because it won't last. My mother

always said it's the chase that fascinates men. Once a man has caught a woman, he tires quickly and moves on to another. Like my father. Once he was certain of my mother's love, he moved on to someone else. She always said that was her biggest mistake. She let him know how much she loved him."

"I'm not your father," Trey said.

Sophie scooped up some beans with a cracker, then put them into her mouth. "No," she said, shaking her head as she chewed. "But you are a man."

Trey stared at her for a long moment, before reaching out and smoothing his hand over her cheek. Was she really that cynical? "And you're a very special woman. There's something very exotic about your eyes." He ran his finger along her collarbone and let it drift down to a spot between her breasts. "And about the way your skin feels." He leaned forward and kissed her, taking his time to tease a response out of her. "And you taste better than any woman I've ever kissed."

"I think the oysters are working," she said, a tiny smile playing at the corners of her mouth. "Either that, or you're too charming for your own good."

He should have put aside his doubts right then and pulled her into his arms. But instead, her words brought his past crashing back to the present. How many times had he heard that? Peter Shelton the Third was all charm and no substance. "Do you really think this is just a game?" Trey asked, his mood darkening suddenly. "That I'm just interested in the chase?"

"I—I don't know what to think. I think maybe you're used to getting what you want from women."

"And you don't get what you want from men?"

Sophie shook her head. "Not usually." She picked another oyster out of the tin and held it out to him. Trey shook his head. "At least, not until now."

The rest of the meal passed in more subdued conversation, Trey's mind occupied by the admissions spoken between them. He may be good at sex and even better at seduction. But it was the other stuff he needed now. He wished he were better at the whole romance thing.

For the first time in his life, he wasn't quite sure what to do. How could he get Sophie to look at him as more than just the man who satisfied her sexual needs? A man only interested in the chase?

SOPHIE GUZZLED THE LAST of the bottled water, hoping that it would ease the tiny hangover she'd gotten from the wine. Trey had found an old coffee tin in the cottage and had used it to collect rainwater to refill their bottles before the night set in.

He truly seemed to be enjoying their exercise in survival. He'd made a hammock, started a fire, cooked dinner and was now replenishing their supply of drinking water. Sophie had to admit she could have been stuck on this island with a far less useful guy than Trey Shelton.

And far less sexy, as well. Dressed only in his ragged shorts, Trey might have looked a bit disreputable to some. But Sophie couldn't take her eyes off him. His skin had been burnished by a day of Polynesian sun filtered through the cloud cover, and the thin sheen of sweat on his torso only highlighted the muscles of his shoulders and back.

Sophie drew a ragged breath as she let her gaze drop to his butt. It wasn't difficult to imagine what would happen between them that night. What else was there to do in the dark but continue the seduction that had begun the moment the plane landed?

She wondered if there might come a point when his touch didn't cause her to respond so intensely. He seemed to know what she needed even before she did. And when he set out to bring her pleasure, Sophie could do nothing but be swept up in the moment.

Brushing the cracker crumbs off her fingertips, Sophie stood. Right now, she wanted to be kissed by him. And after that, touched. She didn't want to wait until dark. She needed to look into his eyes when they made love and know that he needed her as much as she needed him.

Slowly, she descended the steps, wincing at the residual pain from the jellyfish sting and the tingles that shot up her other leg from a foot that had fallen asleep. But as she took the last step, her leg wobbled and she tumbled face forward onto the sandy ground.

Trey turned and quickly crossed to where she was lying. He bent down and helped her to her feet, holding firm until she regained her balance. "Are you determined to kill yourself?"

"My foot was asleep," she murmured.

"And you've had too much wine. I should have re-plenished our water supply a lot earlier." He held tight to her elbow. "Maybe we should take a walk. Get you some fresh air."

The suggestion struck Sophie as silly. They were practically living outside. How could she get any more air than she already had? A giggle bubbled from her lips and she covered her mouth as a hiccup escaped, as well.

He turned his back to her. "Hop on."

"Where are we going?"

"We're going to the beach. To watch the sunset."

"How romantic," she said with a sarcastic edge. "But I think it's going to start raining again. Look at those clouds."

"Yeah, well, it's about time we do something roman-tic, don't you think?"

Sophie blinked, surprised by his words. Though romance might be nice for a couple that was actually in a relationship, she and Trey were just having sex. A lot of sex. Romance should have nothing at all to do with it.

"Come on," Trey insisted. "Hop on. We're going to miss the sunset and we'll have to walk back in the dark."

"I can walk," she murmured. Sophie slipped into her flip-flops and started off in the direction of the beach, limping on her sore foot and tugging at her pareu as she circled the cottage.

He hurried up beside her and took her hand in his, lacing his fingers through hers. "We're not running a race here," he said. "We can stroll. Or I can stroll and you can continue to limp along."

The whole idea of romance frightened her, Sophie admitted to herself. With romance came expectations. And then disappointments. And regrets and recriminations. She wasn't good at romance. She never had been.

Why couldn't they just concentrate on what they were both good at—sex? It was so much simpler. She didn't need to think about other things when they were together. She only needed to respond to his touch.

"All right," she muttered. "I'll take that ride."

He bent down and Sophie hopped on his back, her legs straddling his waist, her arms wrapped around his neck. As he walked, she rested her chin on his shoulder.

"Tell me, if you were home right now, what would you be doing?" she asked.

"Home? Home has always been a rather vague concept for me. I usually don't stay in one place too long."

"You don't have a home?" Sophie asked.

"Sometimes I live in hotels. Or stay with friends. Sometimes, if I'm in Europe, I rent a house. Lately, I've been living in the Shelton in Manhattan. And if it was dinnertime, I'd probably be watching a ball game and eating something from room service." He paused. "At least here, I've got a plan, a purpose. I like that."

"You're better suited for island life than I am," she murmured, pressing a kiss to the nape of his neck.

"I'm going to find a spot for my resort and I'm going

to get it built," he said. "It's funny. I was waiting around for something in my life to change. And now it has, thanks to you."

"I didn't have anything to do with it," Sophie said.

"I think landing on this island was the best thing in the world for me," Trey said. "It woke me up. Made me realize that life was just passing me by."

Sophie had been feeling that same way for years, as if the world was spinning so fast and she was standing still. Exciting things were happening to everyone *but* her. But crash-landing on Suaneva hadn't made things any clearer to her. Instead, it made everything more confusing.

"I've been waiting, too. For my father to stop being so stubborn, for my mother to decide to come back home, for me to get a life of my own."

"Aren't we supposed to know what we want by now?"

"Maybe there's something wrong with us," Sophie said.

"Or maybe it's just the opposite," he said.

She thought about his comment for a long moment. Was he saying there was something "right" about them? Or was he saying that they shouldn't know what they wanted? Sophie opened her mouth to ask, but then snapped it shut. She really didn't want to know the answer.

By the time they reached the beach, the sun was hanging low on the horizon. To the south the clouds were building, the reflection of the sun creating a riot of pink and orange and purple.

"Wow," he said, coming to a dead stop. "Look at that sky."

"You act like you've never seen a sunset before," Sophie said, hopping down.

"I haven't. I mean, I have, but I haven't really taken the time to look. It's beautiful."

Sophie drew in a deep breath and nodded. It was the most beautiful sunset she'd ever seen. Or maybe it was just so wonderful because of the company she had. She wrapped her arms around Trey's waist and tucked herself into the crook of his arm.

Physical contact between them was something she'd almost begun to take for granted. But standing here, she knew she wouldn't always be able to touch him like this. There would come a time when she'd want to remember the feel of his skin, the way the muscle rippled beneath flesh.

She'd never been one to appreciate romantic clichés—candlelit dinners, long walks on the beach, beautiful sunsets. But something had changed. She was seeing these things for the first time, with Trey. And Sophie was glad she could share them with him.

Thunder rumbled in the distance and a wind gust sent a soft spray across the beach. He wrapped his arms more tightly around her, and she felt the goose bumps prickle her smooth skin. "Is it going to be bad?" he asked.

"It'll probably be noisy and rainy and windy, but it probably won't last long."

"I never really notice the weather," he said. "But here, I'm feeling a little vulnerable."

"It's not a cyclone," Sophie said. "I'd be worried if it was. A cyclone would blow the cottage down around us."

"If I hadn't been so anxious to work on Christmas Eve, you'd be at home, safe and sound, enjoying the holiday like you should be, instead of stuck on this island."

"It is Christmas Eve, isn't it?" Sophie murmured. She turned to him and smiled. "Merry Christmas, Trey."

Her hair blew around her face and Trey smoothed his hands over her temples so he could look into her eyes. "I wanted to forget it was Christmas," he said. "I didn't have anywhere to be this year. No one to buy gifts for. I thought if I kept busy, I wouldn't realize I was all alone. But I'm glad I'm here with you."

"Maybe we should sing some carols," Sophie suggested. "Do you know 'Good King Wenceslas'?"

Trey chuckled. "It just doesn't seem right. There's no snow."

"But there's been plenty of rain. The only difference is a few degrees in temperature." She paused. "I know what we can do." Sophie reached for the knot in her pareu and untied it, then let the breeze blow the fabric from her body. She kicked off her sandals and ran to the edge of the water, then turned to face him. "Come on."

Trey watched her for a long moment, his gaze raking her naked body. Then, with a groan, he stripped off his shorts, slipped out of his shoes, and ran after her. As he passed, he grabbed her hand and pulled her into the water, both of them falling head-first into the surf.

Sophie screamed and splashed water at him, but he yanked her into his arms and kissed her long and hard. Their bodies seemed to fit together so perfectly, her breasts pressed against his chest, her legs tangled around his.

He nuzzled her neck, biting her gently as they played. Sophie leaned back in the water and Trey cupped her breast in his hand, his thumb teasing at her nipple. This was paradise, she thought to herself. When she'd wished for a lover, she could never have expected this man.

Sophie kicked away from him, swimming a few strokes then turning to tread water. But he wasn't watching her. Trey's gaze was fixed on the horizon. "Sophie, look." He pointed and she followed his arm to a spot not far offshore. The white sails of a boat were clearly visible against the sunset. Trey turned and looked at her. "The flare gun. I'll go back and get the flare gun."

He spun around and ran out of the water and onto the beach. But before he could get his shorts back on, Sophie called to him. "Don't," she shouted.

He turned to face her, tugging on his khakis over his damp skin. "What do you mean?"

"Don't," she said, shaking her head. "I don't want you to signal them."

"Sophie, I'm not going to put you in danger. There's

a storm coming up. We're here alone. The least they could do would be to radio someone and let them know we're safe."

"The waves are getting pretty high," she said. "I don't think they'll risk coming through the reef. And the sun is almost down. They wouldn't be able to get back out. We'd be putting them in danger."

"They could call for a boat," he said. "Isn't there a coast guard around here?"

"Anyone sent to rescue us would have to deal with the weather, too." She glanced over at him. "We'll be all right for the night. They'll find us in the morning." Sophie stared into his eyes and she saw the indecision there. But there was more. A genuine concern for her safety. He cared about her, enough to put an end to their time together.

"No," he said.

"Yes." She held out her hand and motioned to him as he slowly walked to the water's edge, the waves swirling around his feet. "I want to spend the night with you. I don't want to be anywhere but here."

He waded through the water to where she stood and picked her up, wrapping her legs around his waist. Then he kissed her, his hands tangling in her damp hair, molding her mouth to his.

"All right," he murmured, his lips warm against hers.

She needed this night, Sophie told herself. After that, she'd be able to let him go without any regret. Just this one night.

BY THE TIME THEY GOT BACK to the cottage, they could hear thunder in the distance. The wind had shifted direction and was blowing across the lagoon toward the plane. The pilot-side float had been grounded on the sand, and the plane sat at an odd angle.

"Should we try to tie it down again?" Trey asked.

Sophie stared across the lagoon, squinting into the diminishing light. "There's nothing we can do now," she murmured. "Except hope that the wind doesn't get too high."

The plane probably wasn't worth a whole lot, Trey thought to himself. He suspected that Sophie and her father had sold the most valuable of their assets first, leaving her with something that was held together with chewing gum and duct tape. He probably ought to be grateful they'd had a problem with the engine when and where they did. Hell, they would have been in a lot more trouble had a wing or the propeller fallen off.

"Don't worry," he said.

"If it flips, we'll never be able to get it off this island," she said.

"It'll be fine," he said, reassured that money could solve any problem. If he had to send a boat over and find a mechanic to take the plane apart piece by piece and haul it back to Tahiti, he'd do that for Sophie.

Trey wrapped his arms around her waist and pulled her against him. In truth, there wasn't much that he wouldn't do for her, if she asked.

"Maybe it would be better if we couldn't get it off the

island," she murmured. "Then it would finally be over. The insurance would pay for the plane. My father's business would be done and we could move back to the States."

"Is that what you want?" Trey asked.

She shrugged and slipped out of his embrace. "Yes." She paused and turned to face him. "No."

"If you could have anything you want, any wish, what would it be?" he asked.

"It won't do me any good to wish," she said, climbing the front steps of the cottage. "Wishing can't make it happen."

He stared up at her, studying her enigmatic expression. "Humor me. If you could snap your fingers and have whatever you want. Three wishes."

Sophie leaned against a vine-covered post and stared out at the lagoon. "I'd wish my father would go to a doctor and get his eyes fixed. And then, I'd wish the business was making money again. And finally, I'd wish my mother would come back."

"Nothing for yourself?" Trey asked.

"All those things are for me," she said. She shrugged, her smile fading slightly. "What about you?"

"I'd wish…I had a big, soft bed here on this island. With clean sheets and down pillows."

"And?"

"And a bathtub big enough for two with an endless supply of hot water and bubbles."

"That's two," she said. "What's the third?"

"You. In the bathtub first and then the bed."

Sophie stared at him for a long time, her gaze flitting over his face. Trey could already imagine the scene his three wishes might create. A bath, a bed and Sophie was a fantasy he hoped might come true. He'd make it come true.

Trey felt the first drops of rain on his skin and he looked up at the sky and closed his eyes. It seemed as though they'd spent a lifetime on this island and yet, in so many ways, they were still strangers. He wanted to touch the real Sophie, the lighthearted, silly woman that he sometimes saw, not the indifferent, slightly cynical girl that he was faced with now.

She was so guarded at times, so careful of her emotions that Trey wondered if he'd ever truly know her. He knew she had an incredible inner strength and she was fiercely loyal to those she loved. He knew her parents' divorce had left her with deep scars, making her unable to trust her own feelings.

They'd been intimate, but only with their bodies. He wanted to know this woman, to feel what was in her heart and soul and to touch her there, as well. But how was that possible in just a single day and night?

Trey drew a deep breath and opened his eyes to find her still staring at him.

She held out her hand. "Come in out of the rain," Sophie coaxed.

"Come into the rain," he countered, holding out his hand.

Sophie turned and walked in the open door of the

cottage. Trey knew if he went to her, she'd surrender. He'd run his hands over her shoulders and toss aside her pareu and they'd pleasure each other the way they had since the moment the plane had gone down.

But sex with Sophie wouldn't get him what he wanted. It wasn't just passing pleasure. He needed to know this relationship actually meant something to her, that they weren't simply satisfying a physical craving, but, perhaps, connecting in a deeper way.

Slowly, he climbed the steps, his desire overwhelming his resolve. At least, when he was inside her, he could claim a part of her that no one else could. In those moments before they dissolved into orgasm, the walls fell and she was his completely.

Trey cursed softly, stopping just outside the front door. Once he touched her, there was no going back. She stood at one of the windows, staring out at the rain, her face illuminated by the late-evening light. Her beauty took his breath away and Trey wondered at the stroke of luck that had put him here on this island with her.

He slowly walked across the room and slipped his hands around her waist, gently turning her around and backing her up against the wall. His fingers tangled in her hair as his mouth met hers. Sophie moaned, going pliant in his arms. They couldn't seem to keep their hands off each other for long.

Was it just unbridled lust or did he need to reassure himself that she still wanted him? So many times in the past, the passion he'd felt for a woman faded too quickly. It had always been replaced by the pragmatic notion that love wasn't worth the trouble.

Hell, he didn't even know what love was. He wouldn't know it if it dropped out of the sky and hit him on the head. But this was certainly a lot more than just lust, Trey thought, his lips tracing a path from her jaw to the sweet curve of her neck.

His palms were warm on her naked skin and he found the knot in her pareu. With practiced ease, Trey tossed aside the filmy fabric and it drifted to the floor. She held her breath as he cupped her breast in his hand, rubbing his thumb over her nipple until it peaked.

Bracing his hands on either side of her head, he pinned her body against the wall with his. Another kiss, this one more intense and demanding, brought a moan from Sophie's throat and the silent question he asked was answered. She did want him as much as he wanted her.

She tore at his shorts, hastily unzipping them before shoving them down over his hips. The instant his shaft made contact with her body, Trey knew any thought of stopping would be futile. But he wanted more than just pleasure. Unfortunately, he didn't know just exactly what that was.

Trey hooked his finger beneath her chin and turned her toward the light from the window, his eyes fixed on hers. "You're the most beautiful thing I've ever seen," he groaned.

He grabbed her waist and pulled her up, wrapping her

legs around his hips and using the wall for support. His shaft was hot and hard between them, the length of his erection rubbing along the damp slit between her legs. Pleasure knotted inside him with every stroke and he struggled to keep himself from release. Sophie arched back, pushing against him with each stroke as her need built.

Trey ached to lose himself inside her, to feel her heat as he came. But neither one of them wanted to pause to retrieve a condom and he wasn't even sure where the last one was. The force that had brought them together was too strong for them to deny or to stop.

He probed at her entrance and Sophie shifted above him. For one breathtaking moment, he slipped inside her, then cursed softly. "We shouldn't," he murmured, swallowing hard. "Should we?"

Sophie shook her head, her breath coming in short gasps, her hair tickling his chest. "I don't want you to stop."

"I have some control, but not that much," he said, his voice raw with need. "And not with you."

She moved again and he was inside her and it felt like heaven. But suddenly, reality set in. This woman had stolen the last ounce of his self-control. When he was with her, all he could think of was this, the feel of their bodies joined as one.

Drawing a deep breath, he slowly pulled out, then set Sophie back on her feet. If he expected anything more than sex between them, then the sex would have to stop, at least temporarily. The next time he was intimate with Sophie, Trey wanted it to mean something.

"What's wrong?" she murmured, her lips pressed against his chest.

"Nothing. We just shouldn't do this without a condom." He pulled his shorts back up over his hips and forced a smile, the height of his desire still plainly evident.

"Are you going to go get one?" she asked, her eyes wide.

"Right." Trey nodded. "I'll…go get one."

He walked toward the door, wincing slightly as the zipper from his shorts rubbed against his erection. When he got outside, the last light from the day had nearly faded. The sky was a deep blue and the first stars twinkled through the clouds. The rain had stopped for the moment and the air was fresh with the smell of the island.

Trey leaned back against the weather-worn siding next to the door and closed his eyes. Things were moving far too fast. Emotions he'd kept so closely in check were threatening to break through his usual indifference.

Somehow, this place had worked a kind of magic on him. Civilization, and the real world, seemed miles and miles away. And for the first time in his adult life, Trey was able to live unencumbered by the expectations of others.

Here, on Suaneva, he was able to be himself. And he was beginning to like the guy he'd found.

6

SOPHIE LEANED BACK AGAINST the wood-paneled wall and sighed. The rain had begun again, the soft hiss of raindrops filling the room, the sound amplified by the tin roof. The sun had set and the last traces of light were leaving the sky. In another few minutes, it would be impossible to see.

Trey had walked out a while ago and hadn't come back. She thought about going after him, wondering why he wasn't interested in finishing what they'd begun, but Sophie didn't want to hear the answer. They'd almost done something they could have both been sorry for later. And yet, Sophie was sorry now.

Since their sunset stroll on the beach, something had changed between them. What had begun as a physical relationship was quickly turning into something more. She'd grown desperate to feel him inside her, without anything between them, and not just because it brought physical pleasure. She had wanted him to bury himself deep during his release so that they could share something they hadn't yet experienced, something that would be theirs alone.

It was foolish, Sophie knew. She'd never allowed such an emotional attachment to any other man. But her feelings had somehow become tangled up in all of this and she couldn't help herself. For just a little while, she wanted to believe what she and Trey had was more than just sex.

Ever since her parents' divorce, Sophie's heart had been left nearly paralyzed. It still beat every day, but she'd been unable to feel anything deeper than mild affection for anyone. She couldn't trust herself with emotions that might end up wounding her even more deeply.

Yet the moment she and Trey had faced possible death, the moment they'd stumbled out of the plane and into each other's arms, she'd felt her heart begin to come alive again. Sophie had tried to tell herself it was just the adrenaline rush of landing safely. But the adrenaline had worn off long ago and she realized she was falling for her fellow castaway.

Sophie drew a ragged breath and moaned softly. Sexual attraction and mutual desire had somehow transformed into trust and affection. And though it was dangerous to even explore such emotions, perhaps it might be worth the risk. Maybe this was just a first step, a way for her to find herself. How much could he possibly hurt her in such a short time? She was stronger now and more able to recover. Why not take a chance?

Reaching up, Sophie touched her lips, still bruised from his kiss. No man had ever made her feel this way. Every moment with Trey was like a carnival ride, a mixture of thrills and fear and exhilaration. She wanted to get off, yet she felt compelled to stay for just a little longer, to see what wonderful experience might be next.

"That's the problem," Sophie murmured to herself. "Knowing when to get off."

She bent down and picked up her pareu, then wrapped it around her naked body and knotted it under her arm. When she reached the door, she stepped out onto the porch. Trey was bent over the fire he'd built earlier, trying to coax a flame to life while shielding it from the rain.

Sophie wrapped her arms around the porch post and watched him, wondering what he was thinking. "It's raining too hard," she called. "It won't last."

He glanced over his shoulder. "If it's big enough, I can keep it going," he said. "Besides, your father is going to know something is wrong by now. He might send out a search plane. If they see the fire, it may give him cause to hope."

Sophie smiled, grateful that he understood her father's worries. But she suspected he was working on the fire to avoid talking to her. "In the dark, they could miss the island by miles. They're not likely to see a fire that small."

"Then I'll make it bigger," he snapped. Trey grabbed another branch and tossed it onto the feeble flames, the muscles across his back tight, his fists clenched.

He was angry, Sophie mused. They had let their desire get the better of them, both of them enjoying the feel of each other without a barrier between them. But they'd stopped in time. And it wasn't as if she were trying to trap him with some surprise pregnancy. "You don't have to take it out on me," she replied. "What's your problem?"

He straightened, as if he were about to turn around and face her. But then, he must have thought better of it, as he continued to stare into the fire. "I don't have a problem."

"Why are you angry with me?"

He drew a deep breath, his shoulders rising. "Sophie, just go back inside."

She didn't like being dismissed. And she didn't like being blamed for something she wasn't even sure she'd done. With a muttered curse, she hurried down the porch steps and crossed the short distance to Trey, then grabbed his arm and spun him around to face her.

"You can't just ignore me," she said. "We're stuck on this island together."

"I'm not trying to ignore you. I—I just need some space right now."

"If you didn't want to have sex, you could have just said so."

His sharp laugh split the damp night air. "That's not the problem. All I want to do is make love to you. It's all I think about. I can't get enough of you. The moment I touch you, I lose all capacity to resist." He stopped himself, drawing a deep breath. "I don't like that feeling. It scares me."

"It's just sex," Sophie said.

"No, it isn't. And I'm not sure it ever was."

She took a step back. "What is that supposed to mean?"

Trey shrugged. "It means I'm not sure we can just walk away from this when it comes time to leave this island. I'm not sure I want to. And I don't think you do, either."

Sophie shook her head. "I'm not going to talk about this," she muttered. "We were just having some fun. There's no need to make a big deal out of it."

"Come on," Trey countered. "It's more than fun. I feel it. You feel it. I know you do."

Sophie avoided his gaze, as if one look would reveal the truth. Of course she felt it. But that didn't mean it was anything more than just infatuation.

He grabbed her chin and turned her face up to his. "Go ahead. Admit it."

"What? You want me to say I love you? No, I'm not in love with you, Trey. We've spent a day together. No one falls in love in a day."

"I didn't say love." He paused. "You did."

Thunder rumbled in the sky and she felt her temper rise. Was this all a game to him? "What were you going to say?"

He opened his mouth, then closed it again as he measured his words. "I've never felt this way about any woman," he replied. "There's something there. It's…different."

"Right. Different. Oh, that tells me a lot." She spun on her heel and stalked back to the porch, cursing to herself in French. "That something is lust, pure and simple," she said, shouting through the rain.

She stepped through the door and slammed it behind her, but the moisture had made the wood swell and it refused to close. With a frustrated growl, Sophie shut it, then leaned back against it, her breath coming in tiny gasps, her heart slamming in her chest.

She hadn't meant to say it out loud. All along, from the moment they'd first kissed, Sophie had warned herself against just this moment. She'd been a fool to believe either one of them could keep emotion from creeping into their relationship. And now that it had, everything was ruined.

She wanted to run away, to hide until all these feelings evaporated. But she was trapped here with him, at least until morning…and maybe even longer.

A knock sounded on the door. "Sophie?" He tried the doorknob, then gave the door a push, but she braced her shoulder against it.

"Go away," she called.

"Let me in."

"I just want to be alone for a while." She closed her eyes, trying to stem a flood of tears. Great. Now she was crying over him. What was wrong with her? "I need some space."

"All right," he finally said. "But we are going to talk about this again."

Sophie slid down along the rough wood door until she was sitting on the floor, her knees tucked under her chin.

It had been so simple to avoid attachments. Trey had been right, she could have left her father and found a place for herself in the world. But instead, she'd hidden from her future, from love, in one of the remotest places she could find. Was it any wonder she had no one to love?

In her mind, she rewound the memories of her previous relationships and Sophie recognized a disturbing pattern. Whenever her feelings became too intense, she'd walk away. Her motives weren't difficult to interpret. Her father had been a notorious philanderer and though she loved him, she'd never really trusted him. But all men weren't like her father, were they?

There were people in the world who had wonderful marriages, people who loved the same person for their whole life without infidelity ever entering the picture. Had she already found a love like that and carelessly tossed it aside because of her fears? Or was that man here, on this island, with her?

Sophie covered her face with her hands, trying to restore a sense of order to her crazy thoughts. Someday, she'd have to face all her doubts and insecurities about love. But now wasn't that time. How could she afford to risk her heart with a man she didn't even know? Though they'd shared the most incredible intimacy, Trey was a complete stranger. She knew nothing of him beyond what she'd learned on this island.

Sophie silently cataloged the things that she did know. He cared about her and in more than just a sexual way. He wanted to protect her. He found her interesting and amusing and attractive. And when he touched her, he made her feel as if she were the only woman in the world he could ever want.

Inside the cottage, it was now dark and she could barely see any light coming through the windows. It would be a long, lonely night with Trey outside and her alone inside. But right now, facing Trey meant facing her feelings. And she just wasn't ready to deal with that. Not yet.

TREY HEARD THE HINGES SQUEAK and the soft footsteps on the porch floor. He lay in the hammock, his arm thrown over his eyes, blocking his view. He slowed his breathing, wondering if she intended to speak first or reach out and touch him.

He felt her fingertips brush his shoulder and he pulled his arm back. He could just barely see her as his eyes adjusted to the dark. Trey held out his hand and she wove her fingers through his, repairing the break between them in that single instant.

He gently pulled her to the hammock and she crawled in beside him, stretching her body along his. They lay together silently, the hammock swinging back and forth, the warmth of her body seeping into his skin. Sophie nestled beneath his arm, then threw her leg across his, wriggling until she was comfortable.

"I'm sorry," he whispered, his lips brushing her forehead as he stroked her hair. "I didn't mean to snap."

Sophie nodded. "And I'm sorry for getting angry."

"I shouldn't have walked out."

"It wasn't you," she continued, a trace of hesitation in her voice.

"What was it?"

"Past mistakes," she said. "What do you call it? Luggage?"

"Baggage," Trey corrected.

"Yes. Baggage. I have a lot of baggage."

"You and me both." He kissed her again, but this time it wasn't out of desire, but pure affection. She hadn't really opened up to him, keeping details of her personal life to herself. But now, he felt desperate to know what had formed this extraordinarily fascinating female. "Sometimes, it's better to just open it up and examine it."

A long silence grew between them and Trey wasn't sure she was willing to enlighten him. But then, she drew a ragged breath and began to speak.

"When I was young, we lived in Pape'ete, in a little house near the water. My mother worked as a pastry chef in one of the big hotels and my father ran the air-charter business. I was pretty much in charge of myself and I'd come and go as I wanted. We had a wonderful life and I was happy. And my parents were like this…golden couple. Everyone loved them. My father was handsome and dashing and my mother was sophisticated and beautiful. They were proof that opposites could attract."

She paused and for a moment, Trey wondered if she intended to stop there. But then, the next words came out in a rush. "After school, I'd usually go to the airport and work at the hangar with my father, helping to keep the books or clean the planes." Her fingers traced lines over his bare chest, as if the distraction helped her to explain. "I'm not sure when it first happened. But one day, I walked into his office and there was a woman there, sitting on his lap, kissing him. I didn't know what they were doing at the time, but when I got older, I understood."

Trey could hear the pain in her voice and he pulled her closer, wrapping his arms tightly around her shoulders. "I'm sorry," he murmured.

"My father told me I couldn't say anything to my mother or she would be so upset she might leave us both and never come back."

"He made you keep his secret?"

Sophie nodded. "I was so confused. I mean, I assumed he was telling the truth—that if my mother walked out on their marriage, she'd leave me behind. So I didn't say anything. But it kept happening, with that woman, and with others. Sometimes he'd use me to make excuses to my mother. And I kept my mouth shut. Even after my mother suspected, when I could see it in her eyes, I still didn't say anything. Then one day, she was gone."

"That's it? She just walked out?"

"She went back to Paris, to her family. It was a separation at first. And I thought, it's right she leaves me, because it was my fault, too. The funny thing was, from the moment she left, my father just fell apart. He didn't know what to do without her. And when she finally sent for me, he begged me to stay with him and I did. I thought my mother would never be able to forgive me and I just couldn't face her."

"Why?" Trey asked. "It wasn't your fault. You didn't know."

"It was me who'd done it, too," Sophie said. "I could have asked him to stop. I could have made him stop. I could have told her when it first happened. But I didn't."

Trey reached down and cupped her cheek in his palm, feeling the tears that dampened her cheeks. "Oh, sweetheart, you can't blame yourself for any of that. You were just a kid. Your father was wrong to make you keep that secret. And your mother was wrong to leave you behind."

She drew a ragged breath and then let it out. After another, he did the same along with her, until her breathing had slowed and the tears had stopped. "Better?" he asked.

Sophie nodded. "You're right. Now that I've said it out loud, it feels like I can leave it behind." She placed her palm on his cheek and kissed him. "Is that how you deal with your luggage?"

"Baggage," he said. "I've got a lot of it. Steamer trunks full. But I usually pack it all up and leave it behind. I've got trunks all over the world—Paris, Tokyo, London, New York. I usually just abandon my baggage."

"Is that a good idea?"

"It's worked for me in the past," Trey admitted. But

now that he thought about it, walking away from his problems had never really solved them. He'd never taken responsibility for his life, for the mess he'd made of it. Maybe it was time for him to open some of those trunks, too, and look at what was inside.

"I didn't have the most perfect parents in the world," he said, deciding to open up, too. "My mother and father are still married, after thirty-five years. But they barely speak to each other. Most times, they're living in separate houses. My mother lives for her charity work and my father concentrates on business. They go out in public all dressed up and looking happy for the cameras, but they don't have a marriage, either."

"Do you know anyone who is married and happy?" Sophie asked.

"My grandparents. My grandfather was the one who bought the first hotel, and he and my grandmother built the business together. They were always so content, so solid. They never spent a night apart throughout their whole marriage. When he was sick at the end, she slept at the hospital with him. They were devoted to each other." Trey smiled. "That's what I'd like. But maybe that's just asking for too much."

"So, I guess we're both pretty screwed up," Sophie finally said with a soft laugh.

"Maybe. Or maybe we know just enough not to make the same mistakes our parents did."

Sophie pushed up, bracing her hand on his chest, and looked into his eyes. "Do you really think so?"

"Yes, I do," he said. Trey smoothed her hair out of her eyes, trying to read her expression through the darkness. "Whatever happens with us begins here, Sophie. It doesn't start back when we were kids. It begins now."

She snuggled against him again and sighed. "Merry Christmas," she murmured.

"Merry Christmas," Trey said. He chuckled softly. "Speaking of Christmas, I have presents for you."

This brought her upright again and Trey could detect a smile on her face. "You do?"

"Of course I do. Since it's Christmas, I thought we ought to have gifts."

"But I didn't get you—"

Trey reached out and touched his finger to her lips. "No need. You kind of saved my life this morning, so I'll count that as a very big gift."

"I saved my life, too," she said. "You just happened to be along for the ride."

Trey chuckled. "You also gave me a story I can tell for years to come. About how I was marooned on a deserted tropical island with a beautiful woman."

"Can we open them now?" she asked.

"Oh, you're one of those." Trey shook his head. "Nope. Can't do it. Presents are for Christmas morning. This whole idea of opening them on Christmas Eve is just wrong."

Sophie curled up beside him again. "You're probably right," she said. "Besides, I wouldn't be able to see anything, anyway. It's very dark."

"Oh, well. I can take care of that."

"Now you command the sun and the moon?"

Trey rolled out of the hammock, then walked across the porch. He'd found a lantern earlier that day, hung above the porch rail, but hidden by the twisted vines. It was full of kerosene, probably replenished by a passing boater. He retrieved the matches from his pocket and lit one, touching it to the wick.

Holding it aloft, Trey turned to see Sophie standing beside the hammock, a surprised expression on her face. "Just what I wanted for Christmas," she teased. "Light."

"This isn't one of my presents. Although, it is nice to see you again, Miss Madigan."

"Where did you find it?"

"Hanging from that hook behind you. I figure it will last us a good part of the night."

"So, we can have a celebration," she said.

Trey nodded. "Why not? We don't have any other pressing engagements, do we? No parties, no caroling. Church is pretty much out of the question. A celebration would be nice."

"Then, I need some time," Sophie said. She hurried up to him and took the lantern from his fingers, then walked back to the door of the cottage. "You wait out here and I'll get things ready."

"What am I supposed to do in the dark?"

"You could work on your fire," Sophie suggested.

"I think that fire is a lost cause," he said. Trey smiled as he watched her slip inside the cottage. How quickly the mood had changed. Hell, he'd been with plenty of women who could hold a grudge for weeks. But all he'd had to do was find out what was on Sophie's mind and allow her to talk. Once she'd unloaded her worries, things went right back to the way they'd once been with them—easy.

Was it really that simple? He'd been prepared to play the typical games, the abject apologies followed by the standard groveling. But this time, he listened and things were set right.

Trey walked down the steps to the fire. He grabbed a stick and stirred the embers, surprised to see an orange glow beneath the ashes. Like the fire between him and Sophie, this one refused to die, even in the pouring rain. He tossed a few more branches into the center of the flames and watched as sparks rose into the air and were quickly snuffed out.

Trey turned his face up to the sky and let the soft drizzle fall on his sunburned face. Raking his hands through his hair, he drew a deep breath. What happened between them tonight would probably set the course for the rest of their relationship, he mused. Either he'd be able to convince Sophie what they had was real, or he'd fail to prove his case and they'd go their separate ways in the morning.

Trey wasn't even sure how this would all work out, even if they decided they wanted it to. He lived in Los Angeles now and she lived in the South Pacific. And then there was her father, although perhaps he could be convinced to move back to the States given proper incentive.

Still, there was always the resort. If he could find a way to build it, then he'd be here with Sophie for at least a year or two. Living on an island in the middle of the South Pacific certainly wouldn't seem so bad if Sophie was with him. Maybe they could build something together, like his grandparents had.

But he was getting ahead of himself. Trey wasn't about to put all his hopes out there and risk Sophie rejecting him out of hand. No, he had to at least be certain she'd consider the possibility of a future together, permanent or otherwise, before he made any plans.

He'd come to this island unsure of his future. Now, if things went well, he'd be leaving with a purpose. That was a lot more than he'd been able to achieve in the first twenty-nine years of his life.

Sure, the thought of allowing himself to fall in love was a little scary. And he wasn't sure he wouldn't want to take off after just a few months. But the possibility of finding a woman to spend his life with was intriguing, especially if that woman was Sophie.

SOPHIE SMOOTHED HER HANDS through her damp hair and tugged on her T-shirt. It was Christmas and she and Trey were going to have a date—of sorts. It was only proper that she dressed for the occasion. And though she might have preferred a sparkling party dress with a low-cut back and a high-cut hem, this outfit was what she had available.

She glanced at the preparations she'd made for a

light meal, laid out on the cabinets at the back of the cottage. They had wine, the rest of the crackers, another tin of oysters and a can of what seemed to be ham salad. Though they weren't the most sophisticated hors d'oeuvres, they'd do in a pinch.

A knock sounded on the door and Sophie turned. Trey had been outside for the past half hour, biding his time and tending to the fire. But the rain had increased in intensity again, evident from the sound of it on the tin roof. She took a deep breath and walked over to the front door, then pulled it open.

But instead of setting eyes on Trey, she found herself staring at a clump of palm fronds tied together at the base with a short length of rope. Interwoven in the fronds were blooms picked from the vines on the porch. "Oh, you've brought me flowers," she exclaimed.

He slowly lowered the fronds to reveal his face. "It's supposed to be a Christmas tree," Trey admitted.

Sophie smiled. It did look a bit like a tree, if she didn't look too closely. And he'd done the best he could in their circumstances for ornaments. "It's lovely," she said, stepping aside to let him enter. "Thank you."

He crossed the room to the lantern, then set the "tree" on the counter, leaning it up against the wall until it was balanced upright. He'd found his shirt and put it on, buttoning it properly and rolling up the sleeves, but his hair was still wet and his shorts soaked. "Not bad," he murmured.

"It does look festive," she said.

Trey plucked a blossom from the tree and turned to her, then tucked it behind her right ear. She fixed her gaze on his face, then reached up and turned the flower around. It was clear by the look in his eyes that he understood the signal. He bent closer, wrapping his arm around her waist and dropping a soft kiss on her lips.

"Merry Christmas, Sophie," he murmured.

"Merry Christmas, Trey," she replied, desire humming in her veins. Now that they were both dressed as they had been when they'd met, the thought of getting naked was even more exciting. She couldn't just look at Trey and admire his body as she had for most of the day. Now, she was left to imagine what was hidden beneath the clothes.

"Would you like some champagne?"

He blinked in surprise. "We have champagne?"

Sophie picked up the bottle and held it out to him. "It was on the bottom, beneath the other bottles. Someone was thoughtful to leave it behind."

"Very," Trey said as he pulled the foil off the cork. "Let's hope it's still good."

A moment later, the cork popped. He sniffed at the bottle. "It still smells okay." Tipping it to his mouth, Trey took a sip and smiled. "It would probably be better chilled, but I'm not going to complain." Trey held out the bottle. "A toast. To my lovely pilot and castaway companion. I can't think of another person I would have wanted on this island with me."

His words were incredibly sweet and Sophie couldn't

help but blush. Everything seemed so different now, as if they'd brushed aside a curtain hanging between them. It was all right to admit she cared about him and that her feelings were more than just lust. Trey Shelton was a man any woman would be lucky to claim as her own.

"We don't have much time left here," she said. "They'll send out planes at first light. And they'll probably come here first."

"If they don't?"

"They will. Sooner or later, they'll find us. Or another boat will come along. If all else fails, we could try to fly out. I can drain the fuel sumps and we can hand prop the plane to start it. But I don't really want to do that without knowing what's wrong. Hand propping can be dangerous."

"Hand propping? What is that?"

"That's when I sit in the plane and you spin the propeller. If you don't pull your hands back in time, they— well, you don't have hands anymore."

Trey held up his hands. "I kind of like these things. Besides, I don't mind staying a few more days."

Sophie smiled. "Your family will come looking for you, no doubt. Whether we like it or not, I'm afraid, we're going to be rescued tomorrow."

Trey gave her a reluctant smile. "Yeah. I know. But a guy can dream, can't he?"

"It hasn't been all bad," she said, taking a sip of the champagne, the bubbles tickling her nose. "The landing wasn't so much fun, but after that, it's been pretty nice."

He nuzzled her neck, biting softly. "Just nice?"

"Better than nice." She shivered as his lips trailed to her shoulder. "It's been interesting."

"Oh, no, not *interesting*. Watching someone pet a puppy is nice. Watching someone build a house is interesting. Certainly, you have a better word than that for us."

Sophie took another sip of the champagne and handed him the bottle. "All right. How about intoxicating?"

"How about tantalizing?"

"Enthralling?"

"Mind-blowing?"

"Earth-shattering."

"We are good together," he admitted. He set the bottle down on the counter and pulled her into his arms. A heartbeat later, his mouth was on hers, soft, yet demanding. His fingers ran through her hair, and he molded her lips to his.

Sophie had come to know his kiss so well. She could walk into a pitch-black room, filled with a hundred men and pick him out of the lot by just the fleeting touch of his mouth. How was it that she could know this part of him so well, the way he seduced her, the way he made her body ache with need, yet not even know what he liked to eat for breakfast or how he took his coffee?

She stepped out of his embrace and grabbed his hand, then led him over to the counter. Boosting herself up, Sophie drew him between her legs, her hands clutching the front of his shirt. "We've been on this island together for a day, but I don't know anything about you."

"I'm not very complicated," Trey said. "But if you're curious, ask away. I'll answer any question you have. As long as you do the same for me."

"This doesn't have to be the Spanish Inquisition," Sophie said. She turned and picked an oyster out of the tin and placed it on a cracker, then held it out to him. "We'll pretend that we've just met at a holiday party. Your friend Bob and my friend Danielle introduced us. We find ourselves sitting together…on a terrace. Under the moonlight." Sophie held out her hand. "It's a pleasure to meet you," she said. "What did you say your name was again?"

"Peter," he said. "But my friends call me Trey."

"Peter." Sophie gave him a coy smile. "I'll call you Pete. My name is Ann-Marie. But my friends call me Sophie."

"Your name is really Ann-Marie?"

She nodded. "Sophie is my middle name. My mother is Ann-Marie. My father insisted I be named after her. But she always called me Sophie, so it stuck."

Trey nodded. "I like this," he said. "So, Sophie, what do you say we blow this boring party and find a place where we can be alone?"

"Where are you going to take me?" she asked, toying with the top button of his shirt.

"I have a really fast car outside. We'll put the top down and ride up to Malibu."

"Malibu? What is that?"

"A beach in California."

"Oh, we're in California?" she teased. "I just assumed we'd be in Tahiti."

"No, we're in L.A.," Trey said.

"Well, if we're not going to be in Tahiti, then I'd rather be in Paris. We can take a ride along the Seine in your convertible."

"You're making this really difficult," Trey said, frowning.

"Then maybe we should stay at this boring party a little longer," Sophie suggested. "And get to know each other better."

"So I'm going to have to charm you?"

Sophie nodded slowly, a smile curling her lips. "Yes. And maybe, if you're lucky, I'll let you take me home at the end of the evening." She smoothed her hands over the front of his shirt. "So, Pete, what do you do for a living? I want to know everything about you."

7

THE STORM RAGED OUTSIDE, the wind rattling at the old shutters and threatening to blow in the front door. It was raining so hard the sound from the tin roof had almost become background music. The darkness was broken only by the flashes of lightning and a wavering light from the old lantern Trey had found.

Sophie handed Trey the empty champagne bottle, then launched into another verse of "The Twelve Days of Christmas." They'd begun singing Christmas carols after the effects of the champagne had set in, Sophie standing before him in her pareu and fumbling through "pipers piping" and "geese a-laying."

Though Sophie wasn't much of a singer, Trey found her performance endlessly charming. But when she got to "five golden rings," Trey pushed off the wall and playfully covered her mouth with his hand. "No more," he cried. "I can't take it."

She threw her arms around his neck and kissed him playfully. "It's Christmas Eve. What else are we going to do?"

In truth, there were plenty of things that they could have been doing. They had one condom left and Trey intended to make passionate love to Sophie before the sun came up in the morning. And this time, he was determined it would be more than just a physical release for them both.

The doubts and insecurities that they'd both felt building had been banished by their argument. Like a valve releasing steam, they'd simply let go. They were laughing and having fun, dissolving into silly giggles and outrageous teasing, then taking time out to kiss and tease each other.

Trey couldn't remember the last time he'd felt this close to a woman. Maybe he'd never experienced it. He felt her laughter in the depths of his soul, as if the sound of her voice was vital to life. Like eating or breathing.

He couldn't stop touching her, couldn't seem to stop watching her every move. Every time she looked at him, he found some new facet of her beauty to explore. And when he finally realized what was happening, Trey wasn't surprised or even concerned. He was falling in love with Sophie and it was the most natural thing in the world.

"Damn," he said, rubbing his forehead. "I forgot my presents." He pressed his finger to her lips before she could begin another song. "Stay right here."

"I thought we weren't going to open them until tomorrow morning," she said.

"If it will get you to stop singing that ridiculous song, then you can open them tonight." He walked over to the front door, where they'd piled all their belongings to get them out of the rain. Bending down, Trey grabbed his bag then returned to the center of the room. He sat down on the floor, pulling her down with him, then handed her three small packages. They looked rather festive, wrapped in yellow legal paper and tied with palm fronds.

"Where did you get presents?" she said.

"Didn't I tell you? There's a Bloomingdale's on the other side of the island. You can take the subway right to the front door."

"What is Bloomingdale's?"

He nodded. "A department store? In New York City? At Christmas, they have the most wonderful window decorations. Someday, maybe we'll go there and see them together." He pointed to the smallest package. "Go ahead. Open that one first."

The thought of them spending Christmas together in New York was almost enough to make up for the pathetic trove of gifts he'd managed to find. He wanted to show Sophie the world, all the wonderful things she hadn't yet seen. And then he wanted to show her all those that she had, so they might experience them together.

"Pretty wrapping paper," she said as she tore open the first package. Inside, she found a chocolate bar. A gasp slipped from her lips and she seemed genuinely surprised. "Where did you get this? Oh, this is wonderful."

"It was in my bag. But it had your name on it." He'd given expensive jewelry to women and never gotten such an enthusiastic reaction.

Sophie wrapped her arms around his neck and kissed him, lingering over his lips for a long time. "Thank you. We'll have it for dessert."

Trey handed her the next package. "And what's this?" she asked.

"That's actually yours already," he said. "I figured, at least you'd like it."

She pulled away the paper to discover a bottle of nail polish that had been sitting at the bottom of her purse for the past few months.

"It fell out of your purse when you pulled out the *monoi*. If we run out of things to do, I can paint your toes. I was really good at art when I was a kid."

"I'd like that," she said with a laugh. "What a nice present." Sophie held up the last package. "Maybe I should save this for tomorrow morning."

"Open it now," he said.

Trey had thought long and hard about this gift, but in the end decided to give it to her anyway. After all, at this point, he had nothing to lose. She glanced up at him as she ran her fingertip over the plastic card.

"It's my frequent-flyer card," he said. "I have a lot of miles. I thought you could decide where you wanted to go and…just go. I'll get you a ticket. Paris, London. Wherever you want." He paused, then reached out and took her hand. "We could meet. I could show you the sights. We could drive up to Malibu or shop at Bloom-ingdale's or visit the Eiffel Tower."

She stared down at the card and Trey said a silent prayer. If she accepted, then he knew there would be a time for them off this island—a chance at just a few days, maybe a week together in the real world.

"Thank you," she murmured, her voice soft and filled with emotion. "It's a wonderful gift." Sophie glanced up, tears glistening in her eyes. "I'm sorry, I don't have anything for you."

He shrugged, surprised by her sudden emotion. "That's all right. It was just something silly to do."

"But it was nice," Sophie said. "It was a very nice thing to do. It feels like Christmas now."

"All right, continue with the song," he said, hoping to cheer her mood again. "I believe you had stopped at five golden rings."

"I don't feel like singing." She slowly got to her feet and walked to one of the windows, peering through the shutters at the storm outside. "This isn't how I expected to spend Christmas Eve." She glanced back at him, forcing a smile.

"You miss your father?"

"Yes. But that's not it. The past few Christmases, my father and I would open gifts and then he'd drink too much and fall asleep in his chair. And I'd sit there and wonder if there was anyone else in the world quite as lonely as I was." She sniffled, brushing away her tears with the back of her hand. Then a smile broke through.

"But I'm not lonely now. This is the best Christmas I've had in a long time."

The truth was, Trey didn't want to be anywhere but here, with Sophie. And try as he might, he couldn't feel guilty for finding some kind of pleasure in this time marooned on the island.

Trey got to his feet and joined her at the window. "Everything is going to be all right, Sophie. I promise." It was the only thing he could think to say that might stop her tears. And yet Trey knew it was the truth. He would make everything right for her. And she'd never have another lonely Christmas again. Not if he had anything to say about it.

Sophie wrapped her arms around his waist and nuzzled her face into his chest. Running his hand over her hair, Trey kissed the top of her head. It was so easy to lose himself in the feel of her body touching his. But every kiss, every embrace was filled with more meaning and more intensity.

He drew back and wiped her cheeks with his thumbs. "Don't cry." He wrapped his arm around her waist, then took her hand in his. "Come on. There's a band playing. Let's dance." Slowly, he began to move, gliding her around the floor as he hummed "White Christmas."

Sophie was reluctant to participate at first, but then he picked up the tempo and pulled her into a swing dance to "Jingle Bell Rock." Trey didn't know half the words and hummed almost everything but the chorus. And before long, they were laughing again.

He didn't like to see Sophie sad. When she hurt, he felt almost frantic to soothe her. But then he realized it was all right to let her cry, or yell or pout if she wanted to. She'd held her emotions in for so long that letting them out was a good thing. If she could feel passionately enough to get angry at him or to weep in front of him, then she could feel passionately enough to love him.

"Look out," he warned. "Dip coming up." Holding tight to her waist, he leaned Sophie back, then yanked her up again. Before long, they were moving easily around the floor, their steps strangely in sync with each other. "We're not too bad, are we?"

"You're a good dancer," she said.

"My mother made me take dancing lessons when I was a kid. She said someday I'd appreciate knowing how. She's right." He glanced down at her, then dropped a kiss on her lips. "Feeling better?"

She rested her head on his shoulder as he moved her slowly around the room, this time singing "Silent Night." "I wish I'd known you when you were a little boy," she murmured. "I wish I'd known you when you were a young man."

"You wouldn't have liked me very much," he said.

"Why not?"

They continued to dance in silence, Trey wondering how much he ought to tell her about his life before Suaneva. "I suppose you'll find out anyway, once we get off this island."

"It can't be that bad."

"It's not good. I have a bit of a reputation around town. Actually, around the world. Some journalists have called me a wastrel. Others, a playboy. A boy toy. A himbo."

"A himbo?"

"The male equivalent of a bimbo," Trey explained. "All looks, no brains. I don't think I deserved that label, but then, the press is never really interested in the truth."

"I don't understand. Why would they call you that?"

He opened his mouth, ready to change the subject. But then, Trey decided to tell her everything. He wanted to be honest with her, to let her know that he'd left that life behind. "Because that's what I am, Sophie," he said. "I'm famous for spending money. And for being with famous women. You said that once they realized I was missing, they'd call my parents. In twenty-four hours, the whole world is going to know that you and I spent the night on this island. They're going to want to talk to you and take your picture and get all the salacious details."

"Why would they be interested in me?" Sophie asked, staring up at him in disbelief.

"Because you were with me." Trey grabbed her arms and set her back from him, so he could look into her eyes. "Don't believe anything they tell you, Sophie. What happened here was real. What goes on everywhere else isn't. Promise me you won't listen to any of it."

"But I—"

"Promise!" he demanded, a desperate edge to his voice.

"All right," she murmured. "I promise."

He cupped her face in his hands and kissed her gently. "Good. As long as I know you believe in me, then everything will be all right."

There was an apprehension in her expression that frightened him. How could he protect her from that? Public opinion had never been on his side. But Sophie had lived so far from what went on in the rest of the world. Maybe it wouldn't make a difference.

He'd face that problem when it came. For now, he had an entire night to convince her he wasn't the man the rest of the world believed him to be. Instead, he'd be the man she wanted him to be.

SOPHIE SNUGGLED INTO THE CURVE of Trey's arm. They sat on the top step of the porch, staring out at the lagoon in the night. The squall had passed, the rain had stopped and every now and then, the moon would peek out from behind a cloud.

It was late, probably well after midnight. Trey's fire had been doused long ago, but there was no need for it now. In six hours, the sun would come up and a new day would begin. She took a deep breath of the damp night air, a cool breeze blowing in from the ocean. She was afraid to go to sleep, afraid that when she woke up, everything would have changed.

For now, she wanted things to remain exactly as they were, for just a few more hours…until the sun rose and this magical night came to an end. She'd always remember this Christmas. Every detail would remain etched in her mind—the presents, Trey's tree, the storm, the dancing and singing. Though it wasn't a traditional celebration, it was perfect in her eyes.

Sophie turned to Trey and smiled. "I do have a Christmas gift for you," she said.

"What is it?"

She slowly stood, then pulled her T-shirt over her head. A moment later, her pareu fluttered to the ground. He stared at her, unblinking, in the moonlight. As she shed her clothes, Sophie felt as if she were letting her last inhibition go.

She didn't want to hold anything back, not physically or emotionally. They only had one chance, just a few more hours together, and she didn't want to leave Suaneva with any regrets.

At first, Trey seemed to be afraid to touch her, his gaze skimming her body. Though it was dark, her skin gleamed from the *monoi,* reflecting the white light from the moon. Sophie knew the effect her body had on him. But this time, she wanted him to really see her, not just as a sexual object, but as a woman.

He slowly reached out and spanned her waist with his hands. "That's a nice present," he said, running his palm from her shoulder to her hip.

Sophie shook her head. "I have something else," she murmured.

His eyebrow arched. "What are you giving me, Sophie?"

She took his hand and placed it over her heart.

Sophie could feel the pounding of her pulse and she wondered if he could, too. Drawing a deep breath, she met his gaze. "Just for tonight, I'll love you."

He looked at her, a frown furrowing his brow. "What?"

"I'll love you. Tonight, I'll be completely yours, my heart and my body. I'll do anything you want, be anything you want."

"What if I want you to love me for more than just one night?" Trey asked.

"I don't know what's going to happen once we leave Suaneva," Sophie said. "You don't, either."

"But I know what I want, Sophie. And it's you."

"When we wake up tomorrow morning, everything might be different. We might feel different."

"That's not going to happen. I know how I feel. And I think I know how you feel."

"It's all I can give, Trey. Tonight, I'm yours, completely. It has to be enough for now."

Trey stood and took her hand, drawing it up to his lips and kissing each fingertip. "Then for tonight, I love you, too."

He laced her fingers through his, then led her back up the porch steps. After slipping out of his shirt and tossing it aside, Trey took off his shorts, as well. Sophie held her breath, watching as the light from the moon played off the planes and angles of his naked body. He bent down and dug through his pocket, then held up the condom they'd been saving. He pressed it into her hand as he led her to the hammock.

It was damp from the rain, but Sophie liked the feel of their bodies cradled so closely together, as if there were nothing between them at all. They could barely move, but it didn't make a difference. He kissed her, softly at first, teasing at her tongue until she moaned in frustration.

Sophie ran her fingers through the hair at his nape and drew him into a longer, deeper kiss, a kiss meant more as an invitation than a challenge. He was already hard, the heat of his erection pressed against her belly. But this time, she was in no hurry. Sophie wanted the night to last forever.

It was a long, slow seduction. Sophie focused on the warm spot beneath his ear, rough with a day's growth of his beard. Then she moved to the notch in his collarbone, tracing the soft dusting of hair there.

All the while, her hands roamed over his lean but muscular body, smoothing over hard flesh and warm skin. Though she'd touched him before, this time she felt a measure of possession. His body was hers, at least for tonight. And in turn, she surrendered herself to him.

They held off for as long as they could, each of them bringing the other closer and closer to release, touching and teasing. When she finally sheathed him, Sophie was almost dizzy from the need. He turned her away from him, tucking her against his body, his lips pressed to her nape. Then, ever so slowly, Trey entered her.

The sensation was more powerful that she'd ever experienced before. And as he began to move, Sophie had to keep herself from dissolving into her orgasm. Trey whispered her name softly, telling her how much he wanted her, how much he needed her.

His hands drifted to her breasts and then to the damp spot between her legs. But Sophie was so close that she couldn't bear to have him touch her. She wanted the feelings to last far longer than they ever could. Days, weeks, months would never be enough.

"Tell me you want me," he murmured, his breath warm against her shoulder.

"I do," Sophie said, arching back against him. "Oh, God, I want you so much."

It was nearly impossible to get any closer to him, the hammock cradling them both. Sophie knew he was almost there and this time, when his hands drifted lower, she allowed him to touch her.

Her orgasm came quickly, like a bolt of lightning, sending a current through her limbs until she trembled with ecstasy. Spasm after spasm rocked her body and a moment later, Trey followed after her, moaning her name as he surrendered.

The pleasure seemed to go on and on, long after they'd both been satisfied. For Sophie, this time had been different. This wasn't just sex. It was an expression of her feelings for Trey, of her trust and her affection for him.

Sophie listened as his breathing gradually slowed. Trey pressed a kiss to her shoulder and sighed. "Say it," he whispered.

"I love you." The words were so simple, yet so powerful. But she barely had to think before they formed a sentence and became true.

"I love you," he replied.

Sophie didn't care whether it was the truth or not. For now, in this moment, it was. And though their feelings for each other might not last past morning light, they would last the rest of the night and that was enough.

TREY SLEPT SO SOUNDLY, he didn't stir when Sophie crawled out of the hammock. As he opened his eyes to the early morning light, he realized she wasn't lying next to him anymore. He raked his hands through his hair and brushed the sleep out of his eyes before swinging his feet to the floor.

He was still naked and the breeze off the ocean was cool on his skin. He rubbed his chest, surprised at how smooth his skin was from the *monoi* that Sophie had rubbed all over their bodies yesterday.

Trey smiled sleepily. It was odd to wake up and find himself alone. Usually, he was the one who crept out well before dawn, preferring to finish out the night in his own bed, alone.

Drawing a deep breath, he stretched his arms over his head and worked a kink out of his back. Though the hammock had kept them close, it wasn't the most comfortable place to sleep. His thoughts shifted to the big four-poster in his hotel suite, with the down pillows and crisp cotton sheets. He'd like to wake up with Sophie there.

Trey walked to the door of the cottage and peeked inside, then turned and stared out over the lagoon. There was just enough light to see the outline of the atoll, and Sophie standing at the edge of the water.

She was naked, the low light creating a silhouette over her curves. The stiff breeze tangled her hair, whipping it around her head. For a moment, Trey wished he'd had a camera with him to capture the scene. She looked like an island princess, a sacrifice to the gods of passion, her tanned limbs and dark hair a contrast to the white sand that surrounded her.

He'd thought the sunset had been beautiful the evening before, but this was just breathtaking. Closing his eyes, he committed the scene to memory, burning the image into his brain so it would be there for years to come.

What was she thinking? Was she looking for the rescue plane to come and take them both off the island? Or was she thinking about last night and the pleasure they'd shared? Her words still echoed in his head. *I love you.*

It was just a silly sentence, a Christmas gift that expired at the end of the evening. But it felt so real, he mused. And when he had returned the sentiment, there was no guilt or regret in his heart. He'd wanted to say those words again and again. But now, in the light of day, Trey wasn't sure what to do.

Now he knew what it was like to make love to a woman. Though he'd seduced more than his fair share, love had never been part of the equation. Sophie had changed that. The connection between them had been so intense, so perfect and pure, that Trey couldn't imagine ever feeling that same way again with anyone else.

He slowly sat down on the top step, his eyes fixed on her, his mind running through what might happen in the next four or five hours. In truth, he would have been happy to kidnap her, to take her back to Tahiti, lock her in a hotel suite with him, and figure out exactly how they felt about each other.

But Trey was afraid the moment they returned to civilization, they'd both realize what they'd shared was some silly fantasy. People didn't fall in love in the course of a day. Their situation had merely made them vulnerable to the illusion of love.

It seemed like the perfect solution, but only if Sophie went along willingly. But would forcing the issue be the right choice? Or should he take a few steps back and woo her slowly? He could find more than enough excuses to stay in the islands for a week or two. Certainly, after that, he'd know where they stood.

Hell, he'd never really had to work to get what he'd wanted from a woman. It had always been so simple. They went after him and he was happy to oblige for as long as it suited his fancy. But with Sophie, he felt like a rookie, desperate to get into the game, yet not fully aware of the strategy.

Trey groaned softly. How the hell had he managed to go through nearly thirty years of living without ever figuring out how to fall in love? He wanted her in his life, but he wasn't sure what he had to offer. A marriage proposal was beyond his current capabilities. A simple promise to make her happy might work.

Maybe it was best to just wait, until they got back. Then, everything was sure to make sense in his head. He pushed off the steps and walked to the edge of the lagoon. Standing behind her, Trey slipped his arms around her waist.

His touch didn't startle her. Instead, she reached back and wrapped her arm around his head, twisting her fingers through the hair at his nape. "They'll be coming for us soon," she murmured.

Her backside nestled against his hips, the soft flesh pressed into his cock. He closed his eyes and drew in a slow breath. "I know. I'm going to miss this place."

Sophie laughed softly. "Me, too." She turned in his arms. "We could always come back."

Trey gazed down into her mesmerizing eyes. It was the first time she'd ever acknowledged the possibility of a future together and he took it as a hopeful sign. "We could. But next time, we're going to bring better food. And wine. And ice for the champagne."

"And a softer place to sleep," she mentioned.

"And more clothes," he said.

Sophie shook her head. "I was just thinking maybe we had too many clothes. It might be nice to spend the whole vacation naked."

"You're right," he said, glancing down at her naked

body. He dropped a kiss on her lips, his palm cupping her breast. "Who needs clothes?"

"We will today," she said. "They won't take us back to Tahiti if we're naked."

Trey smoothed his hands from her torso down to her thighs. "So where are your clothes, Sophie? If we don't get dressed, they might just leave us both here for a little longer."

She turned in his arms again, wrapping his embrace more tightly around her. "Will you buy this island for your resort?" she asked, her gaze scanning the landscape.

"I don't think it's right for the resort," Trey answered. "But I wouldn't mind making a personal investment in the local real estate."

She looked at him over her shoulder, frowning. "I don't understand."

"I'd buy it so we could come back here. It could be ours. A place to come when we wanted to be alone, and run around naked, and make love on the beach." He paused, pressing a kiss to her ear. "We could renovate the cottage. Bring in a bed and some other furniture. A stove for cooking."

"And you would come here, a few times a year, to visit?"

"Yes," Trey said. "I would."

"I'd like that," Sophie agreed. "I'd like to come back here with you someday."

Trey took her hand and led her out into the water. When it was deep enough, Sophie wrapped her arms around his neck and her legs around his waist and they bobbed in the water, neither one of them speaking.

It was enough to just hold her close, to feel her body against his. They didn't have to say anything. The mood was palpable. He felt a knot of regret in his gut, regret that they didn't have more time, that the end was coming soon. But as long as he could touch her, they could still communicate.

"What's the first thing you're going to do when you get back?" Trey asked, running his hands through her hair as it floated on the surface of the water.

"Kiss my father. Tell him I'm sorry for all the worry I caused him. Then I'll figure out how to get the plane back to Pape'ete."

"I told you I'd help out with that."

She smiled, then dropped a gentle kiss on his lips. "Thank you. It's probably just a minor problem. We'll fly a mechanic over and he can fix it. And then I'll fly the plane back."

Trey frowned, not happy with the prospect of her getting back into that plane. "Maybe you should get someone else to fly it back," he suggested.

She gave him an odd look. "Why? No one knows that plane better than I do."

"What if the guy doesn't fix it right? I don't want you going down again. This time there might not be a safe place to land."

"I'd never go up if I wasn't sure the plane was ready to fly."

"The plane wasn't ready to fly when you took me up," he said. "The engine died and the radio didn't work."

"The engine cutting out was probably caused by moisture in the fuel. That happens during the rainy season. And I suspect that I couldn't restart the engine because the alternator belt broke. Which drained the battery for the radio and the ignition. So, it's just a broken belt, that's all."

Trey knew he shouldn't push the issue. But the last thing he wanted was for Sophie to go up in that plane again. When he got back to Pape'ete, he'd discuss the matter with her father. He'd hire a mechanic and another pilot to do the job. Hell, he'd buy the damn plane and set it on fire before he let Sophie risk her life again. She shouldn't be flying around in that old rattletrap.

He nodded. "Just find a good mechanic. Make sure he knows what he's doing," Trey insisted.

She kissed him again and a moment later, they were lost in a rush of desire. Trey had grown to love the taste of her. With just a simple flick of her tongue, she could make him crazy. Holding tight, he walked out of the lagoon and carried her up to the porch. Then, he gently put her back into the hammock and he joined her there.

They had at least a few more hours until someone came looking. Trey intended to use the time wisely.

8

SOPHIE COULD SMELL THE SCENT of warm bread baking, of sweet pastries in the oven and fresh croissants. She drew a deep breath, her mouth watering. Oh, and coffee. A moan slipped from her lips. Hot, black coffee. It was enough to make her stomach rumble with hunger.

She sighed, snuggling into the comfortable depths of her bed. But her bed wasn't so comfortable anymore. And the sounds of the birds and the waves that usually woke her up were distinctly different. Sophie slowly opened her eyes, then realized where she was.

"Are you hungry?"

She pushed up on her elbows to find Trey standing on the porch, dressed in his shorts and shirt. He was holding a banana leaf. On it, he'd cut up fresh fruit and piled canned cashews, arranging them in a pretty pattern. "Is that my breakfast?"

"Yes. Breakfast in a hammock."

Sophie crawled out and grabbed her pareu, then wrapped it around her naked body. She followed him over to the steps and sat down beside him. The sun was up and though the day was cloudy, there was blue sky to be seen through the haze.

Trey held out the fruit and she picked a piece of mango and popped it in her mouth. It was sinfully sweet and juicy. This island had the best mangoes she'd ever tasted. If that wasn't a good reason to come back, nothing else was. "I wonder what time it is?"

"It's a little past seven," Trey said.

"I thought your watch broke when you got it wet."

He shrugged. "I looked on my cell phone."

Sophie gasped. "You have a cell phone? Here? On the island?"

Trey nodded. "Yeah. But it doesn't work. There's no signal. I tried yesterday, while you were messing with the radio."

"Oh," Sophie murmured. "All right then."

He chuckled, bending closer to catch her gaze. "Did you think I would have let your father worry over you or kept us stuck on this island if the phone had worked?"

"We didn't use the flare gun," she said. "We could have signaled that boat."

He pulled her against him, giving her a hug. "Yeah, you're right. Even if it had worked, I probably would have waited until sunset to call." He grabbed his bag and pulled his cell phone out. "But I forgot about one feature of this phone." He flipped it open and held it out. "It's a camera."

Sophie covered her face. "No! Don't take a picture of me. I just got up."

"There," Trey said, showing her the display. "Look at how beautiful you are."

Her hair was mussed and fell in careless waves around her face. She took the phone from his hand and stared at her image. She was beautiful. Sophie barely recognized the woman in the photo. Was this how he saw her?

"How do I take a photo of you?"

Trey took the phone from her hand, then stood next to her and pressed a kiss to her cheek. A moment later, the photo came up on the display. Sophie laughed, delighted with the shot. It was so silly, but it reminded her of all the fun they'd had together.

"Now a serious one," she said.

Trey wrapped his arm around her shoulder and they both smiled at the camera. As Sophie examined the third photograph, she stared at Trey's face. He was a handsome man, a beautiful man.

"You're very pretty," she said.

He grabbed the phone from her and began to take pictures, one after another. Caught up in the fun, Sophie posed, throwing her arms out and giving Trey a series of sexy looks.

She gave him one last smile, then held a piece of papaya in front of his lips. "We should probably make a list of all the things we've consumed so that I can replace them when I come back for the plane."

"Three bottles of wine, including a bottle of champagne," Trey said.

"Funny, I don't feel that hungover. And that's the most I've had to drink in years."

"You handled yourself well," he teased. "Except for the 'Twelve Days of Christmas.' That was bad."

She munched on a cashew. "I think I'll bring back all sorts of good things. So the next people to stop here will have a gourmet feast." She paused. "You're going to have to get another charter service," she said. "There's an outfit called Tiare Air. They have the hangar next to ours. Gabe Aubert is a really good pilot and they have very nice planes. I'm sure I can arrange to have him take you up."

"I'll wait until you can take me up," Trey said.

"I don't know how long it will be before I can get the plane back in the air," Sophie said.

"I'll wait," he repeated.

She didn't want to lose the fee, but if he was willing to stay in Tahiti for a week, then she wasn't going to fight with him. In truth, Sophie liked the idea that they'd have a little more time together.

They both nibbled on the fruit and cashews. Trey's mood was a bit subdued but Sophie thought it might be due to a lack of sleep. Or perhaps he didn't want to leave the island any more than she did.

They'd been together for less than twenty-four hours and already, they'd grown so comfortable with each other, sharing breakfast as if they'd done so for years. Sophie finished the last of the mango, then stood up. "I'm going to go get more," she said. "Do you have the knife?"

"It's on the counter," he said. "There's a couple more mangoes in there. And another papaya. Do you want me to help?"

She smiled and shook her head. "No. I'll get it." She picked up the banana leaf and walked to the front door, then turned and looked back at Trey. How would it be between them if they actually lived together? Would they wake up in each other's arms every morning? Would they make breakfast together before going off to work? Would there come a time when they had children running around at their feet?

Sophie found the mangoes where he'd left them, along with the knife and a few more banana leaves. She sliced through the ripe fruit and arranged it on the shiny green leaf. But as she was cleaning up after herself, writing on the wall just above the counter caught her eye.

Unlike the rest of the inscriptions around the room, this one appeared unfaded and fresh, written with a thick black marker. "Here on this island," she read, "Trey fell in love with Sophie. Christmas Eve, 2008. We will be back."

Sophie glanced around, certain that she'd misread the writing. But it was her name and Trey's there on the wall. Reaching out, she ran her sticky fingers over the inscription, aware that she was looking at Trey's own handwriting for the first time.

They knew so little about each other. She wouldn't have even recognized his writing had their names not been evident. And yet, he'd fallen in love with her. Sophie drew a shaky breath. Should she ask him about the inscription or should she pretend she never saw it? Had he meant for her to see it?

With shaky hands, Sophie picked up the fruit and carried it to the front door of the cottage. For now, she wouldn't say anything. Maybe he would—

Trey's shout startled her as she walked through the door. "Sophie!" He was standing near the lagoon, staring up at the sky.

"What? I'm here."

"I think I hear a plane," he said. He turned to face her, the flare gun clutched in his hand. "Do you hear that? Or am I imagining things?"

Sophie set the fruit down on the porch step and joined him near the lagoon. She closed her eyes and listened, then nodded. "I think so."

"What should we do? Should I shoot a flare?"

"It's too soon. If it is search and rescue, they'll fly over and probably be able to see us from the air. At the least, they'll see the plane."

Sophie scanned the horizon. The sound was too far away to pinpoint the direction. But it was definitely a small plane. Was it part of a search-and-rescue team or just a passing pilot on his way to another island?

A few minutes later, the plane was visible to the south of the atoll. Trey reached out and took her hand, as they waited silently. Gradually, the plane began to descend and Trey held up a hand and waved.

The pilot circled once, then came down low. "That's Franc Aubert," Sophie said, waving. "He owns Tiare Air." Sophie took the flare gun and aimed it over the lagoon, then pulled the trigger. "There. Now he'll know we need help."

"Is he going to land?" Trey asked.

Sophie shook her head. "No. He doesn't have floats on that plane. He'll radio back and they'll send someone with a float or amphibious plane, one that can land in the lagoon. His son, Gabe, flies an amphibious plane like ours." She turned to him and smiled. "I guess we're going to be rescued."

"I guess so."

They both turned and started for the cottage, their fingers linked, their arms swinging between them. Suddenly, Trey pulled her to a stop. "I don't want to be rescued," he said.

Sophie laughed. "Neither do I."

He yanked her into his arms and brought his mouth down on hers, his kiss fierce and possessive. It was clear to Sophie what he wanted beyond no rescue. Stumbling toward the cottage, they tore at each other's clothes, the same way they had that very first time.

"How much time?" he whispered, untying her pareu.

"Maybe minutes," she replied, breathless with anticipation. "Maybe an hour." Sophie pushed his hands away and she unknotted the filmy fabric and tossed it aside. Then she tugged his shirt over his head and dropped it at their feet.

"I don't have another condom," he whispered as he watched her unzip his shorts.

"I don't care." Sophie knew her body well enough to know that there wasn't much chance it would matter. "I'm safe. Are you?"

"Yes," he said. "Always."

She skimmed his shorts and his boxers down over his hips and calves, then pushed him gently back to sit on the step. After she'd stripped off her T-shirt, Sophie straddled his legs and sat down on his lap.

Trey groaned as he glanced down. With a sly smile, Sophie wrapped her fingers around his shaft and began to stroke him. "You could ask me for anything right now and I'd give it to you," he said.

"All I want is you," Sophie replied. "Nothing else."

He leaned back and braced himself on the step behind him, watching her every move. And when he was hard and ready, Sophie lowered herself onto him, burying his shaft to the hilt.

The sensation was so exquisite that for a long time, she was afraid to move. She closed her eyes and arched back, burying him even deeper. And then, unable to stop herself, she pushed up until he was outside of her again.

It was a tantalizing game and she was in complete control of his desire. When she felt him nearing the edge, she slowed her pace and when he'd regained his control, she quickened it. But all the while, she knew she was drawing him closer and closer to an explosive orgasm.

If this was the last time they made love, Sophie wanted it to be the one he remembered for the rest of his life.

She didn't know what tomorrow would bring. Or where they would be in a few days' time. But this was the way she wanted to spend their last hour together…swept into a vortex of pleasure.

BY THE TIME THEY WERE completely sated, Trey and Sophie were both drenched with perspiration. She grabbed his hand and pulled him along to the water tanks behind the cottage, then showed him the shower.

The water was a bit cooler than that in the lagoon and it was fresh. He turned his back to Sophie and she smoothed her hands across his shoulders, gently massaging. He loved the feel of her touch and the sensations she caused. He tipped his head back, letting the warm water rush over him.

Sophie circled around him and began to wash his chest. Trey rested his hands on her shoulders. Her skin was warm and smooth beneath his touch, her limbs lean and supple, yet soft and feminine. She hadn't been toned by a trainer, but kept beautiful by living a healthy life in lush surroundings.

His gaze fixed on her fingers as they skimmed over his chest. Her nails were clipped short and were unpainted. Sophie was beyond the rules of feminine primping, but he'd come to admire that about her. She wore no makeup, yet she was the most beautiful woman he'd ever set eyes upon. She hadn't been spoiled by the modern world. Sophie was completely unaware of her own beauty.

His gaze slowly drifted down to her breasts and Trey watched, fascinated, as the water sluiced between them. Natural, that's what she was. Perfect and natural, the way God had intended a woman to be.

He grinned as her hands drifted lower, lingering just below his waist. "We don't have time for that," he warned, grabbing her hands and bringing them back to his lips. Trey kissed her fingers.

"If they come while we're busy, we'll just signal them to circle the island until we're ready to leave."

"How about we make some plans," he said, cupping her face in his hands. "Dinner tonight at my hotel. You wear your sexiest dress, I'll order the best bottle of champagne and we'll continue where we left off."

"All right," she said. "It's a date."

"Yes, it is a date." He dropped a kiss on her lips. "I'm going to go gather up our stuff while you finish your shower."

"No," Sophie cried. "I need you to scrub my back."

"If I start running my hands all over your body, then we are going to have a problem."

She looked down at his crotch, then back up, a wicked smile curling her lips. "I know how to make that go away."

Trey shook his head and stepped out from beneath the water. "Take your shower, Sophie. I'll be waiting for you when you're done."

He walked back toward the cottage, the sand clinging

to his bare feet. Though the shower did a bit to cool him off, there was no escaping the heat and humidity on the island. The temperature really didn't vary a whole lot. It only seemed cooler when he remained absolutely still for an hour or two. And Sophie didn't make that easy.

When they got back to Pape'ete, they'd have an air-conditioned room and clean sheets and all the food they'd care to eat. Living on the island with Sophie for a day had been a little bit of heaven. But when they got back, they'd be in paradise.

Trey turned to take one last look at Sophie, knowing that from now on, they'd be dressed. She smoothed her hair back, then opened her eyes to catch him staring at her. She smiled coyly, then reached over and turned off the water. Slowly, she walked toward him, the water glistening on her skin. As she passed by, she let her hand drift along his belly, just low enough to tease him.

"I'm in the mood for a pedicure," she said. "I think we'll have just enough time to take advantage of my Christmas present."

Trey groaned. This wasn't fair. He'd always thought he was the one in control when it came to sexual relationships. But here on this island, he had completely lost it.

It was getting ridiculous, or pathetic, he wasn't sure which. He'd enjoyed a very satisfying orgasm fifteen minutes ago and just watching her shower had made him ready for another. A guy had to wonder how many more times his body could react before it just gave out.

Trey followed her back to the cottage, his gaze fixed on her curvy backside. A cold shower would have done the trick in a matter of a minute or two. But there were no cold showers on Suaneva.

"YOU HAVE VERY PRETTY FEET."

Sophie dipped the brush into the nail polish and carefully painted Trey's big toe. He'd finished her pedicure and with nothing better to do, she'd decided to treat him to pale pink toenails.

"You're lucky I'm wearing boat shoes home."

"What are you worried about? You're manly enough to carry off pink. Coral might be a bit much, but…" She glanced at the bottom of the bottle. "Bubblegum Baby is definitely your color."

They sat on either side of the porch steps, their backs braced against the posts, their legs stretched out in front of them. Trey idly massaged her feet as she painted his toes. But it wasn't enough to just focus on the pedicure. Instead, she rubbed her foot gently against his crotch. He was hard again and if she teased him much longer, he'd need to seduce her again.

It wasn't the worst use of their time, Sophie mused. They'd been expecting the plane for the past hour, but it hadn't come. Neither one of them seemed particularly concerned about rescue. Sophie informed Trey that calling up a floatplane from Tahiti could take at least an hour or two. By her calculations they had about thirty minutes left.

There was a tiny sliver of fear inside her, a feeling that the moment they lifted off from the lagoon, everything would change. She knew there wasn't anything magical about the island. It was just a deserted atoll in the middle of the South Pacific.

But something wonderful had happened here, something very unexpected. She'd gotten on the plane in Pape'ete thinking she'd like to seduce Trey Shelton. A night in his bed was all she was looking for. But now, Sophie was sure that a single night together was just the beginning for them.

They had a date for that evening. She wouldn't have time to go home, so she'd run out from the airport and find herself a nice dress, then shower at the hangar. She made a mental note to buy some sexy underwear, too.

"What is this?"

Sophie glanced up from her painting to find Trey rubbing his hand over the tattoo on her ankle. "It's a sunrise," she said, "with a hibiscus flower."

"Why did you choose that?"

Sophie shrugged. "I didn't. The tattoo artist did. In Tahiti, some of the artists are like…mystical. They read your aura and they create a tattoo to symbolize who you are. He saw the sunrise because I was beginning a new phase of my life. And the hibiscus was to remind me of my life on the islands."

"Did it hurt?"

She shook her head, then laughed. "Yeah. It hurt

like hell. But it only took about a half hour, so I tried to be brave."

"I like it," Trey said. "It's sexy."

"When my mother saw it, she was so angry with me. But I've always felt as if I lived between two worlds with my parents. My mother is French, my father American, but I feel Polynesian. I grew up in Tahiti. It's home."

"Maybe I should get a tattoo," Trey said. "My mother would probably kill me, too." He paused. "Although, I've done a lot of stupid things in my life. A tattoo wouldn't be the worst of it."

"You have to get a tattoo for a reason," Sophie explained. "It's like a rite of passage. You get it when you undergo a change in your life. I got mine after I lost my virginity."

"Going down in that plane was a big moment in my life," he said. "Things kind of changed after that."

"What changed?"

Trey thought about his answer. He wanted to say, "everything." "I'm just looking at things a little differently. Taking stock of my life. Thinking about making a few changes."

"Like with your resort?"

"Yeah, that. And other things."

Sophie considered his story for a long moment, then nodded. "That's worth a tattoo," she said. "When we get back, I'll take you. I'll even hold your hand."

She finished with his right foot, then blew on his

toes. "It's so damp, this isn't going to dry very fast. If you walk in the sand, it'll stick to the polish."

"How do I get this off?"

"It never comes off," she teased. "Your toes will be pink for the next year."

"Pink toes would definitely scare my mother," he said.

Sophie put the top back on the bottle, then handed it to him. "For touch-ups," she teased. "And you'll have to get some polish remover and some—" She stopped, a distant sound catching her attention. "The plane is coming."

Trey swung his feet off her lap and stood, then held out his hand and helped her up. Sophie pointed across the lagoon. "They'll come in from that way," she said.

"How do you know?"

"The wind. They'll land into the wind."

They stood on the step and waited. Just as Sophie had predicted, ten minutes later, they saw the plane circle twice before lining up for a landing. Sophie smiled as she recognized Gabriel Aubert's plane from Tiare Air. Both Gabriel and Franc were excellent pilots and Sophie wasn't surprised that her father had called on them both to lead the search. Besides, Gabe and Sophie had also dated for a time three or four years ago and Sophie suspected he still harbored a small crush.

Gabriel made a perfect landing with the amphibious plane, maneuvering so it glided slowly up toward the beach. He cut the engine and the propeller stopped. A moment later, the plane came to a halt about twenty feet from the shore. Sophie strolled down to the lagoon, Trey walking a few feet behind her.

Gabriel hopped out of the plane and waded through the water, a wide smile on his handsome face. "Sophie Madigan, you have caused a lot of worry," he scolded, his French accent thick. "Your father was frantic when you didn't return last night."

Sophie threw her arms around Gabe's neck and gave him a hug. "Thank you for coming for us. We had a problem with the plane and I had to put it down."

"She put it down without the engine," Trey said.

Gabe glanced back and forth between the two of them. "Really? This is true?"

"It was nothing," Sophie said.

"It was something," Trey contradicted. "I've never seen anything like it."

"*Alors,* let's get you home," Gabe said, draping his arm over Sophie's shoulders. "You can tell me all about it on the way. Your papa is anxious to see you, Sophie." He looked over at Trey. "And so is yours, Mr. Shelton."

"My father?"

Gabe nodded. "He's waiting at the Madigan hangar at Faaa. He came in on a Learjet. Nice plane. I've always wanted to fly one of those." He glanced around. "Do you have your belongings?"

Trey held up his bag and Sophie nodded. "We're ready to go." It was obvious from Gabe's attitude toward her that he didn't suspect anything had gone on between Trey and her. And it was obvious from Trey's expression that he didn't like Gabe touching her. But Sophie wasn't ready to explain to anyone what had happened on Suaneva.

They waded out into the water. Gabe grabbed her around the waist and lifted her into the plane. Sophie crawled into the copilot's seat, then turned to watch Trey and Gabe spin the plane around. When they were finished, Trey took the spot behind the pilot's seat while Gabe strapped himself in. Sophie sent Trey a smile, but he didn't return it.

She turned back to the controls, wondering what was going through Trey's mind. Though she and Gabe had dated, they'd realized early on they were much better off as friends. And now, they were more like siblings, sharing their interest in flying and their frustrations with working for their fathers. Trey really had no cause to be jealous.

Maybe he was just sad to leave the island, she mused. Sophie sat silently as Gabe started the engine and when they were ready to take off, Sophie fastened her seat belt and glanced back at Trey. "You okay?"

"Yeah," he said, staring at her with an enigmatic smile.

Gabe pushed the throttle forward and the plane began to skim over the lagoon. Her father had been right. Though landing was always tricky on Suaneva, taking off required a very steep bank at the end of the lagoon to avoid the tops of the coconut palms. When they were in the air, Gabe grabbed the radio and flipped to the channel that her father used for Madigan Air.

"Madigan Air, this is Tiare Air 2269. I have both passengers on board and we're on our way to Faaa. Estimated flying time, ninety minutes. Over."

Sophie heard her father's voice crackling over the distance between them. "Let me talk to my daughter. Over."

Gabe handed her the radio and she pushed the transmit button. "Hello, Papa. I'm so sorry to have worried you."

"You don't know how frantic I was," he said. She could hear it in his voice, the same emotion that she heard whenever he talked about her mother. "I didn't know what to think. What went wrong? Over."

"I think there was moisture in the fuel line. The engine cut out and I couldn't get it started again. I'm pretty sure the belt on the alternator broke. That's why the radio didn't work. Over."

"You made a dead-stick landing?"

"Yes, Papa. Just like you taught me."

"Good girl, Sophie."

She could hear how upset he was, so Sophie decided to cut the conversation short. "Papa, I'll see you when we land. Tell Trey's—I mean, Mr. Shelton's father that he's fine. I love you, Papa."

"Love you, too, Sophie."

She handed the radio back to Gabe, then brushed a tear from her cheek. Drawing a ragged breath, she fixed her gaze out on the horizon. Sophie had to believe everything would be fine when they got back.

But as Gabe chatted about his plans to buy a new plane for his father's business, Sophie realized that she really wasn't interested. She longed to hear Trey's voice, even if he was reciting the alphabet or reading the phone book.

In fact, she was starting to seriously regret they'd ever left the island at all.

9

TREY KNEW IT WAS GOING to be bad as they taxied up to the Madigan Air hangar. He could see a group of photographers hurrying toward the plane, their cameras flashing. Cursing softly, he wondered if Sophie was prepared to handle this.

He'd been wading through the celebrity cesspool his entire adult life. The press had finally begun to back off now that he was keeping a lower profile, but a story like this was too juicy to resist. Plane crash, castaway on a tropical island and a beautiful woman. All elements the tabloids could exploit.

"Look at that," Gabe said. "*Les Nouvelles* has sent out reporters. Sophie, you must be famous."

"No," Trey muttered. "I think they're looking for me."

Sophie glanced back at him, their gazes meeting for the first time since the flight began. Trey sent her a weak smile. "When you get out of the plane, go right to your father," he said. "Lock yourself in the hangar until the press leaves. Do you understand?"

She nodded, then turned back to stare at the growing

mob outside. Sophie had spent the past hour chatting with her handsome pilot while Trey had pretended to work, scribbling illegible notes on his legal pad as he tried to figure out the true nature of the relationship between Sophie and Gabe.

It had become so easy to think of Sophie as his own. But after just a few minutes off the island, Trey was forced to admit there were other people who cared about her, too. Her father. And obviously this Gabe character.

Trey had known men like him, Frenchmen, who were well schooled in the art of charm. Even with his faded T-shirt and battered cap, Trey could see through the act. This guy was smooth. And from what Trey could tell, he'd set his sights on Sophie.

"Look," Gabe said, "there is your father." He took Sophie's hand and gave it a squeeze. Trey bristled at the gesture and he bit back a curse. For the first time in his life, he was jealous and he didn't like the way that felt.

"See, this is the Lear I was talking about," Gabe said, pointing to Trey's father's plane. "Nice, *n'est-ce pas?*"

"Very nice," Sophie murmured.

The plane drew to a stop and Gabe shut off the engine, then crawled out the pilot's side, leaving Trey and Sophie alone for the first time. "Don't say anything to the reporters," Trey warned. "Just do as I said and everything will be all right. I'll come back later, after everything has cooled down."

Sophie nodded, giving him a weak smile. Then the passenger-side door opened and Gabe reached in to help Sophie out. "What is lost is now found," Gabe said as he grabbed her waist and lifted her from the plane.

Trey found his bag and prepared himself for the crush of photographers and reporters. If he was able to draw their attention away from Sophie by answering a few questions, then maybe she could get away. He waited until she'd reached her father, then, taking a deep breath, Trey stepped out of the plane to the flash of cameras.

"Trey, tell us about your time as a castaway!"

"Are you all right, Trey? Do you have any injuries?"

"They say your pilot was a woman. Was the crash her fault?"

"There was no crash," Trey said with a warm smile. "We had to make an emergency landing, that's all." He kept his eye on Sophie, watching as she threw herself into her father's embrace. "There was a minor mechanical problem with the plane and the pilot did an amazing job putting us down on the lagoon at Suaneva."

"My son will answer all your questions later!" Trey stopped at the sound of his father's voice, then turned to watch Peter Shelton the Second emerge from the Learjet. He slowly strolled down the steps as the cameras turned their attention toward him.

"Mr. Shelton, were you worried about your son?"

"Did you think he was dead?"

"Tell us how you felt when you got the call."

"I said we'd answer questions later," Trey's father said. "I've arranged for a press conference at the Sofitel in a couple of hours. You can get all the photos you want and ask all your questions then. Right now, I'd like to talk to my son."

His father crossed the tarmac to where Trey stood, then pulled him into a fierce hug. Trey couldn't recall the last time his father had showed the least bit of affection toward him. "A press conference?" Trey muttered.

"Good to see you, Trey," he said. "I was worried."

"How did you get here so fast?" Trey asked.

"I got the call late last night while I was in Tokyo. It didn't take me long. Your mother is on her way. She's flying in from New York and should be here early this evening. I chartered a plane for her."

"That wasn't necessary. I'm fine."

"Well, good." He clapped Trey on the shoulder and to his surprise, Trey saw tears glistening in his father's eyes.

"I'm glad you came," Trey said. "And it will be nice to see Mom. We haven't spent a Christmas together in years."

His father smiled. "We'll have a big celebration."

Trey thought back to the simple *celebration* he and Sophie had enjoyed the night before. His father's parties were always overblown affairs. "Maybe we could just have a drink and talk?"

A taxi screeched to a halt near the hangar and Trey turned to watch as an oddly familiar woman crawled out of the back. She pulled off her sunglasses and surveyed the crowd, immediately catching the interest of the photographers. "It's Tania!" one of the reporters shouted.

"Oh my God! Oh, Trey, thank God you're alive."

Trey cringed. Tania Richardson. What the hell was she doing here? Though he'd broken off the relationship six months ago, since that time, Tania had managed to perpetuate the rumor that she and Trey were about to announce their engagement. Obviously this was some silly publicity stunt.

Tania came from a famous acting family in Britain and was rather used to over-the-top dramatics. But this was too much. She rushed over to him, making sure to stop a few times for photographs. Tania was wearing clothes more suitable for a nightclub—a skimpy little dress that left nothing to the imagination.

When she reached him, Tania threw herself into his arms and the flashes began popping continuously. Trey tried to extract himself from her embrace, but she wouldn't let go. "Stop," he gasped, unwrapping her arms from around his neck.

"I'm so glad you're alive, darling."

Trey glanced over to see Sophie watching them both, her eyes wide, her expression marked with confusion. "How did you get here, Tania?"

She stepped back and gave him a plastic smile. "Well, darling, when I heard you were going to be here for the holidays, I thought it would be nice if we'd spend some time together. With your schedule and mine, we've been apart for too long. Imagine my horror when I heard you were missing. So of course, I called the press. News like this is important."

"No doubt you were anxious to try out a new role—

that of the grieving fiancée," Trey said. "It would have been a good part, Tania, but unfortunately, I survived. And I suppose now would be a good time to tell the press we're not really engaged."

In fact, now would be the *perfect* time, Trey thought. He glanced around at the small crowd gathered around him. He'd lost track of Sophie and he stepped away from Tania, searching for her. A moment later, he saw her, standing at the door of the hangar.

"Sophie!"

The reporters and photographers immediately turned their attention to her. He tried to walk toward her but no matter which way he moved, they stepped into his path. Trey gave one of the reporters a shove and the guy stumbled back, falling against a photographer. "Sorry," Trey muttered. "Just let me get by."

"Son, come on." Peter Shelton grabbed Trey's arm and pulled him back. "I have a car waiting to take us to the hotel."

Trey glanced back and forth between his father and Sophie. His gaze met hers and held and for a moment; he felt as though they were back on the island, all alone. He could read the confusion in her eyes and he wanted to explain. But not here and not with everyone watching.

Sophie gave him a little wave goodbye, then turned and walked inside the hangar. The moment she was gone, Trey felt an incredible loneliness set in. He knew things might be bad when they got back. But he'd never imagined this.

"Come on, darling," Tania said. "Let's get out of here. You need to change out of those awful clothes and have something decent to eat." She turned to Trey's father and gave him a blinding smile. "You don't mind if I ride with you, do you?" She looped her arm through Trey's and pulled him toward the waiting town car.

"By the way, who was the girl?" Tania murmured through clenched teeth as they wove back through the photographers.

"She was the pilot," Trey said. "Her name is Sophie." Tania had a jealous streak a mile long. It had been one of the things that had quickly put an end to their short relationship.

"I think you should sue," she added in a clipped tone. "The girl is obviously incompetent. You could have been killed."

Trey crawled in the backseat of the car, Tania getting in after him. His father brought up the rear, scowling as if he wasn't pleased they had an extra passenger, either. But Trey couldn't think about the politics of what was going on. All he could think about was getting back to Sophie.

They pulled away from the hangar and the reporters and photographers quickly gave chase, some in cars, some on motorcycles. Trey sank back into the soft leather seats, not listening to the incessant chatter coming from Tania. Sophie was always so careful with her words. She never wasted any and everything she said was endlessly interesting. Tania talked because she loved the sound of her own voice.

He'd get back to the hotel, get changed and then find a way to leave without the reporters following. He knew Sophie and her father lived on an outlying island, but maybe, without their plane, they'd be forced to stay in Tahiti for the day.

Or perhaps Gabe would take them home. If that was the case, then Trey would simply hire Gabe to fly him to Sophie. That part of his plan would be easy to accomplish. After Tania's little stunt, convincing Sophie that they belonged together might be a bit more difficult.

Trey pushed up from his seat and crawled over Tania, squeezing in next to his father. "I have something I want to talk to you about," he said. "An idea I have for a resort."

"We can talk about business later," his father said.

"No, I need to talk about this now," Trey insisted. "My future depends on it. I don't have time to waste."

SOPHIE SAT DOWN AT the battered desk inside the hangar of Madigan Air. She'd been back for two hours and it hadn't taken long for her life to return to exactly what it had been a few days ago.

Her father, Franc and Gabe had insisted she accompany them into town for a celebratory breakfast at their favorite patisserie. Sophie had begged off, wanting nothing more than to get home and back to her normal routine. But the three men had been up all night and wanted something to eat, so she'd stayed behind to make arrangements for a mechanic to fly to Suaneva the following morning.

The thought of going back to Suaneva without Trey was difficult to imagine. But the reception they got on arrival was enough to convince her they'd never be going back there together. Her thoughts wound back to the scene she'd witnessed.

One of the reporters had come over to ask her a few questions about the "incident," as he had called it. She carefully explained what had happened and he seemed satisfied with her answers. But then, Sophie had risked a question of her own, asking about the woman who had greeted Trey so enthusiastically.

The reporter had looked at her as if she'd just asked him what that big bright ball of fire was in the sky. He'd quickly informed Sophie that Tania Richardson was both a famous British starlet and Trey Shelton's fiancée.

Sophie had never heard of her, but then, she'd been stuck on an island in the middle of the South Pacific her whole life. And Tahiti wasn't exactly a hotbed of celebrity activity, either.

As Sophie searched the desk for the phone book, anger bubbled up inside her. She cursed loudly first in French, and then in English for good measure. How could she have been so stupid as to trust him? The whole time they'd been on the island, he'd been playing her for a fool. When he'd said he was unattached, he'd lied. And everything after that was a lie, too.

Merde, she should have known. A man as handsome and charming as Trey Shelton was never single for long. Besides that, he was rich. But after observing his fiancée for no more than just a few minutes, Sophie had to wonder if she ever knew anything about Trey at all.

She and Tania Richardson had absolutely nothing in common. Tania was glamorous and aloof and probably rich, too. She wore expensive jewelry and designer clothes, she had a snooty accent and seemed a bit…obnoxious.

If Trey was in love with Tania, what could he find remotely fascinating about Sophie Madigan? "I was convenient," she finally said, throwing up her hands at the revelation. "He was horny and I was convenient. And easy. And more than willing to seduce him."

Well, she'd gotten the lover she'd wanted. Sophie bit her bottom lip to stem a flood of emotion. Falling apart was not going to do her any good. She needed to accept that what they'd enjoyed had only been temporary. Before landing on the island, that would have been exactly what she needed. So what had really changed?

"Everything," Sophie murmured. After only twenty-four hours, she'd imagined a whole future with Trey, an exciting life where she looked forward to every day—and every night. Unfortunately, his future was with someone else.

Sophie finally found the phone book and rifled through it, searching for the number of Trey's hotel. Before he left the island, she intended to tell him exactly how she felt about his deception, if only to prove to herself she was strong enough to do it. Once that was accomplished, she could move on with her life.

But as she punched in the digits, Sophie realized her true motives for calling Trey. She wanted him to tell her it wasn't true, that he didn't love Tania Richardson and that he hadn't lied to her. She wanted him to say he loved her.

Sophie dropped the phone back into the cradle and sighed. Maybe it was best to just get on with her life. If she got back to work, she'd forget all about Trey and what happened on the island. But why should she forget? He'd betrayed her and she deserved an apology.

His father had said they'd be holding a press conference at the Sofitel. Maybe she could get some answers to her questions there. She pushed away from the desk and crossed to the mirror hanging on the back of the office door. She was still dressed in the clothes she wore on the island.

Even after just a day of saltwater and sand, they looked a bit ragged. But she didn't have time to buy something new. Maybe it was best to remind him of their time together. He'd worn her pareu and removed her T-shirt. If he saw her dressed in these clothes, he'd remember.

Sophie raked her hands through her hair. She'd lost the scarf she'd worn that day in the plane, but it didn't matter. Staring at herself in the mirror, she gathered herself, calmed her emotions and thought about what she'd say to him.

"Sophie?"

She recognized the voice as soon as he said her name. Sophie closed her eyes and cursed softly because it wasn't the voice she wanted to hear. Gabe stood outside the office door, his cap in one hand and a small bouquet of flowers in the other.

"Hi," Sophie murmured. Gabe held out the flowers and she took them. "What are these for?"

He shifted on his feet, twisting his cap back and forth in his hands. "When I found out your plane had gone down, I was very worried, Sophie. And sad. Very sad because it made me realize how much you mean to me. And how I never really told you this."

Sophie held up her hand. "You don't have to—"

"I know we said we would not see each other anymore, but I want you to know my feelings haven't changed. I am still very fond of you, Sophie. And I thought, perhaps, we might go out some night and…talk. Or eat. Or both."

Sophie opened her mouth, prepared to make some feeble excuse. Though Gabe was incredibly attractive, very available and one of the nicest people she'd ever met, there had never been a spark between them. Not like there had been with Trey.

But then, Trey wasn't available. Was this how it was to be? Sophie wondered. Would she compare every man she met to Trey Shelton? Maybe it was time to open herself up to new possibilities. Though Trey had allowed her to trust again, she wasn't about to let his behavior set her back. She was stronger than that.

Sophie held the flowers up to her nose and drew a deep breath. It was time to get out there and try again. Even if it was with a man who seemed more like a brother than a lover. "All right. But I'm going to be very busy this week trying to get the plane back from Suaneva. How about next week?"

Gabe nodded, a warm smile breaking across his face. "Sure," he said. "And I can help you with the plane. I'll fly you out there and take a look at it. We'll get it back up in the air in no time."

"Yes," Sophie said, warmed by his thoughtful offer.

Gabe glanced around nervously. "Well, I promised your father I'd fly you both home. I'll go pick him up from the patisserie and we'll be on our way."

"Thank you," Sophie said, reaching out to touch his hand. "For coming to get me. And for the flowers."

He nodded, then turned and walked to the door. When it slammed behind him, Sophie let out a tightly held breath. She returned to the office and plopped down in the chair, then put her head down on the desk.

Suddenly, she felt exhausted. It was no wonder. A life-and-death landing in the lagoon, followed by nonstop sex was enough to make anyone want to curl up in bed and sleep for three or four days. In truth, she wanted to sleep so she wouldn't have to think about Trey.

Tears pressed at the corners of her eyes, but she stubbornly pushed them back. She wouldn't get emotional about this. Instead, Sophie would look at their relationship for what it was—short, sweet and incredibly satisfying. She closed her eyes and let her thoughts drift, back to the island, back to the man who'd made her body ache with desire.

"Sophie?"

At first she thought she was dreaming. But then Sophie opened her eyes and saw him standing in the doorway of the office.

"Are you all right?" Trey asked.

Pressing her hand to her heart, Sophie felt her pulse begin to race. He'd showered and changed and he looked so different from the man she'd grown to love on the island. He wore a loose cotton shirt with a flower tucked into the pocket and shorts that revealed his long, muscular legs.

His face was a bit sunburned and his hair looked a little lighter than she remembered. But his eyes were the same beautiful shade of hazel and his smile still made her blood warm.

"I—I didn't think I'd find you here," he said.

"I'm here." Sophie slowly stood, twisting her fingers together in front of her, holding tight to calm her nerves.

Trey reached out to touch her, then let his hand drop to his side. "I'm sorry."

"Yes," Sophie murmured, staring down at her feet. "You probably are. She's very pretty. I can understand why you're with her. And it's fine. We don't have any claim on each other and—"

"I'm not with Tania."

"Then she's back at the hotel?"

"Yes." He frowned. "I mean, no. She's not here. She's not with me. She's not *with* me." He reached out and took her shoulders in his hands, giving her a gentle squeeze. "Sophie, Tania and I haven't seen each other for six months. There's nothing between us."

"But one of the reporters told me—"

"He's wrong. Trust me on this. Do you honestly think I'd choose her before you?"

"She's beautiful," Sophie said.

"You're beautiful," he countered. "You are everything I've been looking for all my life. The funny thing is, I didn't know I was looking until I found you. And now that I have, I'm not going to let you go."

Sophie swallowed hard. Was she hearing this right? She'd been so stunned to learn Trey wasn't engaged that she'd forgotten to listen to the rest. "You want me?"

"Yes." He bent close and kissed her gently. "Yes, yes, yes."

A long silence grew between them as Sophie regarded him suspiciously. She wanted to believe him. The truth was there in his eyes. "I want you, too," she said softly.

It was a risk she had to take, but for the first time in her life, Sophie knew it was the right risk. A giggle slipped from her lips. "I was going to go to your press conference and demand you tell me the truth."

He grinned. "That would have been nice. We could always drive back to the hotel and you could do that. Tell them what a great guy I am and how I built fire on the island and made a hammock."

"You're missing your press conference?"

"I don't need a press conference," he said. "I'm going

to be out of the public eye for a while. For the next fifty or sixty years. I'm hoping they'll soon forget about me."

"What are you going to do?"

"Well, first, I'm going to take you out to lunch and then we're going to go back to my hotel and we're going to take a long bubble bath. And then, I need you to take the nail polish off my toes."

"No, I meant what are you going to do. About your work, your job," Sophie said.

"I'm going to build my resort. I told my father about my idea and he thought it was a good one. He's going to back me on it financially. I'm going to move here while it's being built. And after that, we'll see what happens."

"You're staying here?"

He nodded and Sophie felt a smile break across her face. She couldn't help it. She wanted to pretend she didn't care, but she did. And if Trey was here on the island, they'd have plenty of time to explore all these new and wonderful feelings.

"So, now that I'm staying, I was wondering if you'd be my girl."

"What would that mean?"

"It would mean that when Gabe puts his arm around your shoulder, you'll tell him you've got a boyfriend. And when I have to go back to the States for business, you'll come with me. And we'll maybe spend the night with each other occasionally. Or always. Your choice."

Sophie wrapped her arms around Trey's neck and pressed her body against his. She gave him a sweet, tantalizing kiss. "I think that sounds like a good idea. Especially the always part."

Trey nodded. "Then there's only one thing to do." He stepped out of her embrace and reached for the flower he'd tucked in his pocket. He brushed it across her lower lip, before tucking it behind Sophie's left ear. "There. That makes it official. You're taken."

"Yes, I am," Sophie said. With a laugh, she threw herself into his arms and kissed him fiercely. She would have a man for the New Year, and not just a lover, but a friend. And if all went well, they'd have many New Years to come. Suddenly, life seemed full of possibilities. And the islands didn't seem so small after all.

* * * * *

NO HOLDING BACK

BY
ISABEL SHARPE

First published in Great Britain 2010
Harlequin Mills & Boon Limited,
Eton House, 18-24 Paradise Road, Richmond, Surrey TW9 1SR

© Muna Shehadi Sill 2009

ISBN: 978 0 263 88148 6

14-1110

Harlequin Mills & Boon policy is to use papers that are natural, renewable and recyclable products and made from wood grown in sustainable forests. The logging and manufacturing processes conform to the legal environmental regulations of the country of origin.

Printed and bound in Spain
by Litografia Rosés S.A., Barcelona

Isabel Sharpe was not born pen in hand like so many of her fellow writers. After she quit work in 1994 to stay home with her first-born son and nearly went out of her mind, she started writing. After more than twenty novels—along with another son—Isabel is more than happy with her choice these days. She loves hearing from readers. Write to her at www. IsabelSharpe.com.

To Lori H,
for being there every day to whine to

1

"SO THERE I WAS IN PARIS at one of the greatest restaurants in the world, and stomach flu picks *that night* to turn on me, between the *pigeon aux olives* and the *baba au rhum*."

"Oh, no. Imagine that." Hannah O'Reilly swallowed another mouthful of tepid champagne and glanced desperately behind the large pallid lump named Frank who'd inflicted himself on this portion of her evening. At a New Year's Eve party in an ostentatious mansion outside of her home city of Philadelphia, wearing one of those dresses saved all year for parties like this, she should be dancing wildly with a hot stranger. If she wanted boredom, she could have stayed home.

A waiter wafted by with a tray of tidbits. Hannah grabbed one, not sure what was in it, but assuming it cost more than her daily food allowance. Gerard Banks, owner of both this house and the newspaper that employed her, *The Philadelphia Sentinel,* threw a fancy New Year's Eve party every year for his staff, friends and family. Hannah didn't know which category this guy Frank belonged in, staff, friend or family, but she wished he'd bludgeon someone else with his stories. She was here for a healthy serving of hedonism.

"Another time, in London, I ate an oyster and felt movement between my teeth." He mimicked checking in his large mouth and pretended to hold something up. "Turned out to be a worm. Never ate oysters after that."

"I don't blame you." She laid her hand on his jacket sleeve to cushion the rejection. "You know…I think I'd like a refill on my champagne. It was great talking to you."

"Sure." He sighed and lifted his soda in a resigned toast. "Happy New Year."

"Same to you, Frank." She escaped, breathing a guilty sigh of relief, maneuvered between a chatting couple and a chartreuse settee, set her glass on a table full of similar empties next to the stone hearth and went searching for a champagne-bearing waiter. Then she was going to find some wild single hottie and flirt her head off. Because she was determined that this new year would launch a fabulous new chapter of her life. Careerwise, familywise and manwise. Out of the rut, into the rutting.

Bingo. Tuxedoed waiter ten paces ahead, carrying a tray of fizzing delight. She dodged between a ficus and a ceramic statue of a leopard. With any luck she could cut him off on the other side of the orange suede couch, and—

"Hannah, how's the year winding down for you?" Tragically, her boss, Lester Wanefield, neither wild nor single nor with an extra glass of champagne, stepped into the few remaining feet between her and her next dose of bubbly. "Hey, now don't *you* do good things for red sequins."

"Oh. Thanks." She loved how she looked in this dress, but enticing her boss made her wish she'd worn sackcloth.

"Great party, huh?"

"Mmm, yeah." If she could keep herself from thinking the money should be used for something more worthy. Like charity or education or disease research or Hannah's bank account.

She kept her eye on the waiter. This could still work. If he moved a few feet to his right and glanced her way…

"I've been thinking about your next assignment. Not for your Lowbrow column, but a feature story. Maybe start it on the front page."

Lester had her full attention then—all rotund, gray-bearded, bespectacled, five-foot-six-inches of him. Now that she'd been at the paper over a year, she'd been pestering him—well, hinting first, suggesting second, pestering third—for more substantial assignments than the powder-puff stories he'd been tossing at her and burying in the back sections. "That would be fabulous, Lester. You know, I've actually been researching a story. There's a little-known side effect of the drug Penz—"

"A story about boobs."

If she punched him in his large stomach, would he squeal like the pig he was? "Boobs."

"Women who've had boob jobs, to be precise. How does having a bigger rack alter their dating habits, their sex lives, their ability to attract men and does it change the type of men they score with?"

"How…interesting." He had to be kidding. "But I was actually hoping to do—"

"We'll call it 'Rack of Glam.' And I want lots of pictures." He leered at a well-endowed woman strutting past. "*Lots* of pictures."

"I'd rather—"

"I know you would, O'Reilly. But you don't get your 'rathers' in this business until you've been around a lot longer than you have."

"So you've said." *Ad nauseam.* "But I—"

"No butts." He gave her bare shoulder a condescending squeeze and winked. "Just boobs."

Ew.

She approximated a smile, knowing further argument would only cement his opposition. But grrrrrr. How much girly news could a nongirly woman stand? Girly dress tonight aside.

She needed to find a story on her own, something bigger

and sexier than the drug side effects, something so compel-
ling that even Pig Lester couldn't turn it down. A huge scoop
with enough popular appeal to hook him, but enough substance to further her career and get her on such sound finan-
cial footing that if her parents' lives imploded again she could
be the one they could depend on.

Like…

Like…

Yeah. Like that.

She blew out a breath and spotted another waiter, wished
her boss a Happy New Year that she barely managed to keep
from sounding like *Damn You and Your Family to Hell,* and
followed, determined to score more alcohol, this time to numb
the frustration. A story about boobs. Whoopee. The year
ended in approximately fifteen minutes and as far as she was
concerned, good riddance. Landing what she thought would
be her dream job hadn't worked out. Again. Her last boyfriend
hadn't worked out. Again. Her determination to lose ten
pounds hadn't worked out. Again. Twenty-nine years old and
she thought she'd be set for life by thirty.

At least circumstances had miraculously turned around for
Mom and Dad. Though fat lot of help she'd been able to be.

The waiter stopped to serve an evening-gowned trio. This
was her chance.

"Hannah." Her closest work-friend, business reporter
Daphne Baldwin, snagged her hand and dragged her into the
library. "You have to meet this person…Dee-Dee something.
Royco or Rosmer or Rrrrr…I forget. But you have to meet her."

"Why?" Hannah glanced wistfully at the top of the retreat-
ing waiter's head, his tantalizing tray just visible above the
crush of people. So close, and yet…

"Because, she's…wait." Daphne searched the room and
frowned. "She was just here."

"Where's Paul?"

Daphne made a face. "He wouldn't come. Said he didn't see why he should get dressed up in uncomfortable clothes and hang around people he didn't know and didn't want to know, when he could stay home and be comfortable drinking without having to worry about driving drunk."

He had a point, though Hannah wouldn't dare admit it out loud. There were times she felt Daphne's mellower half would be happier with a woman who matched his nonenergy, and that Daphne needed more of a live wire, but Daphne insisted he was her life's ballast. Hannah thought he was more her life's punching bag. "So you're a wild single tonight. He better watch out."

"I don't know, Hannah, he's been acting weird lately. Doesn't want to do anything with me."

"You mean he no longer jumps to do everything *you* want to do?"

"Ha ha ha." Daphne continued to scan the crowd, unperturbed by Hannah's bull's-eye zinger. "I'm serious. He's been distant and…I don't know, unresponsive. Like there's something really bugging him, but he won't tell me."

"Do you think he's cheating?"

"What?" Daphne's horror was immediate, and so impressive that nearby heads turned.

Oops. Where was the Reverse button on this conversation? Obviously Hannah had struck a nerve, and it wasn't her place to torture her friend by planting suspicions. "No, no, I don't think he is, I just… Isn't that what you always suspect when—"

"Paul would never cheat. He doesn't have the time. Or the initiative."

Oof. As much as Hannah loved Daphne, sometimes she thought Paul *should* cheat, just to stop her from taking him for granted. "Something at work?"

"He'd tell me that. It's probably a midlife crisis. Men get those all the time, don't they? Serves them right for not being slaves to hormones every month like we are." She frowned and plunked her hands onto her enviably trim hips. "Now where the heck is that woman?"

"Why do I need to meet this person?" Hannah sighed, queasy over her friend's relationship attitudes and feeling generally cranky. She didn't want to make small talk with any strangers, not even Mr. Hot-Wild-Single-Whoever. The dress was wasted. The night was wasted. The year was wasted. Her life was on its way to being wasted. Only *she* wasn't wasted because the damn waiters were avoiding her.

Fine. She'd ring in the New Year, butt-kiss Gerard for spending gazillions on people he underpaid, and get home to the city before the predicted ice storm hit. Too bad about her fantasy of spending the night enraptured with a new love, but probably just as well. It was always the same tired story. She fell for men like stemware during an earthquake, then when they sensed the depth of her passion and excitement and hope for the future, they abruptly moved on. No matter how hard she tried to act indifferent, men could always tell. Maybe she should make a resolution tonight to avoid the gender altogether.

"Come on." Daphne dragged her out of the library into another room, some sort of study, then another huge garish living room, as if the front living area the size of Hannah's entire apartment wasn't enough. "Don't see her here, either. Let's go back."

"Ooh, wait." Hannah caught a glimpse of Rory, the VP of advertising whom she had a minicrush on, standing alone, looking a little lost. At the office Rory barely acknowledged her in her usual attire of jeans and baggy sweaters. Should she test her slinky red-sequined minidress out on him and see if he—

Argh! What was she, some kind of addict? Ten seconds and

she'd already forgotten her resolution. *Men bad, Hannah. Alone good. Alone safe.*

Alone, boring and predictable.

"Let's try this way."

Hannah dug in her feet before Daphne could continue bull-dozing. "Would you mind telling me what is so thrilling about this person?"

"Oh. Right. Duh." Daphne thwacked her forehead, making her fabulous brown curls bounce. "She's close to Jack Brattle."

Zip. Hannah's gaze left Rory's tall form at light speed and fixed on her friend. *"Jack Brattle?"*

"Knew that'd get your attention."

"Where is she?" Hannah grabbed Daphne's rock-muscled arm, not even indulging her usual envy for Daphne's disci-pline in the gym. "Find her. An interview with Jack Brattle could get me—"

"I know, I know, world renown and riches galore. Why do you think I wanted you to meet her?" Daphne pulled Hannah—or was Hannah now pulling Daphne?—toward the house's huge foyer into which spilled a staircase worthy of Scarlett O'Hara's Tara. And at this staircase, oh happy day, Daphne proceeded to point. "There she is."

And there she was, a little-black-dress-clad platinum-blond bombshell cliché, sauntering down the steps on requi-site spike heels. A perfect candidate for Lester's "Rack of Glam" article.

"I'm sorry, is there a Pamela Anderson look-alike contest tonight?"

"Shh." Daphne positioned herself at the bottom of the staircase. "Hi, Dee-Dee."

"Hey." Dee-Dee reached them, shook back her mane of peroxide and flicked a glance at Hannah. "Cool dress."

"Thanks. Thank you." Hannah gave her best ingratiating grin. "I love yours, too."

"This is Hannah O'Reilly. She works with me at the *Sentinel*."

"Yeah?" Another shake of overcooked hair.

"She writes the Lowbrow column."

"Oh!" Something approaching life quivered in her too-taut face. "I love your column! You're always fighting with that guy who writes the Highbrow column, D. G. Jackson. Too funny!"

"Yes!" Hannah gritted her teeth. Way too funny. Mr. Jackson took malicious delight in thumbing his nose at her column, which extolled the virtues of inexpensive food and entertainment around the city of brotherly love, while his dwelt on places and things no normal person could afford and no sane person would waste that much money on. She'd responded to one particularly degrading remark by sending him a case of Grey Poupon and blogging about it. He'd reciprocated with cans of spray-cheese. Word got out, and now both their editors were fanning the flames…all in the name of circulation and buzz.

Circulation and buzz. Yeah, superdeedooper. What about the news? She wanted to write news.

"So…what does this D.G. guy look like?" Dee-Dee tipped her head and started playing girlishly with a fried strand, making Hannah want to tell her D.G. could be Liberace's surviving twin. "His articles are so charming and funny and classy all at the same time."

"I've actually never met him." Hannah smiled, aching to change the subject to Jack Brattle—where was he, how soon could she meet him? "But maybe I can arrange to set you up sometime for lunch."

"Oooh, I'd love that. I have this feeling about him…" She giggled. "Would you really do that for me?"

"Sure, no problem." Hannah hadn't been serious, but it

didn't hurt to promise one favor right before she asked for another. And maybe she could work a date with the grievously tacky Dee-Dee into another joke on Mr. Highbrow. "So…Daphne tells me you're best buddies with Jack Brattle."

"Oh." Blink-blink of false eyelashes. "I don't know about best buddies. I shouldn't even have told—"

"Friends, though?"

"Well." She looked uneasily between Hannah and Daphne. "I've…met him."

Hannah sent Daphne a sidelong glance. *Met* was a far cry from *close to.* "When was this?"

"Oh, a while back." She gestured vaguely. "I'm really not supposed to tell. It just sort of slipped out."

And thank God for that. Jack Brattle had kept himself out of the public eye as effectively as his late gazillionaire father had kept himself in it, which meant the absence of a Brattle in the news left that much bigger a hole.

An interview with Harold Brattle's son and heir… Or, given that Dee-Dee was full of hot air as well as silicone, even snippets of inside information on Jack's whereabouts, his habits, tastes, sexual preference… Any reporter would give up major organs for that scoop.

Many had tried, none had succeeded. Not since the disappearance of Howard Hughes had a missing person generated this much mystery and excitement. Yet by all accounts Jack Brattle continued to run his father's empire while remaining invisible. From time to time people claimed to have encountered him—like people kept seeing Elvis—but the sightings always turned out to be hoaxes or misidentification.

"Whatever you can tell me would be great. I'll handle it all very discreetly. No one will ever be able to trace anything back to you."

"Oh gosh. I'm *so* not supposed to."

"I know." She laid a sympathetic hand on Dee-Dee's soft arm, wanting to pinch her. "I completely understand. I've put you in a really tough position."

"Well…" Dee-Dee bit her bee-stung lip. "I do know where he lives. A guy I met once took me by his house. I guess it wouldn't hurt to tell you that."

"Really?" Hannah's droopy spirits perked up. Rumors had been flying that Jack owned property in the area, but his cover had been scrupulously complete. Or at least he hadn't walked down any local streets with a giant name tag on. "You are amazing, wow."

"In West Chester." Apparently now that Dee-Dee had started, the confession had gotten easier. "My friend said he's abroad until spring, but the house is not that far from here."

Hannah's reporter lust started rising. Around them the chatter intensified as enormous flat-screen TVs in several rooms flickered on, and crowds gathered to watch midnight approach.

"Can you tell me how to get there?"

"Well…yeah. I could. But he's away. And I'm really not supposed to."

"Simple curiosity on my part. I wouldn't try to go in or bother anyone. Just drive past. No one would ever know I'd been by." She smiled her most innocent smile, shrugging as if it didn't matter all that much if Dee-Dee spilled or not. *Please. Please. Please.*

"Well…okay. You got paper or anything?"

"I have a BlackBerry." She nearly gasped out her relief, fishing the life-organizing electronic device out of her adorable dress-matching red-sequined bag as fast as she could before Dee-Dee changed what there was of her mind. "So what does he look like?"

"Oh, he's…" Dee-Dee gestured expansively and raised her eyes to the ceiling. "You know."

"Ah. Yes." Hannah's heart sank even as she opened a new memo, ready to write down directions. Dee-Dee definitely hadn't met him. Probably didn't even know which house was his. This would turn out to be another attention-grabbing hoax. She better prepare herself for the disappointment right now. And yet, on the crazy minuscule chance this could be legit… "So where does he live?"

She poised her fingers over the tiny keyboard and waited. Several minutes later, she'd written down Dee-Dee's directions, which consisted mostly of phrases like "turn left at that big stone thing" and "stay on the road even when it looks like you shouldn't."

A miracle if she found it. And an even bigger one if there was anything to find.

Excitement swelled in the room. Someone started a countdown from sixty seconds. Hannah slipped the BlackBerry back into her evening bag, then snagged—*finally*—a second glass of the slightly sour champagne from a passing waiter and turned to face the screen, counting along with everyone else.

As soon as midnight came and went she'd find Gerard, thank him for a wonderful evening and set out on her hunt for the wild and elusive Jack Brattle, heir to his father's real estate fortune which could, of course, given that Dee-Dee didn't seem qualified for Mensa, be nothing but a wild-goose chase.

She lifted her glass as the shouting started. *Five, four, three, two, one…*

Or…she could scoop every other reporter in the country and make this a really phenomenal start to the rest of her life.

2

HANNAH PRESSED HER FOOT gingerly on the accelerator, peering through the windshield into a curtain of sleet, bouncing *tzap-tzap* off the glass and tinkling on the roof of her beloved bright red Mazda, which she'd named Matilda. Hannah considered herself a very persistent investigator, but even she was questioning how smart it was to be out here so late in this mess with no one around. Pennsylvania's gentle rolling countryside surrounded her car. Despite the beauty of the fields, forests and sloping hills, she did not want to slide off the road and end up spending the night in any of them.

Amazingly, Dee-Dee's directions had held up so far, which fueled her determination to keep going. Hannah had found "the stone thing" and she even recognized the "amazing tree." The woman might not radiate brainpower, but, whether or not Hannah found the Jack Brattle pot of gold at the end of this rainbow, Dee-Dee obviously had a sharp eye and a killer memory. All Hannah had to do now was turn down a driveway where the gates were "kind of creepy and jail-like." Not to mention, "not very visible from the road unless you were looking."

She was looking; she just wasn't seeing.

The sleet fell harder. A driveway crept by; Hannah peered toward it. No gates.

"Come on, Jack's house." At this point, she just wanted to

see the damn thing, mark the address so her BlackBerry could find it again, and come back when the weather wasn't intent on killing her. Of course hindsight was now sitting on her shoulder whispering that she would have done a lot better to come back later in the first place.

Next driveway. No gates. Phooey. Properties weren't exactly close together out here in Billionaireland. Everyone needed his own private stable, pool, tennis court, golf course…all the basic necessities of survival.

Her BlackBerry rang. She dragged it from her bag, which she'd flung onto the passenger's seat, and glanced at the screen. Dad, calling to wish her Happy New Year. If she didn't answer, he'd worry. She eased Matilda over to the side of the road and turned on her flashers.

"Happy New Year, Dad."

"Happy New Year to you, sweetheart." His rough slow voice crackled over the tenuous connection. "Why don't I hear party noise, you didn't go? Or do fancy parties not make noise?"

"I left after midnight. Wanted to get home before the weather turned bad."

"Is it bad now? I haven't looked outside in a while."

"Uuh, no. Not bad yet." The tinkles of ice crystals on her roof turned to sharp taps. In the white beam of her headlights pea-sized balls bounced and rolled on the asphalt. Hail to the chief. "The roads are fine."

"Okay. But call me when you get home. The storm is supposed to come on fierce."

Tell me about it. "I'm…seconds away, Dad. In fact, turning on my street now. How's Mom?"

"Better, still better. Always better, thank God. I don't know what we would have done without Susie."

"She's a blessing, for sure."

"Mom even fed herself part of her dinner tonight. I made lasagna."

"Good for her! Her favorite. That's wonderful." She smiled, ashamed of herself for not being grateful enough as the clock ticked toward midnight for the few good events of the past year. Dad's latest employer, The Broadway Symphony, on the brink of collapse, had been saved by a generous donor who wiped out the orchestra's debt and allowed her father to keep the first job he'd ever held down this long—going on five years now. And Susie, a nursing angel of mercy, had showed up at their door, highly recommended by Mom's doctor, offering to help out with Mom's rehabilitation right there in their home for practically slave wages, saying she needed the experience.

Before those miracles, Hannah had gone through agonizing feelings of helplessness with her own bank account in no shape to help. Prey to addiction and poverty, her parents hadn't done much to give her a secure childhood, but especially now that they'd climbed out of the pit, she wanted them to have a secure retirement. "Tell Mom I love her and that I know this year will have her back to her old self. I'll call tomorrow."

"I'll tell her. I hope it's a good year for you, too, Hannah-Banana." He coughed to clear his throat—a legacy of lifelong smoking. "Maybe a nice young man will come along."

"Maybe." She rolled her eyes. Yeah, maybe. Maybe he'd even stick around longer than a few weeks or a month. And maybe cancer would start curing itself and global warming spontaneously reverse.

"You take care of yourself. Drive safely."

"I will. Love you, Dad." She ended the call with another pang of guilt as the sleet continued to bombard Matilda, collecting on the roads at an alarming rate. This was crazy. If anything happened to her, what would it do to her poor father who'd already had his relatively new sobriety and stability threatened with her way-too-young mom's shocking stroke and his livelihood nearly yanked out from under him?

Hannah was being selfish. She should turn around now and crawl home, give up this crazy quest until the weather was better.

Except she'd already come this far… And it was *Jack Brattle*. What if someone else in the business had overheard Dee-Dee? What if Hannah lost this huge long shot at a scoop? What if? What if? What if?

She put Matilda in gear and moved slowly forward, wheels crunching ice. A flash of lightning made her jump and hold on to a wince while waiting for the expected thunder. Thundersnow. Whee. This only added to the fun.

Next driveway… No gates.

The wind started whipping in earnest, sending Matilda into a shimmy. Hannah narrowly avoided a largish branch on the road. Snow mixed with the sleet to reduce visibility further.

Oh goody.

Next driveway. She had to turn in and focus her headlights to see…

Gates! Creepy dark jail-like ones! Eureka. She'd found it. Or found something.

Out came her trusty BlackBerry. She called up the GPS system and noted her location. Bingo. Adrenaline rushed out to party. She had Jack Brattle's address. 523 Hilltop Lane, West Chester, Pennsylvania.

Tomorrow she'd come back to—

More lightning. Close. A mere beat later thunder cracked the sky over her car. Wind gusted.

Hannah went rigid in her seat. The gate had opened a crack, then swung back. She swore it had. Matilda inched forward, Hannah peering through the torrential snow-sleet.

There. There it went again. Unlocked? It certainly looked that way. And, according to Dee-Dee, who seemed to be on the up-and-up since her directions had panned out so far, Jack Brattle wasn't in residence. Hmm…

Wait, what was she thinking? He must have a full staff living on the estate and security up the wazoo. If she even crossed the property line she'd probably be surrounded by guard dogs and torn to shreds.

But maybe before they quite devoured her, she could get a glimpse of the house. After all, by now she had the perfect excuse. A lone disoriented traveler, lost on her way back from a party and… Help! Where was she? Could she depend on the kindness of strangers until the worst of the storm passed?

And by the way, while she waited, could she whip out her BlackBerry, take pictures of every room in the house and interview everyone old enough to speak?

They'd go for it. Sure they would.

Now. The gates. She fumbled under her seat for the umbrella she kept in the car. Of course it wasn't there. Where had she lost this one? Who knew?

No umbrella. And since she'd been to a party she was wearing her couple-times-a-year wool coat and not her everyday water-resistant parka with hood. Not to mention open-toed heels instead of warm fleece-lined boots.

Uof.

But okay, for Jack Brattle…

She dashed out of the car, whistling "This Could Be the Start of Something Big," one arm up to keep from being pelted, which accomplished pretty much nothing. But oh joy, it was worth every thwacking and stinging and drenching moment because, hot damn, the gate was really and truly unlocked!

Not only that, the hinges were beautifully oiled, so the

huge structure moved soundlessly and easily with one good shove. Was breaking and entering meant to be or what?

Back in the car, giggling with cold and nervous excitement and residual champagne, she applied her wet foot to Matilda's accelerator and then…

She, reporter Hannah O'Reilly, gained admittance to what she was starting to dare believe was Jack Brattle's estate, and got thwacked, stung and drenched pushing the gate nearly closed behind her.

Woohoo!

The long driveway curved through a wooded area thick with tall evergreens that blocked out the worst of the assault. A good thing because otherwise, given the current visibility, she could easily have ended up bumper to bark at some point.

Two or three tensely expectant minutes later—no attack dogs yet—the trees gave way to a large grassy lawn already frosted white. Matilda slid gracefully sideways on the last turn; Hannah reduced her speed, heart thumping even harder than it had been. She definitely did not want to get stuck here.

Another gust of wind rocked the car and sent snow flying nearly horizontal. Hannah pined briefly for her cozy—the politically correct term for *tiny*—apartment, for sitting safely in bed with her warming blanket heating the sheets, a good book in her hand, a hot mug of tea on her nightstand.

But then…no Jack Brattle scoop. After years of an unsatisfying career fund-raising while writing too-often rejected magazine articles and pieces for her neighborhood paper on the side, she'd managed to land a job in journalism, which she'd wanted since she was a kid and had written and produced her own paper: *Hannah's Daily News,* circulation, approximately four, including herself; number of issues: twenty. She still had them somewhere.

Another flash of lightning, a clap of thunder. The sleet rattled her roof in earnest now—could it really hail during a snow-storm?

She guided Matilda around the circular driveway, came to a stop opposite the grand front steps, complete with stone Grecian urns. Snow obscured the view, but it wasn't hard to tell the house was a colossal Colonial.

This wasn't how the other half lived, this was how the other millionth lived.

So…

Car in Park, she sat for a minute before switching off the engine. She really didn't want to drive all the way back to Philly in this mess. The roads were dangerous and the trip could take hours. Options were either to wait out the storm right here in Matilda…she had plenty of gas to run the heater periodically…or see if anyone was home. No lamps glowed in any windows, at least not in the front of the house, at least as far as she could see. The light shining over the entrance could be on a timer.

Nothing ventured…

She pulled the handle and nearly had her arm torn off as a gust of wind wrenched Matilda's door wide open. Her excitement gave way to jitters. This storm took itself quite seriously. Now she hoped someone *was* home, not only for the sake of her immortality-guaranteeing article, but to make sure she survived this.

Up the steps, she nearly slipped twice, squinting through the sting of ice, finally reaching the front door. Holding her breath, she rang the bell, then crossed her fingers for good measure and crossed her arms over her chest, strands of her ruined upsweep whipping her cheek, earrings turning into tiny daggers repeatedly flung at her neck. Another gust rocked her back on her probably ruined heels. Hannah made a grab at the house's front-door handle and miraculously stayed upright.

This was not that much fun. At least not yet.

Another poke at the bell, another shivery icy minute or so waiting, though by now she knew it was ludicrous. On New Year's Eve with the master abroad any remaining staff would have the night off, and if there were some type of butler or housekeeper on duty, he-she would have answered by now.

She stepped away and craned up at the facade to see if any lights had gone on in response to her ring. Though housekeeper-butler rooms would be in the back, wouldn't they? She wasn't that up on her mansion architecture.

A horrifically bright flash of lightning, a massive crack of thunder, a truly terrifying assault of wind. Hannah yelled and leapt toward the door, pressing herself against it for the tiny bit of shelter theoretically offered by the ledge above.

Then the odd impression of something dark swooping through the air in her peripheral vision, and the open-mouthed disbelief as the limb of a tree—large enough to be a tree itself—landed on her car.

Crash.

Hannah stared. Her mouth opened, but no sound came out. *Oh, Matilda.*

Her roof and hood were crumpled down to the seats, the windshield smashed. If Hannah had still been inside, she could be dead now.

Dear God. Delayed shock hit, funny breathing and all-over-body shaking that wasn't only from the cold this time. This was really, really not good. Really. When was she going to learn to curb her impulsive behavior? She knew this storm was coming. Jack Brattle's estate was not going to disappear overnight. Her parents and friends would say it again. *How many times do we have to tell you, look before you leap? Think before you act.*

Think, period.

Okay, okay. Staying calm. She had other more important things to worry about. Like not freezing to death.

Down the treacherous steps again, she tugged at poor sweet Matilda's door. It didn't budge. Slipping and sliding her way around to the other side, she pushed her arm through cold scratching branches to yank on the other door, even knowing the frame was too crunched to be able to open.

Oh Cheez Whiz. Her evening bag containing her Black-Berry was still in that car. Her GPS system would broadcast her location, but not until someone realized she was missing and tried to find her. Why had she told Dad she was already home safely?

Because he had enough to worry about.

She staggered back up the steps, huddled against the house's cold uncaring door again. Not for the first time she envied her mother and father their renewed commitment to each other after they got their lives back on track, their mutual caring and support. If she had someone now, the kind of man she dreamed about finding, he'd stop at nothing to bring her home safely.

Or he would have stopped her being such an idiot coming here tonight in the first place, and she'd be home safely in bed with him now, ringing in the New Year in one of her very favorite ways.

Tears came to her eyes and she blinked them away in disgust. Okay, game plan. She was responsible for herself and had been as far back as she could remember. Maybe there was a service entrance? Maybe someone in the house would hear her ring or knock from there? Maybe there was a cottage behind the house she could break into, or maybe her amazing luck would hold and there'd be a garage with the door left co-incidentally open…

Oh dear.

Another flash of lightning. Hannah turned away from it, burying her face in her hands, shoulders hunched, waiting for the smash of thunder.

Boom. More wind. Sleet pelting her back.

"*Stop.*" She grabbed the door handle and twisted desperately, knowing it would be locked and the gesture was completely—

The handle turned.

The door swung open.

She tumbled in, gasping with surprise, then relief, slammed the door behind her, closing out the terrible storm.

Did that really just happen?

Who the hell went abroad and left his front door open? More than that, what house of this size and value didn't have a dead bolt and a security system? She waited with held breath for the ear-splitting shriek of an alarm. *Whoop-whoop, intruder alert.*

Nothing.

Maybe he had a system that only sounded at the police station. One could only hope. Rescue would be welcome if the cops took long enough so she had plenty of time to look around. Because it was slowly dawning on her, now she'd escaped the possibility of hypothermia, that she could very well be *in Jack Brattle's house.*

Of course it was possible the door was open because someone had already broken in. Maybe some terribly dangerous criminal was right now prowling the floors above her.

She listened, listened some more, kept listening…and heard nothing, besides the distant hum of the heating system. Really, what kind of idiot would be out on a night like this?

Ha ha ha.

Maybe someone was asleep upstairs? Maybe he or she forgot to lock the gate and the front door after a particularly fun party?

"Hello?" She wandered closer to the staircase, barely visible from the light coming in through the front windows. "*Hello?*"

Nothing. She climbed halfway up, peering into the darkness of the second floor, and prepared to shout as loudly as she could. "*Anyone home?*"

Still nothing.

Most likely careless—or tipsy—staff or service people were responsible for the unlocked entrances. Maybe they'd intended to come right back and the storm had held them up or held them off. Whoever they were, she owed them a huge juicy kiss for inadvertently offering her shelter. Bless their irresponsibility. She was not only going to survive the night, she was going to survive the night *inside Jack Brattle's house*—because she just had to say that again. *Inside Jack Brattle's house.*

That was assuming Dee-Dee was telling the truth, which Hannah would, because why would she go to all that trouble to send Hannah anywhere else?

Of course Mr. Brattle would have a phone so she could call for help right away, but…she didn't need it right away. Later would be fine. Far be it from her to make someone risk his or her life coming to rescue her now in this terrible weather. Right? Right.

Oh, this was a night for her memoirs. First, she needed out of these wet shoes and to hang her coat somewhere waterproof so drips from melting ice bits wouldn't stain the hardwood.

She fumbled at the wall near the door and struck pay dirt with a light switch that threw a soft chandelier-glow over the breathtaking entranceway. Hannah let her eyes feast in a slow circle around her. Parquet flooring, and thick vivid Oriental rugs that she lost no time in exploring with frozen toes after she kicked off her shoes and stripped off her sodden stockings. Mmm, bliss.

The house was warm—deliciously warm—so obviously whoever left was planning to come back soon. At least when he or she did, the storm, the open gates, open door and Hannah's devastatingly destroyed car provided the ideal justifiable excuse for her presence.

This could not possibly have been more perfect. Maybe being impulsive hadn't been so bad for once. Matilda—God rest her engine—would not have given her life in vain.

A promising set of louvered doors slid open to reveal, just as she'd hoped, a vast closet with an array of expensive coats—men's coats—in conservative shades of brown, black, gray and tan, suitable for the average heir. She brushed her hand over the textures—wool, cashmere, leather—sniffed the lingering hint of their owner's very nice cologne, then pushed past the wooden hangers for a metal one her damp coat wouldn't ruin. Down the hall to her left she discovered a first-floor bathroom in whose shower she hung her dripping woolen mess.

And now…to explore. *Jack Brattle's house.*

Kitchen first, glimpsed as she'd passed in search of the bathroom. *Ooh la la.* State of the art, but not detracting from the nineteenth-century feel of the entranceway. She skimmed her fingers over the built-in paneled refrigerator. Wouldn't she love to microwave a hot dog in a room like this? She bet it had never seen one.

Out of the kitchen, exploring room after room, not unlike Gerard Banks's house—and hey, how often did she score a two-mansion day?—but here there were no leopard statues, no large-screen TVs or—dare she say—gaudy furniture. Jack Brattle was all dark wood, leather, brick fireplaces, rich subdued colors in rugs, books, cushions. True old-money class.

She had to admit, in spite of her aversion to opulence, the house was incredible. The kind of place that brought to mind every fabulous manor she'd imagined while reading, from *The*

Secret Garden to *Jane Eyre*. And yet, a home she could imagine someone actually lived in, not redecorated every season to show off to visitors and lifestyle magazines.

Up the curving staircase to a landing with a comfortable-looking burgundy couch and gold patterned chair, another shelf of books and a window seat beside it. Down the hallway lined with portraits and landscapes, passing at least four bedrooms, a workout room, a study, another bedroom, apparently unoccupied like the others, and then, what she suspected was the master bedroom suite. Was this where Jack Brattle slept?

The glimmer of light under the door registered at the same time she pushed it open…

And came face-to-face with the wettest, handsomest naked man she'd ever been startled out of her wits to meet.

3

"OH! I'M SO SORRY!" HANNAH jammed her eyes shut and reared back into the dim hallway, slapping a hand over her closed lids for good measure. Oh, *no.* Oh my goodness, oh my...*goodness* what a sight. Even with her eyes closed she could still see—

No, stop. She could be arrested for breaking and entering, this was not the time to go lusty-wench. He could be calling the cops right now. *Reporter Busted for Ogling Billionaire's Bodacious Bod.*

"Sorry. I'm really sorry. I, um, got lost and your entrance was open and my car is—"

She sensed the door moving in front of her, slid two fingers apart and peeked through.

Gulp.

He was standing, towel wrapped around his, um, hips, ohhh, yeah, and, um, his chest was...whew. He... Wait. He was smirking. She apparently amused him. Or maybe he thought it was funny because he'd called a SWAT team, which was pulling into his driveway right now and unloading bazookas.

"I was, um...just saying that your door was open."

"You pushed it open."

"It was—" She realized just in time what he meant. "No. Downstairs. The front door. Was open. My car is outside with a tree on it. What I mean is, I got lost and the roads are bad and then, so I saw your gate open and then the car-crushing thing happened and I came in because you're unlocked in front, and I was freezing and thought the place was empty, so I started looking around, but…uh…but it's not, is it. Empty that is."

Silence. He looked even more amused, but as if he were trying hard not to be. God, he was gorgeous. Gor-gee-usss. If this was Jack Brattle, then he had to be emotionally bankrupt or deeply miserable because it was just not fair that anyone could have all that money and all that…everything *and* look the way he did.

"No, the house isn't empty. I'm here."

"Right. Right. I see that. I'm so sorry. I just needed shelter because I didn't…have any."

"Okay."

Are you Jack Brattle? She couldn't ask, because she wasn't supposed to know this was his house. But, of course, who else could be naked in the master bedroom? Stunningly naked, she might add.

"I'm Hannah."

"Jack."

Jack! *Jack!* It took every ounce of energy not to light up like a tree angel, blast off like a rocket, or fizz like a shaken Coke. Bless Dee-Dee and her gravity-defying boobs.

"Nice to meet you, Jack. I'm truly sorry to barge in on you like this. Especially—" She gestured to his towel without looking at it even though she really wanted to look at it, and at him. All of him. "—like this. My phone is in my car, which I can't get into. If I could use yours to call the—"

"Wait here."

She nodded demurely, then when he went back into his room and closed the door, she did a silent, hopping, fist-pumping victory dance in his hallway. Besides a front-page spread in Lester's "Rack of Glam" article, she owed Dee-Dee a hundred lunches with D. G. "Highbrow" Jackson for this. No, a thousand.

Hannah stopped dancing and put a hand to her hammering heart. Regroup. She was a pro. He was her subject. When he came back out, she needed to talk less—since she'd just broken the world record for disjointed babbling—and observe more. So far she'd observed that he wasn't very chatty, not that she'd given him much of a chance, and that he had no problem giving orders. "Wait here" was not the most charming way she'd ever been asked to linger. Though for all he knew she was a lying con-artist thief, so maybe a lapse in manners was forgivable.

She had also observed that he was the kind of male eye candy she liked best. Thick dark hair, none of this California surfer-dude stuff for her. A strong face, very masculine, stopping short of head-clubbing-caveman. Tall. Dark brown eyes that sent out a shock of attraction on contact, and that indicated copious brainpower behind them.

And—gravy on her stuffing—the man obviously worked out. Good shoulders, flat stomach and that great sculpted butt that—

"Sorry to keep you waiting."

"Oh. Well. That's okay." He'd put jeans over the great sculpted butt, which was disappointing because while she liked him naked just fine, she always thought of Jack Brattle in a tuxedo, kind of James Bondish. Were they thousand-dollar designer denim? Looked like Lees to her. "You certainly don't need to apologize. I'm the one who intruded on your—"

"I saw your car out my window. Impressive."

"I do things thoroughly."

"Uh-huh." He moved forward unexpectedly and took hold of her wrist—not very gently. "So what are you really here for?"

She gasped at his harsh tone, which took her completely

by surprise after his initial pleasantness. "To keep from freezing to death?"

"You're sure that's all?"

"Yes." In spite of her shock over his Jekyll-Hyde act, she felt a crazy pang of sympathy and a dose of guilt. Guys like Jack Brattle probably had people with ulterior motives surrounding them 24-7. Including her at the moment. "Why else would I be here?"

"You're not a reporter, are you?"

She laughed nervously, unable to lie to this man's face. "Of course I am. Breaking into strangers' houses on major holidays is how I work."

"I see." His lips half smiled, and she realized with more guilt and a twinge of satisfaction that he thought she was joking. Advantage Hannah. Except then he started looking her leisurely up and down in the short clingy sequined dress and she didn't feel like she had an advantage anymore. At all. "You didn't come here with…other ideas?"

"*What? Why would I do that? I didn't even know you were going to be home.*" Oops. *Because I thought you'd be in Europe, Jack Brattle.* "I mean here."

His brow went up. "Where did you think I'd be?"

"I have no idea. I thought the house was empty, then I found out it wasn't. You left your door unlocked, so I—"

"You told me. I'm sorry if I insulted you. Women have— It's happened before, though not at this house."

"You have others?"

"Yes." He started looking her over again, and she got all flustered and a little heated up, when she really wanted to be annoyed and insulted. "And that *is* a very seductive dress."

"I was at a party."

"Where?"

"Malvern."

"You live in Philly?"

"Yes."

"Strange way of heading back to the city from there."

"I got lost, I told you."

"Yes, you did." He held her eyes and she controlled her hot and flustered self enough to look back fairly steadily.

Except the second she relaxed her guard, she started thinking about how much she wanted him to kiss her, and how sexy and romantic it would be right here in his twilit hallway. He could back her up against the wall and have his multi-billion-dollar way with her.

Mmm.

What would he do if she leaned forward right now and— *Stop it. Just stop.* Had she learned nothing about herself and about men in the years since puberty? Not to mention she'd just become outraged when he suggested she was thinking exactly what she was thinking.

"Sorry about that." He relaxed his interrogation-stare, so apparently she'd passed the test. "I just have to be careful."

"Why?"

He winked. "Double-O-Seven stuff."

"Seriously?" She nearly swallowed her tongue. Had she not just been thinking James Bond? And here he was, the legend come to life, though she doubted he was actually doing anything but running his late father's business. A business, of course, she knew nothing about as far as he was concerned, so she'd play along. "You're a *spy?*"

"Not even close. What are we going to do with you?"

She had many ideas by now, none of which she could say out loud. But his abrupt change of subject away from the personal meant this could be a tough interview. "If you'll point me to a phone I can call Triple A and have my car towed."

Say no, say no, say no.

"Why don't you wait until this weather clears? I'm sure Triple A will have its hands full rescuing motorists who couldn't find conveniently unlocked, apparently deserted houses."

"If you're sure…" Stranded in a mansion with a hot über-rich playboy who could make her career? A miracle. Though she had no idea if Jack Brattle actually was a playboy. She could rule out gay now that she'd met him and had been on the receiving end of those eyes. If he was a playboy, he certainly kept his conquests as thoroughly out of the press as he kept himself. Maybe he sold his discarded women into slavery to ensure their silence.

She did think it was odd he wasn't more disconcerted about his door being left unlocked.

"Are you hungry?" He put a hand to his sadly now-covered stomach. "I'm starved. Hardly got a thing to eat tonight."

"Were you out?"

"For a while. The forecast convinced me to ring in the New Year at home."

"Considering the state of my car, you made the right choice. Home would have been a lot simpler."

And one-eighth the fun.

"Where in Philly is home?"

"Ah." She glanced pointedly at her surroundings. "A stunning three-room estate above a shoe-repair shop."

"Location, location, location."

"So they say. Did you grow up in this…hut?"

"Yes. You never did tell me if you were hungry."

"Famished." Another abrupt change of subject. He wasn't going to make this easy by volunteering long tales of his childhood, was he.

"This way to the kitchen." He pointed down the hall and curved his other arm behind her as if he were going to touch her, but ohh, not quite. "Or maybe you've already been there."

"I…took a peek, yes. Couldn't resist. This is so not my life."

"Don't assume that's a bad thing."

"No?" She turned at the top of the stairs to see his face. Reserved as usual. "Why? Most people would die to—"

"Most people have no idea."

Billionaire's Bitter Secret. "Tell me then."

"It's not what you think."

"What do you think I think?" She knew he thought she'd gone too far when he shot her a look and started down the stairs ahead of her. "You think I ask too many questions."

"You do sound like a reporter."

"Didn't I tell you I was one?" She laughed again, ha ha ha, watching him closely, but he only laughed, too, ha ha ha. Wow. Obviously he wasn't as suspicious as he seemed or he'd have been all over that one. "Just naturally curious I guess."

He ushered her into the kitchen and turned on subtle track lighting around the tops of the cabinets that lit the room one might almost say romantically, if one was thinking along those lines, but, of course, Hannah wasn't. She wasn't going to fall in the blink of an eye for any more toads who happened to be wearing prince's clothing. Might as well become infatuated with movie actors.

Of course, she did that, too.

"Have a seat." He indicated a tall stool pulled up to the space-age-looking island in the center of a vast area that would set any chef drooling, then rubbed his palms together. "What do you feel like?"

"Surprise me."

"Okay. Let's see." He narrowed his eyes, looked her up and down speculatively, which made her hope her stomach wasn't pooching out in doughy rolls. "You don't look like a peanut-butter-and-jelly woman…"

"Ha!" She put on a deeply offended look. "I'm a prime, grade A, number-one peanut-butter-and-jelly woman. My desert island food."

His smile made the corners of his deep brown eyes crinkle. "Then let's go in another direction. You game?"

"Sure." When he looked at her like that she'd agree to anything.

"Any foods you hate?"

"Tofu hot dogs. They taste like how my dentist's office smells."

He chuckled, which made him look twice as charming, she should mention, and worse, making him laugh gave her a stupid silly thrill. "Crossing tofu hot dogs off the list. Now…"

He looked around, as if choosing which cabinet to open and amaze her with first. Then he opened one with a flourish…and apparently struck out. As he did also on his second try. One more, and he made a sound of satisfaction and pulled out a couple of plates.

Hannah kept on her polite smile. He didn't know where he kept his plates? Did this man do nothing for himself?

Powerful Billionaire Helpless in His Own Home.

Two drawers later he'd located knives, forks and spoons. Quite a while passed before he found champagne glasses. The champagne, however, he scored on his first try, and she'd just say that wow, it was not Asti Spumante, and it made her uncomfortable thinking of how much the bottle cost and how much her parents could have used the money she and…*Jack*…would drink up in such a short time. Probably a week's groceries in that bottle. Maybe two.

"To start us off." He removed the cork expertly and just as expertly poured her a glass. Clearly he had more experience with bartending than cooking, she'd guess with bottles exactly this expensive and more. "Happy New Year, Hannah."

"Thank you, Jack." She lifted her glass and toasted him, feeling a fizz of excitement even before she'd started drinking, a feeling she recognized all too well. No, no. No crushes. She was here as a professional first, not a female, and never the twain should meet. "You're not having any?"

"After I get the food ready."

"Cheers, then." She took her first sip tentatively, hoping to be able to sneer and assure herself a bottle of bubbles couldn't possibly be worth that much money.

Oh wow.

Not that she was an expert, in fact, she prided herself on being an expert on all things *not* likely to be in Jack Brattle's palace, but even she could tell the champagne was exquisite. Nothing like the swill Gerard served at the party, not that she'd blame him with that many people drinking that much. But this…tiny bubbles that streamed daintily upward, a smooth delicate flavor that changed over the course of the sip-swallow, and no sour aftertaste to ruin the experience. This was why champagne existed, and what everybody was after while making do with inferior stuff.

"I don't need to ask what you think, I can see it in your face."

"I was that obvious? How unchic of me. But, yes." She turned the glass reverently. "I'll have to work not to guzzle."

"Feel free." One eyebrow quirked. "I enjoy watching that much pleasure."

Ohh my. Except instead of arching an eyebrow back and saying something sultry like, *I'd love to show you exactly how much pleasure I can feel, Jack,* she gave a snort of nervous laughter and then made an even more revolting noise to get champagne out of her sinuses.

"You okay?"

"Mm, yeah. Sure. Fine." She thumped her chest and took another more cautious sip.

"I'll put the bottle where you can reach." He took a slim elegant wine cooler from under the island and slid the champagne inside, putting it on the counter next to her. "There's more where that came from."

"Thank you." There was more. More hundreds-of-dollars bottles of champagne. Not just this one, carefully saved for the occasion, of course not. The idea both thrilled and repelled her.

"Let's see what's in here." He rummaged through his refrigerator, mumbling to himself—which tickled her since she did the same thing—occasionally withdrawing cans or jars or various other containers, and placing them on the counter next to him. Hannah's bid to check out what billionaires had in their refrigerators besides not-Asti Spumante champagne was foiled when she couldn't stop checking out the pull of his wide shoulders under the soft-looking shirt and the shape of his beautiful you-know-what—yes, they were Lee jeans and, oh, he did such lovely things for them. They should be grateful. She certainly was.

A few minutes slicing this and that, arranging that and the other, another few minutes at the gleaming toaster, then he loaded up his haul onto a large lacquered tray and bore it triumphantly to the island. "Seems we've done pretty well."

"Um…yes." She put down her champagne and gaped. Suffice to say what was in his refrigerator bore absolutely no resemblance to what she had in hers. A glass jar of foie gras with slices of toasted brioche and thin slices of what looked like apple or pear but wasn't—maybe quince?; tins of osetra and beluga caviar to be served with delicate bone spoons alongside toasted pita bread squares, and a satiny white cream of some sort to spread over them; translucent slices of prosciutto next to a silver bowl of fresh green and black figs; cheeses whose names she didn't know on a polished elegantly grained wooden tray; olives in three colors; flawless miniature vegetables—tiny carrots, yellow squash, cucumbers and elongated radishes—with a green creamy herb dip; perfect maroon grapes the size of peas, tangerines the size of golf balls; plump raspberries whose gorgeous perfume made her want to bury her face in them; assorted miniature pastries…

"Are you expecting a crowd?"

"You said you were hungry."

"You eat like this all the time?"

He looked blank. "Doesn't everyone?"

Billionaire Out of Touch With Reality. She was about to roll her eyes when he winked, and she blushed instead, because the wink made it seem as if they were alone in a highly intimate situation. The fact that they *were* alone in a highly intimate situation only made her blush harder. But that wink would do it even in a crowd of thousands. And yet…how could she eat this? Enough for twenty people. What would he do with the leftovers? Toss them? To waste money and food…she hated the idea of both. However, no, she couldn't help herself. She was dying to try everything. Would he let her take some to share with Mom and Dad? With her friends. Her landlady? The whole block? Everyone should be able to eat like this.

"Now, the final touch." He fumbled with buttons on an under-cabinet music system and soft jazz floated into the room. Oh my. Oh my my my. You could absolutely not beat the cheesesteaks at Jake's Corner Bar, or the fresh almond cookies at Mama Fortunato's Bakery, or the sizzling shrimp at Hu Min's Dragon but…

Oh, but…

Mr. Amazing then rummaged in another three drawers before he found what he was looking for, which turned out to be candles. *Candles.* What kind of man thought of candles?

Perfection in a Male: My Evening with Jack Brattle.

Was this his typical evening at home? He couldn't have been expecting her. Maybe just a typical New Year's? But why would he haul it all out for her if he was planning a party later?

Was he…trying to *seduce* her?

She shouldn't, but with half a glass of excellent champagne in her, on top of a couple of glasses of not-so-excellent champagne, and dazzled by the man and the occasion, she sort of hoped so. Not that she could give in and sleep with *Jack Brattle* when she was planning to publish an article about him. She had her limits. What fun though to hold this memory close to her heart, and place it reverently into her best friends' voice mails and long e-mails to people she didn't know that well, for the rest of her life.

"Do you often throw impromptu candlelight suppers in the middle of the night for strange women?"

"I might make it a habit after tonight." He considered her carefully. "So far, no signs that you're a deranged killer…are you?"

"Ah, no. I gave up deranged killing. Hell on a girl's nails. And those dry-cleaning bills…" She made a tsk-tsk noise and shook her head.

"I hear you." He pulled up another stool close to hers, so what could she do but wiggle around until she faced him? "I'm glad you showed up."

"Really?" Fishing, fishing, she was shameless.

"Really." He poured himself champagne, topped hers off and put the bottle back in the fancy chill-thing, which undoubtedly kept it at the perfect temperature. "Since I left my party early, the evening didn't feel finished. I'm glad to have company to salvage it."

I Need a Woman: Billionaire's Sad Tale of Deprivation.

He clinked his glass to hers. "Dig in."

Maybe she shouldn't have, maybe she should have at least

hesitated and spent another minute or two contemplating the plight of the poor, but she didn't. She dug.

Oh my. Dug again. And again, and where was her shovel? If D. G. Jackson could see her, he'd never stop saying told-you-so. She'd deserve it, too.

"Caviar?" He passed it, amusement in his eyes.

Caviar…who knew? She'd had the jarred preserved stuff from the supermarket once and decided the fish should have been able to keep it.

"Foie gras?" The amusement became a smile.

Foie gras…she'd cheerfully gain forty pounds on the stuff given the chance.

"Prosciutto with figs?" This time he was outright smirking.

Prosciutto with fresh figs…sign her up for that action every day. And on and on, while they talked about the food she was eating: him discussing the various types of caviar, she bringing up overfishing in the Caspian Sea; he regaling her with memories of his first taste of foie gras, her mentioning the controversy involved in force-feeding the geese and ducks; him painting a picture of the summer he spent in Lebanon and the fig tree outside his bedroom window from which he could pick ripe figs first thing in the morning, to which she had no politically correct objections. All the while their champagne glasses were emptying and refilling until finally she couldn't eat or drink another bite and what a horrible shame that was.

"I have reached my absolute limit."

He drained the last of the bottle into her glass. "C'mon, I dare you."

"Oh, you Satan."

He picked up her practically licked-clean plate, grinning triumphantly. "Enjoyed it?"

"Ya think?" She gathered up dishes and bowls and placed

them in the sink. "I've never had a feast like that. I'm not much of a luxury foods person."

"Ah."

Something about the way he spoke made her glance at him suspiciously, though he was concentrating apparently innocently, on rinsing plates. What was that about? Had she disgraced herself with her greed? Maybe, but everything was so good she couldn't regret it. And he'd been eating quite healthily himself. Best of all, with Mr. Jack Brattle's notorious aversion to publicity, this multidollar-binge could remain her guilty secret.

"I feel like I should run about five miles to atone for those calories."

"There's a pool if you want to do laps."

Of course there was. "No suit."

"I'm sure you'd look great in one of mine…"

She giggled and blamed it on the champagne. "Um. Minor coverage problem."

"If you're sure…"

"No women in the house?" She tried to ask casually, and succeeded. She thought.

"Not for a long time."

"Are you divorced?" A natural question, wasn't it?

"No." He walked toward her, drying his hands.

"Never married?"

"Never. You?"

"Never. Girlfriend?"

"No. Boyfriend?"

"No."

And there they stood. If he was feeling anything like what she was feeling, the obvious circumstances of their proximity and their mutual singlehood were suggesting a number of delightful possibilities. Unfortunately there was that damn ethics thing because getting romantic with a man and then publishing an article about him was taking kissing and telling way further than she was comfortable taking it. But ohh, his mouth was so tempting, his lips full and sharply drawn, surrounded by the faint masculine gray of stubble-to-come.

A song came on, a smooth velvety jazz lullaby sung by a female artist whose voice she didn't recognize.

He took a step forward and she took one, too. His arms went up, one at her shoulder height, one at her waist. "Dance with me, Hannah."

Jack Brattle: All the Right Moves.

"Love to." Mmm, she hadn't been in a man's arms since Norberto, the smooth-tongued, talented-in-bed, charming, absolute cheating idiot creep jerk butthead...

Okay, she'd ignored all the warning signs and leapt happily into his arms and gotten her heart smacked down yet again. She should have known better.

But now, Jack Brattle smelled soooo good. And he moved like a dream. Under her hand, his shoulder was solid and warm, his chin also warm and smoothly close-shaven when it occasionally brushed her forehead. His fingers held hers lightly, but he kept his body close.

Hannah should know better right now. She'd have to crash down into reality all too soon. Somehow that seemed so deliciously far away, though, and he was so deliciously near.

"You dance divinely, Ms....what?"

"O'Reilly. Thank you. As do you, Mr....?"

She knew he wouldn't answer, but she lifted her head from where it had pillowed itself on the smooth comfortable front of his shirt and looked up expectantly.

"...Brattle." He stopped their dance. Looked down intently.

Her reaction was perfect, since she was actually shocked

and could do a convincing double take. She couldn't believe he'd told her. What about keeping himself such a tremendous secret all those years? All that trouble to stay hidden, and now he was telling her, a complete stranger who'd already joked she was a reporter and had been asking all kinds of questions?

Why would he do that?

Her treacherous imagination immediately supplied the kind of answer that was always getting her in trouble. Maybe he'd fallen for her, same as she'd fallen for him and therefore he had given her this incredible gift of trusting her with his identity.

She sighed. Nice story, but it never happened. At least not to her.

Something was definitely odd about the confession, but her brain discarded those thoughts because he was still inches away, their hands were still on each other's bodies, champagne fizzed through her veins, and since somewhere there must be someone for whom the name Jack Brattle rang only the faintest of bells, she decided the best possible course of action was to pretend to be that person, go on tiptoe and kiss him.

Of course, of *course* he kissed like a dream. The first was soft and quick, probably a surprised response to her typical lack of self-control. Then another at his initiation, longer and sweeter…then gradually hotter. Her body warmed, she felt his next kiss right down where kisses went when doled out by seriously sexy men. And when she pressed closer—and who could help it when his strong arms slid around her so completely—she could tell that he was…er, enjoying the kiss, too.

Mayday. She was completely crazed with lust, unbearably infatuated with everything about this man and this evening. This was where she should back up, think this through and make sure she understood every possible ramification of her—ooh.

He'd nudged her legs apart and put his thigh between hers,

which made her skirt ride upward. His hand dipped to caress her rear, which she faintly hoped, with the last glimmer of her sanity, had gotten firmer since she'd been going to the gym.

What had she been thinking? Something about pulling away. Something about…

Aw, hell.

He guided her back a few steps and lifted her onto the edge of his counter stool, stepped between her thighs and kissed her exactly how women all over the world longed to be kissed whether they knew it or not. He was very hard now, pushing the swollen heat against her thin, red, lace panties, making her nearly ready to come just thinking about being in bed with him.

Wasn't she supposed to stop this? Something about a story, about ethics…

His lips left hers to explore her neck; his hands drew her skirt slowly up, building her arousal with the expectation of more intimate touch. He slid those same warm hands back and forth on her hips as more and more of her skin became available to his fingers.

Must…hang on…to brain. "Jack."

"Mmm."

"This is a little…unreal."

"How so?"

"You and this amazing house and the incredible food and the champagne and now…this."

"What 'this'?"

"Nothing that should be happening." Her voice was low and breathless, making it damn clear how serious she was about stopping. Which would be not enough.

"I know. It's a lousy idea."

"You do? It is?" She opened her eyes. "Why shouldn't you be doing it?"

"Shh. Pretend it's not happening." He trailed his fingers

across the lower edge of her abdomen, then along the lacy sides of her panties. "What happens tonight stays there. In the morning, it will all be erased."

"So…this isn't happening?"

"No." He urged her legs farther apart, slid fingers teasingly inside the lace edge. "It's not happening."

"Mmm, Jack, but it…really does feel like it's happening." She braced her feet on the chair rungs, lifted her hips. He took his cue and slid her panties down, got them over one leg and let them fall down the other.

"No, don't worry." He knelt and she leaned her elbows behind her on the counter, tipped her head back, open and vulnerable to him, feeling his warm breath on her sex, closing her eyes in delicious impatience for his even warmer tongue. "I promise it's not happening."

"If you say so—*oh!*" She gasped, let her hips lift and retreat under his talented thrusts, so close to coming so soon that she had to take deep breaths and open her eyes to slow the process down. She wanted him with her. She wanted this to last forever. But, no, she wasn't going to hold out much longer. "Are you sure this isn't happening? It really *really* feels like it is. Any second now."

"Let it happen, Hannah."

"I want you with me."

"I don't have a condom downstairs."

"But if this isn't happening…" She was panting, trying desperately to hold on to some kind of logic. "Then we don't need…oh!"

He'd moved to kiss her inner thighs, but now settled firmly back on her clit and she was lost. The orgasm started in a dark rush, then boom, steam engine blowing past, making everything rattle and roll in its wake, subsiding eventually to the distance and the past.

"Oh my goodness." She slowly unclenched her muscles, slumped wearily back on the counter, staring at him with what was certainly a worshipful look as he stood up, smiling male triumph.

Then the impact of what she'd just done hit nearly as hard as the orgasm, creating a serious rupture in her afterglow. Sex with an interviewee who didn't know yet that he was an interviewee…absolutely not. He'd think she'd slept with him for the story.

Jack Brattle—*Jack Brattle*—stepped forward and scooped her back to upright, bent and kissed her hard, once, then again and nearly overwhelmed her dismayed and blissful heart by gazing into her eyes and smoothing back what must by now be a rat's-nest hairdo. "You know they say what happens to you New Year's Day predicts how you'll spend your whole year?"

"Does it?" She smiled wistfully up at him, already in love with this perfect, beautiful, incredibly talented-tongued man. "Then this is going to be the best year of my life."

"I haven't had a perfect night like this in a long time."

Something about how he said it made her think that instead of being polite, he meant the words literally. "Me, neither."

She meant them literally, too.

"I have a brilliant idea." He held out his hand. "Come upstairs with me and we'll make more things not happen."

"That *is* a brilliant idea." Hannah accepted his hand, slid off the stool, picked up her panties and took a moment to get her hips working while he supported her. "As soon as I can walk again."

Up the stairs, then, resting her fingers in his, anticipation mixing with dread, mixing with elation, mixing with sadness. Maybe none of this would have happened by morning as far as he was concerned, but she doubted she'd ever forget a single second.

Not only that, but morning was going to come way too soon. And with it the dismal certainty that once again she'd done plenty of leaping without the slightest bit of looking beforehand. And once again she'd have to pay—this time by having to give up the career opportunity of a lifetime.

4

HE WAS SO SCREWED. NO MATTER how he played the rest of this evening, Derek was screwed. Everything had gone as planned, but nothing was working out as it should.

Obviously Dee-Dee had played her role perfectly at Gerard Banks's party, dangling the Jack Brattle interview in front of Hannah and supplying her with directions to the house. He'd had no doubt she'd take the bait. However, once the weather had changed so dramatically for the worse, he'd never dreamed she'd risk driving out tonight. After his shower earlier in the evening, he'd been about to relock the gate and front door.

Instead, he'd met Hannah for the first time stark naked. That hadn't been part of the plan. Nor had been his immediate attraction, which only compounded the interest and curiosity that was sparked by the provocative wit she revealed in her Lowbrow column, blogs and occasional features in *The Philadelphia Sentinel*.

He'd started the Highbrow column as D. G. Jackson when Philly's restaurant scene began to take off, wanting to indulge his passion for food on the one hand, and on the other, wanting to introduce the average man and woman to dishes, flavors and establishments he or she might otherwise be intimidated by. In his view, good food was one of life's greatest joys. But once Hannah began countering his "highbrow" suggestions with her "lowbrow" alternatives, he quickly learned that she knew what she was talking about as well as he did. He took great pleasure in going—incognito, of course—to every hole-in-the-wall and mom-and-pop joint she recommended, all of which satisfied as she promised.

His interest only intensified along with their public rivalry. Who was Hannah O'Reilly? What was she like? How could he find out? He wouldn't call her an obsession, but he certainly thought about her more than was normal, certainly more than any woman he'd met since he'd been forced by circumstances in his early twenties to grow up practically overnight. Okay, maybe obsessed. But not being the kind of man who tolerated unanswered questions, he'd come up with tonight's plan.

The chance for Hannah to experience the lifestyle of the elusive Jack Brattle was his bait. Lure hungry journalist with promises of the interview of a lifetime, then make her the most "highbrow" meal he could whip up, secretly document her enjoyment, and in his last column before he left Philadelphia for good, skewer her as a closet gourmet. Anyone with taste buds as unerring as hers would be an easy mark.

Hannah had shown up, Derek played the Suspicious Heir act apparently convincingly and she'd gone down without a fight—though he wished he could have captured photographic evidence of her shoving in the foie gras and washing it down ecstatically with Pol Roger Cuvée Sir Winston Churchill 1985.

After the "impromptu" meal, perfectly poised for a wrap to the ultimate checkmate, what did he do? He asked her to dance. Nice one. What did he think, he'd have her gorgeous body pressed against his and remain completely impassive, then *Hey, thanks for the dance, I'm off to bed, choose a room, and see you in the morning?* He'd immediately started getting ideas involving a lot more than dancing, fueled wilder when it became apparent she was getting the same ones.

Now…with this beautiful, sexy, willing woman stranded in his house, to say that things had gotten out of hand was like saying winter got chilly in Antarctica. Lure her, yes, feed her, yes, dance with her…okay. Kiss her? Bad idea. Succumb to the sexual promise of her blue eyes, rose lips and slender body?

He'd already said he was screwed.

Worse, he was leading her upstairs, unsatisfied lust driving out common sense. Once she got into his bedroom…

Well, *she'd* be screwed. He didn't want to think about how low this was for him to go. He might be fascinated by Hannah way beyond the typical male interest in boobs and a great ass, but nothing he could say would convince her of that if she knew who he was and why she was here.

His only hope of going through with the rest of the night without feeling like total scum was to ditch the idea of the article. At least she hadn't admitted yet that she was a reporter, so he wasn't the only one holding back truths. Granted, she'd dipped a cautious toe in honesty, but quickly gave up total immersion when he pretended to think she was joking.

What a pair. *I'll lie to you, you lie to me, come into bed, and we'll lie together.*

He got to the end of the hall, pushed open the dark door— so much dark in this house to accompany the dark memories—pulled her into the room and into his arms. She nestled against him; he lowered his chin onto her hair, inhaling her light perfume, more tropical and exotic than he would have expected on a woman whose face could be in an Ivory soap commercial…and whose body could be in an X-rated movie—okay, the perfume made sense.

Either way, Ivory or triple X, she was driving him wild.

Watching her come… He was going to have to do some serious soul-searching if he wanted his ego to regain control of his id.

Did he? He wasn't sure. Because the alternative would be very, very sweet.

"So…" She drew back, keeping her hands linked lightly behind his neck. "What's not going to happen now?"

Oh, the choice of words. If he had any sense of honor, he'd tell her everything wasn't going to happen now, he was D. G. Jackson, he'd set her up for this entire evening, though he hadn't planned the sexual part, and—

"Hmm?" She started rotating her pelvis seductively against his erection.

"Hannah."

"Ye-e-es?"

"I can't think while you're doing that."

"Do you need to?"

Yes. He needed to. But thought wouldn't be easy. Hell, it might not even be possible. Her lips were parted, eyes half-closed, head tipped back as she gazed at him. Her skin was so smooth, her neck so long and graceful, the clingy dress sparkled and winked at him so enticingly…

"I'm thinking that—"

"No." She moved forward again; her tongue painted a short line on his throat, then she closed her lips over the moisture in a brief biting kiss that made him want to pick her up, throw her on the bed and visit heaven. "Don't think, Jack. Just do…me."

Her whisper made him groan. He couldn't take advantage of her like this. Someday in some form even though he was leaving *The Herald,* she might find out what D. G. Jackson looked like and loathe him forever. Either he told her right now, or—

She let go of his neck abruptly, backed up a few steps, reached to the hem of her dress and pulled it slowly up.

Oh, no. No no no. If she did that, he was—

Long thighs came into view, widening into round hips un-interrupted by the red lace panties that unhinged him earlier. A curving female waist, full breasts barely contained in a red lace demibra.

—lost. He was lost.

The dress dangled from her triumphant fingers, then dropped. She arched her soft brown brows. "What are you thinking now?"

"Ungh." His caveman grunt made her laugh. To hell with it. Buy now, pay later. He'd make love to her until she begged him to stop, have her sign an I'll-never-tell document she'd assume typical of Jack Brattle, have her towed home as soon as the weather cooperated and change his planned final Highbrow article. He'd be selling the house soon. Hannah would never meet D. G. Jackson or Jack Brattle in person. Or maybe if she ever did, by then she'd think this was funny.

Right. Maybe.

The plan had flaws wide enough to drive a Hummer through, but with a half-drunk horny woman wearing nearly nothing— no, with *this particular* half-drunk horny woman wearing nearly nothing, anything sounded better than turning her down.

"You have on too many clothes." He shrugged clumsily out of his shirt, yanked his undershirt over his head, still uneasy over his lame justification. Where was his nobility?

"I was so hoping that's what you were thinking." She put her hands to the back of her bra.

To hell with nobility. Nobility would leave him more frustrated tonight than he'd probably ever been in his life. The promise of those breasts…

"No." He waggled his finger at her, the stern taskmaster. "My job."

"Yes, sir." Her arms fell to her sides. Her sexy mouth, crimson lipstick by now only a faint hue, looked all the more tempting for the smile that spread it. "Your job."

He'd never make it. He'd get within an inch of her, and he'd come just from that smile. Out of his jeans, impatiently out of his briefs, he strode toward her, stopping inches away, not coming, but more than ready to start trying.

"Make it all not happen, Jack. All of it." She spoke with earnest passion. "Any way you want it not to happen works for me."

He grinned, slowly, enjoying her humor, her obvious eagerness. The last woman he'd made love to had the body of a Playboy Bunny and the brain of a squid. Suffice to say, he'd had too much to drink that night and been embarrassingly desperate for sexual contact. But Hannah was Hannah, and he wanted this to be good even if it was going to be their one and only night together. Even if they were both lying through their teeth about who they really were. At least they were honest about wanting this.

What a way to meet.

His hands found her waist, followed her smooth firm lines back and around, wandered up her undulating spine-trail to the closure of her bra. He unhooked it slowly, his eyes anticipating the glorious moment of her full breasts' release from the confining lace.

Ohh, man. The thought of being able to see this body naked only this one time made him want to weep.

And the thought took him aback. With women these days he was absorbed only in the erotic present. No emotions had been involved since his first girlfriend, Amy, back in college, before his father's life shattered and brought his mother's down with it. How often and how deeply he traced losses back to that hellish year. Loss of trust, loss of the desire and capacity for true intimacy. Was it possible to break the cycle if the right woman came along?

Derek pushed the thoughts away. *Lighten up, dude,* as his Oberlin roommate would say. It was New Year's Eve, he'd been seduced by champagne and this woman, with all her possibilities. By morning, she'd have to be another brief conquest like the rest of them. In the meantime…he'd give her what they both wanted before he disappeared.

He lifted her and set her down on the edge of his bed, savoring the way her arms came around him to help support her weight. Starved for female touch, he knelt to worship her body, rubbing his cheek around each heavy breast, glad he'd shaved to spare her feeling sandpaper. Her scent was exquisite, the voluptuous softness of her skin enticing, the smooth weight against his face thrilling. Her nipples responded to his tongue and teeth; she moaned and didn't resist when he pushed her gently back on the quilt-covered mattress and climbed over her, settling between her legs, not entering yet, though his cock was in a frenzy. Too soon. He wanted this to last forever. As if anything could.

She pushed her hands up the columns of his arms, met his eyes unwillingly, hers unexpectedly shy and vulnerable. "Hi."

"Hi." He was undone by those eyes, suddenly and fiercely protective of her, naked underneath him, opening herself willingly to a stranger. Crazy old-fashioned idea. For all he knew, she spread for every guy she met. Boatloads of them a week. Though he didn't think so, didn't know why not, just instinct, about the only thing he trusted anymore.

"This is still not happening, right?"

Suddenly he felt a longing so fierce it startled him. He kissed her forehead, her cheeks, then her mouth, long lingering kisses, hoping the vulnerability he'd glimpsed in her eyes meant she felt the same.

"Nope. Not happening."

"Whew. Good."

Yeah. Great. He reached for a condom from his night table to hide the surge of anger he recognized as disappointment in her reaction, then settled back over her. If he kept his brain on tits, ass and pussy, he'd be fine.

Except he wanted much more out of this night with her, all the more so since it would be their only one together. So he took his time, tasted her mouth leisurely, willing her to be seduced by his lips and tongue until she wanted this to be "not happening" as much as he did. She responded warmly, her arms encircling his shoulders. His hand wandered to her breast; he slid his palm back and forth, brushing her nipple gently side to side. Her kisses grew hotter; her hands clenched in his hair. Triumph swelled. Her control was wavering. She wanted him as much as he wanted her. And he wanted her more apparently than he wanted his own integrity intact.

His erection found her sex, barely nudged into her opening, forward, back, forward, back, no more than half an inch. Her legs spread; her hips lifted; she made an impatient sound. Still he teased, press, release, press, release.

She wrapped one arm around his back, brought her knees up beside his shoulders, reached down and spread herself wide with her fingers. "Jack."

"Something you wanted?"

"Um." She gave a short hoarse laugh. "Yeah."

"What's that?" He whispered the words in her hair, lifted his hips to give his hand access to the sweet moisture between her legs, trailing his fingers up and down her sex, loving the way she hissed in breath when he lingered over her clitoris. She was so responsive. So uninhibited. He wanted to believe she was like this only with him.

"Er… I find that sex is a lot better…" Hiss of incoming

breath. He slid a finger inside her and she gasped the air out again. "When you actually have it."

"Really." He wasn't going to be able to hold back much longer. The calm and cool act would be completely blown if she could feel his heart thudding, hear the lust-roaring of his too-long denied body. She was so beautiful. "Interesting idea."

"Do it. Now." She took hold of his cock and guided it straight where it most wanted to be, wriggling her hips up and around, trying deliciously to impale herself.

His control vaporized; he lowered and let his muscles do the work they were so desperate to do, sliding into her as gradually as he could manage, trying not to dwell on the smooth tight feel of her gripping his length or he'd come too soon.

Her blissful sigh nearly undid him.

"Like that?"

"Mmm, like that."

He moved slowly, against all instincts urging him to pump until his orgasm had its way, made sure he stimulated her, concentrated on making her as crazy for him as he was for her.

She fell in with his rhythm, her body flushing, her eyes glazed and sensual. He had to look away. She was too perfect. Too beautiful. Too close and too intimate like this. His chest ached dangerously; he wanted, insanely, to possess her in a far more lasting way than just this one night.

In defense, he closed his eyes, sped his rhythm, trying to finish before he lost his heart—or his mind. He wasn't sure which was in danger, maybe both. She whimpered, and he tried to block out the sound, wanting her over the edge ahead of him. Her legs locked around his back; her head made swishing noises on his pillow; her breath grew rapid and hoarse. He loved what he was doing to her. He wanted to do this to her every day; he didn't want another man touching her ever, no one ever making her feel like this but him.

Tension locked her body; he opened his eyes so he could watch the ecstasy on her face as he felt her pulsing around his cock. Her cheeks were pink, lips parted, expression awed and blissful.

His own climax tore through him; at its peak he joined their mouths and kissed her with every shred of passion he could feel, more than he knew possible.

Then it was over. Lost, he rolled them to one side, still inside her, gathered her to him, his chin resting on her hair, listening to their breathing gradually slow, feeling their hearts still pounding.

He'd been a fool to think he could make love to this woman and call it over. He wanted more. He wanted to talk to her every day, eat with her every day, to make her laugh, give her everything she wanted and things she didn't even know she wanted.

Where had these emotions come from? How had he gone from seeing sex as an occasional human necessity with whomever appealed, to wanting to devour everything about this woman? Had she drugged him? Bewitched him? Had he become such an emotional hermit that the need in him exploded retroactively? He didn't know.

But he had to tell her at least some of the truth or nothing more than tonight would be possible. After the power of what just passed between them, maybe she could forgive and forget…and want more, as well.

Though no doubt his confession would make for a rough few hours.

"Hey." She stretched and started stroking and massaging his neck and shoulders, making him want to handcuff her to his bed so she could do the same every night.

"Mmm?"

"That was incredible."

"It was certainly that."

"And totally unexpected."

"Totally." He caught her hand, kissed her fingers and set them back down to continue their magic. "You should get lost in more snowstorms."

"I should, if they lead me to you." Her hands worked their way up onto his scalp. Pure heaven. "You said other women showed up to seduce you. Did you ever take advantage?"

"Never."

"Really?"

"I guess you caught me in a moment of weakness."

"Which you now regret."

He chuckled. "Not in a million years."

"Did any of them know who you were?"

"Some might have suspected."

"Jack…" Something in her tone kept him from the complete relaxation her fingers promised. "Why did you tell me your last name?"

Derek shrugged, not sure why he'd carried it that far himself. "You asked."

"But you've been hiding from the world for so long."

"You're not the world."

"Seriously." She stopped her magic, got up on one elbow to see his face. "How do you know I won't go out there and tell everyone where you are?"

He didn't like this turn to the conversation at all. He winked and gave her an über-villain stare. "Because, my schveet-haht, you vouldn't enjoy ze consequences."

She giggled, looking slightly nervous. "Tell me you're kidding."

"Ah, Hannah. Let's not go into it." Her apparent excitement

about Jack Brattle made him uneasy. She was a reporter after all… "Instinct told me I could trust you. Let's leave it at that."

"Okay." She smiled and snuggled against him, her body molded to his, head fitting comfortably on his shoulder. "I'm glad you trust me."

He did. Implicitly. But he wasn't going to ask if she trusted him. Because he couldn't bear to hear that she did, knowing how much he was betraying that trust. He needed to tell her. He would…

But right now she was so warm against him, and the room felt so peaceful and complete while outside the storm still buffeted the house. His eyes were getting heavy. Her breathing had already slowed.

Later. There was time for truth later…

He didn't know how long he'd slept but couldn't be bothered to lift his head and check the clock. Light was showing around the edges of his shades. Late morning? Early afternoon? A rush of wind drove sleet against the windows. Good. The snow was still raging. Hannah would have to stay. They'd have time to argue out his confession, let the anger settle, and then…?

She stirred against him, her soft thigh came across the top of his. His cock responded. She made a small sound and stirred again. He followed the line of her back with his fingers, over the curve of her firm and fantasy-fulfilling ass, and into the crevasse, stroking the sensitive area gently.

"Mmm. G'morning."

Her voice made him smile. Her body made him hard. He respected her brain, admired her spirit, loved her humor. Was there anything else before he found himself in too deep?

He turned on his side, adjusted her thigh over him, reached for the condom he'd stashed under his pillow, just in case, then got busy making sure she was as turned on as he was. She kept her eyes closed, but her body responded with motions, whimpers, moisture between her legs. He still held off, teasing her, listening for her breathing to gauge what she liked best. When she finally opened her eyes pleadingly, he knew. How many women had he been able to understand this well this soon? Not many. Maybe not any.

Inside her, he started a sleepy rhythm to match their moods, gripping her hips to give him control. Slow and sweet. The perfect way to start a—

She pushed hard, rolled him over to his back, climbed on and started riding, pinning his wrists to the mattress with her weight, her heavy breasts swinging, her skin gradually flushing, strong thighs working on either side of his body.

Oh, man. "This isn't tiring you?"

"At the moment—" she arched her back, panting, ground her pelvis against him, then rode harder "—I don't care."

The way she was making him feel, her insistent rhythm, the triple X sight of her made him almost not care, either. Almost.

He freed his hands, put them to her hips to help her along, try to keep some of the pressure off her legs. "Are you sure you—"

"I'm sure." She accepted his help, raised her arms over her head, eyes closed, breasts bouncing, stomach pulled taut. It was too much.

"Hannah." He gritted his teeth.

She put one arm down, found her clitoris and started adding to her own pleasure.

He lifted his hands, cupped the beautiful rounds of her breasts. The feel of her warm flesh in his palms, the sight of her face flushed with desire sent him over the edge. He grabbed her hips again, practically lifted off the bed with the force of his orgasm.

His beautiful, ethereal porn queen gasped; her fingers sped; she gasped again, then opened her eyes and looked into his as he felt her contracting.

There was no way, no way, this one day with her, this one incredible night with her, was going to be remotely enough. Why the hell, when her articles and blogs had intrigued him so much, hadn't he just called her and asked her out? Why put them both through this elaborate and underhanded charade? Had he gotten so used to not trusting people, to approaching them with suspicion after his father's betrayal, that he couldn't even ask a girl he was interested in out to dinner?

Something told him this time with Hannah was going to change his life. He wasn't sure how, or whether his future would involve her still, but he knew he wouldn't be the same after this experience. He'd make sure of it.

She collapsed onto him. He waited until they could both breathe more normally, then rolled her carefully back next to him. "You okay?"

"More than okay." Her voice was languorous, sated. He wanted her to feel that all the time. But only if it was because of him. "Tremendously okay."

"You're amazing, Hannah."

"No, you."

He chuckled, stroking her hair, wishing again there was another way they could have met.

"Jack."

The name stabbed into his happiness. He still had a small matter to clear up. "Mm?"

"Now that you have given my body more pleasure than it has ever had with food and incredible sex, it's time to get down to business."

"Business?" He didn't like that word. "What do you mean?"

"I want you to tell me more about you." She put a possessive hand on his chest. "I want to know everything about Jack Brattle. Absolutely everything."

Derek stopped stroking. Dread started leaching away the afterglow. She couldn't be— Not after what they'd shared. "Dull stuff, all of it."

"I'm sure it's fascinating." She lifted her head, eyes alight. "Tell me. Your life, your childhood, your job, everything. Pretend I'm…oh, I don't know…"

"Going to write an article about me?"

Her face froze, then fell. "No. I…no. Of course not."

Derek disentangled himself and sat up abruptly. "Back in a minute."

In the bathroom, he wrapped the condom in a tissue, tossed it into the garbage, ran hot water onto a washcloth and cleaned himself off. Cleaned her off of him. He was a fool. Hannah had slept with him as Jack Brattle in order to get a story.

What kind of naive idiot had he been? He'd set her up for the sake of his own story, but he'd cancelled that plan after what happened between them. Now looky here, she'd set him up, too. Pouring on the charm, not asking too many questions too early, waiting for after the big seduction when she'd hooked him and her curiosity would seem more natural.

He should have realized she'd do anything to get the scoop. He'd been so smug about his clever trump-card joke, so ego-centric once it backfired, thinking only of how she made him feel and how much he wanted her. He hadn't been thinking of her motives. What a sick joke, arrogantly assuming he was as irresistible to her as she was to him. Worse, for a man as cynical as he was, he'd assumed she felt the strong pull between them and had fallen under its spell to the same degree he had. Apparently that strong pull was pure fantasy on his part, born of reading too many of her columns and imagining in a too-lonely life that they'd share a connection. Not much better than a kid with a celebrity crush.

An interview with the infamous Jack Brattle. The big prize, the brass ring. Sex was merely the means. Derek wasn't a man, he was a stand-in for a celebrity scoop, a pawn in her quest for the story to launch her career.

A story he was about to bring to a swift and unhappy ending.

5

HE WAS *WHO?*

This was not happening. This was so not happening. This was so completely not—

Again with the "not happening"? This horror *was* happening. And it made her wish the sex hadn't. Except rolling around in the sheets with…this man…was so amazing, that Hannah had convinced herself she was hours away from falling irrevocably for…someone she thought was someone else.

Not again, this pain and disappointment in matters of the heart. Not again! And yet…what did she expect going instantly gaga over a complete stranger?

"So…you're actually D. G. Jackson?"

"Yes." He stared at her moodily.

"Not Jack Brattle."

He kept staring. She could not get her brain around this at all. She'd just spent one of the best nights of her life—and had the best first-time sex of her life—with D. G. Jackson, the columnist. *Not* Jack Brattle, the billionaire.

It made no sense. What was D. G. Jackson doing in Jack Brattle's house, besides seducing her under an assumed identity? And why instead of looking like an abashed sinner now, was he giving *her* a contemptuous sneer as if she'd somehow tricked *him?* In an incredibly vile and disgraceful way, she might add.

Oh, this hurt. Horribly. Were men ever who they seemed? Ever, ever, *ever?*

Worse, she was so wonderfully naked alone with him three minutes ago, and now he had on black silk boxers, and she wanted nothing more than to grab his—or whoever's—sheets from the bed, cover herself and go fetal on the floor, whimpering. But she didn't want to show any weakness. Didn't want him to see how much he'd hurt her. All she wanted was to rise from the bed and with considerable dignity, set his pubic hair on fire.

"Would you mind telling me what the hell is going on?"

"I set you up." He spoke matter-of-factly, as if he tricked people into his bed every day of the week, which was entirely possible. "Dee-Dee is a friend of mine."

"Dee-Dee." She could barely gasp out the syllables. This was…odious! A supremely sick joke, except D.G.—*D.G.!*— wasn't laughing. He didn't look as if he enjoyed this at all. Which made two of them. "You tricked me into thinking you were Jack Brattle."

How ghastly. How low and vicious and mean. She wasn't sobbing with rage only because shock still held her rigid.

"Yes, I did." He didn't sound anything but angry.

Luckily she'd already suffered the loss of the Brattle interview since *she* had principles that prevented her from acting like a slimebag butthead, or she'd want to run outside and beg another branch to fall, this time on her. Or, hell, why not just order one up for a crash landing on the head of D. G. Jackson?

"What are you doing in Jack Brattle's house?"

"The house is mine."

"*Yours.*" She was hopelessly confused. He said that as if she *had* really trespassed instead of showing up at his Jack Brattle-worthy mansion exactly as he intended she should. And what the hell kind of salary did *The Philadelphia Herald* pay, anyway? "So Jack Brattle…"

"Is completely out of the picture."

No Jack Brattle. Just D. G. Jackson, a newspaper colum-nist with a mansion and apparently a Paul Bunyan-sized ax to grind with her. Had he really been that put out by Grey Poupon? It was excellent mustard. "Why did you do this?"

"The meal you ate downstairs was going to be the subject of my next Highbrow piece. *Lowbrow Columnist is Closet Gourmet.*"

Her face grew hot. The room looked wrong, too bright or something. A weird high pitch played in her ears. She didn't think she'd *ever* been this furious. Not even with another man. She was a good sport. Objectively she could see the humor in the situation. She could see how luring her to eat everything her column was opposed to would be a really good score.

Except for one rather overwhelming detail.

"You *slept* with me. Was that going in the article, too? Any hidden cameras for pictures you're planning to run with the column?"

"No." He glanced away, the first sign that he might be feeling at least some guilt over what he'd done. Thank God. She was beginning to think he was a sociopath.

"That's why you were so insistent anything physical between us 'wasn't happening.' I get it. How practical. Just delete the inconvenient aspects of responsibility and still get what you want." She bounced off the bed to avoid the pain of sitting there feeling sick and rejected, made a futile grab for her panties, missed them through her tears, and had to lunge for them again.

"You were willing to screw Jack Brattle for a story."

His flat accusation stopped her. She gaped at him, panties dangling from her clenched fingers. Screw Jack Brattle for a story? Ha! If only she'd been smart enough to do it for that reason. But, no. She'd started out wanting the story, but ended up wanting only him. Because he was funny and sexy and charming and had set the stage for one of the most wonderful and romantic nights of her life. Because in spite of his wealth making him stand for everything she'd been brought up not to value, he'd gotten under her skin and, while he was inside her body, also into her heart. Because she was an idiot, but okay, no point belaboring that.

Afterward, she'd been greedy to know everything about him, to absorb his background, likes, dislikes, routines, hobbies, no longer for a story—because how could she publish anything after sleeping with him?—but to immerse herself in him, to draw them closer so her knowledge could catch up at least partway to her feelings.

When would she learn?

So he'd taken her questions about him as a sign she could play dirty, too. Fine. She wasn't stupid enough to show more vulnerability now. "What's it to you who I screw or why?"

"Nothing." He shrugged carelessly. "It's nothing to me either way."

"Super." She yanked the panties right side out, wondering how much more pain she could stand before she split in half from the pressure. "Well, thanks for the orgasms. I've gotta go."

He gestured toward the ice-covered window. "Out in that?"

"Nothing—" she nearly lost her balance when her toes tangled in red lace "—is going to keep me from leaving this house."

"Without a car? You'll freeze to death."

"If you want to be concerned over my welfare, you should turn back time and rethink some of this disgusting little trick you pulled last night.'

"Ah, right. Just one question."

"What." Panties finally on, she jammed her hands on her hips, then realized she was still topless and crossed her arms over her chest.

"When were you planning to tell Jack you were a reporter? After you left his bed and published his life story?"

In her outrage she forgot to keep her breasts covered and had to hug herself again. "*How* hypocritical. *You* set me up from the beginning to get a story under false pretenses. I fell into this situation. And I actually did tell him—you—that I was—am—a reporter."

His eyebrows lifted.

"Okay, only sort of, but I did." She looked around for her bra, kicking herself for not realizing that's why he let the ha-ha joke about her job pass so easily, when anyone as vulturously protective of his privacy as Jack Brattle wouldn't have let her get away with even the most obvious lie about it. Nor would he have admitted who he was in the first place. She'd noticed and wondered, yet she wanted so desperately to believe in the fantasy, just like she always wanted to believe in fantasy and romance and fairy tales and probably even Santa Claus if her bratty cousin Tom hadn't burst that particular bubble. A career-catapulting interview with a sexy billionaire who couldn't help falling desperately in love with her and she with him? Are you kidding? Who could resist that?

Get real, Hannah. Not even in the movies did they make stories that fantastic.

"Anyway, D.G., you—"

"Derek."

"What?"

"My name is Derek."

"You're changing it again?"

His expression didn't waver. "It's Derek."

"Fine. *Derek.* Whatever. You knew I was a reporter when

we slept together. I didn't know you weren't Jack. And what kind of life story was I going to publish when you don't even have the right life?"

"That's not the point."

"It is to me." She found her bra sticking halfway under the bed, put it on inside out and had to take it off again, turning her back when she noticed Derek's—*Derek's, not Jack's*—eyes lingering on her breasts, which, in spite of her one-hundred-degrees-in-the-shade rage, remembered his touch and wanted more.

Super. She'd reached a new low in falling for lowlifes. *The more they abuse me, the harder I fall. Humiliate me. Trick me. Lie to me. I'm yours, baby, and keep up the pain.*

"You can't go anywhere in this weather, Hannah."

"Try and stop me." She snatched her dress off the floor and jammed it over her head, not caring if it ended up wrong-way around. Her shoes were downstairs, her coat was in the—

Hands landed on her shoulders; she ducked and whirled to face him. "What are you doing?"

"Trying to stop you."

"Do me a favor and don't do anything else to me for the rest of your life."

He put his hands on his hips and regarded her darkly. Which of course made him look intense and masculine and even more gorgeous than he did looking cheerful, which was already too gorgeous for her sanity. "What's the plan, walking the rest of the day through an ice storm?"

"Give me a phone, I'll call Triple A."

"No phones."

"Oh, be serious." She scanned the furniture and walls, tried to remember one in any of the rooms she'd been in. "What is this, *The Shining?*"

"It's a cell-only house."

She didn't buy that for a microsecond. "Then give me your cell."

"Gee." He crossed his arms over his broad, bare, fantasy-perfect chest. "I forget where it is."

"I thought you'd want me to leave."

"I don't want your death on my conscience."

"But my humiliation is resting there quite comfortably?"

"Hannah…" Was it her imagination or had his voice become slightly conciliatory? "The joke was meant to be just that. A joke."

"Once you slept with me it became very not funny."

"Sex was not part of the plan." His voice had definitely gentled. "And trust me, that part was no joke."

Oh, no. She fought against the warm fuzzies and the stupid, *stupid* hope. She'd never learn. "What was it, then?"

"It was…" He rubbed his hand over his forehead, looking suddenly tired, which made her anger ebb further and her desire rise to put him to bed and give him a backrub. Honestly! She should still be wanting to kick him where it counted. "Let's call it the intersection of attraction, opportunity and good champagne."

"Ah." She took in a huge breath and let it out quickly. She had to stop listening to him right now. Because once he started, he'd make it all sound so reasonable. How often had she been through this… She'd listen, empathize with every-thing from his point of view, see how she was partly if not mostly at fault and forgive him. In the process, once again she'd forget that her needs and emotions had been completely left out of the equation. How often had she done that? Too many times to count. No more. No more. Neither of them had acted with impeccable integrity, however in her book he'd crossed a much bigger line than she had, and she wasn't going to play forgiving doormat anymore.

"I'll need a crowbar."

Very understandably he looked startled. "For my skull?"

"For my car windows. So I can get my own phone."

"Uh, fresh out of crowbars."

"I'll find something." She glanced around. A couple of porcelain lamps, which would shatter. She wasn't quite up to throwing a bureau or his king-size bed. Her mind went over the house's layout. Fireplace poker? There must be one. She headed for the door.

"You can't be serious."

"If you say so." Out of the room, she jogged down the hall—Derek G. Jackson's hall, damn him all to hell—down the steps, not hearing any furious signs of pursuit and feeling oddly triumphant and disappointed at the same time.

In the living room, as she grabbed, yes, a poker, she heard him at the top of the stairs and rushed to jam on her damp high heels, longing for the gray fuzzy-lined boots sitting in her apartment's front hallway. No time for a coat. She'd run out and bash the window, grab her phone, and call for help in getting away ASAP from Mr. Not-Jack-Brattle.

She flung the front door open. The cold and wind hit her like an air bag. Ice crystals stung. Hannah stopped on the threshold. This was stupid, wasn't it. Another Harebrained Hannah move. But what choice did she have, other than to sacrifice her pride by crawling back inside and staying until the storm abated? If she couldn't retrieve the phone, she could lock herself in his bathroom or something equally mature.

This was awful.

Over the wind she barely heard feet thudding down the stairs. "Hannah, for God's sake, don't be an idiot."

That did it. Out the front door, closing it behind her. Wobbling across the front stoop. One step down the staircase and she hit ice. Her foot twisted. Slipped.

Bam. Bam. Bam. Down the stairs and landing hard at the bottom. Very hard. Cold. Very cold.

Pain.

When would she learn?

DEREK COULD NOT GET DOWN the stairs fast enough. What was Hannah thinking, going out in an ice storm in spiky heels? To break a car window, no less! She was crazy. He'd been convinced she was bluffing or he would have made sure she stayed inside.

A dash across the foyer, the door opened, a wince at the blast of cold and the icy pellets dive-bombing his chest. At least he'd taken the time to drag on a T-shirt before he followed her. God, what a mess. He squinted out into the blizzard conditions toward her car.

Where the hell was she? "*Hannah.*"

The wind gusted, whipping her name back down his throat and reminding him in no uncertain terms that his legs and feet were bare. He stepped carefully forward and saw her. His heart jumped. She lay on her back at the bottom of the front steps—only three of them, but they were concrete. Damn it. He'd never forgive himself for not trying harder to stop her. Ignoring the cold and wet, he made it down the icy steps as quickly as possible and knelt beside her. Up close, her ragged breathing was obvious; her eyes opened in a squint; she grunted. One of the most beautiful sounds he'd ever heard.

"Hey there." He moved to shield her body from the blast and was doubly relieved when she struggled to roll up on one elbow, blinking snow from her beautiful long lashes. No major injury, to her body at least. "Did you hit your head?"

"No." She rotated her right shoulder painfully then rubbed her lower back. "Took the fall on my hip."

"Much better choice. Everything else working? Nothing broken?"

"Don't think so."

"Can you stand?" He took her wrist, helped her up, hoping she'd forget the angry words between them and let him help her. "Come inside, and I'll—"

"Oh!"

He got a sudden armful of snow-covered red-sequin-clad woman when she stumbled against him. "What is it?"

"My ankle— *Ow.*" She let loose a couple of words not allowed in either of their newspapers.

If he hadn't been so concerned, he would have rolled his eyes. Rushing out into slippery weather on shoes that no human should be able to walk in under any circumstances…just crazy. She was lucky she wasn't comatose or worse. "Is it broken?"

"I think just twisted. Maybe sprained." Her teeth chattered around her words. Her body shook.

"Come inside." He supported her into the house, thank God without resistance. In the sudden calm and blessed warmth, he kicked the door shut behind them and lowered her gently onto a chair, grabbed his black cashmere coat from the front closet, and draped it around her shivering shoulders. Then he did what he should have done the night before, punched in the code to close and lock the estate gate.

"S-stupid idea, huh."

"I've encountered better." Yet…he'd loved that same impulsive spirit in Hannah's columns. She came across as someone who danced through life trying everything that occurred to her, and while she might strike out more often than not, she also discovered places and had experiences too many other people would overlook. Or not consider possible. Or practical. Or safe.

He'd spent his whole life practical and safe. No wonder she attracted him. And astounded him. And infuriated him.

"Let me look." He took off her impractical unsafe shoes as carefully as he could. "Can you wiggle your toes? Bend your ankle? Circle it?"

"Yes. Yes. *Ow.*"

"*Ow.* Okay, let's get you upstairs. RICE for sprains, isn't it."

"R-rice?" Clutching the coat at her throat, she leaned her head against the wall, pale and drawn, snowflakes melting on her cheeks into drops he wanted to kiss dry.

"Rest, ice…something that begins with *C*…"

"Ch-champagne?"

He grinned. "Don't think so. At least not until we're sure you're okay."

"I'm okay."

"You don't look okay."

"Thanks."

"You're welcome. Let's get you into bed."

She came instantly to life, sent him a sidelong glare. "You're not g-getting me into—"

"Medical reasons, Hannah. I want you warmed up and calmed down." He slid an arm around her waist, maneuvered hers around his neck. He felt the tension in her body. "I know you're angry, but this time you can trust me."

"Only this t-time?"

He growled in frustration. "Come on."

She let him support her on the stairs to the landing, where he swept her up and carried her the rest of the way down the hall, Rhett Butler-like but with more honorable intentions. Unfortunately.

Given their recent battle, he hadn't thought he'd ever have Hannah in his arms again, which hadn't seemed such a loss until now, retroactively, when he was hit by the deep pleasure of holding her again. Wasn't he supposed to be furious still?

He didn't seem able to be when she needed him. Not to mention the genuine shock and pain on her face when he accused her of sleeping with "Jack" for a story that had undermined his confidence in her guilt. Maybe he hadn't imagined the emotion that had bloomed between them upstairs under his covers. "You'd better get out of that wet dress."

"Okay." She was shaking in earnest. He didn't stand on ceremony, set her down onto her feet, pulled the material over her head, and swept the rumpled bedcovers out of the way so she could climb carefully in, grimacing when she moved her right leg. He covered her meticulously with the sheet, then the comforter, feeling again that overwhelming sense of protectiveness, of deep satisfaction that she was with him, that he could keep her safe, help her get warm and recover.

"Better?" He crossed to his bureau to pull on a dry T-shirt, sweats and thick socks, and to escape the disturbing emotions. "I'll make you some tea."

She blinked at him. "Tea."

"You don't like tea?"

"I love tea."

"So…?"

She gave a weak but grateful smile. "Tea would be nice. I'm a little shaky. Thank you."

"Cold and shock. And you're welcome."

He went downstairs, filled the kettle that was always sitting on the stove, and put it on to heat. Maybe she'd like a couple of cookies? Rita always had shortbread somewhere, the Scottish kind made with real butter, because she knew how much he liked it. Which cabinet? And where were the tea bags?

He'd gotten too much in the habit of immersing himself in work, letting Rita and Ray take care of the house and of him, on the too-rare occasions he was here. He understood his life had been different from the average man's, but the surprise in Hannah's eyes when he could barely find the china in his own kitchen had been disconcerting and unwelcome.

He put a generous helping of the cookies he found on a plate. He and Hannah had eaten a huge meal in the wee hours, but it was near lunchtime now and, *ahem,* they'd burned quite a few calories in the interim. He glanced at the clock. Twelve-thirty. Not much sleep, and he was as full of energy as he'd been yesterday when after eight full hours he started his morning routine—exercise, shower, shave, dress, breakfast, work, work, work…

In the downstairs bathroom he found a first-aid kit he'd seen Rita taking out of the vanity. Inside, an ice pack and an Ace bandage. He added a bottle of ibuprofen to his haul and went back to the kitchen, searched for mugs and tea bags.

Mugs, he found quickly. Tea bags took longer, but he managed. At least he could make good tea, thanks to his English mother's absolute rules of how-to and how-not-to. She'd be horrified he wasn't brewing a "proper pot" with loose tea. The thought made him smile. Sometimes he did manage to smile at the memories of his mother. Too often they were too tainted with grief and bitterness at his father.

Tea bag in the mug, already rinsed with boiling water to heat it, more water poured in, he set the timer for five minutes. Even ineptly, he found he liked doing these little things for Hannah. Not that he could be glad she'd hurt herself, but…maybe she'd have time to cool off and not be in such a hurry to leave. She was right that he didn't have a leg to stand on blaming her for doing the same thing he'd done. He hadn't been completely open. But he'd have to trust her a lot more than he did now to reveal more.

He still wished she'd immediately denied having sex with

"Jack" to further her career, but a potential interview with someone like Jack Brattle might have led her over boundaries she'd not otherwise cross—and he was pretty sure she'd found more in bed with him than interview material.

Plus it was so like Hannah to jump right in at the hint of an opportunity—her blogs as well as her columns reflected that aspect of her personality. She was always first in line when new shops and restaurants opened up around the city, always immediate with her opinions and emotions. He couldn't fault her for being herself.

Or was he excusing her simply because he wanted to be closer to her than any other woman he'd ever known?

He grimaced. Men really hadn't evolved past Neanderthals. Why else would he have dragged her off to bed, knowing how complicated making love to her could turn out to be—and did turn out to be?

Complicated, yes. Yet he liked this complication. All the other complications in his life in recent years related to work. It had been a long time since his life was emotionally complicated, partly from not leaving himself open to anything or anyone in so long. Even now, half of him wanted to run, the other half felt on the verge of being reborn. Why now? Why her? He didn't know. And wasn't likely to figure it out any time soon. His next challenge, though, faced him immediately: he needed a tray.

In a narrow cabinet next to the oven he found one, and arranged the medical supplies, tea—milk and sugar in case she wanted either—and the plate of cookies, adding a bowl of the tiny tangerines she'd liked so much at dinner and some leftover raspberries. For the final touch, he went into the greenhouse—a breath of warm, fragrant summer in the midst of a New Year's Day storm—and cut a perfect champagne rose, which he laid on the tray.

During his childhood while his parents were gone or distracted, which was too often the same thing, there had always been people—most recently and for the longest stretch Rita and Ray—kind enough to nurture him as best as they could. A flower wasn't much, but the little extra touches had made him feel someone cared enough to go to that trouble on his behalf. Though Hannah's life was probably already full of people who loved and cared for her.

The timer rang. Derek jerked out the tea bags and tossed them into the garbage, then picked up the tray. He didn't like feeling jealous, of all those people or of her. And of course the sick irony hadn't escaped him that millions of people would kill to be in his expensive shoes.

Feeling uncomfortably vulnerable, he carried his little offering up the stairs, hoping his ministrations would make her feel better. Except if she felt better, Hannah would most likely try to leave again, he hoped in a less dramatic way. Maybe it was just as well. They could put the strange and wonderful night behind them and pretend, as they'd joked, that none of it had happened. Maybe next time he was in Philadelphia he could call her, they could go out on a normal date and start over. Though with his company's Philadelphia office closing, this house selling and his leaving *The Herald*, time for trips to the city would be rare.

He reached the end of the hallway and stepped into his bedroom. One look at Hannah propped on his pillows, blond hair glistening on the dark green Egyptian cotton, her eyes sleepy, mouth soft and pink, smooth bare shoulders visible above his comforter, and he knew he had to find some way, any way—fighting fair or fighting dirty—to keep her there a whole lot longer.

6

TEA. JACK-DEREK WAS BRINGING her tea. She'd yelled at and insulted him—even if he did deserve it—what's more she'd been an impulsive idiot again and forced him outside into frigid temperatures and a raging storm in his underwear. Instead of rolling his eyes and smashing her car window to retrieve her phone himself so she could leave faster, he'd tucked her into his bed with concern and brought her tea and cookies.

And a rose. A perfect, perfect rose that smelled like summer at her aunt's house in New Jersey. No, better than that, like her high-school best friend's wedding bouquet, or like a romantic evening stroll through Society Hill's rose garden.

Aw, geez. She was still angry, her ankle hurt like hell, her shoulder and hip were bruised and stiff, she couldn't seem to get warm, yet she lost no time feeling fluttery. In her experience, men at their best made good companions and lovers, but not good nurturers. Their idea of spoiling Hannah rotten was not making her cook them dinner.

Maybe she needed to change the type of guy she dated.

"Wow." She tried to drag herself to sitting and winced.

"Easy. I brought you ice packs and an elastic bandage, too."

"Thank you." Her voice came out soft and tremulous. No, no, no, this was not the way to behave around a liar. Around liars she needed to be frosty and superior and remove herself from their company as soon as possible.

But "as soon as possible" was in a who-knew-how-long delay due to ghastly weather, said liar's lack of cooperation in handing over a phone, her car being impenetrable, her ankle having been injured... *Intrepid Reporter a Helpless Prisoner*. She sighed deeply. Helpless prisoner in a glorious mansion in the bed of a sexy handsome man who was being very, very sweet to her. Quick, someone remind her why this was horrible.

Derek laid the tray on the edge of the bed, then carefully offered her the steaming mug. "Milk? Sugar?"

"Neither. Fine straight up." She kept her eyes on the mug so she wouldn't spill and so she wouldn't betray how delighted her traitor heart was with the whole setup. Even with her brain reminding her the sexy-handsome-mansioned guy lured her here under false pretenses and slept with her without mentioning his real identity.

So? She could drink his tea and allow him to fuss over her ankle. She didn't have to fall in love with him. Again. Maybe she'd already started down that road with Jack, but she could at least be strong where Derek was concerned.

Okay? Yes, okay. As long as he'd traded in manipulator for Boy Scout, she could let him help her. After all, she was in this mess through her own clumsiness and lack of judgment, and he hadn't blinked once.

"Let's see what we can do about that ankle." He strode to the back of the room and disappeared into what must be a walk-in closet, probably the size of her entire bedroom. He reemerged carrying a thick navy bathrobe which, when placed over her chest, felt incredibly soft and smelled of Jack-Derek, which was way too pleasant for her peace of mind. She wanted to bring it home with her and take long guilty sniffs on lonely nights. Not that she was pathetic or anything. "Thanks."

"You're welcome." He slid back the covers so her body was exposed briefly to the cool air before the bathrobe came to her rescue, spread quickly over the rest of her. "Oh. Wait. I brought you ibuprofen."

He struggled briefly with the bottle, muttering, popped the top off, shook out too many pills, put two back, and presented her the others with a flourish. Then he made a face. "I forgot water."

"It's okay, I have the tea." She held up the mug and took the pills. Something about his lack of ease in certain areas contrasted appealingly with his utter confidence and suavity in others, like caring for her and food. And sex.

No, not thinking about that. Boy Scout, remember?

While he concentrated on taking the Ace bandage out of its box, she took another sip of tea, savoring the hot comforting liquid. The mug wore clusters of oversize blueberries which reminded her of pottery she'd seen at a restaurant store on a family trip to Maine. Hannah had asked for a pretty plate of this type, but her parents had been drunk and arguing, and they'd ignored her, then cruelly snapped at her when she persisted. Months later, by way of apology, a similar plate had appeared under the Christmas tree. Hannah had been pleased, but the memory of that initial unpleasantness tainted the gift. When her college roommate had broken the plate during a party, Hannah hadn't been all that upset.

"Here." Derek grabbed a burgundy throw pillow from the black mission sofa under the windows, lifted her leg, keeping her ankle straight with a hand under her heel and lowered her calf onto the pillow, while she clutched her mug and anticipated pain.

There was very little. He was very gentle.

Mmm.

"Hold there."

She sipped more tea, feeling its warmth spreading through her body, luxuriating under the softness of his robe, enjoying the feeling of being taken care of way more than a liberated twenty-first-century woman should. Tough. Let him fuss. She was due.

He wrapped her ankle a few times, molded two cleverly flexible ice packs around the swelling, wrapped those firmly in place, then removed the bathrobe and drew the lovely warm comforter back over her.

"Twenty minutes, then I'll take away the ice. You don't want frostbite on top of everything else you've been through."

"Thank you."

"You're welcome." He stood beside the bed, watching her with a slight frown.

For some bizarre reason Hannah felt suddenly and ridiculously shy. For heaven's sake, she'd been thrashing around in his bed totally naked without the slightest bit of shame all night long, now she was sensibly covered and drinking tea. What was the problem?

Maybe that she wasn't sure about the current terms of their…association. Should she ask to use his phone again? Should she yell at him some more? Apologize for her behavior? Should she—

"Cookie?" He held one in front of her mouth so she could take a bite.

"Thanks." She reluctantly took the arm not holding the mug out from under the heavenly cloud of goose down.

"Stay covered. I'll help."

"I can certainly feed myself."

"I know, I've seen you. You're very good at it." He held the cookie out insistently, then when she hesitated, brushed it across her lips, back and forth, leaving tiny crumbs she wanted to lick off. The buttery smell reached her nostrils.

Oh, she was weak. Maybe just one bite…

"Mmm."

"Good, huh. Take another one."

Another bite, the cookie crumbling marvelously between her teeth.

Another. Then she looked into his eyes, which were focused on her lips, and saw something she shouldn't have seen there. Something rather primal and possessive. And speculative. As if he were wondering what those lips of hers could be doing other than chewing a cookie.

No, no. No longer manipulator, Boy Scout. Her nurse, not her seducer. After their fight he wouldn't dare go there again.

He fed her until the cookie was gone; she felt an odd combination of satisfaction and vulnerability at being so pampered.

"Raspberry?" He held one up to her lips.

Oh gosh. She should stop this game, she felt it instinctively, but her rational brain couldn't come up with a solid enough reason. He was feeding her. She was eating. And yet… And yet… There was something more going on. "Ja— Derek, I can feed my—"

"Raspberry?"

Hannah couldn't help half a smile. Nor could she resist opening her mouth. They were talking raspberries in January. Good ones, too, fragrant and sweet. Probably had a carbon footprint the size of Sasquatch's, but as long as they were already here…

She parted her lips. He leisurely painted the ripe soft berry over them before allowing her to draw it into her mouth.

Hannah didn't look at him. Derek "Nightingale." Simply helping her get well…

"Another?"

She glanced up to find him looking a little too determinedly innocent. "I think it would be more efficient if I ate them myself."

"I'm sure it would be." He didn't offer to give the berry up.

"Um." She couldn't help a sizzle of temper. "Then, no, thanks."

"Okay." He brought the raspberry to his own mouth and against her will, she watched, trying not to get to a low point in her love life where she envied fruit. His full masculine lips parted, opened…enveloped.

Oh my. The ice and pain reliever were starting to take away the throbbing in her ankle. Her body was warming. Definitely warming. She gulped more tea. "I should go soon."

"Sure." He started peeling a tangerine.

"So…you'll let me use your cell to call out?"

"Sure." A section of the peel landed on the plate. The fresh scent rose toward her. "In a while. When you're fully recovered."

"I'm feeling fine now. Much better."

He separated a section of the orange and held it out to her. She frowned at him even while her mouth was watering.

"No?" He waved it back and forth. "Vitamin C is good for you."

Fine. It was just food. She opened her mouth, and accepted the juicy section, all business. Even so, every sense seemed to be on high alert, registering with unusual intensity the burst of pulp, the chewy membrane, the sweet tangy flavor. She wasn't going to go into what her senses were picking up about Derek. She had to get out of here before she did something stupid like beg him to make love to her again. Then she could doubly humiliate herself by falling in love with Jack Brattle and Derek Jackson on the same day.

"Tell you what."

"What?"

"Neither of us was acting completely honestly."

"True."

"So how about we clean the slate and start over?" He put the plate on the floor and held out his hand. "I'm Derek G. Jackson. Among other things I write for *The Herald*."

She contemplated the offered hand for a second or two, then nodded and took it. At least by being friendly she'd have a better chance of using his phone and escaping to save her sanity. "Hannah O'Reilly. I write for *The Philadelphia Sentinel*, not among other things."

"Nice to meet you." His eyes were warm and brimming with mischief, which made him extremely hard to regard as merely the ticket to her exit. "Maybe you've read my Highbrow column, which helps educate Philadelphians about food worth eating."

"I might have. Once." She affected a narrow-eyed look of accusation, which didn't do anything to wipe the sexy look off his face, or to dull her reaction. "I write the Lowbrow column, which shows you don't have to be a millionaire to enjoy delicious high-quality food. Maybe you've read that one?"

"I've noticed it…"

"Hmph." Her glare became a smile in answer to his. How could she do otherwise? His grin was as contagious as a yawn.

"How did you decide to be a reporter, Hannah?"

"Oh." She waved the question into insignificance. "It was one of those childhood dreams. Other kids wanted to be actors, rock stars, firemen, I wanted to be a reporter."

He pretended to be taking notes. "And why was that?"

"Well, Doctor, in case you didn't notice, I have a passion for communicating."

"Hmm." He scribbled a few pretend words. "I did notice the passion part…"

"And why did *you* start writing, among all your 'other things.'"

"You will be shocked to learn it was a passion for communicating. The rest of my job is pretty dry. I'd written for my high-school and college paper, and it seemed like a fun and useful way to connect with people in this city, so I submitted the column idea to the *Herald* editor, Clyde Ortiz, and he went for it. Then you showed up in *The Sentinel*, people began comparing—"

"Then all my readers started reading you, and—"

"All my readers started reading you, so we both benefited." He leaned closer, focusing on her lips. "I think it's time, Hannah."

"Time?" Her voice was oddly breathless. Air wasn't going in and out of her lungs in its usual quiet way.

"To take off your ice pack."

"Oh." She didn't sound disappointed. She was sure. Not at all. Which was good because she was relieved. She'd thought he was going to use his lame apology—which now that she thought about it, hadn't even been an apology, just a plea for a truce—to seduce her again. What kind of highbrow did something lowbrow like that?

"Here." He took off the comforter, leaving her lying there again in her underwear. Only this time her modesty was not preserved with the bathrobe. He unwound the bandage, removed the ice pack and rewound the stretchy material, leaving his hand warm and strong on her shin. Nothing objectively erotic about that. Nothing. But…oh goodness. Why was the touch of a new lover so incredibly potent, where another man's hand on her shin—her shin for heaven's sake—would make her want a nap?

"Thank you."

"You're welcome." His hand traveled upward, slowly, deliberately.

She brought her good leg close, trapping the tips of his fingers just above her knees. He wouldn't. He couldn't. "What are you doing?"

"Sitting in bed with you, with my hand on your knee?"

She glared at him, fluttery all over again but determined not to show it. "Your hand is not on my knee."

"No?" He looked down in mock surprise at his fingers, which had escaped and traveled farther up her thigh.

She grabbed his hand and flung it onto the mattress. "Please cover me back up."

He shook his head, politely regretful. "I'm sorry, I can't do that."

"Why not?"

"Because I get headaches when I'm under blankets."

She gave him an are-you-crazy look. "What does that have to do with covering me up?"

"This." He put one hand on the mattress by her left hip, leaned to the right and kissed her outer thigh, lingering on her chilly skin with warm lips.

"No. Oh, no. No, you don't." She pushed at his shoulders which involuntarily jarred her leg. "Ow. You're hurting my ankle."

"No, you're hurting it." He kissed the top of her thigh, nuzzled the skin, trailed his tongue gently along the leg elastic of her panties, heading for—

"No." She tried to move away and let out a soft cry of pain.

"Don't move."

"Stop this."

"Sorry, no. Medical necessity."

"Derek."

He pressed his lips gently over the smooth fabric of her panties, unerringly landing on the small swell of her clitoris.

Fire. She was on fire. *Woman Spontaneously Bursts into*

Flames. How did this man affect her so strongly? She wanted to rip off her panties so he could plunge his tongue inside her and make her come like crazy. But she was still annoyed with him for earlier manipulation, and here he was manipulating again. If she gave in…

She'd get to come violently.

Damn it, no. That was not how she should be thinking. If she gave in, he'd get his way again, through trickery, and she'd lose every advantage of pride and probably another big chunk of her heart, too. Wasn't that always how things went with her?

"Stop. Please." She was squirming, arching, trying to figure out how to get away from him without moving her leg, trying to figure out how to get him inside her as quickly as possible. He was tearing her in half. "I don't want this."

"Your body's telling me diffcrently."

"It has no authority to speak for me." She had to stop this. "I need to leave. *Ow.*"

Leaving was not an option. The pain was worse that time.

"Lie still, Hannah. Lie still, and it won't hurt." He deepened the pressure of his lips through her panties, biting kisses that transferred sensation and warmth where she most wanted it.

"Derek…"

"Mmm?" He slid his hand between the soft tops of her thighs, tried gently to pry her good leg away from its injured counterpart. She resisted fiercely, fists clenched, eyes screwed shut, coping with the pain in her ankle and the deep pleasure of his mouth on her.

"Open for me."

"No."

He nudged again, then his finger followed the crotch of her panties and discovered her moisture, already soaking through the material. For the first time in her life she wished for fatter thighs so he wouldn't have access between them.

"Hannah, let me in." His mouth picked up its pace along with her breathing. He found the elastic side of her panties and slid under, managed to push a finger, slowly, inevitably inside her.

She whimpered, not daring to move, but needing to desperately, so turned on she was past the point of pretending she wasn't, insistent on not letting him have his way, at the same time acknowledging the battle was all but lost. He bit gently through the red satin and lace, then rubbed in a regular rhythm with his lips, pumped inside her with his finger, and she lost control, came in a burning, overwhelming wave that drew an unfamiliar animal sound from her throat and a familiar thought from her brain.

I'm falling for you.

No. No. *No!* What had she done?

The contractions subsided. Her breathing slowed. He kissed her in a lazy line up her stomach, between her breasts and on her mouth, warm sweet kisses that made her want to wrap her arms around his shoulders and give in as she had to her desire. But she didn't want desire from his kisses or his closeness, she wanted something more, and that, for once, kept her arms at her sides.

"Angry?" He looked down quizzically, but she could sense his triumph and wasn't sure whom she was more annoyed at, him or herself.

"Not angry."

"But not happy."

"I don't know what I am. Sated, anyway."

He grinned. "Um, yes."

"That was a dirty trick. Your second dirty trick, I'd like to point out."

"Mmm, thank you."

She couldn't help laughing. "You're proud."

"But not sated."

"Well, I'm injured, so you're just going to have to suffer."

"Hmm. I don't think so." He raised himself onto his knees, removed his T-shirt, pulled down his briefs. Just the sight of his broad chest and strong thighs was enough to turn her on again, but his erection, which had made her very, very happy a couple of times already during the night, turned her on even more. Anyone would have to admit it was a thing of beauty. Not overly long, but smooth, soft and thick, the kind that let a woman know in no uncertain terms a man was inside her. In spite of her recent Richter-scale orgasm, Hannah was becoming aroused again. Especially when he met her eyes in challenge, curled his fingers around his manly thing-o'-beauty and started a graceful and experienced rhythm.

Oh, oh, oh. Everything was sexy on him. In spite of herself, she reached to help, cupping and manipulating the soft sacs of his testicles, pleased at the sharp intake of breath and speeding of his fingers that showed she had power after all.

She could do more.

Her hand trailed down his thigh, then over to her own, up to the sides of her panties. She eased them gradually down, intending to tantalize him into the same helpless lust she'd experienced.

He watched hungrily, let out a low moan.

Playtime. She let her fingers wander through her pubic curls, then drew a zigzag line up to her breasts, lifted her bra, arching to slip it off over her head. His breath came out in a rush; he said her name as if the syllables had been wrenched from his throat.

She lay back, cupped her breasts, stroked them sensually, then licked her finger and painted first one, then the other nipple with the moisture, drew another finger again between her lips, farther, in and out as if she were going down on him. His rhythm accelerated, he drew his thighs farther apart. His color was high, his lips parted, he gazed at her with feral intensity.

Hannah loved this. She'd never dreamed watching a man pleasure himself would make her feel anything but left out. But here—*she* was so clearly fueling his desire. And he was so clearly losing his mind.

Her fingers left her mouth, painted a trail down her stomach to her lower abdomen, parting her soft hair, then she slid them farther, watching his face as she slowly spread the lips of her sex open to him.

His reaction was immediate, a low hoarse sound, and the warm raining of his climax on her stomach and breasts, again and again, while his eyes locked on to hers. She felt as if the world had dwindled to this man and the intense chemistry between them.

Wasn't this supposed to feel like some kind of victory?

It didn't.

"Hannah." He rubbed his fingers through his hair, making it stand in a thick tangled mess, which made him look rumpled and sexy, and even more masculine.

A dangerous possessive sweetness spread through her heart. Oh, no. First Jack. Now Derek? She was hopeless. *Mansion Captive Becomes Prisoner of Love.*

He pulled a couple of tissues from the box on the nightstand—camouflaged by a black lacquered cover showing a flaming red dragon—and cleaned her up tenderly, then disappeared into the bathroom, returned with a warm damp washcloth and repeated the action, lingering over her breasts.

She stirred on the bed—carefully so she wouldn't hurt her ankle. The warm cloth followed by the cool air was quite, er, stimulating. So, it seemed, was anything this man did to her.

"Now." He tossed the washcloth into a wicker hamper with perfect aim and crossed his arms over his chest. "What are we going to do with you today?"

She knew what she wanted to say. But the depth of her

feeling was making her panic a little. Leaving was a good idea. Whoever came to tow poor Matilda could give her a ride home. She could ask Daphne to help if she needed anything before she made it to a doctor.

A gust of wind shook the house; ice tinkled against the windows. The thought of leaving, of the trip back in the storm, of her empty apartment, made her feel cold and lonely already. Nothing wrong with her place, it was just so…not-a-mansion-with-a-sexy-man-in-it.

She twisted her lip. Mansion? What about her refusal to worship any and all things overpriced or overwrought? Sexy man? Even though she'd given in to lust and helped generate his, she couldn't forget what he'd done to get her here.

Argh! This was all too complicated and confusing to sort out immediately and nearly impossible to do with his deep eyes and warm smile and hot bod fogging her brain.

"I should call Triple A."

"Okay." To her disappointment, he crossed to his massive dark wooden bureau without a fight and extracted a phone from one of the small top drawers.

"I wasn't kidding about not having a landline in this house." He held the cell out, too far away for her to reach it, but close enough to see that it was a BlackBerry, exactly the same model as hers. She made no move to try to grab it. "I want to make you an offer."

"Okay."

"First, I am sorry for thinking my original plan for you tonight was a good idea."

She shrugged. "I admit, it was a pretty good joke. Or it would have been…"

"If we hadn't gone animal at the sight of each other."

"Yeah, that." She couldn't stop herself from grinning.

"I'm sorry I made love to you the first time without being

clearer about who I am and what you were here for. But I'm not sorry we made love."

Hannah nodded, wishing she could sit up; lying there felt too vulnerable. She wanted desperately to accept and forget, but she couldn't decide if accepting his apology—because it really was an apology this time—would make her generous and wise, or once again a man-doormat.

"I hope you'll forgive me." His eyes were dark, sincere— he was asking, not begging. He still retained that proud quality she admired so much, yet she also got the feeling her forgiveness mattered to him. She couldn't resist that. None of it.

"You had me at *first*."

"Thank you." He chuckled, his expression warm and relieved. "Now I want to—"

"Wait." She owed him, too. Admitting the truth would strip her of her last defense, but she couldn't leave the lie out there. "I'm sorry I let you think I slept with 'Jack' only for a story. That wasn't true. I'm not like that. As soon as things, uh, heated up, I knew I wouldn't write the article. I should have admitted it right away, but I was angry. And too…proud, I guess."

"Thank you."

She had to turn away from his pleasure and the thrilling feeling that they'd crossed a line and moved closer to something wonderful. "So what's the offer?"

"Spend the day with me here. We'll start over, without the manipulation and lies, and enjoy what's left of New Year's Day together. There's plenty of food, and the roads are a mess." He tossed the phone so it lay within her reach. "If you want to, you can call and leave now. This time I won't try to stop you."

Hannah gazed at the familiar phone. So. She was free to

go. And she was free to stay. It meant a lot that he'd wanted to clear the air and that now he was letting her choose. No manipulation, no guilt trip.

She'd definitely been dating the wrong type of guy…not that this counted as dating, really. And she'd just ignore the immediate pang of longing and loss at that thought. Because that deep hunger for more of him should be enough to panic her into leaving all by itself.

Though Derek wouldn't ask her to stay unless he wanted her here, and well, it was possible for men to fall in love, too. Or so she'd heard.

She picked up the phone, registered the instant of naked disappointment on Derek's face before he dressed it with impartiality. She smiled and handed the cell back to him.

"I'd love to stay. Thank you." The flash of relief and his wide grin went straight to her heart, making her so happy she refused to listen to the voice warning her of inevitable heartbreak ahead. Again.

Sometimes she thought being smart about love was the one lesson she was doomed never to learn.

7

"WAIT." HANNAH RETRACTED her arm just before Derek took back his cell phone. "I told my father I'd call him today, is that okay? He'll worry if I don't."

"Whew." He grinned, then lunged forward unexpectedly and kissed her. "I thought you wanted the phone because you'd changed your mind about staying. Absolutely call Dad. I'll be back in a few minutes."

"Okay. Thanks."

His gloriously naked body strolled out of the bedroom into the hall. Hannah clutched his phone in her fingers, little tweety-birds chirp-chirping around her head while heart-shaped fireworks exploded in the sky…and every other cliché she could think of.

Clearly she lacked a grip on reality, if not on herself. Calling Dad was a good idea for lots of reasons. Not the least of which was that she needed to remind herself that the rest of the real world and the rest of her real life still existed out there, minus truffles and pâté and a dozen bedrooms, and that whether or not she and Derek saw each other again, she'd be returning to that reality after this fantasy New Year was over.

Bummer.

She dialed hurriedly. "Dad, hi, Happy New Year."

"Hannah?" His slow voice rose uncertainly. "I didn't recognize the number. Almost didn't answer."

"I…can't get to my phone, so I'm using a friend's."

"Ah, okay."

For once she appreciated that her dad wasn't, nor had he ever been as far as she remembered, curious about her life. Anyone else she knew would jump all over the bizarre circumstance of Hannah being separated from her beloved phone. "How's Mom doing today?"

"Good. She had Cream of Wheat for breakfast. Ate it herself."

"Terrific. That is wonderful. Can I talk to her?"

"Sure." He cleared his throat, and she heard him telling her mom about the call, then extended fumbling as the receiver was handed over.

"Hannah, dear, Happy New Year."

"Same to you, Mom." Hannah's words caught in her clenched throat. She hated hearing her mother sounding so old and weak when she wasn't the former and shouldn't be the latter.

"How was the big-money party last night?"

"Big and monied. You would have hated it on both counts. I hear you're eating on your own. Congratulations."

Her mother snorted. "Yes, I'm a big girl now. Eating all by myself."

Hannah laughed, though the amusement was bittersweet. For her mother to finally confront and control her alcoholism, make it through law school, get a decent job in a prestigious firm, finally get a leg up on the family's debts, and then be reduced to pride in spooning Cream of Wheat into her own mouth…

"You'll be going off to kindergarten before you know it."

"Big fun ahead, I'll tell you. In the meantime, Susie and your father are taking good care of me."

"That's great, Mom. Good for Dad. Though I know you'd do the same for him."

"I would, yes. But caretaking doesn't come naturally to most men." She paused for a slow breath. "You don't think about that when you're choosing a partner. You think you'll be young and healthy forever."

Hannah squeezed her eyes shut. Her mother's situation was so desperately unfair. "You'll keep getting better, Mom."

"That's what they say."

"Look how far you've come already."

"Yes." She sighed. "I guess I'm saying forget sex appeal when you choose a man, Hannah. It's so unimportant in the long run. Find someone who will feed you when you can't do it yourself."

Hannah instantly flashed back to the soft, sensual feel of the raspberry painted over her lips, the crumbly rough sensation of cookie. Mmm…

Oops. Not what Mom had in mind.

Another flashback to Derek carrying her into the bedroom, bringing her tea…

No. *No.* She had to stop imagining herself halfway down the aisle in her bridal white when she'd only just met someone. Worse than that, after what her mother said, with only a little effort she could imagine her and Derek fifty years from now, drinking Metamucil out of matching glasses. "I'll remember that, Mom. On my very next date I'll hand the guy a bowl of Cream of Wheat and a spoon and see how he does."

Her mom gave a rusty giggle, music to Hannah's ears. "Let me know how that works for you."

"Happy New Year, Mom. Say 'hi' to Nurse Susie."

"I will. I don't know how we'd have managed without her. You know how important work is to your father."

"Yes." Hannah managed to keep the irony out of her voice. Now that he could actually hold down a job, it was. "I do. Give him a kiss from me and sending love to you, too."

"I wish you only the best and most wonderful things this year, Hannah."

"You, too, Mom. By next New Year's Day you'll be back to taking on the legal world by storm."

"That would be very nice." She sighed again. "Goodbye, sweetie. We'll talk soon."

Hannah hung up, feeling the combination joy-sadness that wrestled in her chest these days after talking to her mom. Joy that she was alive and still her old self and sadness at the long road she still had to travel. Why couldn't the world operate perfectly all the time?

Okay, maybe that would be boring. Certainly it was unlikely. At least the troubles should be distributed more fairly. Miracle rescues aside, her parents had been through enough.

She closed the phone, then thought about calling Daphne. Her friend would have called by now and might worry when Hannah didn't return her call. Plus, Hannah wanted to check and see what was new with her boyfriend, Paul. He had been bartending when they'd met three years earlier and now worked in a bank, resisting Daphne's plan that he attend law school. Hannah wondered again if he was just rebelling against her…um, enthusiasm for ordering his life. She meant well, wanted him to fulfill his potential and all that, but…he was a grown man. All the same, Hannah would hate to see anything go wrong after three years together. Three years. Astronomically longer than any of Hannah's relationships had lasted. Maybe in the process of asking about Paul, Hannah could hint at where she was and what she was up to right now. About time she had some truly promising news where men were concerned.

An odd thump and a muttered curse made her glance toward the bedroom door. There was Derek triumphantly pushing a wheelchair. So much for Daphne. Hannah would call when she got home. At least her parents knew she was safe.

"I'd forgotten we had this chair until you needed it. Mom

used it toward the end. I'd much rather see you in it on the way to recovery."

"Derek…" His words had jolted her. "I'm sorry about your mom. When did she die?"

"Over ten years ago, and thanks." He spoke abruptly, strode over to the opposite side of the bed and dragged on the sweats and T-shirt he'd been wearing before her delicious seduction. Evidently now that he was no longer Jack Brattle, he still didn't want to share his past. Hannah tried not to feel rejected, while reminding herself wryly, again, that they weren't quite engaged yet. He didn't owe her his secrets.

But she still wanted to know them.

"Now." He returned to the wheelchair and pushed it up to the bed. "Your throne awaits. I thought you might like a guided tour of the house."

"I'd love it." She reluctantly bit off further questions—for now—and eased herself to sitting against his fabulous down pillows, clutching the comforter over her chest. Maybe he'd confide in her later. She craved more of that intimacy, to indulge more of her fantasy that he hadn't told many people the things he was telling her.

Hannah, Hannah. Always looking for signs she meant more to men than she did.

"Maybe I could borrow some clothes? Unless pushing naked women in wheelchairs is a thing for you."

He laughed and she was ridiculously happy to have put cheer back on his face.

"Fun for me, chilly for you." He crossed to his bureau and dug around in a drawer. "I looked outside. The wind has diminished, but the snow is coming down pretty hard. It's beautiful, actually. I'll show you once you're dressed."

"Just leave out the view that includes my poor car. I can't handle the carnage."

"She's got a nice blanket over her, too."

"And a tree."

"Yeah. You know, I'm not sure Triple A does trees." He shot her a mischievous look over his shoulder. "You might have to stay quite a while."

"Oh, that would be horrible." She shuddered exaggeratedly, trying her best not to grin. "With all that incredible food to finish and this big house to explore and you to…ahem, explore, too."

He opened his arms wide. "Explore me, baby."

Like she needed any more encouragement? "Okay. What do you do besides work for *The Herald*? Do you get to travel a lot? Stay in one place?"

Derek scowled. "I thought you meant ex-*plo-o-ore*. Not interrogate."

"We did ex-*plo-o-ore*. Now we interrogate."

"My luck." He rolled his eyes and tossed her a pair of sweatpants and a T-shirt like the ones he had on. "My job is to manage a family business that came to me after my parents died."

She winced. "Your dad is gone, too?"

"Yes." His face became robotic again. "He died shortly before my mom."

"Oh, no." She couldn't stand it. Ten years ago. He must have been barely out of college, if that. All that on his shoulders so young. *Man Who Has Everything Deprived of Youth.*

"But, yes, I travel. Some for pleasure as well as business. I try to mix the two whenever possible."

"I would, too, if I could." She pulled the sweatpants over her good leg, grimacing when she had to lift her bad one. In three steps he was there, helping, making her gooey inside. Making her try not to think any more about what her mother had said about snapping up caretaking men.

Travel. They were talking about travel. And she'd been back to envying his current lifestyle and all the opportunities that went with money. Sadly, no one had ever offered her all-expense-paid trips to Paris. Which they really should. "Where do you go next?"

"China. Next month." He gave her a teasing glance. "Wanna come?"

"Ooh, again?"

"I meant to China."

She rolled her eyes to douse the hot thrill and took refuge for a few seconds under the T-shirt she dragged over her head. *He was kidding, Hannah.* "Sure! I'll just cash in my checking account and let my boss know. He'll be fine."

"It's settled."

"I can do a piece on nail salons and communism and call it a business trip."

"Nail salons…"

"My boss." She lifted her hand and let it thwack his mattress on the way down. "He won't give me anything that isn't girlie. My next assignment is on women who've had boob jobs."

"Now that's a weighty topic."

She snorted. "One might say meaty."

"Ponderous."

"*Pen*dulous."

"One of the breast ideas I've heard in…I don't know."

"Recent mammary?" She mimed a quick drum-cymbal *ba-da-ba* beat. "I was thinking the lovely Dee-Dee would be a perfect subject."

"Mmm, yes."

"Mmm?" She turned on him witheringly. "Don't tell me you and she…"

"Never. I swear." He leaned forward, hands raised in

Boy Scout trust-me salute, until his mouth was an inch from hers. "Jealous?"

"No." She spoke too loudly, which plainly meant yes. All-over green with it. Though she felt a bit better when he kissed her. Okay, no, a lot better.

"You have less than no reason to be. Let's get you ready to roll." He helped her on with a much-too-big pair of thick gray cotton socks. "And I want to hear more about what you want to write. Though I can't imagine anything more satisfying than breasts."

She let him know with her eyes exactly what she thought of that comment. "Obviously I want to write about more substantive things."

He paused, leaving his hand on her good ankle, good humor dissolving into a frown aimed down at the loose floppy sock. "Like…Jack Brattle?"

"Oh. Well, yeah." She sighed wistfully. "That would have been a dream come true. After a scoop like that, I could have had the clout to write about… Well, never mind."

"About what?"

"About anything."

"Hey." He raised his eyebrows expectantly. "This is my interrogation. Answer the question."

"Yes, *sir*." She saluted, pleased he really wanted to know. "I found out this drug, Penzyne, used for treating depression, has shown promising results as a treatment for diabetes. However, it's ten times cheaper than the drugs sold now, and the company doesn't want to decrease their profit margin. Seems to me that's important information a lot of suffering people should know."

He put his hands on his hips, staring with a perplexed look on his face, until she started to feel as if she should tell a joke to break the tension. "It was…selfish of me to play the Highbrow trick, Hannah. I was thinking of the one-up-on-you score, not of what pulling Jack out from under you would represent to your life and career. Or how it would feel. I'm sorry."

Whoa. She had to look away from his sincerity. Instinct told her he didn't make apologies a habit, that this had been a rare and painful event. The fact that he'd done it for her…

Well, gee whiz, she should tell him her ring size and be done with it.

"Thank you, Derek. It's okay. The joke would have been great if it hadn't gotten…" She gestured aimlessly.

"Complicated."

"That's one way of putting it." Very complicated. More than he knew.

"You ready?"

"For anything." She let him lift her into the chair, though she probably could have managed on her own. But who could resist the chance to feel the power in those arms and shoulders and to be held, all too briefly this time, against that magnificent chest?

Clearly not her.

"Let's go." He turned her chair, then paused. She peeked back and caught him putting a couple of condoms into the pockets of his sweatpants.

"Excuse me, what kind of tour is this going to be?"

"I hope a really, really fun one."

She laughed as he maneuvered her out of the bedroom and pushed her down the hall. She was eager for the tour, not only because she was interested in finding out more about the house and exploring it leisurely, but also because this would be her first normal time with Derek, time when they weren't either feasting, flirting, fighting or—

That other *f* thing. Though maybe those condoms would come in handy…

"Now, this…" He stopped outside the first door on the left,

which gave onto an attractive masculine room done in royal-blue and hunter-green. "This bedroom is where my uncle Chris grew up. You can find dirty words and limericks carved on the inside of the closet door. He used to hide in there for hours."

"Wow. Go, Chris." She loved it. *Black Sheep in the Jackson Pasture.*

He rolled her farther down the hall and to the right, by another bedroom in muted crimson and powder-blue with pale pink sprigged wallpaper.

"This one belonged to my Aunt Sue. Knocked up at seventeen. My very conservative grandfather disinherited her. No one knows where she is now."

"Ouch. Poor girl." An even blacker sheep. Obviously Hannah had assumed people with so much money lived charmed lives. Ridiculous now she thought about it. Life happened to everyone. Though she still maintained the bad times would hurt less if you could pay for anything you needed.

"And this one." He pushed open the door to reveal an absolutely minuscule room, which meant it was practically the size of hers. Most likely meant to be a closet, it had a bed-sized mat on the floor, a set of bare metal shelves and a wooden bench. Period. "This was Uncle Frank's room. Weird kid. Grew up to be a weird adult."

"Why doesn't that surprise me?" She examined the unusual furnishings, wondering why they hadn't been changed. "Is anyone apple-pie normal in this family?"

"Nope," he said cheerfully.

"You, anyway."

"Don't be too sure."

"Which was your room?"

"Ahh." He pushed the chair down the hall and opened a large door to the left of the stairs.

Hannah gaped. "You have an *elevator* in your house?"

"What, not everyone does?"

She rolled her eyes and let him push her on. "Oh. Yeah. Um, I guess ours was always being fixed."

"See?" He grinned at her expression and rotated a lever on a dial set into the wall toward the number three. "My great-grandfather had terrible arthritis, so he had this installed. And look, it's coming in handy."

"True enough." She listened to the appealing rattle-clank of the ancient machinery and hoped it had been inspected fairly recently. "I guess money goes back generations in your family."

"You don't think I earned all this as a newspaper man?"

She snorted. "Trust me, that never occurred to me."

"Well, Hannah, the ugly truth is that the family has never lacked for cash. Great-great-grandfather made the fortune."

"In what?"

"Here we are." He slid back the gate and opened the door onto the third floor.

Hannah stared, openmouthed, trying to process what she was seeing. "Oh my gosh."

"Thought you'd like it."

She wasn't sure she had moved to *like*. She was still stuck on *flabbergasted*. "*This* was your *room?*"

"Yes."

Would she ever be able to take this in? Rooms opened one into another, so the effect was of one continuous space—make that an entire mansion floor of continuous space. To the left, a normal bedroom area, or rather a normal rich kid's bedroom area, in navy and white, with a beautiful sleigh bed, matching dresser and table, a multilevel desk and a smart navy and white rug covering the hardwood. Branching off from there, the "bedroom" left off, and the fantasy began.

A large central area directly off the elevator had a jukebox, soda and snack vending machines along one wall, and a glossy wooden dance floor, ready for action. In the next room she could see the corner of a Ping-Pong table and most of a small trampoline. After that, a mini-movie house with rows of theater-style seats and a popcorn maker. The place should be in Wikipedia to define *overindulged*.

But wait! There was more…

Derek rolled her forward past a wall of stereo equipment and floor-to-ceiling shelves of CDs; a room with a stage, a puppet theater and racks and boxes of costumes; a room with gymnastic equipment and mats, security harness dangling from a complicated track on the ceiling; a music room with piano, guitars, drums and karaoke machine. An elaborate setup in the next, with electric trains that ran around mountain and valley landscaping and several villages with assorted vehicles and tiny figures. A room with tables, easels, art supplies and a whole wall of board games. Finally a library with half-a-dozen long, four-tier bookcases bursting with books, a computer, a study carrel and chairs and table arranged around a fireplace.

She was exhausted just looking. Nothing prepared her to equate what she'd just seen with the words *my room*. And yet for all its splendor, it had an abandoned quality, as if it had spent too many years as a sad museum instead of the play space it should be.

"I spent a lot of time in this library." He parked her by the fireplace and crossed to one of the shelves, running his large strong hands over what were doubtless familiar titles. "I was kind of a nerd, I guess."

"You didn't have brothers or sisters?" She bet she already knew the answer. She was just trying to wrap her mind around one person having all this, when there were so many kids for whom any one piece would be a fantasy so far out of reach, they could dream about it for an entire childhood. Like her, about two decades ago. Heck, her now.

"Nope." He dropped into one of the armchairs and thoughtfully traced an ink stain on the upholstery, maybe remembering how it got there. "I'm sure it looks…extreme for one boy."

"Yuh." He had no idea. Her big-thrill toy was a set of chipped metal doll furniture that had been her grandmother's.

Derek sat back in the chair, watching her too closely, probably sensing her discomfort. Then he leaned forward, resting his elbows on his thighs, and her greedy body lost no time feeling the hum of sexual electricity at his nearness. "It's too much. I know. My parents…they thought if they gave me enough toys it wouldn't matter that they had no interest in being parents."

Hannah nodded. She knew what it felt like to have parents too distracted to parent. But…he had *this*. My God. "You must have had friends over constantly."

"Occasionally. I was a loner. And we didn't live here that often."

A loner. Surrounded by a kid paradise. And they didn't live there often? Why not? What did that mean? "So all this just sits here?"

"Yeah." Her question obviously puzzled him. "Why, you want to play with me?"

"I'm not really in shape for gymnastics at the moment."

"You managed fine downstairs." He grinned, and she blushed idiotically. "The truth is, I don't spend much time at this house, and I'm constantly busy with…" He tightened his lips. "Things that don't matter to me very much."

She couldn't understand that. "*I* know what that feels like. But with your money you'd have to be free to do whatever you want."

"You'd think so."

But…

The word stayed unspoken. Obviously the little people like her didn't understand his world. She wouldn't pretend to.

"I'm selling the house."

Hannah jerked her head back to him, instantly dismayed. She didn't expect that. At all. The revelations about his great-grandfather, his batty uncles and wayward aunt had made her feel the house was steeped in Jackson tradition and always would be.

"You're moving."

"We're closing our Philadelphia office, so I—"

"Where are you moving to?" How could he? She'd just found him. And he was *leaving?* The dating gods had gotten her once again. What a joke. Ha ha ha.

"I don't really live anywhere, Hannah. My parents were restless. When the family troubles hit, they found moving around honored their privacy more than staying in one place. And they wanted this original family house protected as much as possible from the media. I was mostly alone here, in the charge of the property caretakers." He glanced around moodily. "I guess I inherited Mom and Dad's taste for roaming."

But…he'd still be visiting, wouldn't he? "Why sell?"

"Now the office is closing I have no reason to return."

All her strength was needed not to look as if she'd been sucker punched. "Well, but…it's your home."

"I don't have great memories of my childhood. My parents and I weren't exactly best friends."

"I didn't have that, either."

He looked surprised. "You seem so close to them."

"Uh…" Her turn to look surprised. How would he know? "I do?"

"After your mom's stroke and your dad's orchestra nearly going under…you sounded deeply concerned."

"How did you…" She stared at him, mind spinning furiously. The newspaper world was small, but not that small. How could—

Her mental lightbulb switched on. "You read my blog."

He nodded. "Frequently over the past year."

"Really." She was astonished…then pleased. Then *thrilled*. If he'd read her blog, that meant—

"I enjoy it a lot. Another reason I wanted to meet you." He gave a crooked smile. "Though I went about it in a pretty underhanded way."

"You should have shown up at *The Sentinel* and jumped me."

"I wish I had."

She laughed automatically, her mind processing the new information, trying in her typical way to make it point toward something that would bring them together. He'd been reading her blog. He wanted to meet her. He hadn't just been out to trick her, then been overcome by lust on the spur of the moment. He'd actually admired, liked, been curious about her before tonight—or, well, make that yesterday night.

Steady, Hannah. That didn't mean he'd fallen for her or that he was going to. But…it sure beat unreasoning lust on sight. And with the way he'd looked at her, handled her as if she was the most precious gift he'd ever been given… *Hope Springs Eternal in Oft-Trampled Heart. "I Can't Help Myself," Woman Says.*

"I'm…glad things are better for your mom and dad." He cleared his throat, looking self-conscious.

"Thanks. It was miraculous that they got help when they needed it."

"Life is messed up no matter what your circumstances." He got to his feet, but she pushed the wheelchair back before he could walk past her.

"Hold on, we need to change that attitude."

Derek's eyebrows rose. "We do?"

"Oh." She felt herself blushing. *Nice going, Hannah.* Every man's worst nightmare: a woman who'd try to change him. She hadn't really meant it that way. She just…aw, hell, she just wanted him to be happy. "No, I mean—"

"I know what you mean, Hannah." He bent and kissed her, causing electric crackles that soothed to sweetness when he stroked her hair back from her face. "I'm afraid my problems go deeper than the time we'll have together to solve them."

Ouch. She hadn't wanted to hear before, but there it was. Of course. They'd just met, had a lovely promising beginning and, oh, look, here came The End. Story of Hannah's life. Not for her the series of normal pleasant dates everyone else expected and got, followed by a natural commitment to an exclusive relationship and an investment in hope for a future together.

No. She dove straight in—to arms, to bed, to love, lured by the promise of The One, Her Soul Mate. And always she found out she was wrong.

But this was worse. Because beyond the usual attraction, and I-can't-wait sexual drive, she saw how he needed her and how he could make her happy. And she saw how their differences could complement and teach each other, instead of driving them apart. Enough there to be worth exploring. More than enough.

He'd said he had no reason to return. But…

Sparks of determination lit a corner of her gloom. It was a long shot. A very long one. Maybe, though, over the next hours, days, or weeks, whatever time they still had together, she could convince Derek Jackson he had the very best reason of all.

Her.

8

DEREK ROLLED HANNAH BACK into the elevator, closed the gates and turned the control lever to the first floor. Seeing his childhood room through her eyes had been an educational experience. He was so used to the awed and envious reactions of the few friends he'd shown it to—mostly kids in grade school—that he was unprepared for how an adult stranger would judge it. And him.

So much of his childhood he'd spent alone that he felt he'd been anything but spoiled. Sure, he had a lot of toys. A lot of cool stuff. But the toys his parents bought never came close to giving him what he needed from them.

Now, however, he saw the room as something new. A waste, for one. Her disapproval had made him want to redeem himself. Ha! Since when did other people's opinions of him count? His parents had disdain for nearly everyone. And here he was, the apple close to a tree he'd wanted to chop down for as long as he could remember.

The elevator stopped. He pulled the gate, pushed open the door and wheeled Hannah through, his enthusiasm for the tour dampened. She wouldn't enjoy the lavish ballroom, the formal dining room, the pool, or indoor tennis court, either. Why had he thought they'd impress her? Because they did most people? He should have figured out by now that Hannah was anything but "most people."

"Where next, Captain?"

However… "Would you like to see the greenhouse?"

"I'd love to. Unless it's full of snow and icy steps."

"Neither. I promise." He guided her down the hall past the kitchen, the second parlor and to the left to bring them to the back of the house. Ahead, the door to the greenhouse promised warmth and greenery. This he knew she'd like.

"Here we are." He opened the door and rolled her in, felt a wave of satisfaction when she gave an exclamation that showed, yes, she thought this, at least, was money well-spent. He had to agree.

Rita handled the household duties, and Ray, a green-thumbed genius workaholic, tackled the handyman jobs and the grounds. The greenhouse was and always had been his pride and joy. Derek's mother had loved flowers, especially orchids and roses, and had given him carte blanche in select-ing and maintaining whatever he thought would please her. Which was too often whatever she thought other people wouldn't have and would envy.

"Who takes care of all this?" Hannah breathed in the humidity and floral scents rapturously. "I'd spend my whole day here if I were you."

"You like to garden?"

"I'm sure I would if I had one. I tried to grow a few flowers indoors, but I don't get enough light in my apartment, and they all died eventually. I tried again outdoors, but someone stole the pots off the fire escape, and that was that."

He frowned, not liking the idea of her cooped up in a tiny dark home. Nor did he like the idea of her being around thieves, even just plant thieves. "Ray takes care of the green-house. He and Rita manage the estate."

"What will they do when you move?"

He smiled wryly. Did she think he'd kick lifelong staff—

and friends—out into the cold when he no longer had use for them? He'd be disturbed by her accepting the cliché of cold-hearted wealth, except too often his family embodied it.

"They were provided for in my parents' wills. They're planning to retire to Oregon." He gestured to the snow, still coming down hard. "Ray wants a longer growing season."

"Don't blame him."

He pushed her forward amid the greenery, seedlings in pots on small tables of varying heights and areas landscaped by Ray's gifted eye for color, texture and composition. Derek found himself talking about the plants, pointing out the rare ones, showing her how Ray had molded and tended others, how he'd grouped them according to countries and regions of origin. He was surprised how much he remembered from those days when he'd tagged along behind Ray as he made his rounds, watering, pruning, sensing what each plant needed in a way Derek could never hope to intuit.

"Oh, roses." Hannah clapped her hands. They'd stopped at his mother's favorite spot, a small stone bench surrounded by various fragrant and colorful species. "This must be where you got the one for my tray. They're exquisite. I could spend the next several hours just smelling them."

"And so you shall." He strode to the back wall of the green-house, to the neatly organized storage area that held Ray's tools, and retrieved the pruning shears, filled an etched crystal vase with tepid water to immerse the stems in. The way he felt right now—like Christmas morning did to children—he wouldn't rest until he'd cut every rose in the whole place and presented them to her. Somehow making her happy had become the same thing as making himself happy.

His hand stilled on the vase handle. Unless he was wrong he was well on his way to falling unexpectedly and irration-ally in love with Hannah. He'd probably been halfway there when he'd arranged to lure her to the estate in the first place. His obsession with her blog and columns wasn't only due to his admiration for her writing skills and her intimate knowledge and love of the city. He hadn't hired a nurse for her mother and bailed out her father's orchestra because he was noble. Something about her had inspired him, attracted him, gotten to him deeply from the very start, had him acting in ways he'd never acted before. New acts, new thoughts, new feelings…new Derek.

Even the thought of the word *love* made him what another man might consider giddy but on him felt finally and completely alive. Maybe Hannah was sent by a guardian angel to kick his lame ass back into the land of the living.

Fanciful, but that's the kind of mood he was in, very uncharacteristic. Too many happenings during this night had been magical for it to seem like a normal series of events. Though there was one other possible explanation, which would probably never have occurred to his old self. Maybe *he'd* been sent by *her* guardian angel, to help make her life into more of what it should be. To help her family, yes, but money wasn't the only thing she needed. He had the means to provide exactly what she wanted, to take her where she wanted to be.

He could get her the interview with Jack Brattle.

Back at her side, he perused the roses, hardly seeing them. It would be tough to have Jack's story out there for the world to read, when Mr. Brattle had kept himself and his life so private for so long. Derek wasn't sure he'd be willing to make that sacrifice, even for a journalist as worthy as Hannah.

"Derek?"

He blinked and realized he'd gone frozen staring at the roses with shears raised in his hand, probably looking as if he were posing for a horror movie poster. "Sorry. What colors do you like?"

"I'd hate for you to cut them." She shook her head at the array of bushes, her eyes glowing with wistful pleasure. "They're so beautiful here."

"They'll be more beautiful in your home, with you." He didn't like thinking of her going back there. He didn't like thinking of her going anywhere. Maybe it could snow for the rest of her life.

Safety catch released, pruners ready, he started cutting, laying the blooms in her lap as he went. White, burgundy, pink in two shades, yellow, lavender, red, peach—

"Derek, stop." Her protest was made while laughing. "There won't be any left."

He knelt in front of her, picked up a rose, holding her gaze so she'd really listen and really understand each one was selected for her. "Pink for grace."

Her laughter stilled. She watched him put the stem into the vase of warm water, suddenly shy.

"White…for youthfulness and humility."

"Hmph." Her show of petulance didn't completely hide her pleasure. "I notice you didn't say purity or innocence."

"*And*—" he glared in mock reproach "—white also stands for silence."

A giggle transformed her faux pout. "Shutting up. Go on."

"Burgundy." He drew the velvet bud down her face. "For unconscious beauty."

A blush started where the rose had traveled, as if it had transferred its beautiful color to her cheek.

"Peach for sincerity. Pale pink for joy." He arranged the blooms carefully beside the others in the vase and selected the next, praying she didn't think he was a total sap. He wasn't so sure he wasn't one. Her fault entirely.

"Yellow…" He smiled into her eyes. "For the promise of a new beginning."

Her breath went in; her gaze dropped to her hands. He was pretty sure she didn't think he was a sap.

"Red for courage and passion." His voice had lowered, become thicker. He set the red rose in the vase, almost completing the riot of color he wanted. One more.

"Lavender." Nearly whispering now, he rested the perfect bloom against her perfect lips. "Lavender for love at first sight."

She didn't move, didn't even raise her eyes. He held his breath. If she laughed or worse, withdrew politely, he'd want to lock his life away again, forever.

Then a tear slid slowly down her left cheek, and his heart melted. He dropped the flower in her lap, took her shoulders and kissed her with everything he felt in his heart.

She responded tentatively, then her arms crept around his shoulders, and her mouth softened, opened, her tongue swept his, and passion erupted. He drew back, ran his hands down her sides, drawing his thumbs deliberately over her breasts. Her breath caught; her body arched into his touch. At her hips he stopped, eased her to the front edge of the wheelchair seat.

"Will it hurt if I lift you?"

"Tour's over?" She blinked in innocent mischief.

"No, we're just getting to the climax."

She laughed, drew his head down as if for a kiss, then surprised him by painting his lips, slowly and sensually with her tongue. His cock hardened further. He lifted her as gently as he could, heard her quick inhale signifying pain.

"I'm sorry."

"I'm fine." She wrapped her arms around his neck, wrapped her good leg around his back. He walked slowly, careful not to bang her foot, and settled her onto Ray's potting table, kept meticulously clean as usual.

Hmm. He'd never thought about the table being the ideal height for sex, but now he'd never see it any other way.

"Derek."

"Yes." He stepped between her legs, moved her thick hair to one side and tasted the soft pale skin of her neck.

"Are you…did you mean…" Her voice trembled. "The lavender rose…"

He kept her face next to his, sure vulnerability would overwhelm him if he met her eyes. "Did you feel it?"

"Yes." She kissed his throat, his chin, finally hovered a fraction of an inch from his mouth. "I did."

He moved that fraction of an inch and met her lips again, felt his brain turn to pudding. Nothing he'd experienced with a woman had ever approached this tornado of want and need and fear and joy.

Being a guy, however, he knew what he wanted next, how to show her what he felt without having to resort to more words or more flowers. And frankly, the sight of her breasts against the material of his T-shirt was liquifying his pudding-brains further.

She was attractive, intelligent, talented, he respected her, yes—but, oh man, she was also one of the hottest women he'd ever met.

The T-shirt had to go first. It surrendered easily as he pulled it up and over her head, leaving her breasts bare, open to him, for him. He palmed them greedily, taking one, then the other into his mouth, tuning in to her moans and gasps of pleasure.

The snow might end—it was slowing already—she might leave the house, but she wasn't leaving his life. Not any time soon. Not until they both found a damn good reason they wouldn't suit—or until one of them died of old age.

Her hands tugged at his shirt, and he obliged her by taking it off, letting out moans of his own as her teeth and lips closed over his nipple and her hands slid down into his sweats, cupping his buttocks, bringing his erection closer to where it wanted to be.

Their kisses turned hot, eager, tinged with desperation. He loved her. He wanted her. He needed to be inside her so badly he was ready to scream.

She swayed side to side, edging her sweatpants over her hips, letting them fall. He knelt and eased the elastic cuffs over the ridiculously large socks he'd loaned her—a look he'd find incredibly sexy from now on—kissed his way up her bare smooth legs, pausing to bury his face between them, to arouse her, and to sate his need to taste. But this wasn't how he wanted her to come. He wanted her to come while they were face-to-face, so he could experience her climax with her, make sure she knew he was the one bringing her the ecstasy.

He stood, dug a condom out of the pocket of his sweats before he pushed them down around his ankles. He'd take it slow, stimulate her carefully to make up for the lack of foreplay, but he wanted and needed that more intimate connection now.

The condom went on swiftly. He stood watching her for a few long seconds, memorizing her face as if this was the last time they'd be together. He knew it wasn't. But he wanted to remember this moment forever, the first time he'd made love to a woman he cared for more than anything else he'd ever cared for. His life felt new, and he intended Hannah to be part of it.

All this in less than twenty-four hours.

"Hi." He grinned at her, pretty sure he hadn't felt this happy in…ever.

"Hi." The way her face glowed made him dare to think she felt the same way. Was there anything better than this?

Yes.

He moved close, caught her upper lip, then her lower between his, leisurely biting kisses that made her whimper. "Something you want?"

"You."

He put his forehead against hers, stroked her cheek. "You've got me, Hannah."

"I want nothing less." Her fingers traveled through his hair, down his back; she smiled suggestively. "But I also want something more."

"It's yours." He guided his erection against her, concentrating on every sensation, then pushed deeper with each gentle thrust. She was tight—he hadn't spent enough time. "Am I hurting you?"

"Mmm, no. No." She wrapped her arms around his back, urged him on.

He pulled back, moved forward slightly farther, pulled back and did it again, making sure he wasn't forcing, making sure his erection glided gently where it belonged, inch by slow inch.

One final pull back, another long thrust that made her groan in pleasure, and he was in to the hilt and could relax and start his rhythm. In and out. The scents of the greenhouse surrounded them; humidity made sweat dew their bodies. In and out. In and out. Outside them, everything was cold and white and severe; around them only green and warmth and life; between them heat and passion.

In and out, he made love to her, catching her chin sometimes to gaze into her eyes, seeing his feelings and his arousal reflected there. In and out, hands spreading her legs wider, leaning back so they could both look down and watch the beauty of what they were doing.

In and out, thumb to her clitoris, bringing her to the brink then letting her down again.

In and out. Nothing in his life had ever been as precious as this moment, the two of them together, stranded in the cocoon of a summer paradise.

This was the one thing he had never been able to find. The

one thing his money couldn't buy. The one thing he'd been hungering for, the thing that had drawn him to Hannah, and the reason he'd pursued her. Her vitality. Her joy. A chance to relive his lost youth as he approached the middle of his life.

In and out. He gathered her closer, murmured words into her hair, sweet tender words he wouldn't have thought himself capable of. Always in and out, stroking her, and with the movement stroking himself as nature intended.

"Derek?"

"Yes." He drew light circular designs down her back.

"I…don't— I've never…" She made a sound of frustration. "I don't know how to say this."

"You don't have to say anything."

"It's…this is so amazing," she whispered. "Don't move away. Don't leave."

He wanted to say he wouldn't. He wanted to reassure her, but in the middle of this overwhelming sensual and emotional experience, wasn't a good time to rethink a major life decision.

"Hannah…"

"It's okay. You don't have to answer. I… It was the only way I could think of to tell you how this feels."

He only had one way to respond. He kissed her, over and over, accelerating his rhythm until he started breathing in short bursts. He felt his pleasure rising to where it would soon be out of hand.

Hannah. He drew his body back just far enough to slip a finger between them. In less than a minute he had her slippery and writhing around his cock.

"Oh." She gasped; her nails dug into his shoulders. Her body flushed, and he knew she was close. *"Oh."*

He took his finger away, dug his hands under her beautiful firm hips and plunged harder. He felt her coming a second before he lost his own control.

Hannah.

He stayed inside her for a long time, holding her, not wanting to break the connection either physically or emotionally, not wanting to return to reality, to the tough and complicated decisions ahead, half-afraid that once the spell of her presence was removed, the decisions would be made for him, like most of the decisions in his life. That when given the chance to ditch his past and start out new, the tentacles of habit and duty would clutch at him, and he'd be unable to break free.

Now, though, wasn't the time to think about that. Now was the time to think about Hannah's soft skin and eager lips, her beautiful body and her gift for bringing happiness, the dozens of ways he wanted to bring happiness back to her.

Like giving her Jack Brattle.

He opened his mouth to offer the interview…and couldn't. Not now. Not yet. In a moment like this, he didn't want to introduce a man who had something Derek Jackson couldn't give her. Not for the first time, and only for a few useless bitter seconds, he hated Jack Brattle and everything he stood for.

Because giving Jack to Hannah meant losing part of himself.

9

THERE WAS NO DOUBT NOW. None. Hannah was in love. Again. Only more. As far as she was concerned all the other men had been warm-ups, appetizers, *amuse-bouches*. With Derek she felt ten times the passion, ten times the respect, ten times the enjoyment, ten times the surety.

He was The One. *Woman Finds True Love in Hothouse Sexfest.*

"Going up." He pushed her wheelchair onto the elevator and turned the control lever to take her back upstairs.

Yes, she knew she thought one or two other guys might have been The One before him, but, no, really, that had only been briefly, say after two dates and sex once or maybe twice. She and Derek had been together all night and nearly an entire day, which counted as three or four dates at least, and they'd had sex many times. Yes? Yes. See?

Maybe under twenty-four hours seemed too quick, even for her, but Derek was quality over quantity. Besides, everyone said you just knew when you met the right man, and she did. *This* time for real.

Really.

Not only that, but he felt the same way. He must. Because he'd given her the lavender rose and whispered, "Love at first sight." For once she wasn't the only one struck by an instant thunderbolt. For once Eros had aimed arrows at the man, as well. Took him long enough. Little bastard.

But then, she shouldn't be too hard on him. Maybe the demigod had a plan all along. To drag her through the dating dregs so that when she met Derek she'd be sure he was right, having had so many wrong experiences, and so that he'd be more than worth the wait.

"Second floor. Everybody out." He opened the gate and door and wheeled her into the hall.

Bliss! Perfection!

Well, near-perfection. When she stopped to think about it, the whole "I'm Jack Brattle" deception still stung, but not like a thorn, more like a grain of sand she'd turn into a pearl. And of course, in her typical fashion she was coping by trying not to think about it. Denial could be a very good and useful friend. Besides, that incident had happened wa-a-ay back then. Yesterday. Before she and Derek had started to trust each other, before they'd gotten this close.

Hannah blew out a breath that made her bangs sail outward. All that sounded so lovely and felt so right and so true. So why were her inner demons starting a cynical chant in her head?

She fought to shut them out. No, she wasn't just being stupid again. This time she wasn't. This time…

Well…she trusted this man more than she trusted herself.

"Now arriving. Bedroom on track four."

In the greenhouse after they'd made love in every sense of the phrase, she'd leaned against him for a long time, feeling his heart thumping under her cheek, his arms holding her securely, breathing in the wonderful fragrances around them. Oh la la, could someone please invent a moment-preserver? Because that particular moment didn't deserve to happen once and be lost forever.

Hannah had wanted time to stop, didn't want anything about her life or their relationship—and oh, how sweet to use that word without fear—to get more complicated or less beautiful than it was right then.

Silly, she knew, unreal for sure, because no relationship could grow and bloom without its share of troubles, but that was what she'd wanted. Minutes had ticked by with neither of them moving. Finally, a load of snow had rumbled off the roof and thudded onto the yard, startling them both, breaking the spell, leading them to smiles, kisses and, since they'd both agreed to shower before dinner, up here to the—

"Bathroom. Last stop."

Oh my lord.

By now she would have been shocked and probably disappointed if his bathroom—or what had been his parents' bathroom—was anything but amazing. The room was enormous of course, tiled in elegant gray and cream. Rich mahogany cabinets. Muted wallpaper with a tiny gray pattern. Cream towels about twice the size and thickness of hers, hanging on what looked like an electric warming rack near the shower door. Brass faucets, cream sink and toilet, thick gray rugs, and the whole effect brightened by a fresh green air fern growing from a brass pot on a small glass table near the sink.

Then…the shower, which was the size of her entire bathroom for starters, made of slightly frosted glass that echoed the gray in the rest of the room.

"Gee." She looked around as if she were deeply disappointed. "I expected it to be fancy."

"Yeah, Mom and Dad were noted for their frugality." He stepped around the chair, helped her up and out of her clothes, the perfect gentleman except for a tendency for his talented, lovely hands to linger affectionately on her naked skin, which she found, coming from this gentleman, not at all objection-able. And in fact, she herself was ladylike enough to keep from jumping his body as it emerged from its clothes, but when he bent to take off his socks, she felt it extremely nec-essary to trail her palm over the smooth solid platform of his back.

"We're ready." He put an arm around her, supporting her as she limped toward the shower door. "I know the third floor overkill was more shock than pleasure, but you liked the greenhouse, and—"

"I *loved* the greenhouse. Especially your table manners."

"Mm, yes." He kissed her temple. "I think you are going to enjoy this, too."

Oh, yes, she was. Inside the stall, a bench where she could sit comfortably, and on the walls, the ceiling—everywhere it seemed—about a dozen showerheads, wide ones. When he turned them all on, she insisted on standing, stretching out her arms, lifting her face. It was like being caught in a glorious spring deluge, the kind that is so warm and inviting you don't care if your clothes get wet. Only they weren't wearing any, which was even better.

She could get used to this. And to the way they leisurely soaped and shampooed each other, hands always in motion over slick skin. At every touch of his fingers, she expected their chemistry to kick in, but it never did. Instead, she fell into a quiet sensual contentment more satisfying than if they'd gone at it again in the shower. Which, mmm, maybe sometime they'd get to. But together like this, they weren't doing, or wanting, or needing anything from each other, they were just being. It felt so right, she couldn't fathom that twenty-four hours earlier they hadn't even met. She'd almost believe in past-life existences if they explained the degree to which she felt she'd always known him.

They rinsed off for far too long, given that water, especially water pouring down in such delicious torrents, shouldn't be squandered. But even though she believed firmly in conservation and took quick no-nonsense showers at home—where one showerhead seemed plenty, *ahem*—here amidst all this luxury she felt there couldn't possibly be a shortage of anything anywhere. As if the planet's rules applied to other people who lived in the real sad world, not here. Maybe that was part of his heritage, part of the entitlement he'd grown up with. Maybe that was why the room upstairs had been left undisturbed. Because in his mind, it was just his room, to preserve or destroy as he wanted.

"Having fun?" He grinned down at her, water droplets on his cheeks, dripping from the ends of his hair, running in streams down his chest and arms.

Her heart started to swell and then bypassed love into unexpectedly deep vulnerability tinged with panic. What if he really did move away? What if his flower speech in the greenhouse was a rehearsed routine? Or the opposite, a whim of the moment, Derek carried away by the circumstances? What if he woke up after she went home and thought, *Hmm, good lay, time to move on…*?

He might. Men did. Especially with her. *She* wouldn't, she knew that. She'd carry some part of this man with her until the day she died.

"Had enough? Your ankle bothering you?" He put steadying hands around her waist, moved her closer to help support her weight. He must have mistaken the fear on her face for pain.

"No, I'm okay." She clung to him, savoring the warm hard length of his body braced against hers. "I was thinking I need a shower like this in my apartment. Maybe if I took out the living room it would fit."

He reached and turned off the water, grabbed a towel from

outside the stall, and wrapped it around her shoulders. Yes, she'd been right about the warming rack.

"Does my money bother you?"

"No. Of course not." Her denial came out too quickly.

"Really."

Hannah sighed. *Tell the truth.* They were all about truth now. "It's…not what I'm used to. It's not who you are, either."

"Not totally." He was watching her intently. "But it is part of me."

"And abject poverty is part of me." She grinned and used a corner of the towel to dry a drip traveling down his forehead. "Though not so much anymore."

"The cliché is true, Hannah, there's more to life than money." He grabbed the edges of her towel and drew her close, grinning mischievously, then bent his head toward her. "For example, there's this…"

Oh, yes, there was, and thank goodness. She could happily be kissed by him for the rest of the day. She wouldn't need food, sleep, nothing…the kissing equivalent of his air fern.

When he drew back, she could barely remember what they'd been discussing except that it had been serious. Not as serious as how gorgeous he looked with his eyes alight, hair in wet curls, cheek rough with masculine stubble.

"You know, you never told me how your family made its fortune."

"I didn't, no." He turned away and grabbed a towel for himself, draped it around his hips. "I also didn't tell you, which I've been meaning to, that I've been to every restaurant and shop you've recommended since I started reading your column last summer."

She was so astonished she let him get away with the second avoidance of her question and gaped at him. "You have? *Every* one? All of them? For months?"

He looked pained. "Now you think I'm a stalker freak."

"No, no!" She laughed and kissed as high as she could reach, which was somewhere on his sandpapery chin. "I'm amazed. Flattered. Delighted."

More than that. She was going to float up and bounce around the shower walls like a balloon letting out its air. This connection between them went way back. Even the antagonism in their columns had been part of it. She could see that now. Like those great old movies, *His Girl Friday* and *Pillow Talk,* where the hero and heroine fought and bickered to deny their true and growing feelings.

Yet all the while he'd been sneaking out to act on her recommendations. *All* of them.

"You have great taste, Ms. Lowbrow."

She tipped her head coyly. "I like you, don't I?"

"Will I be the subject of your next column?"

"Oh, yes." She paused thoughtfully as she composed the perfect review. "'For those of you hankering after a tasty hunk of beefcake, hanker no more. Proceed to Five Twenty-Three Hilltop Lane in West Chester and feast upon the finest quality male this reporter has ever had. Perfect buns. Plenty of meat. Many condom-ents available. The pleasure will make you want to come again.'"

His laughter rang out in the tiled room, the first time she'd heard him really let loose. The sound made her laugh, too, and feel the world could not become any more perfect than it was just then. It had better stay that way for once.

"I won't even try a response." He let out a last chuckle. "Anything after that would be lame copycatting."

"Thanks." She couldn't seem to smile hard enough.

He opened the shower door and helped her into the warm—even the tile floors felt gently heated—but mysteriously not steamy bathroom. There must be some state-of-the-art dehumidifying gizmo installed. Imagine not having to put up with even the smallest of life's inconveniences. The idea still made her a little queasy.

He dragged his towel over his body, which was so beautiful she felt it impolite not to stare. "So you want to know what my favorite article was of yours?"

"Of course."

"The one about the Lone Star Diner in South Philly."

"You went there?" She couldn't begin to imagine him among the eclectic assortment of South Philadelphians.

"One of the worst entrées of my life." He hung his towel on the rack, took hers from her shoulders and hung that, too.

She arched an eyebrow. "Considering what you have to compare it to, that could still be a compliment for most people."

"Ouch." He handed her a clean T-shirt. "Touché. However, you were absolutely right about the pie."

"Apple?"

"Best I've ever had anywhere."

"Yes!" She grinned and pulled on the shirt, bubbling with excitement. Most of her friends didn't get her deep love—nearly worship—of good food. Even Daphne, who'd grown up in a middle-class Italian family which ate very well, didn't get her obsession. And judging by what Hannah was fed growing up, her parents didn't even inhabit the same dietary planet. "Isn't it incredible? Not too sweet, plenty of apples, minimal goo. They use brown sugar I'm sure."

"Maybe some maple, too."

"That perfect touch of nutmeg with the cinnamon."

"And ginger."

"And the crust…oh my God, it could inspire its own religion."

"The Church of Crust? You were right about all of it. *And…*" he patted his stomach "—about the egg rolls at Ken Han's."

"Yes!" She was practically salivating, not only from hunger but from the thrill of being able to share her passion. "You can taste the individual ingredients in the filling, unlike normal egg rolls."

"Which taste like salty cabbage."

"Exactly."

"You know…" He waggled his eyebrows. "I think I'm getting turned on."

Hannah burst out laughing. "I know! I know. It's crazy."

"Not to mention hungry. Are you? I don't know what time it is, practically evening, I bet."

"I am hungry, believe it or not. Even though all we've done is eat and…that other thing."

"So…what's your point?"

She giggled. "Nothing. Not a thing. Two of my favorite activities."

"Same here. Let's get our traveling circus on the road."

He rewrapped her ankle and helped her on with his sweats, while she was, very uncharacteristically, too full of happiness to speak. Look what they shared. And look how he respected her opinions, even though his true love was food produced on a much different plane.

"I need to take you to some of the places I discovered around the city." He helped her carefully into the wheelchair.

"I'll have to go incognito or lose my reputation." She was glad he couldn't see her face. He'd take her *places*. Places was plural. Which meant he planned for them to go out more than once. Even though he was moving. Or maybe he'd change his mind and stay. Maybe he'd keep the house. Maybe someday they'd have mini-Dereks and mini-Hannahs who could play their hearts out in the rooms upstairs, bring them back to life.

Okay. She was getting ahead of herself again. "I'll dress up. No one will recognize me looking fancy."

"Anyone who saw you in that red dress would. No man could forget a woman like that. Ever."

Hannah laughed so she wouldn't cry at the reverence that showed through his teasing. "Why, thank you, sir."

"You're most welcome." He wheeled her back through the bedroom and toward the elevator. "I didn't advertise who I was at your greasy spoons, either."

"Dark glasses…mustache."

"Trench coat, floodwater pants, sneakers with dark socks."

"Hot, hot, hot."

They did the elevator routine again and arrived back in the kitchen, the scene of the previous night's crime of overeating. Tonight she was in the mood for something simpler. Easier on the stomach and the ethics.

"You know what there is in the cupboard. What sounds good?"

"Well…"

He turned at her less-than-enthusiastic voice. "Something entirely different?"

Hannah decided right then that there was nothing in the world sexier than a man who could read her mind. "I'd like to cook for you, will you let me?"

He looked surprised, then nodded. "You're on. If your ankle can take it."

"It can. And after all—" she smiled sweetly "—I can probably figure out where things are as well as you can."

"Um, yeah. About that…" He rubbed his chin. "I never needed to know my way around a kitchen so I never learned. A terrible flaw."

"Terrible."

"But how about since you're incapacitated, you tell me what you need and I'll find it. Somehow."

"It's a deal. Eggs?"

He found them. And went on to find bread and everything else she called out...eventually. Preparing the meal was the most fun she'd ever had in a kitchen. Sometimes it took them a while to locate something, and drawers and cabinets would be opened and closed all over the room until his shout of triumph would crack them both up. Hannah stood, with his gallant help, to do the cooking, ogling the sleek high-quality pots, and tentative around the flat-topped induction range that heated instantly in contact with the cookware. *The Future Is Now: My Day as Judy Jetson.*

She'd grown up using her mom's temperamental electric range and random-temperature oven to prepare meals when her parents were out or out of it. Amazing what you could do when you mastered an appliance. And when you had no other choice.

The meal was one of her comfort-food favorites, grilled cheese, tomato and ham made with french toast instead of plain bread, honey mustard and a sprinkle of oregano. Add to that a big pot of strong coffee and bananas sliced with a drizzle of cream and a touch of vanilla and cinnamon. Of course, in his kitchen, the bread was artisanal, the cheese was Gruyère rather than Swiss, and the cheddar was encased in black wax and imported from England, not plastic-wrapped in Wisconsin. The tomatoes were fancy vine-ripened ones with actual flavor, and the oregano he disappeared to snip, fresh from the herb garden in the greenhouse. Coffee came, no doubt, blended from beans picked personally for his family. Bananas, thank goodness, were bananas.

But so much for true lowbrow.

She had to admit, however, that the sandwiches were pretty spectacular, the perfect melding of her lowbrow and his highbrow tastes. And judging by the way he inhaled his and made another one on his own, following her instructions, he'd enjoyed them, too. Which satisfied her even more deeply than knowing he'd taken advantage of the recommendations in her column and online. This was something close to her, made with her own hands, part of her past. And he'd not only accepted it, but loved it, too.

Most importantly, as they talked, it turned out they had everything in common except income levels. They liked the same movies—oldies and indie films, occasional action flicks and comedies, but no horror or gore—took the same shots at the same politicians, had read many of the same books and had similar reactions.

Should she perhaps pinch herself? This whole day-night-day had started to feel like a dream. All those years beating herself up for not being cautious enough with men, for trusting too much, for falling too quickly—she'd done all those things here, once again, but what a difference it made when she'd found the right man and they'd dived in together.

"Did you ever have a pet? I bet it got lonely for you in this house." She looked around, frowning. "I know you don't have one now. No pet hairs, no fuzzy mice, no slobbered-on tennis balls."

"That's what the house needs. Fuzzy mice and slobber." He waited for her to stop laughing. "I had a dog as a kid. Toby. Short for Toblerone—like the chocolate. Needless to say, he was a chocolate Lab."

"Of course he was." She grinned. "Is he still around or…no, probably not."

"Long gone. He was a great dog. I have pictures somewhere of the two of us."

"Can I see?" She contained most of her eagerness and still sounded overexcited. She'd bet Derek was positively edible as a child. "I mean when you've finished your coffee."

"Sure. I even know where they are…probably. My dad bought Toby for me, I think mostly to drive my mother crazy."

"How sweet."

"Wasn't it. Toby was great company." He scooped the last of the cream from his bowl and set the spoon down, stared into his coffee, looked up a couple of times as if about to say something, then stood abruptly and took their dishes to the sink.

Hmm. Something about the conversation must be making him uncomfortable. Like… She had no idea. Did he miss his dog that much?

"Your turn." He squirted dish soap into a mixing bowl and ran warm water into it. "Did you have a dog?"

"My parents didn't want the hassle. They could barely feed themselves and me, and could barely get up and out of the house every day. Sometimes they couldn't even do that." She took a sip of coffee to ease the tightness that still cropped up in her throat.

"You had to grow up early."

"I did." She spoke matter-of-factly, as he had. It was incredible to be able to talk to someone who really understood. "As did you."

"I had Rita and Ray."

"And I had Mrs. Babbidge who lived next door. When things got…loud at my house, she'd knock and invite me over for cookies or to watch TV with her. She was like a grandmother."

"I'm glad you had that." He held her eyes, started to speak again, then turned back to the dishes.

Um… So… She finished her coffee and limped over to give him her cup, grabbed a linen dish towel over his objections, and helped dry. What was it he found so hard to say? She was too chicken to ask.

He finished the last dish, rinsed, and handed it to her, dried his hands slowly on a blue-and-white striped towel, then threw it down and cleared his throat, bracing his hands on the counter. "I was thinking…"

"About?" She waited, reminding herself to breathe. If he dumped her, she'd have a mental breakdown. If he said he loved her and had decided not to sell the house, she'd have a mental breakdown, too. Only the good kind.

"Here. So your ankle doesn't get tired." He insisted she sit back on the counter stool, then sat next to her, took her hand and played idly with her fingers. "I was thinking that I'd like to do something for you."

"Okay." That didn't sound like prelude to a dumping, did it? "Does it involve food or sex?"

"You might thing it's better."

"Better than food or sex?" Her heart leapt at a few romantic possibilities, all of which she knew were ridiculous. "I am not sure I'm ready for this."

"How would you like an interview…" He watched her warily. "With Jack Brattle. For real this time."

Hannah's mouth opened, her eyes shot wide, a caricature of the surprise she was feeling genuinely. "Who? Whah? You know him?"

"Yes."

"Oh my gosh." Heat flooded her cheeks. She felt near tears. "I'm…I don't know what to say."

"How about 'sure, that'd be good.'"

"Sure. Yes. Sure. *Thank* you. That would be…way more than good." She took his hand in both of hers and hung on for dear life. This was completely unexpected. Completely…unreal. She wouldn't even have to make up a clever headline because that one would speak for itself: *Interview with Jack Brattle by Hannah O'Reilly.* "What…made you want to do this for me? I mean, before you could have but didn't, and now…"

"It's about trust."

"Trust. Yes. Okay." She took a deep breath, still feeling that this was slightly surreal. "You mean you need to trust I won't tell anyone you know him?"

"And that you'll respect his privacy in what you do write."

"Of course. Of *course*." At this point she'd only write about his shoelaces if that's what he wanted. Derek knew Jack Brattle! Were they neighbors? Very possible. Or maybe rich people just knew each other. Bumped into each other incessantly at parties in Paris. Maybe their families had done business together, which would mean Derek's family did something related to real estate development. "So…when? I mean where is he? I mean what kind of interview, phone or…"

She hardly dared hope.

"In person. When is good for you?"

"Wow. Wow." She laughed simply because she couldn't keep the emotion back. "Is he in town? Next week? Monday?"

"I'll…check and let you know."

"Wow. *Wow*." *Stop saying wow, Hannah.* "So…you'll just call him and ask? Just like that?"

He chuckled and touched her cheek with the hand she wasn't squeezing the blood from. "He has a phone just like us mortals."

She loosened her grip. "Okay, yes, I know, sorry. I'm a little…starstruck."

"Hmm." He narrowed his eyes, and she got the impression he meant to tease her, but the look didn't quite come off. "You're going to make me jealous."

"Oh, no. I mean…no way." She shook her head emphatically. "I just want him for his story. You I want for…everything else."

"Make sure it stays that way." His grin seemed halfhearted. His eyes were no longer bright.

She searched his face with concern. Something about this wasn't right. "You're sure this is okay? I mean...you're not going to be calling in some favor you'll need for yourself later?"

"It's fine." He still looked odd. Nervous, but something else, too. He couldn't possibly think she'd fall for Jack Brattle, could he? How many gorgeous rich guys could a woman fit into her life? One was plenty for her. This one, and only this one.

He removed his hand from hers and stood. "I'll go look for those pictures now."

"I'd love to see them." She really didn't like that he was leaving the room so suddenly. "You're sure everything is good?"

"Everything."

"Derek."

He turned back, eyebrows raised questioningly.

"Can I...tell my friend Daphne? She's a reporter and knows about keeping quiet. I'd just love her to know because we're close and...she'd understand what this means to me."

"If you trust her, then it's fine." He walked back toward her, taking his phone out of his sweats. "Because I trust you."

She beamed, sure there were more hearts shooting out the top of her head.

He put the cell on the counter. "Go wild."

"Thank you. So much." She watched him walk out of the kitchen, hoping he'd tell her soon what was bothering him. If something about her interviewing Mr. Brattle would cause him trouble, even she would think twice. But he wouldn't offer if he didn't want her to have the story. Would he?

She dialed Daphne eagerly on the familiar BlackBerry keypad. Luckily her friend picked up immediately.

"Daphne, hi, Happy New Year."

"Hannah? Where are you?" She sounded worried, and her voice was thick, as if she'd come down with a cold. "I've been calling you all day. You didn't answer your phone or your cell."

"I'm not home. I went to check out the Jack Brattle tip."

"Today? In this weather?"

"No, last night."

Her friend gasped. "And you're still not home? What happened?"

"Oh ho *ho* what *didn't* happen." She swirled luxuriously on the stool and nearly whacked her ankle on the kitchen island.

"Hannah." Her friend's exasperation was all too obvious. "Cut the drama. Did you find his house?"

"Yup."

"And? You're not still there, are you?" Another gasp. "Was someone home? Was *he* home?"

Hannah took pity on her poor not-in-love-with-the-perfect-millionaire friend and told her the story. All of it. Well, almost all of it. The roses belonged to her.

"Hannah, Hannah, Hannah." Her friend didn't sound as dreamy and excited as she was supposed to. In fact she sounded exasperated all over again. "You're telling me you're in love *again?*"

"But this time—"

"With a man you met *yesterday* who lied to you and manipulated you into his house and bed?"

"Daphne, it's not like that."

"You didn't meet him yesterday?"

"I did, but—"

"He didn't lie?"

"Well, he…not any more than I did."

"And he didn't manipulate?"

"Look, we've been over this. I mean he and I have. It's water under the bridge—we've gotten past it. I trust him."

"Hannah, honey, this plays like an old tune. You trusted Mr. Can't-Keep-It-Zipped Norberto. Remember what you said? 'I just know this is right, Daphne. This one is going to—'"

"That was different."

"Aw, Hannah. You said that, too." She was trying to keep her tone gentle, but Hannah could hear the frustration.

"I know. I *know*. But this time…" She rolled her eyes. "Forget it. I know you won't believe me. And I guess I don't blame you. But listen, there's more."

Her friend sighed. "I'm not sure I want to hear this."

"Ha ha ha." Daphne must have some serious cranky hangover going at the moment. If anything would get her out of her bad mood, this would. "Get this. He is going to get me an interview with Jack Brattle. For real this time."

"Oh, really." To say her enthusiasm was lacking would be a major understatement.

"I'm serious! This is huge."

"Hang on." She blew her nose, cleared her throat. "Do you have proof he knows Jack Brattle or has access to him?"

"Geez, you believed *Dee-Dee,* why can't you believe him?"

"Well…don't you think it's a little too coincidental? Two offers of Jack Brattle in one day? From your professional nemesis who elaborately planned to humiliate you in print? I'm sorry, but this guy makes me nervous."

"Daphne, listen…"

"Think about it. When was Jack Brattle's last interview with the press?" Her voice rose and started shaking. "Let me think. Last…never. But this guy, who has already lied to you once, is going to produce the man himself on a silver platter and hand him over on bended knee, just because you asked him to?"

"I didn't ask him to. He offered."

"Hannah." She spoke more calmly, trying to be nice to her clearly insane girlfriend. "Jack Brattle has guarded his privacy ferociously for the past decade since his family imploded. How likely is it that this guy has that kind of power?"

"He said it, and I believe him." She put her elbow on the counter, leaned her head in her hand. She did believe him. She did. But it sounded so lame out of context like this. Her temple started pounding.

Daphne sighed again. The sigh of a long-suffering friend. "When is this miracle going to happen?"

"Next week."

"Has Mr. Jack Brattle confirmed this? Within your hearing?"

"It's New Year's Day." She suddenly felt terribly weary, her stomach a bit sick. "Derek can't call him now. Give me a break, Daphne. I know I've screwed up in the past, but you need to trust me this time. You can't keep treating me like I'm some kind of idiot."

A long silence, and a soft hiccup. Was she crying? Hannah's body tensed in alarm.

"Daphne? What's wrong?"

"Paul." A broken sob. "His New Year's Day present was to dump me. After three years."

"*Dump you?* But Daphne…" She struggled for words, found none that fit. "Men don't leave *you*."

"This one did." She barely got the words out.

"But why? I mean what did he say?"

"He was tired of me expecting him to jump. I never thought I was doing that. I mean I…I don't know, I guess I screwed up. He was pretty angry. I just thought after three years… Well, you want to talk about trust? I thought I could trust in what we had."

"Oh my God, I'm so, so sorry." Tears came to Hannah's eyes. She knew what that felt like. No wonder Daphne was so cynical. "Are you home? When the roads are plowed I'll come right away."

"No. I want to be alone." Her voice was so low and miserable Hannah had to turn up her phone's volume. "I'll call you tomorrow. I just need to cry now."

"Daphne, no, don't—"

The line clicked off. Hannah gritted her teeth, feeling her friend's pain. The last thing Daphne needed was to hear Hannah bragging about her new man when Daphne's had just kicked her in the teeth. Hannah needed to call back and apologize.

She started to key in the shortcut for Daphne's number when her phone started vibrating. Good. Daphne, calling back. "Hello?"

"…Who is this?" The voice was female, older, unfamiliar and a bit harsh. Hannah barely stifled a sound of annoyance. She should have checked the number.

"Hannah. Who is this?"

"Where is Jack?"

She rolled her eyes. At least this would be quick. "You have the wrong number."

"No. I don't. Where is he? He hasn't answered all day."

"Uh…sorry, but this isn't his number. Why don't you check—" Hannah froze, realizing her mistake. The phone wasn't hers; it was Derek's. She'd been so upset by Daphne, and his phone was so much like hers, she'd forgotten.

"I'm quite sure it *is* his phone. I'd like to know why *you* answered."

Her stomach grew sicker. Her skin grew clammy. "Did you say…Jack?"

"*Yes*. Where is he? Has something happened? Are you at the house with him?"

Hannah slumped onto the counter, the granite cool under

her hot forehead. The call was for Jack. She didn't need to ask for his last name.

"Answer me." The voice had grown sharper, more suspicious. "Where is Mr. Brattle and what are you doing with his phone?"

10

DEREK STARED MOODILY into his closet. He knew exactly where to find the pictures of Toby. The only things he'd kept from childhood were jumbled in an Adidas shoe box that sat on the far right of the upper shelf, next to his shoe-polishing kit. Inside were the pictures; his lucky pebble, found when he was six and imbued by him with powers for reasons he could no longer remember; his ninth-birthday card from his grandma, which arrived the day after she died; the bouton-niere Amy gave him for the spring dance at Oberlin; the stub from his first paycheck from Brattle, Inc…. Other stuff, too, he couldn't remember the rest.

But he still hadn't taken the box down. Because if he took it down he'd have to go back to the kitchen and face his failure with Hannah. He'd fallen in love for the first time in over ten years, and managed to screw it up in as many ways as he possibly could before twenty-four hours had passed.

Offering her the interview with Jack Brattle was the right thing to do. Failing to mention at the same time, given what she meant to him and what he hoped he was starting to mean to her, that *he* was Jack Brattle was a terrible idea.

How could he explain the pain involved in opening up that part of his life to her, or to anyone outside of the very few who knew of his twinned existence? Since childhood, as a boarding school student and as an employee of Brattle, Inc., he'd been Derek Gibson, for security reasons and to avoid charges of nepotism as he worked his way up.

Now "Derek Gibson" was Mr. Brattle's personal representative, charged by the reclusive hermit himself with the power to run his family's company. A few people knew; there were always risks. But the way his parents had controlled and isolated him in his youth, the way he'd controlled and isolated himself since they died, plus a little luck, meant so far no one had blown his cover. When he'd started to write for *The Herald*, he'd taken still another identity to avoid any connection between his writing and the Brattle company and name.

How could he explain that encountering Hannah's columns and blogs had brought to the surface what must have been a suppressed yearning to connect with someone, with life, with at least a piece of the world as his true self. How could he explain to someone so full of the joy of life that he'd chosen to live so long without it?

And how could he explain how excruciatingly difficult it was, after a lifetime of self-protection, to offer himself up now, even as his certainty had only grown over the last months and finally this last incredible day, that this was what he wanted with her. Even offering the interview while she still thought of him as Derek had been tough. Like a turtle emerging from its shell, he felt he'd be left with no protection. Taking that last step, leaving the shell completely behind by confessing who he was had been too much all at once. Stupidly, he'd panicked.

The public eye had tortured his family, eventually driven his father to emotional ruin and early death, and his mother to suicide. Not hiding anymore, not his past, not his present, not his future…he knew it was what he wanted for his and for Hannah's sake, but he hadn't expected the habit of holding himself close and safe to die so hard.

People would look. People would talk, most people would move on eventually to the next celebrity *du jour*, but many people wouldn't. Until his father's betrayal by a man he'd always considered his best friend, Derek's dad had relished the public role, relished the world's attention. Jack had always hated it. So much so that he'd spent his life denying who he was.

He reached for the shoe box, cradled it in his arms without opening it. The pictures would still be in there. He'd taken them with his own camera, had Rita take the ones of him and Toby together. After they'd been developed, he'd shown them to Rita and Ray and maybe his parents, he couldn't remember. No one else had seen them or moved them, he was sure.

On his way out, he closed the closet door so the light would go out. Step by step he crossed the room. Fear of losing his privacy wasn't the only reason he was anxious. Hannah would have every reason to be furious that he'd held back his identity—again. He'd told the truth when he said he was Jack, told the truth again that he was Derek, and now would tell the truth that he was both. But from her perspective...three lies, not even counting the D. G. Jackson pseudonym. Last time he'd confessed she'd bolted. This time...she couldn't run physically, but she might not be willing to listen to his explanation, to try to understand what his bizarre life had been like.

More than that, while he was indulging in useless pessimism, anyway, Hannah hadn't made it a secret that his fortune bothered her. How would she feel knowing he was not only obscenely wealthy, but part of a notorious family doomed to be in the public eye?

He started heavily down the stairs. Obviously he'd soon find out. His feelings for her had grown to the point where any type of deception had become impossible. And finally, gratefully, he was sick of hiding, sick of lying, sick of being ashamed of who he was. Ready to open himself up to her, he could only hope she wouldn't immediately shut him out.

Hearing a noise at the bottom of the landing, he paused and looked outside. Darkness had come, but the outdoor lights shone through the still air. The snow, slowing for a while, had now stopped completely. The noise grew louder, the hum of an engine. The man Ray had hired to plow the driveway must have started, which meant the roads were passable. Rita and Ray would return to check on the house and on him. There would be nothing keeping Hannah here. After what he'd put her through, and what he was about to put her through, without the storm keeping her prisoner, Derek, Jack, D.G....all of him might not be enough to stay for.

He took a deep breath and moved on to the kitchen. She would have called her friend by now, her friend would be thrilled about the Brattle interview, and her excitement would have buoyed Hannah up even higher. Now he got to burst that bubble hard.

How had he allowed this to happen?

Easy. He didn't know he was going to fall in love with her, and he didn't realize to what extent he was a shutdown prisoner of habit. And something of a coward.

He turned the corner into the kitchen, holding up the box, smiling as naturally as he could. "I found the—"

The smile dropped off his face.

"Hannah." He walked toward her, tossed the box aside on the counter, shocked at the sight of her tearstained face. "What happened, what's the—"

"Don't." She held up her hand and he stopped on the other side of the island, aching to touch her. "Here's your phone back."

He took it, fear keeping him speechless. What had happened? Illness? Accident? Death? Her parents? Her friend?

"You got a call while you were upstairs. I was confused since our phones are so similar and I answered it."

"No problem." His fear started turning sick. "Who was it?"

"A woman. She wanted to know where you were. Apparently it's not like you not to answer calls right away, and with the storm and you having been out last night…"

"Rita." He guessed what was coming, but couldn't process it, as if his brain was protecting him from the bad news for as long as possible.

"She was very worried about you…" She turned her head finally; her eyes were wounded and hostile. "*Jack*."

He didn't flinch. He deserved this. He was going to get it one way or another, though he desperately wished he'd been able to tell her himself. "Yes. Jack Derek Gibson Brattle. My mother's maiden name was Gibson. My grandmother's maiden name was Jackson, which is why I chose it for the column."

"Ah." Her face crumpled, then hardened. "All in the family. How sweet."

His eyes didn't leave hers. "I was going to tell you. Just now in fact. I went upstairs to get the pictures because I needed to figure out how I—"

"Please. Give me some credit."

He said nothing. He wouldn't have believed himself, either. "Hannah—"

"Remember how you told me no one in your family was normal?"

He put his hands far apart on the counter, leaned forward. "You need to let me—"

"Because I was thinking… You told me about the uncles and aunts—the pervert, the slut and the psycho. Your father was a closeted homosexual with a preference for teenagers, ruined when his best friend outed him, and your mom was clinically depressed and eventually ended her own life."

"Please." He clenched his teeth. Even now it hurt hearing his parents' tragedies discussed as gossip. He knew she was trying to wound him. He hated that she'd succeeded so well. "Don't go there."

"Then *you* came along." She pointed at him, a Salem towns-person accusing a witch. "And you chose 'compulsive liar'? Am I right? Maybe 'drug addict' was too clichéd for a Brattle."

He bowed his head, reminding himself to be patient. Re-minding himself what she'd been through in the past twenty-four hours, how often he'd raised her hopes and how often she felt he'd disappointed her. "This might be a technicality, but—"

"Just out of curiosity, was *anything* you told me true?"

"Everything was. I told you I was Jack Brattle. I am. I told you I was D. G. Jackson. I'm him, too. I also run the Brattle company and live for the most part as Derek Gibson."

"Oh, right. Of course. Derek Gibson, Jack Brattle's right-hand man. You knew I might piece the whole story together, so you couldn't even tell me that."

"Hannah, it sounds ludicrous, I know, but this is my life and has been for—"

"You know the story of the three blind men who have hold of three different parts of an elephant and each describe a completely different animal? You didn't bother to show me the big picture." Tears started flowing again; she fought them so bravely he wanted to wrap her in his arms and protect her from any pain ever again. Instead he got the box of tissues from beside the sink and placed them within her reach. "But then maybe it's all my fault, like Daphne said, for trusting again."

"She said this was *your* fault?" He made a sound of derision. "Nice friend."

Hannah jerked her head up. "*She's* trying to protect me. Which is much more than you did. I thought you were different. I can't believe I fell for that fairy-tale love-at-first-sight bullshit *again*. Daphne was right. She was right. I need to become a nun."

He was helpless in front of her grief, knowing he caused it, knowing she had every right to be furious. Like a wounded animal lashing out at people trying to help, she was in no position to hear anything he had to say that could make it easier on her. All he could do was weather the storm, wait until she calmed down, and then hope for the chance to explain.

"I called Triple A." She blew her nose, reached for another tissue. "They'll be here as soon as they can."

"No." He drew his hands together on the counter, stood straight. "I need to explain. We need to work this out."

"It's simple. You got what you wanted, I got betrayed and disillusioned."

"I didn't get what I wanted."

"No? What, I didn't give you a blow job?"

"Not fair."

She ducked her head, nodded reluctantly. "No. It wasn't. I'm sorry."

"Look, I know you've been hurt. But this has nothing to do with whatever the other guys' problems were."

"I don't want to hear this."

"You need to. Blocking out trouble, running away from it, isn't the way to—"

"Why not, it's the only thing I haven't tried. And it's what you did."

"So I know what I'm talking about. Shutting people out feels safe, but it isn't really living. The way you put yourself out there again and again, Hannah, with articles, restaurants, your family, your relationships…is how you should live, how everyone should. With enthusiasm and, yeah, a few risks. You inspired me." He studied her face for any sign that she was taking any of his words in. "You brought me back to life."

"Oh, that's ironic. Because now I want to kill you."

He laughed bitterly, he couldn't help it. And his heart rose when he saw she was laughing, too, though through her tears.

"Hannah." He touched her sleeve. "Don't go yet. Let Triple A rescue your car, and I'll drive you home later."

"Why?" She turned to face him, and he hated the dull blank pain in her eyes. "So you can tell me I don't know all the facts? So you can tell me, 'No, it wasn't *like* that. I know how it seems, but if you'd just listen I can *explain…*'"

He gritted his teeth. That was exactly what he'd been going to say.

"I've heard it all before." She wiped her eyes, blew her nose again, calmer now and resigned. He couldn't stand this. "I've been in this situation before. Though you're more creative than most."

"I am not those other men, Hannah."

"No. You're worse."

"I'm not sure I want to know, but how?"

"Because." She ducked her head again, nervously rubbed one thumb over the other. "Because I really, stupidly, thought I was in love with you."

He understood what people said when they claimed to be melting. His heart was a runny mess in his chest. He wanted to touch her, embrace her, carry her back up to his room and make love to her for the rest of their lives. Even in this much pain he was ten times more alive than he'd been for too many years.

I really, stupidly, think I'm in love with you, too, Hannah. He couldn't say it. What had been easy in the greenhouse was impossible now.

"It's a start. Not an end. Just give me time to—"

"No." She carefully got down off the stool and limped toward the door. "I forgave the first deception. I was willing to overlook the fact that you slept with me without telling the truth. But fool me once, shame on you, fool me twice… I can't forgive this time. At least, not this soon. Maybe not ever."

"Hannah…" He felt like a helpless fool. Was this what love was? Would he rather have this pathetic vulnerability and pain than peace and control? If it meant knowing Hannah, then yes. "Don't turn your back on everything that happened between us. Remember the dinner, the dancing, the greenhouse…"

"You can't get me with nice words and flowers now. You can insist you told me the truth all along, but you know what you did." She waved a hand at him, as if he was a bug she wanted out of her face. "I'm not going to argue because I'm terrible at it, and guys always manage to confuse me and make me feel like *I'm* the one who is messed up."

"Oh. So Daphne's a guy?"

He was lucky Hannah only scowled at that comment. But Daphne was not currently on his list of favorite people if she'd made Hannah feel this situation was her fault.

"You didn't deserve what I did. Or didn't do. But I had reasons, and I want you to understand them because of…how I feel about you. And how you feel about me. And because…" His throat cut him off completely. The romantic in him needed more practice with her, especially when she was angry at him. Years and years of practice. Maybe a lifetime. "And because of…what I want us to have…together."

"Us? Which us? Which am I paired with? D. G. Jackson the journalist? Derek Gibson the CEO? Jack Brattle the recluse? Or all three. Is a foursome even legal?" She shook her head in disgust and limped out of the kitchen.

He was after her immediately. "Don't tell me you're going to run outside again."

"I'm going to find my clothes and coat, my shoes and my purse. And wait for the truck. And not talk to you." She stumbled going around the corner and steadied herself against the wall, foot lifted, in obvious pain.

In one more stride he caught up with her, bent, and swept her up. "You can do what you want, you can ignore me, you can detest me, but you can't expect me to let you hurt yourself like this."

"No, of course not. Hurting me is *your* job."

He set his jaw, relieved at least that she wasn't struggling. "Put your arms around my neck. You'll be easier to carry."

For a second he thought she'd refuse and was relieved when she conceded, though she acted as if he were a bag of garbage she was forced to embrace.

Even so, holding her body this close, smelling his shampoo in her hair, made him realize all the more searingly what he had and what he might lose. His gut tightened. This, then, was hell, a new one, very private, designed just for him. Finding the woman of his dreams, finally becoming ready to exit the self-pitying closet of grief and anger to experience life again—or maybe for the first time, given his claustrophobic childhood—and now he was in danger of losing her on the verge of getting it all. Sick, sick irony that the caution he felt had saved and guided his life was currently threatening to ruin it.

"Wait here. I'll get your clothes." He set her down on the dark brown suede armchair in the living room and dragged over the small matching footrest his father had never been without. His chair, his footrest, his scotch and his cigar.

Head down, she mumbled thanks, and he lingered for a quick second, wishing for a miracle to undo the damage.

None came. But one idea did…

He turned and grabbed her shoes from the hallway, went up the stairs, three at a time. In his bedroom he gathered her dress, her underwear and purse, then grabbed a tape recorder off his dresser.

Downstairs he found her coat and laid the clothes in her lap, knelt and put his hands on the armrests on either side of her, boxing her in, wishing he could handcuff her to some piece of furniture until she'd hear him out.

"Hannah."

She hardly looked up. His heart constricted. He couldn't stand her looking so deflated and miserable. But at least she wasn't telling him to go away.

Yet.

Hope rose. He turned on the tape recorder.

"I was born in Philadelphia in 1976, the year of the big bi-centennial celebration. My father had troubled dealings with the mob when he was trying to develop a new casino in Atlantic City in the early eighties, and my parents received kidnapping threats against me and became paranoid. We moved a lot, I had private tutors. Hand-selected friends. When I was fifteen, they sent me to boarding school as Derek Gibson, a name I chose. I was a loner, had a few friends, but no one asked many questions. Same in college at Oberlin.

"I worked with and for my dad also as Derek Gibson, from the time I was old enough to read. He trained me to run the company from the bottom up, told only one or two people I was his son. You know what happened to him. He became greedy, careless, made too many business decisions good for the company and bad for towns and for people.

"In the process, he made enemies, including his best friend, and got caught one too many times with much-younger men. The board got sick of the cover-ups and his friend eventually let him fry. My mother was in bad shape at the time and couldn't handle the scandal or the shame. She killed herself when I was twenty-two.

"I took over Brattle, Inc. with a lot of guidance at the beginning, and vowed to repair the damage, not only to the family name, but to the business. I took the company in a new direction, building affordable housing for lower-income families, investing in already existing properties and renovating them. I put millions into a foundation to award down payments to qualified buyers. In doing so, we stopped making so much money, but we're slowly regaining a decent reputation.

"I'm still downsizing my father's empire. I want to sell this house because I don't like the memories associated with it. For the same reason, I wasn't upset when the good business decision to close our Philadelphia office meant I would be able to sever ties here. I'll miss writing the column as D. G. Jackson, but even we Brattles can't get everything we want all the time.

"I had only one steady girlfriend, in college. Her name was Amy. I never told her I had another life. My father warned me over and over, especially during those horrible weeks of his downfall, before his heart gave out, that I should never trust anyone. Anyone. Even a best friend. Because everyone was capable of betraying me. What he didn't tell me was that by not trusting anyone, I'd be betraying myself—who I was and who I wanted to be.

"But I told you, or was about to before you found out in a case of truly crummy timing on Rita's part. Or maybe the bad timing was mine. I don't claim to have played this all right, or any of it right, but everything I did was because of the incredible, unexpected way you came into my house...and into my heart."

He clicked off the recorder.

"That's it. My story." His voice thickened. "Thank you for letting me tell you."

She stayed silent, staring at her clasped hands, but she was no longer crying.

Hope rose further and stayed, hovering. He wanted to tell her he loved her, beg her to stay, to give him another chance, but the words wouldn't come. He still had too far to go before he could put himself out there the way she could. In any case, she deserved to make the decision on her own, unclouded by pressure from him.

She swallowed, the sound audible in the oppressive silence. And still said nothing. He unclasped her hands and put the recorder in them.

"It wasn't much of an interview, Hannah, but it was with the real Jack Brattle. And now it's yours. That, and whatever you saw and experienced here. If you want any more, let me know."

The noise of an engine, then lights through the front windows, orange flashes sweeping the living-room walls, the furniture and Hannah's stricken face. The plow had come and gone. This was the tow truck.

She nodded almost imperceptibly, then rose, put on her coat and limped toward the front door and toward the truck, her shimmering dress trailing in her hand, sparkling when it caught the light. Derek stood and watched her. His noble speech had been too little, too late. The end of his dream, the beginning of his worst nightmare. Hannah was leaving. The house would feel cavernous when she walked out, devoid of light and joy and life. No way could he lie in that big bed tonight without her. Or shower in the master bathroom, or eat in the kitchen. Might as well sleep on the mat on the floor in his crazy uncle Frank's room. Maybe she'd forgive him and come back someday, maybe sooner, maybe later, maybe never. But he couldn't wait around. His life had been on hold for far too long already.

He'd leave in the morning, sell the house as soon as he possibly could. There was nothing for him here now but painful memories.

11

"MEN SUCK." DAPHNE SHOVED another giant spoonful of rocky road ice cream into her mouth. She lay like an ancient Roman in half recline on her bed, wearing a ratty pink T-shirt that said "I Break for PMS" instead of a toga. Her normally perfect curls stuck out wildly in all directions and her makeup free face sported dark puffy circles under her eyes. She looked exactly the way Hannah felt. "They totally suck."

"You mentioned that." Hannah ate another creamy bite from her own bowl. She'd started their self-pity snackfest virtuously two days earlier with carrot sticks, then slid slowly down the slippery slope with pretzels, low-fat potato chips, full-fat tortilla chips with salsa…then guacamole, then sour cream dip. Finally she gave up all pretense and devolved into a fellow contender for world-record consumption of rocky road.

"They suck."

"I know." Hannah sighed, becoming impatient. A good wallow was vital when things got rough, but Hannah's wallowing abilities had their limit, and that limit was now in sight. She'd gone home from Derek-Jack's house, packed an overnight bag, then Daphne had driven her to rent a car, and Hannah had met her friend at her apartment after a trip to the supermarket for emergency rations. They'd cried together, eaten bad frozen pizza, then had a couple of good slumber party evenings, watching movies, eating chocolate and crying some more. Hannah had slept fitfully on a blow-up mattress on the floor, they'd gotten up around eleven each day and started in again.

By now, sitting here in Daphne's darkened bedroom, Hannah had to admit that, gee, watching the Lifetime channel for the third day straight hadn't made her own pain better, and Daphne's certainly showed no signs of slowing. Not that her friend could get over a three-year relationship in forty-eight hours.

Hannah wasn't sure how long it would take her to get over Derek-Jack. Or if she ever would. No one had ever fit her so well right from the beginning—and face it, a beginning was all they'd had, even if it was an incredibly intense one—shared her tastes, her sense of humor, her view of the world. *And* provided the hottest, sweetest, most passionate sex she'd ever experienced.

Just thinking about it warranted another several spoonfuls of ice cream. From a really big spoon—only because she lacked a trowel.

"They want to live their lives the way they want. We're the ones who are expected to adjust." Daphne sniffed loudly and wiped her eyes. "It makes me sick."

"Yeah." Hannah shifted uncomfortably on the floor-level rocking chair, her body aching to get up and go somewhere, do something. Even exercise. Especially exercise. It was too snowy for a jog, but she could stop by the gym on her way home and work off some of this ice cream. Maybe Daphne would run out of complaints, and she could leave.

"Hey, kids, time for dinner." In the latest weepie on Lifetime, the actress kept up a brave front for her children while crumbling inside from the inattention of her workaholic husband. Once again, he'd missed his daughter's important soccer game.

"Have you ever seen a guy reading a relationship book?" Daphne licked the back of her spoon. "I haven't."

"No. Not me." Hannah's ice cream was starting to taste too sweet.

"Me, neither. It's up to women to figure everything out. And if anything bothers us, if we bring up any issues in the relationship, they act like we're just nagging bitches. Like they're perfect the way they are, and we better shut up and appreciate it."

"Right." Obviously Daphne had never heard herself speaking to Paul as if he were her misbehaving three-year-old.

"It's like they're children, and we have to be their mothers."

"Um, yeah." Could she read minds?

"I mean I want kids someday, but I don't want to have to marry one to get others. I've seen my married friends. The wives do everything, are totally stressed out, and the guys sit there like they're entitled to service their whole lives."

Hannah grimaced. She really wanted to be a good supportive friend, but she couldn't summon the requisite amount of bitterness. "Daphne, I don't think they're *all* that bad."

"Of course *you* don't. If there isn't a bright side, you invent one. Besides, what do you know? You've never had a guy stick around after the initial thrill. Trust me, it's a Jekyll and Hyde experience. Freaks you out the first few times, then you expect it."

"If you say so." Touché…to a point. Hannah's relationships never got the chance to dissolve into boredom. They were always chopped off during the bright hopeful beginning. She'd never seen that as a positive thing. The idea of sitting quietly after work, reading or talking with Der— Ahem. Talking with *someone,* appealed to her tremendously. Imagine a relationship free of uncertainty and fear.

"They want you to be cheerful and supportive *and* sexy all the time. The second you let down your guard or get annoyed, boom, they're done, on to the next one. And chances are their next one is five years younger than you with bigger boobs."

"Yeah." She thought Paul had hung in there for a lot longer than a second, not that he communicated his distaste for Daphne's treatment in a healthier way than scowling and saying, "Go to hell."

"Well, I'm done with them. All of them." Daphne struggled to sitting, frowning thoughtfully. "What are my chances of becoming a lesbian?"

"Good. They're good. About zero."

"Ugh." Daphne fell back on the bed. "That's what I thought."

The actress in the sappy movie fell sobbing into her husband's arms. Miraculously after a near-death experience, he'd realized there was nothing more important to him than family and had arrived home a changed man.

"She's an idiot." Daphne scoffed at the screen. "He'll just screw her over again some other way."

Hannah watched the happy couple, trying not to remember how secure and cherished she'd felt in the arms of Derek…Jack…whatever. "I don't know. I think he really learned something."

"Of course you do, Pollyanna." Daphne heaved herself up and took her bowl to the freezer for a refill. "You think life is a Disney movie, happy ending guaranteed."

Hannah bunched her lips, remembering Derek-Jack's disgust at how Daphne made her feel about herself. About as bad as Norberto and other previous boyfriends had made her feel about herself. While Derek-Jack had made her feel…

She let her spoon thwack back into the bowl of melting ice cream.

Much better than rocky road and Lifetime TV and Daphne.

The movie ended. Daphne's bowl was full again. Another movie came on.

"Men *suck*. The next one I meet, I'm just going to shoot on the first date and save myself and the world a lot of trouble."

"Good plan." Hannah was barely able to sound enthusiastic anymore. Her butt kept falling asleep, her stomach was gurgling unpleasantly from too many empty calories, and her head had started pounding.

An hour earlier she'd had a nearly uncontrollable urge to take her BlackBerry—blessedly unharmed by Matilda's tree trauma—into the other room to check for messages. What if he called? Not that she wanted to hear his voice. Not that she'd weaken and forgive him. At least…not now. *No,* not ever.

This was so confusing. On the one hand, she'd sworn her impulsive behavior had gotten her in trouble for the last time. For the last time she'd fooled herself into thinking she was in love with a man she didn't know at all. So instead of rushing headlong into forgiving him just because she missed him and hated this pain, she was very sensibly and maturely…sitting here. With Daphne. Feeling sick. And bored. And empty of all the good feelings she'd experienced when she was with—

Whatever she was supposed to call him.

"And another thing."

"What?" Hannah was barely listening. She had more interesting things to brood over than Daphne's list of grievances against the male gender. There was the promised interview with Jack Brattle, sitting in the tape recorder in her purse. She still hadn't had the guts to listen to it again, in case his voice propelled her toward more rash stupidity. What would she do about the article? Serve him right if she wrote it. She'd blow his cover wide-open and make a name for herself in the process.

Yeah, that was her all over. Stomping on someone she cared about to climb farther up the career ladder.

"Paul probably thinks he's going to march out there and find someone else. Ha! All he's going to find is how good he had it with me. You watch, he'll come crawling back. And you know what I'll say?"

"No. What." During a commercial break, an attractive woman in a perfect house expressed her joy at being able to clean her floors so easily.

"I'll say, 'You had your chance, Romeo, and you blew it. You don't get a second one with me.'"

Hannah turned in disbelief. "You'd really say that if he realized he'd made a mistake? Don't you think that's kind of harsh?"

"Oh, please." Daphne waved her question away. "Don't you think dumping me instead of trying to work things out was 'kind of harsh'? Whose side are you on?"

"I'm here, aren't I?" And starting to wish she wasn't. "Maybe breaking up was the only way he could get your attention."

"It better not be!" Daphne bounced up to sitting, brandishing her spoon. "Because that trick will backfire right up his ass. I've groveled after that man for three years, I'm not doing it anymore."

"Okay." Hannah pushed the soupy brown lump of ice cream around her bowl. Interesting perspective. Not one Hannah agreed with. But maybe all relationships were complicated like that, a jumble of different people's needs and perceptions.

"And if *I'm* being harsh, what does that make you?"

Hannah shrugged. "Harsh, too."

Too harsh? She didn't know. All she knew was that she'd felt so strong and proud leaving him. Finally she wasn't letting a man walk all over her. Finally she was drawing the line in the sand, saying enough was enough. She'd traveled back home with the tow truck guy in a burst of euphoria. Look what she'd done. Look at her! She'd said, *No, you can't treat me this way,* and for once she'd meant it.

And then…

All the doubts had crept in, like creepy bugs in a horror movie that slip into a house while the owner isn't paying attention, and she doesn't notice until there are so many she can't turn in any direction without stepping on one.

The young mother in the latest movie walked silently into her baby's bedroom, picked up the sleeping infant and cradled him—her?—tenderly. Her husband appeared in the frame, craggy and strong, put his arms around her and joined his wife in gazing at their child. Hannah felt tears rising. Would she ever have that?

"Geez, what kind of idiot does a nursery all in white? Those people are in for some serious cleaning bills."

Hannah sighed, wanting to growl. "Come on, Daphne, it's a movie set. Look how happy they are."

"Sure. He probably just finished banging her best friend."

"Oh, for—" Hannah didn't bother going on. Daphne was clinging to negativity like a shield.

The phone rang. Daphne stiffened hopefully, then caught Hannah's eye and forced herself to look bored and annoyed. "Probably Mom."

She shoved herself out of bed and moved more quickly than she had all day. Her gasp told Hannah the call wasn't from her mother.

"God, Hannah, it's him, what do I do?"

Hannah gave her a withering look. Folded like a house of cards. "How about answer it?"

"But what do I say?"

"You were full of ideas a minute ago."

"Hannah, be serious."

"Okay, okay. You don't have to say anything. But you should really listen and really try to understand."

Something inside her twisted. She hadn't given someone that chance quite recently.

"Right. Good. Okay." Daphne smoothed back her hair, moistened her lips, brushed a chocolate chip off her shirt.

"Uh, Daphne? He can't see you…"

"I know, *I know*. I'm just so nervous. Okay. Here I go." She got a good don't-mess-with-me scowl going, put her hand on her hip for an attitude boost and picked up the phone. "What do *you* want?"

Ah, love. Hannah got up, much to her poor butt's relief, and found the remote to turn down the TV. The young wife was screaming at her shell-shocked husband, who, sad to say, *had* been banging her best friend.

Super.

And yet…by the end of the movie the woman would find someone better for her, who would adore her and love her child as his own, allow her to be herself in a way her husband never had. She'd be happier than she'd ever thought possible and would graciously forgive her ex. Of course Cheater Boy and the best friend would be miserable.

Hannah grabbed her purse. Wouldn't it be nice to know that when bad things happened you had a guaranteed happy ending lurking around the corner?

"Oh, Paul." Daphne was crying, but not miserably. "I miss you, too, sweetie."

Hannah snorted, she couldn't help it, and went into the only other room in the apartment. She was glad Daphne and Paul were working things out, but she did not want to hear the rest of Daphne's happy ending.

In the kitchen area's tiny sink, she rinsed out her ice cream, not caring about the waste, and stuck the bowl in the dishwasher. Where was Hannah's happy ending? Where was the wonderful man who would come to her now that she'd learned her lesson about rushing in where intelligent women feared to tread, and gained the strength to insist on being treated with respect?

Sick dread invaded her mood, along with a picture of a certain handsome billionaire tenderly bringing her tea, gently wrapping her ankle, sensually feeding her raspberries…

What if she'd already found him?

Argh! Uncertainty and confusion were the pits. She opened her phone, sparking adrenaline even as she told herself he wouldn't have called, if for no other reason than he didn't have her number.

One missed call…from her parents, who wanted her to come over some afternoon. Hannah's heart sank. Foolish, foolish heart. Would it ever catch up to her brain?

Daphne's giggle sounded from her bedroom. Hannah didn't smirk this time. She had no reason to when she'd been praying for the same call for herself. But it was time to go. Daphne would want to be alone to prepare for all-night nookie.

Just the thought made Hannah want to smack a pillow over her mouth and let loose with a primal scream. Daphne would get fabulous, passionate makeup sex from the guy she loved…and Hannah got to visit her parents.

She called to let them know she'd see them the next day, and stopped in the doorway of Daphne's bedroom to say goodbye to her now-glowing friend, who'd immediately started stressing over what she'd wear after she ran to take a shower, shaved her legs, plucked her eyebrows, put on gallons of damage-control makeup…

"Have fun."

"I will. I always have fun with— Damn, what goes with these pants? I thought that red sweater was clean, crap!"

"So, uh, men don't suck now?"

"No, they most definitely do. But this one loves me, and I'd be an idiot to let him go." She tossed another sweater on the growing reject pile on her unmade bed. "And, well.

Maybe, okay, maybe, he had just the tiniest, teensiest, little point."

"Which was?"

"Maybe I…" She took a deep breath, as if she really wasn't looking forward to the rest of the sentence and just wanted it over with. "…focus too much on what I need and expect him to produce it. It's just that…he used to. And then he stopped. I don't know. Maybe I…"

"At least you'll get to talk it out now."

"Yes." She grabbed a pink top with a nod of approval, trying to hide her happiness. "Where is my black bra? Crap!"

Hannah finally found it in a corner of Daphne's crammed lingerie drawer, after they'd pawed through enough lace, rayon and marabou to outfit an entire catalog.

"So…you'll take him back?"

"Of course I will." Daphne made a sound of exasperation, but nudged Hannah affectionately with her shoulder. "I love him."

"And that's enough?"

"For me, yeah. It is. I know I get, um, a little enthusiastic about what I want to do and what I'd like him to do. He drives me crazy the way he's so different from me. But we're good for each other. I goose him up, he holds me back when I'm going to shoot off somewhere. Almost losing him…" She shook her head and sank on the bed as if her legs could no longer carry her even at the thought. "I guess the cliché is true, that you don't know what you've got until it's gone."

Hannah checked in with her heart, which still felt as if it were roasting over live coals. "Yeah."

"So what about you? What about Jack?"

"I still don't—"

The phone rang. Daphne's face lit and she lunged for it. "Hi, sweetie. No, not ready yet, but I'm hurrying…"

Hannah let herself out, more confused than ever, which she

wouldn't have thought possible. Back home, she ate better, but that was about all that improved. The frustration and indecisiveness continued. By now she was an expert. *Woman Goes for Gold Medal in Brooding.* No luck working on her next Lowbrow column, either. Slept badly, even in her own bed. By afternoon she was dying to get out of the house and practically ran to her car.

Forty-five minutes later, nervous on the still-wintry roads in her rented car, she arrived in Brookhaven and pulled up to her parents' neat suburban ranch, which they'd bought five years earlier with money inherited from Hannah's grandparents. She let herself in with the key they insisted she keep, and found her mother alone in the small living room, sitting with a simple child's puzzle in front of her on a small wooden table.

"Hey, Mom." She bent to kiss her mother. "You look great."

She meant it. Her mother was dressed in black pants and a pink sweater, her graying hair newly colored auburn and recently cut in a flattering chin-length bob. She looked stronger and less pale, much more her old self. Considering she'd barely been able to move after the stroke, it was nothing short of a miracle.

Hannah and her parents had invested a ton of energy and patience getting to know each other again after Mom and Dad quit drinking, and a whole new relationship had blossomed. She could now happily and honestly say she loved and respected them both unconditionally, not just because they were her parents and she had to. Fate had been nasty and unfair threatening her mother. Hannah wanted years and years more to enjoy her new sense of family.

"Thank you, sweetheart." Her mom smiled, eyes twinkling. "You look horrible."

"Yeah, um, thanks." She pushed her unstyled hair self-consciously behind her ears, wishing in a sudden painful burst that Derek-Jack could experience similar family support.

"So…" Her mom shook her head, lips pressed disapprovingly, eyes still smiling. "When did you last look in a mirror?"

"I was at Daphne's for a sleepover. Or two."

"It shows." She smiled at her plump, pretty, brunette nurse, who came in with a tray of tea and cookies. "Thank you, Susie. Now that Hannah is here, why don't you go relax?"

"I'm not paid to relax, Mrs. O'Reilly." She cleared the half-finished puzzle and set a cup of tea and a small plate of cookies on the table.

"With the peanuts we pay you, you'd be crazy not to when you get the chance."

"It's not a problem." Susie turned the cup handle toward Hannah's mother who had been groping at it in some confusion. "The experience is invaluable, and you know the foundation supplements my income."

"What foundation?" Hannah took a bite of the cookie and had to put it down before she burst into tears. Shortbread. 'Nuff said.

"Brattle, Inc."

Hannah nearly choked on her tea. *Brattle, Inc.?* Was the man going to haunt her everywhere she went?

Her mother sent Hannah an alarmed look, then calmed when she saw her daughter wasn't near death from cookie. "Isn't that the foundation that saved your father's orchestra?"

"Yes, it is," Susie said patiently. "We made that connection, remember?"

"Did we?" Her mother frowned. "I don't remember. I don't remember anything."

"That will change."

Hannah couldn't stop staring, first at her mother, then at Susie, while her brain supplied a picture of Jack in the library section of his third floor after he admitted he'd read about her parents in her blog, uncharacteristically awkward and self-conscious. *I'm…glad things are better for your mom and dad.*

No, she was crazy. It was a coincidence, nothing more. "Does…the foundation sponsor a lot of nurses for home care?"

"Not as far as I know." Susie helped Hannah's mother land her cup back in the saucer. "This was a special grant."

"Ah." Hannah needed help putting her cup down, too. She needed help breathing at the moment. "And…did Dad's symphony apply for a grant from the Brattle foundation?"

"Oh, no." Her mother pounced triumphantly. "I remember that. It was remarkable. A check just showed up one day, after the symphony's troubles had been public for years. The management hadn't approached Brattle because the foundation had no history of funding the arts."

Holy Cheez-Its. Hannah didn't know what to say. She was so close to crying she could only sit there and keep her eyes as wide-open as possible, hoping the teardrops would drain before spilling over onto her cheeks, making her look a tad too invested in symphonic welfare. Jack Brattle had read about her parents in her blog and stepped in to save them? Before he'd even met her? It made no sense. He couldn't have done it for her sake all those months ago. And yet…why else would he?

"Susie, I'd like to talk to my daughter for a few minutes, please. She can help me with the cup."

"Of course." Susie glanced curiously at Hannah, who probably looked like a recently dug-up zombie, and left the room.

Hannah took a seat next to her mother on the blue-and-white striped couch her parents had bought the year before, gradually replacing the older worn and grubby furniture she'd grown up with.

"Hannah, I might not be quite back to myself yet, but I still know when you're upset." She held out her hand. "So…? I'm ready to listen."

Hannah took her mother's hand, blissed out by this new relationship between them, and told her the whole crazed up-and-down tale, managing to keep back the pity-me sobs…for the most part.

When she finished, her mom was quiet for so long Hannah was afraid she hadn't been able to take it all in.

"Mom?"

"Yes, dear." She sat peacefully staring at the print of a Hudson River landscape on the opposite wall, as if no one had been talking at all.

Hannah couldn't help mild panic. "Are you okay?"

"Of course." She squeezed Hannah's hand. "I was just thinking."

"About what?"

"That you're a fool."

Hannah's eyebrows shot up. "Well, thank you."

"You are." Her mother managed a sip of tea. Hannah guided the cup back down and handed her a napkin to wipe a drop from her lips. "If you find a man who loves you that much you should hold tight with both hands and never let go."

Oh. The second time in one day. How often did Daphne and Mom dish the same advice? They couldn't be less alike. Maybe Hannah needed to pay attention.

"I have a man who loves me that much, though he didn't know it for too many years, and therefore, neither did I." She frowned, and then turned her once-again lively eyes on her daughter. "Seriously, what is wrong with you?"

"I…" This wasn't exactly the question Hannah was expecting. "I didn't know about the money he gave you."

"It has nothing to do with money. Look what he offered you."

"The interview?"

"Interview." She spat the word out, as if it were a terrible insult. "He offered you his soul, Hannah. Along with his heart."

For a second Hannah wasn't sure her mother was all there. "He…lied to me."

"What would you have done in his shoes?"

"I wouldn't have lied."

"I don't think you can be so sure." She turned toward the painting again, gazing with faraway eyes. "Since you were a girl, your life's been so full of coping with your own whirl-wind of feelings and wants that you haven't had enough practice absorbing other people's. I take blame. Your father and I forced you to be selfish because of how selfish we were."

Hannah felt tears threatening again and fought not to withdraw her hand from her mother's warm grasp. "So now I'm selfish as well as naive."

"Naive? Who said that?"

"Daphne. I trust too much and forgive too quickly."

Her mother dismissed Daphne with a rude noise. "Neither trust nor forgiveness are faults if the recipient deserves them."

"But how do you know when—"

"Tell the story again from his point of view, Hannah. Not to me, but to yourself." She squeezed Hannah's fingers again and let go. "You're the one who needs to hear it."

She heard it. An hour later she was speeding toward Jack's house, having listened to his tape on the way home from her mother's, once, twice, three times. Each time she'd tried hard to put aside her hurt, her feeling of betrayal, and to apply what she knew about the man, and what she could guess about his past, to the words she was hearing.

Yippee. Her mother was right. Break out the bubbly, Hannah was a certified fool. Always had been. Her problem wasn't necessarily impetuousness, though that didn't help.

Her problem was the same one she'd accused Daphne of so many times. She was only thinking of herself. With other men it had been all about her fantasy, her ideas of what love should be and how it should carry them both away. With Jack, it was all about her pain, her anger.

Halfway home she'd turned to the northwest toward West Chester. No, she didn't love the way Jack—his name was Jack!—had worked every minute of their time together. But there was no doubt that he had his reasons, good ones from his perspective, even if some of them were still incomprehensible.

He hadn't acted out of disregard for her. He'd acted as she had, to protect himself from the big bad heartbreak wolf—until the end when he'd offered her the interview and therefore even his protection. And in reaction to this so-amazing gesture, she'd taken a giant step backward and fled for safety. What she'd called caution, strength, sanity… Nope. Simply impulsive fear.

Hadn't he admitted she was the only woman he'd ever told about his double life? Hadn't he as good as admitted he loved her? Hadn't his actions backed that up, with his astonishing rescue of her parents and his admittedly odd method of coercing her to his house, then his tender and loving and ver-r-ry sexy treatment of her?

Yes, Mom, she was a fool. But she wouldn't be one any longer. This trip back to his house was completely impulsive, totally spontaneous, and exactly what she should be doing.

She arrived at his driveway as twilight fell, heart pounding, and emerged, shaky-legged, into the icy air, to examine the big iron gate. Locked. Without the storm, however, she noticed something she hadn't seen three—could it really only be three?—days earlier: an intercom at the right edge of the drive, set into the gate.

Anxiously, she pressed the buzzer. And waited. Pressed it

again. Waited some more. Her anticipation started dulling. Excuse me, how dare no one be home and ruin her perfect dramatic moment? She had to—

The machine crackled. "Yes?"

Ha! She wanted to shout her relief. A woman's voice. The same one she'd heard on the phone. Rita. "Hi. I'm Hannah. O'Reilly. I was wondering if Jack was home."

"Oh." She sounded surprised and, unless Hannah was nuts, disappointed. "No, he's gone, dear."

"Gone." Hannah drooped. The first time she was sure spontaneity was the right thing to do, the gesture had been wasted. "When do you expect him back?"

A long pause, during which Hannah could swear she heard the woman sigh. "I'm sorry, dear. I don't."

The words didn't register. "You don't…what?"

"I don't expect him." This time Hannah heard the sigh unmistakably. "He isn't coming back."

12

DEREK STARED AT THE SCREEN on his monitor. He'd pulled up a blank document for his final Highbrow column an hour ago and the page was still virgin-white; his deadline arrived in two hours. Thoughts of the column he'd been originally planning to write about Hannah wouldn't leave him alone. Worse, they kept morphing into thoughts of Hannah that had nothing to do with it. *And round and round we go.*

He got up and went over to his office's huge corner window, stared out at the view of Lake Michigan feeling like a guppy in a fish tank. He wasn't used to being unproductive. Didn't like it at all. But then a lot had changed since that night with Hannah less than a week ago.

A week. Geez. He felt as if he'd been with her for years and without her for a lifetime.

A knock sounded behind him. His new secretary, Amanda, hovered at his open door, carrying a load of files and papers. "Mr. Gibson?"

"Come in." He strode back to his chair, wondering how soon he could book a ski vacation and wondering further how much shock he'd cause if people heard he was actually taking time off.

"I have the Parker letter for signature and the report on the Bixby project."

Derek scanned both while she waited patiently. Amanda was a vast improvement over Mrs. Shelby who had been a lovely woman, but flustered easily and let too many typos through, therefore hadn't lasted long. Amanda was also her physical opposite, tall and thin and young, where Mrs. Shelby had been short and plump and of a certain age.

"This looks fine." Derek sat and selected his favorite pen, from a Cross set his father had given him for graduation from Exeter, signed the letter and handed it and the report back to Amanda. "Enclose two copies of the contract, and let me know when they're returned. The report goes to the board."

"Got it."

"My three o'clock conference call…?"

"Set up, all parties expect to be there. And your reservations for China have been confirmed. First class, aisle seat. Also, Jim Schultz can't make your meeting Tuesday, so I cancelled your trip to Dallas."

"Thank you." He made the note on his computer calendar program, then smiled at her, wondering when smiling would come naturally again. "That it?"

"Oh, Rita called."

"Again?" He'd been tied up in meetings all morning.

"She wouldn't leave a message, just asked you to call when you could."

He nodded, relieved. If there was an emergency she would have asked him to call back immediately. "I will, thanks."

"And these are the documents for the Darrin development which Mr. Brattle has to sign."

"Excellent. I'll see him tomorrow."

"Really?" Her curiosity bordered on unprofessional. "Is he…coming here? To Chicago?"

"No." He sighed. The duplicity he'd lived with his whole life was becoming more and more tedious. He wished Hannah would write up the interview and to hell with the consequences. He'd scanned *The Philadelphia Sentinel* daily since

New Year's, but nothing had appeared. Maybe he had an overinflated sense of his own importance, but it seemed to him if the paper had the article, they'd print it in a big hurry. Which meant Hannah hadn't written it. Why not?

"I'm curious." Amanda coyly started playing with a pencil on his desk. "What does he look like?"

Derek blinked. "Who?"

"Mr. Brattle."

"Oh." He shrugged, annoyed. "About my height. About my coloring and build. Yellow teeth, bad skin, two heads…"

She giggled. "Think I'm his type?"

He would have laughed, but her question didn't seem to be part of the joke, which annoyed him more. "He likes petite blondes with lowbrow taste, no sense of caution and little inhibition."

Her nose wrinkled; she threaded pink-tipped nails through her brown bob. "The hair I could dye, but I don't think I can lose height."

"Not worth it."

"From what I hear he's worth a lot."

Derek wearily repressed a childish impulse to say, Oh, shut up. "He's…involved with someone."

"Lucky girl."

"Why do you say that?" He could barely hide his irritation. This was exactly the type of idiocy he'd avoided successfully for so long. And exactly what he'd be inviting back into his life if he fused Derek and Jack into one person. For one intense moment he hoped Hannah wouldn't write the article. "You don't know him. He could be a complete jerk."

"All that money." She sighed wistfully, flicked the pencil so it rolled across the desk and stopped at his elbow. "Who'd care?"

"Right." He picked up the phone, intending to send the

message that the conversation was over. Luckily she got it, gathered up her papers, and left.

Yeah, all that money. Bought you happiness by the truckload, didn't it. Hannah's distaste for his wealth was ten times more attractive than the standard worship of it.

He replaced the receiver, shoved back his chair, and clasped his hands behind his head. What was she doing right now? Writing the article? Not writing it? Missing him? Changing her mind about giving him a second—no, third chance?

Nice thought. More likely she was making a Jack Brattle voodoo doll to roast in her oven. He'd wanted to call her only about a thousand times since New Year's Day. But what was the point? If Hannah had changed her mind, if she'd really understood what he was saying on the tape, what he'd said to her in person, she, of all people, was fully capable of coming after him herself. Jack Brattle might be next to impossible to find, but Derek Gibson was in full public view. Her silence meant only one thing: *I don't want you.*

Another glance at the blank Highbrow column—what the hell was he going to write about? Maybe short and sweet was best. "It's been fun, see ya later." Think that would fill enough space?

Nah, he didn't, either. All week he'd been unable to escape into work, exactly like this. From an early age, he'd trained himself to close off everything but the essentials of what he needed to accomplish at any given moment. But even his disciplined mind couldn't combat the power that was Hannah. She'd derailed his whole existence.

He'd trade in all his money for a time machine so he could go back and do everything differently. Lure Hannah into his house, tell her right away he was Jack Brattle, that he knew who she was because—surprise!—he was also

D. G. Jackson, but that he wanted to give her the interview because he knew she'd do a warm, human, intelligent and tasteful job presenting his truth to the world. Then he'd feed her. Take her to bed, then into the greenhouse and tell her he loved her. Kneel at her feet and offer her the rest of his life. The end.

Right. He rolled his chair back up to the desk, a massive, imposing cherry piece of his father's, which right now he'd like to trade for a golf cart or a safari vehicle. What was the point of wishing for things he couldn't have? He'd done that his whole life and should know better. The only relevant point was that he'd made a mess, had been unable to clean it up, and now faced the rest of his life without Hannah. The only question remaining, did he face it as Derek? Or as Jack? The choice had seemed so clear when he was with her.

He picked up the phone again and dialed Rita. Maybe she had news about selling the house. He wanted the entire transaction over with as soon as possible. With the Brattle mansion off his back, he could tackle how best to move forward.

Damn it. Moving forward was supposed to include Hannah. Without her he risked trading the prison of anonymity for the prison of missing her, and with his offer of the interview, the prison of being Jack Brattle, caged in the public eye, with no one around he could trust the way he trusted her.

Staying Derek was looking better all the time.

"Rita, hi."

"Jack, we have a buyer."

"Already?" A jolt of mild panic surprised him.

"She's very excited." Rita's heartiness sounded forced. "Wants to close as soon as possible."

"Really."

"Her house is already sold. She said she fell in love with

yours the second she walked in the door. Big money, moving down to Philly to be closer to her family. I think the husband is one of those early retirement Wall Street geniuses, and they need a way to spend lots of his money."

Derek's brain tried to celebrate without much luck. "I had no idea we'd find a buyer this soon. I'm…stunned."

"Aha!"

Derek narrowed his eyes. "Aha?"

"You don't really want to sell, do you."

He heard himself laughing strangely. "Come on. I've been plotting to get rid of that albatross for years."

"Uh-huh."

His temper rose. "I know what I'm doing."

"And I've known you since you were a boy, so I can tell when you're lying. Don't forget that."

"Yes, ma'am." His sarcasm was harsh, as was the pain in his chest. "I'll keep that in mind."

"Jack." Her voice gentled. "I'm just saying you don't have to do this. It's okay to change—"

"Thanks for the advice."

She sighed and despite his anger, he felt guilty for snapping at her.

"How soon can you come down for the closing?"

"Earliest would be…" He went back to his desk, brought up his calendar on the screen in place of the not-written Highbrow column. "I had a meeting in Dallas cancelled for Tuesday."

"Tuesday. I'll let her know. You'll make the flight reservations or should I?"

"Amanda will make them." He answered automatically while his brain whirled. Selling the house. Launching himself into a new life, one he wanted, one he was inviting, but…unpredictable. He hated not being in control.

Except the night he spent with Hannah.

Come on, Derek. He yanked himself back from useless mooning. Jitters were normal after so long hiding. He'd push through them, give Hannah another week to write up the interview. If it didn't appear he'd decide once and for all either to come out as Jack Brattle by himself or put the matter to rest and commit to being Derek for the rest of his time on earth. The sale of the house was a good thing. The remainder of his plan and his life would soon fall into place.

"One more thing." Rita paused long enough for Derek to get nervous. "A woman named Hannah came to see you."

Adrenaline burned through his system. "When?"

"Last night. I tried to call while she was here, but you didn't answer your cell."

He bit off a curse. If only he'd known… "I was tired, figured you just had a question about the house. What did she want?"

"She seemed very disappointed you weren't here. She asked how to get in touch with you. I nearly gave her the number, but I know how protective you are."

"Right." He wanted to laugh, but it wasn't funny. She couldn't even give his number to the woman he loved. What kind of half life had he lived? "Did she leave her number?"

"No. But she seemed to want to see you awfully badly."

His heart leapt. But then why hadn't she left a number? "Did she mention an interview?"

Silence, not entirely unexpected. "You mean for the job at the foundation?"

"No. Her interview of me."

More silence. Definitely expected. "She's from the *media?*"

"*Philadelphia Sentinel.*"

"But she asked for Jack."

"Yes." He really didn't want to go into this. He just wanted to know if Hannah wanted *him,* or only more details for her rise to fame.

"Okay, Jack. You better tell me everything."

"Did she say what she wanted?"

Rita made a sound of exasperation. "She said she had a few more questions."

His heart sank. Low. Then lower. More questions. For the interview. "I promised her I'd be available. So she didn't leave any way for me to get in touch?"

"You gave her an interview as Jack Brattle?"

"You said she asked how to reach me?"

"What on earth prompted you to—"

"What did you tell her?"

She growled in frustration. "Fine. I won't ask. I told her you'd moved away and weren't coming back."

"Okay." His voice came out sounding half-strangled.

"Is that a problem?"

"No, not a problem."

"This isn't just about an interview, is it?"

"Rita, I really don't want to—"

"You're involved with her. Personally."

"Not your business."

"And you gave her an interview as *Jack Brattle*. Seems pretty obvious there is a problem."

"No. There's no—"

"I bet I know the solution."

"*Rita*." He put his elbows on his desk, gripping a fistful of hair with his free hand. "I offered her everything. If it was enough she would have stayed."

"Oh, right. The Brattle way. Your conditions, your rules, and if people don't immediately play by them, you cut them off at the knees."

His body turned to stone in his chair. His father's chair. His father's desk. "Excuse me?"

"Just how your dad operated." Typically, she ignored his

warning tone, which usually sent his employees ducking for cover. "Well, let me tell you something about women."

He heard Ray's level voice in the background, Rita shooting something back at him. Derek pictured the two of them: Rita, short, plump and feisty; Ray, tall, quiet and thin. When Derek was a kid, he used to think of them every time he read the poem about Jack Sprat and his wife. "I really don't need to hear this."

"Women can't make snap decisions the same way men can because they think with their heads and feel with their hearts at the same time. They can see both sides of an equation, can absorb larger and more far-reaching implications, while men are good at zipping to the core of a problem and coming to a quick conclusion. I don't judge either way. Both are important.

"But in this case it means you can't take Hannah's initial reaction as her final answer. If asking interview questions was all she wanted, she would have called your office. She didn't. She drove all the way out here and was devastated when she found out you were gone. I could hear it in her voice."

He hated this. The hope Rita was raising and with it the renewed vulnerability and fear. He wanted things calm, ordered, under his control. "Thanks. I'll take that under advice—"

"I'm not finished. You have spent your whole life shutting people out. To the point where people aren't even able to *ask* to come in. This woman wants in, Jack. And you'd be an idiot not to let her. This house is your home. Come make it a home. Take a risk, and let this woman in."

Derek slammed his fist on his desk. For God's sake. He was not a little boy who'd drawn on the walls with crayons. "*Now* are you finished?"

"Yes," she said cheerfully. "So salvage your pride by

hanging up now and telling yourself, 'I'm an idiot.' In the middle of the night when you can't sleep, you can admit I was right, take the house off the market, and call this Hannah person. Even better, transfer me now to your secretary, and I'll have her do it."

He gritted his teeth. If she thought her half-baked psychology would make him toss himself in front of another oncoming Hannah train, she was completely nuts. "I'll do it my way. My risk. The house stays on the market. I'll be there for the closing Tuesday."

She sighed in exasperation. "Okay, Mr. Brattle. See you Tuesday. The buyer sounds like a piece of work. Should be fun."

Right. Fun like a final exam in physics you didn't study for. He stared at the still-blank screen, then at the clock ticking toward his deadline, thinking about his Highbrow column, about Hannah, about leaving Philadelphia, about Hannah, about food and the house, about Hannah, about Hannah…

And he suddenly knew exactly how the article should go.

Highbrow, *The Philadelphia Herald*
Dear readers: Today we bring you D. G. Jackson's final Highbrow column. We at The Herald *wish Mr. Jackson all the best and will miss his humor, insight and talent. Next week we'll start a series on American wines outside of California.*

I've enjoyed writing this column very much over the last three years. Any excuse to explore eating well is worth grabbing. I started with the idea that I could share my passion for good food, maybe inspire a few of you to try some new places, new flavors, new levels of service. Going to the same fast-food or neighborhood restaurant can become a habit. I wanted to challenge people to look beyond the obvious and risk something new. I didn't want this to be preaching to the converted. I hoped to reach people for whom a meal was merely a way to fill the stomach on the way to a movie, and show them that good food is something to be savored, an evening's entertainment all on its own—at its best, an art form.

Given the mail I received from readers, I succeeded with some of you, not others. To be expected.

What I didn't expect was how much I would learn during this process. I learned that aspiring to good food doesn't always mean looking higher, spending more. I learned that focusing on highbrow aspects can be limiting, like wearing blinders. I learned that I was stuck in the same prison and safety of habit as those people who don't venture beyond chain restaurants advertised on TV. The same kind of paralysis can set in at any level.

Judging by my mail, many of you enjoyed the friendly rivalry set up by *The Philadelphia Sentinel* instigation of the Lowbrow column, written by Hannah O'Reilly. I learned from her. I learned to value the perfect grilled cheese sandwich, fresh homemade pie from an all-night diner, perfect pickles from a corner deli. Like the Charlie the Tuna commercials in the seventies, it's not about good taste, but about tasting good.

My hat is off to my formidable opponent. My hope as I wind down this column is that she opens hers, that she joins me in admitting the best of highbrow and lowbrow is when they come together. That true magic happens when grilled cheese is made with Vermont cheddar on *ciabatta* or focaccia. When the apple pie can be a buttery tarte tatin, and the pickles not just cucumbers but mixed vegetables flavored with a variety of herbs. That out-of-season raspberries and pure-butter shortbread cookies can become the love of your life as easily as bananas and Oreos.

That sharing the pleasure with those you love is the real joy and passion of eating and of life.

Lowbrow, *The Philadelphia Sentinel*

Hello, gang, and Happy New Year to all Lowbrow readers. Today's column will be slightly different. I have a new place to review, a place none of you will get to go. It's quite a story and a revelation.

First of all, right up front, let me tell you. I won a few battles, but I ultimately lost the war with the High Priest of Highbrow, D. G. Jackson. He got me so thoroughly that I have to call the contest over and cower in humiliating defeat. Listen and learn.

The setting is New Year's Eve. The bait for poor unsuspecting journalist, Hannah O'Reilly, is the offer of an interview so incredible it would make finding proof of Bigfoot's existence ho-hum, yesterday's news. Off she goes on a stormy night to the assigned place, and what does she find? A near-deserted mansion. A handsome stranger who offers her the meal of a lifetime. Caviar. Foie gras. Prosciutto with fresh figs. A bottle of champagne that would buy her groceries for weeks. What kind of lowbrow could enjoy a meal like this?

Our intrepid reporter betrayed you all. She cheated on you with foodie passion and joy so great that even now she cannot summon the requisite shame. Alas!

But wait, there is hope. Don't hang up your juicy meatball subs and crisp salty hash browns, ladies and gentlemen. Because over the course of the evening, D. G. Jackson confessed—confessed!—to me that he had been a Lowbrow devotee for some time. Imagine!

It's time to rip down borders, dissolve the enmity. Accept the fact that a true foodie is just that. Someone for whom good food is good food, no matter the price, no matter the status. This column will go forward under that umbrella. I'm thinking of calling it Nobrow. Whadya think?

Ending today on a personal note, I thank my colleague

D. G. Jackson for his talent and expertise in his excellent column. I even forgive him for the prank he pulled. Me, the great crusader for lowbrow justice! What he offered to me was far more valuable than the price I had to pay. Over that meal I discovered many new loves that will last me a lifetime. Philadelphia will miss him. So will I. Until next week, readers, whether you go low or go high, make sure you go out and eat!

Live large, live long, live lowbrow. Until next week…

13

DEREK PRESSED HIS REMOTE and the iron gates to the Brattle estate—soon to be the Jansen estate—swung open. He had imagined several times how it would feel to approach his ancestral home—using the term with a certain mixture of irony and bitterness—knowing it would be the last time. He realized that a small amount of grief was normal under the circumstances. Whether or not he'd ever had affection for the house, it did symbolize, along with Rita and Ray, one rare constant in his life, one place where he could be Jack Brattle without fear of discovery. Losing that would understandably involve some pain, pain he would soon overcome when the deed was done, the new owners moved in, and he could look forward to starting over.

No matter what happened after Hannah's article came out—or didn't—he wouldn't be the same man. He'd take more time for himself, spend more time on trips that had nothing to do with business. Choose one place—his condo in Chicago, his house in Dallas or San Francisco—and settle permanently. Try to cultivate a social life. In short, be normal for a change.

He'd found Hannah's home number and called her the day before, left a message on her machine saying he'd be back in town briefly, thanking her for the tribute in her Lowbrow column, saying he was happy to help her out further with the Brattle article. She hadn't responded. Obviously she had worked out whatever questions she'd had and no longer needed any contact with him.

That rejection extinguishing his last foolish hope buoyed by her column was even more crushing since he'd told himself over and over not to try to connect one more time, but hadn't been able to resist.

All the better that he'd be selling the place. If she wanted nothing to do with him, he didn't need the reminders the house evoked of their time together.

The gate closed behind him with a tap on the remote control he'd have to remember to leave here. He'd wanted to hold the closing in his lawyer's office, but the buyer had insisted on having it right here at the house. Apparently she couldn't wait to get her hooks in it.

Fine by him. He pulled up to the front door, sat for a moment, looking out over the still-wintry grounds, the bare trees thickly lined with snow that had fallen the night before, the evergreens powdered with white. He remembered dragging his little sled out here, getting a huge running start as he glided down the lawn's slight incline. Not exactly a daredevil ride. But then he wasn't much of a daredevil.

Yeah, no kidding.

He switched the engine off, scanned the snowy fields broken by fences, trees, low stone walls. A crow flew by, then another.

No point sitting there any longer. He got out of the car, bounded up the front steps, not glancing down at the place Hannah had fallen, not allowing himself to linger on the memories of her body in his arms, the snowflakes on her lashes…

His key went easily into the lock; he'd have to surrender his keys, too. When he drove away, the house would belong to someone else. Rita had contacted the movers who'd start carting off the furniture on Friday, putting it in storage until he felt settled and could decide what he wanted to keep and where.

For an odd confusing moment as he crossed the threshold, he felt he was letting his family down. Ha! The ultimate joke. What loyalty did he owe the Brattle name? Most of his life it hadn't even been his.

Inside, he glanced around, not wanting to dwell on the sights or the past.

"Hey, there." Smiling, Rita hurried to greet him wearing her usual black pants and bright sweater—yellow today. She wrapped her strong plump arms around his ribs, practically as high as she could reach. From the way she'd sounded when he'd spoken to her from Chicago, he expected her to look much more upset on this occasion. "It's wonderful to see you, Jack. How was the flight?"

"Adequate. It's good to see you, too, Rita. You look great. I thought you'd be in mourning."

"I am, but only halfway."

Ray approached from the hallway behind her, tall, bearded, beaming, extending a hand for a hearty shake. "Hello, Jack, welcome."

"Ray and I had our offer accepted on a beautiful house in Eugene, Oregon, this morning, so I'm both happy and not. We're all ready for a change, I guess."

Derek nodded, gripping Ray's hand, a thickening in his throat. "It's time."

"Are you sure, Jack?" Rita's cheery face dimmed with concern. "Really sure?"

"Rita…"

"Okay, okay." She lifted her hands in surrender. "Mrs. Jansen is here already, come on into the study."

He preceded her and Ray into the workroom his father and

grandfather and great-great-grandfather had also used as a cigar-puffery and general male retreat. Dark wood, leather chairs, a manly man's dream. He used to creep in and sit on the floor playing while his father worked, trying to be so quiet that Mr. Brattle Sr. wouldn't notice and kick him out, which he invariably did.

To the left of a thirty-something man in a badly fitting suit clutching a stack of documents, whom Jack assumed was Mrs. Jansen's lawyer, sat Mrs. Jansen herself. One look made his gut tighten. Much younger than he expected, barely thirty if that. Classic trophy wife, he'd bet she was her husband's second or third go-around with marriage—the older the guy got, the younger he married them. She had perfect faux-blond hair. Way too much makeup. Expensive clothing made to look casual. Brittle smile. Even his mother, appearance-obsessed during her good years, had a natural air of class and dignity. This woman was trying way too hard. Not what the house was about.

"Derek Gibson, this is Alice Jansen." Rita gestured to the next owner of the Brattle mansion who was watching him closely. He wouldn't give her the satisfaction of showing what he felt, though she must know. "I've explained that you have power of attorney for Jack Brattle in the sale."

"Yes. You have." The woman rose from the table and smiled the smile of a woman with self-confidence, forced charm and plans for as-needed plastic surgery in order to hang on to her marital meal ticket. "So nice to meet you, Mr. Gibson. I absolutely love your house. I can't wait to get my hands on it."

He forced himself to return her smile, uneasy over her choice of words. Rita and Ray had kept the house in meticulous repair. "Great."

"This room." She gestured around, eyes alight. "Is so wonderful. I absolutely love it."

Derek nodded, pleased. The room was one of his favorites, too. At least she appreciated what she was getting.

"It's going to be my yoga room. I'm going to simplify, simplify, simplify. Tear out all this heavy wood and shelving and paint in a calming sea-green with a hint of pistachio. Then I'm thinking Japanese-style minimalist furniture. Lots of bamboo and painted salvaged metal. Really organic."

Derek's smile froze. The idea of the century-old woodwork being turned into a New Age paean to self-indulgence made him sick.

"That lovely library next door we're going to turn into an entertainment center. We have a seventy-inch plasma TV, and my husband has a collection of over a thousand tapes and DVDs."

There were hundreds of volumes in there, Derek's favorites being those that were leather-bound with gilt lettering, yellowing hand-cut pages, several rare editions. He used to spend hours going through them. Books belonged there. "He doesn't read?"

"Who, Henry?" She let out a peal of laughter that grated on his nerves. "Never. Then the dining room I want to redo in bright red, the kitchen in yellow, the upstairs, oh my gosh, I'm *so* in my primary color phase right now. The whole place needs an update. That third floor, I'm going to transform into one huge space for my interpretive dance studio. I still haven't figured out where to put the pottery or the kiln. Oh, and we're not green thumbs, so we'll put a hot tub and sauna in where your greenhouse is. Or maybe a racquetball court. It's going to be so fabulous. We'll also expand the garage over the back garden to house my husband's collection of antique cars."

"Won't you sit down, Mr. Gibson?" Rita held out a chair to the right of the lawyer. He could see the blame in her eyes, making him feel like a pet owner bringing the vet a young healthy dog to put down because it no longer suited him. She needn't have bothered. The described renovations hit him hard, as well.

He sat, stared blankly at the huge pile of forms the lawyer shoved in front of him and proceeded to explain. He barely listened. A pottery studio? Meditation room? No more greenhouse?

"…if you'll just sign here, first, Mr. Gibson."

He took the offered pen, staring at the signature line. Every instinct in his body was screaming at him not to sign. To tell the tacky trophy wife to go home to her husband and pick on someone else's house. On someone else's *home*.

Was this good instinct or just his natural avoidance of change? His idiotic fear of letting go of his protection? Or a you-don't-know-what-you've-got-till-it's-gone warning he should pay attention to?

"What's the matter, Mr. Gibson?" Mrs. Jansen's voice held a distinct edge. "Having second thoughts?"

He adjusted his grip on the pen, determined to go forward with the sale.

And still couldn't sign.

Hannah in his bedroom, in his shower, in his kitchen, arching in ecstasy on the potting table.

"Derek, it's not too late." Rita put her hand on his shoulder. "You don't have to sell."

If he didn't sell, he'd be saddled with the house. He'd have to keep it up, deal with the memories…

And there it was. Exactly what he needed to do. Stop running away and tackle the house, his memories and his past head-on. Acknowledge who he was, Jack Brattle, and take the damn risk of being himself for once, and forever, whether Hannah's article ever came out or not.

Power rose in him, and optimism. He'd find Hannah, tell her Derek Gibson had an unfortunate accident but that Jack

Brattle had stepped in to take his place. That he had a big house with no one to fill it, with a fabulous place upstairs made for as many kids as she wanted. If she said no, he'd back off, then come at her again and again until she gave in. She loved him. They belonged together. She was worth risking everything for, no matter how many times it took.

He raised his head, looked Mrs. Jansen straight in the eye. "I can't sign this."

"No?" To his complete shock, she smiled, an open, friendly smile of delight, nothing like the toothy grimaces earlier. "Well, that's a relief."

Derek—no, *Jack*—stared at her. "A relief."

"I can't afford the bathroom in a place like this."

Her lawyer gathered up the contract pages, chuckling. "You can't afford a toilet seat in a place like this."

He looked from one to the other, without a clue. "What is going on?"

Rita burst out in a laugh she'd apparently been holding back for a while. "Look at his face. I haven't had so much fun in years. Jack, dear, you've been had."

"I've been…" He stared at her, feeling utterly stupid.

"Had, dear. 'Owned' as the kids say today. 'Punked.'"

A light dawned. "You set me up."

"Mm-hm." She looked happier than he'd seen her in months. Maybe years. "I had a feeling maybe you didn't want to sell as much as you said you did."

"Congratulations." Mrs. Jansen leaned over and offered her hand. "The house is yours. I'm Daphne Baldwin, this is my fiancé, Paul Kronwitz. We're paupers in real life."

"Daphne." Jack's voice came out hoarsely. "Hannah's friend?"

She sent a sidelong wink to her fiancé. "Hannah who? Never heard of her."

"Holy…" He put his hands to his temples. "Rita, what is happening here?"

She put her arm around him, squeezed hard. "Come have something to eat. Now that you're not selling, it turns out I have a house full of food."

This would all make sense someday. He would see the humor, retell the story to his friends, family, grandchildren. For right now he was still disoriented. He'd made the very tough and grand decision not to sell the house and it turned out he was never in danger of selling it anyway. "You knew I'd crack."

"Not for sure." She glanced at her husband who was grinning so hard his beard was sticking out. "Ray was really nervous."

"No, I wasn't." He got up from the chair and joined them, thumped Jack on the back. "Good job, Jack."

He shook his head. "*Et tu,* Ray?"

"I knew you couldn't sell the old girl. Got to keep a Brattle in the Brattle home."

Jack gestured to the papers on the desk. "Forgeries? Boilerplate?"

"A few forms from the Internet." The not-lawyer Paul fanned them out on the wooden table. "Mostly blanks."

Yup. Mostly blanks. He still couldn't quite take this all in. He was relieved and annoyed and happy and something else he couldn't quite get a handle on.

"Come eat. A celebration dinner is set up in here."

He let Rita pull him toward the dining room, still stunned, not only by the trick, but by his own inability to sell the house. "Rita, how did you come up with this scheme? It's not like you to be so sneaky."

"No, it isn't." She grinned at him. "Jack, dear. Your fun is only just beginning. I was all for convincing you not to sell, but the setup wasn't my idea."

"Then who—"

"Aren't you going to come in?" A familiar female voice spoke from his—*his*—dining room. "Food's getting cold."

He froze for two beats, then turned abruptly away from giggling Rita and walked through the doorway. Hannah stood next to the huge table his family had only used on major holidays or for the rare times they'd entertained, wearing jeans, a soft blue sweater that matched her eyes and a nervously welcoming smile. He'd never seen anything more beautiful in his life.

Why was she here? To see the fun? Watch him be on the receiving end of a revenge joke like the one he pulled on her? Or to ask those damn interview questions?

Or…

He couldn't ask in front of everyone. He'd have to play along for now.

"Hello, Derek."

He put his hands in his pockets and gazed at her. "It's Jack."

"Oh, it's *Jack* now?"

"Yes." He hid a cringe. "From now on, Hannah."

"What happened to Derek?"

"Ah, very sad. A fatal illness."

"Ooh." She winced. "Terrible."

"So that charade…" He pointed back over his shoulder. "That was your idea?"

"Rita called me." She smiled at Rita who'd come to stand beside him, that smile women share when they acknowledge between themselves what idiots men are. "She said you needed rescuing from yourself."

"Is that so?" He displayed his best tough-guy face to Rita who shrugged.

"You heard it here."

"So you lured me here under false pretenses." He turned back to Hannah, pretending outrage. "How could you?"

"Yeah, imagine that," she said wryly. "Can't think of *anyone* who would do something that low."

He ambled around to the other side of the table, wanting to touch her, wanting to talk to her in private, but doomed apparently to sharing a meal celebrating his purchase of his own house. "I hear you have more questions for me."

"Oh. Yes."

"For the interview?"

"Yes."

He dragged his eyes away from her, unable to gauge her mood or intentions, aware it was ridiculous to expect her to say, *Forget the interview, I just want you,* when there were four other people with carefully discreet eyes on the Hannah and Jack show.

Frowning, he stared at the meal until he registered what he was seeing and started to laugh.

Deviled eggs, pigs in blankets, tuna macaroni salad, chips, baked beans, all on colored plastic platters he'd never seen before. Bottles of orange soda and root beer. And a bakery cake that said Welcome Home in translucent green icing script on blindingly white frosting.

The most fabulous spread he'd ever seen. "Wow. This looks amazing."

"Rita helped me." Hannah came closer to the table and to him, which made him want to cart her off away from these people and this occasion and make love to her until time ended or he stopped wanting to, which could be a close call.

"Ha! I did nothing but supply our highest quality plastic." Rita waved her comment away. "Dig in, everyone."

"I'm starving." Daphne led Paul to the table. "Bad acting takes a lot out of me."

They ate around the table on paper plates with plastic utensils, laughing and talking. Jack joined in superficially, preoccupied with the situation involving Hannah. Judging by the numerous concerned glances shot in his and her direction from the other side of the table, he wasn't the only one. He tried to keep his own gaze on his food and on his friends, but the need to remind himself Hannah was really there, that she'd really materialized to help make sure he stayed in town—for whatever reason—made it nearly impossible not to stare, not to drink in the sight of her. When she spilled baked beans down her beautiful femininely curving front, it was all he could do not to offer his hands to clean her up.

Finally the last piece of achingly sweet cake had been eaten, the last drop of sugary soda swallowed. Rita and Ray cleaned up with lightning speed, refusing offers of help, then pointedly stayed in the kitchen. Daphne and Paul chatted briefly, made their excuses and left for some dubious appointment in an apparent hurry.

Obviously he and Hannah were supposed to talk alone. He couldn't be more grateful.

"Well."

"So." She smiled, this time with an undercurrent of anxiety. Was she afraid he'd want more or afraid he wouldn't?

He felt himself starting to shut down, to retreat into the protection of impassivity.

No. No. Not anymore.

"Come with me." He got up, took her hand. "Can you do stairs or do you need the elevator?"

"Stairs are fine if we go slowly. Where are we going?"

"You'll see." On the second floor he gestured her toward the continuation of the staircase. "One more."

"Upstairs? To your old room?"

"Yes."

"Why?"

"To play."

She stopped on the staircase. "To play."

"Yup." He gave in to his need to touch her, put his arm around her waist to make her climb easier. Yeah, that was it. Purely thinking of her comfort. "Bet I can beat you at Ping-Pong."

"Ha!" Her head snapped around; she glared at him, eyes shining. "No way. I was a Ping-Pong champion in my high school."

"You were?"

"No." She wrinkled her nose. "Sounded good, though, didn't it?"

"You had me seriously worried." He guided her through to the Ping-Pong room, feeling giddy, as if he'd had a bottle of champagne.

"Prepare to lose." He grabbed a ball and bounced it off the table a few times, then narrowed his eyes threateningly. "No, worse. Prepare to be humiliated."

As it happened, the humiliation was nearly his. Hannah played a mean game, and they were neck and neck to the end until he finally hit a shot she couldn't reach.

"Ha! Mine!"

"Oh, sure, you beat a cripple, congratulations." She put her paddle down, jammed her hands on her hips. "But there is no way you can beat me at pool."

She was right. He didn't have a chance. He also lost at checkers, gin rummy and even at Sorry! He'd never had this much fun, he was sure of it. At some point he'd have to get serious, but right now this time together was too perfect, too right. If nothing else, if she was still hesitating, this reminder of how good they were together couldn't hurt.

"Karaoke time." He strode from the game room toward the party music room.

"Oh, no." Hannah hung back, shaking her head. "You're not getting me to sing. No way."

"Oh, what, so I have to lose at games I'm bad at, but you don't?"

"You can't be *bad* at Sorry!" She limped into the room with him. "Just unlucky. Which also describes anyone who has heard me sing. You've never had that displeasure."

"No, I haven't." He turned on the machine, which sprang to life how many years after its last use? "But I'm about to."

"Derek—"

"Jack."

"Jack." She beamed at him. "Jack Brattle."

"Oh, by the way, that's me. Did I mention that?"

Her laughter lifted him impossibly higher. He knew without a doubt that if she gave them a chance, a hundred years with this woman wasn't going to be enough. "I think so. One of those Spider-Man-to-Mary Jane, Superman-to-Lois Lane confession scenes about the secret identity."

"Sing, Lois." He handed her the microphone.

"Jack, I am not going to—"

"Yes, you are. Here. I picked this just for you." He started the song "Wind Beneath My Wings," backed up and sat expectantly.

Hannah covered her mouth with her hand, the blush spreading up her cheeks. "Oh, man. This is going to be horrible."

"Go."

"Okay, okay. But remember, you asked for this." She started to sing. Or something close to it. Pitch was not her strength. Or tone. Or rhythm. But she stood there for him and sang because he wanted her to, and he didn't think he'd ever loved her as much as he did right then.

The final note she held, a quarter tone flat and wobbling, until the music ended, then put the microphone down in obvious relief. "No matter how long I know you, I am never ever doing that again, so don't even think about asking me."

"Yeah, um, I think you're safe there." He winked and stood to take her place.

She laughed again, face pink, and when she passed him on the way to the spectator seat, it was all he could do not to haul her into his arms and kiss her. But they had a few things to talk over first, and if he started kissing her now, he wasn't going to stop.

He selected a CD, skipped to the last song, "I've Got You Under My Skin," turned up the volume and, praying he didn't make a fool of himself, then suddenly not caring, he sang his heart out.

She giggled nervously at first, seeming unsure where to look. Yes, the moment was pretty sappy, but it was their moment. He walked toward her, holding her gaze, making her understand that this wasn't about the performance, that he meant every word. *So deep you're really a part of me.*

If she was just here for more interview questions, if she didn't want him, okay, but at least he hadn't hidden in safety. He was taking the risk, letting her know how he still felt, that his offer of sharing his life still held, for however long they lasted—and he'd bet on forever.

He reached her, knelt in front of her, laid the microphone on the floor, took her hands, sang the last line of the song, "…under…my…skin."

The music stopped. He waited, watching her. She wasn't laughing. That was good. She wasn't pushing him away. Also good. She looked unsettled, a bit uncertain. He didn't know if that was good or not. A tear appeared in the corner of one mesmerizing blue eye. She shook her head, closing her eyes, and it trailed down her beautiful flushed cheek.

"That was…incredible, Jack. I didn't know you could sing."

"Aw, c'mon." He brushed the tear away, rose and drew her to standing, bent to kiss her forehead, her cheeks. "It's just that after you anyone would sound like Pavarotti."

Hannah burst out laughing, face lit with delight, and his patience ran out. He cupped the back of her head and brought her mouth to his, kissed the laughter out of her until she was clinging to him, panting and sweet.

Then she wrapped her arms around his neck, pressed close and the sweetness was replaced by desire so hot he had to breathe deeply to keep from ravishing her.

"Jack." She tipped her head back to give him better access to her smooth throat. "Make love to me."

"You sure?"

"Oh, yes."

"You're not just here for the interview?"

"Are you serious?" She drew back and gave him an annoyed look. "You're not going to start that sex-for-interview stuff again."

"I want to hear it."

"I don't care if the interview never runs. I just want you."

He grinned, couldn't stop, took both of her hands into his and kissed them together. "That'll work."

"Did you miss the whole symbolism of the meal downstairs?"

"Lowbrow…" He looked to her for further explanation.

"And highbrow. Deviled eggs in a mansion. You and me. Together. See how it works?"

"Do I have to eat that kind of cake? Ever again? Because it was horrible."

She giggled and put her arms back around him where they belonged. "No, but you have to make love to me nearly every day."

"Oh. No." He spoke with flat exaggeration, rolling his eyes. "Anything but that."

"Jack…" She was looking at him seriously now. "Do you want me to run the interview?"

He already knew the answer. "Yes."

"Really?"

"Will you be here with me to share the fallout?"

"Try and get rid of me."

"Not on your life. And, yes, really." The decision was made, what's more, she'd let him make it. It was time for Jack Brattle's life to start. "Now that's settled. What were you saying earlier?"

"About the interview?" She blinked innocently.

"Nope. Before that."

"The cake?"

"Hmm, no. Not that, either." He lifted her sweater, ran his hands up and down her smooth firm skin. "Before."

"Oh, wow, I'm not sure I remember…" She moved seductively against his fly. "Maybe it will come to me."

"Maybe it will come in you."

"Yes, please," she whispered. "Yes, please, Jack."

He undressed her reverently, kissing the skin he uncovered, kneeling to taste where he couldn't resist tasting, so full of emotion at being able to be with her like this that he felt more humble than when she'd beaten him at pretty much everything.

And when she was beautifully and totally naked, he picked her up and carried her to his childhood bed, where he'd spent many adolescent nights dreaming of exactly this scenario—only completely without a clue as to details.

"I missed you." He laid her on the navy-and-white geometric quilt, smiled down at her, taking off his jacket.

"I missed you, too."

"Hmm." He got rid of his shoes, socks, pants. "Disappearing is a strange way of showing it."

"I know." She stroked his thighs, trailed gentle fingers around his hips while he took off his shirt, her face troubled. "At first I felt I was being stronger by leaving you. I was sick and tired of feeling weak with men. Then I realized it wasn't a question of strength, it was a question of getting out of the rut of my own perception and welcoming yours in. Did you read my Lowbrow column?"

"Of course." He shed the rest of his clothes and joined her on the bed, hardly daring to believe he could hold her again.

"Did you get the message?"

"I thought so. When you didn't answer my call, and didn't leave me any way to reach you, I thought…well, I didn't know what to think."

"I wanted to tell you in the column first. And then, um, Rita called me, and by that time…"

He shook his head. "Scheming wench. You knew you'd get me tonight."

"I certainly hoped I'd get you, yes." She pulled his head down for a kiss. He fitted himself to her body, his erection, in its usual base way, desperate to cut to the chase.

"I have a condom in the night table." He whispered into her hair, kissing the strands, inhaling the sweet citrus-Hannah scent.

"Oh, good."

"From the eighties."

She cracked up. "Oh, bad."

"I have a suggestion." He raised up and gazed at her tenderly, drew his hand down between her breasts, lingering over her stomach. "I've used condoms consistently with other women."

She drew in a slow breath, met his eyes and nodded. "I tested clean after my last boyfriend cheated. And I can't get pregnant right now."

"I want this relationship to last a lifetime, Hannah." He took her hand, watching carefully for her reaction.

"I want that, too." Her eyes filled up, but he didn't feel the need to comfort her for those tears.

"Hannah, will you…" he kissed the tip of one finger and gave her an overly sappy stare "…not use a condom with me?"

Her giggles stopped the tears. "I do."

She did. He kissed her, then forgot to stop kissing her, or maybe he was unable to. He touched her everywhere, wanting to own her, to make sure she knew her body belonged to him and only him. Until she wriggled down and her lips surrounded his penis. She sucked in the length of him, then back, then in again, and his caveman impulses were reduced to nothing.

Never mind. He was hers. Completely and helplessly hers, giving in to the pleasure of her mouth on him until he sensed his climax approaching too soon.

"Up here, with me." He took her gently by the shoulders and shifted her back up next to him. "Are you ready?"

"Oh, yes." She spread her legs, naked to him. He moved over her, his erection naked to her, and his heart swelled. They were committing to each other, in a way modern times made significant. He didn't think he could be happier.

Except when he slid slowly inside her, skin to skin, and he realized he could be.

"I love you." The words came out of him before he'd planned to say them. "It's improbable, impossible, insane, but I fell in love with you first through your words. Meeting you only made it official."

"I fell in love with you at first sight, too, Jack." She took a shuddering breath, hugged him to her, buried her face in his neck. "Then, of course, I had to fall in love with Derek, and then with you *again,* but I managed."

"Wow." He smiled and kissed her temple. "So we're actually having a threesome?"

"No." She moaned as he began to move faster. "It's just you and me, Jack Brattle."

"Well, Ms. Hannah O'Reilly." He slid his hands under her perfect ass and made her moan again. "It's pretty risky to commit like this when we don't know each other well. Only twenty-four hours together."

"I know." She opened her eyes, looked deeply into his as he moved inside her. "It's crazy, spontaneous, wild."

"Any doubts?"

"About diving right in?" She smiled and wrapped her legs around his back. "Not a single one."

Epilogue

Transcript of the *Laina Live* show, October 24, Channel 25

Laina: Hello, and welcome to *Laina Live!* I have two very special guests today whose names you know, though you might not know their faces quite as well, since most of the public has only met them on the written page. Mr. Jack Brattle and Ms. Hannah O'Reilly. Welcome to the show!

Jack: Hi, Laina.

Hannah: We're glad to be here.

Laina: So these two have a *stupendously* fascinating past and a totally made-for-movie romance. Unless you lived under a rock for the past year, you already know it. He tricked her into showing up at his house, the frog turned out to be a prince, and they're on their way to happy ever after. Let me start off with you, Hannah. You wrote the article that introduced Jack Brattle to the world. That was *such* a big deal, it seems like every paper in the universe ran it. Now rumor has it you're on the shortlist for the *Pulitzer!* How does that feel?

Hannah: Like there has to be some mistake? No, actually it's amazing. I'm thrilled and terrified.

Laina: I have to tell this audience that if you haven't read the article, *go find it* online. It's so, so much more than a celebrity tell-all. Hannah tackles money issues, social responsibility issues, class issues, materialism, the importance of living life to its fullest, she even takes America to task over its obsession with celebrity. Just a really, really deep article. Go read it. *Go! Now!*

Hannah: Thank you.

Laina: Jack, did you expect the article to be that far-reaching?

Jack: I knew Hannah would write a good article. I watched her slave over it. So I expected to be impressed, but even so, I was blown away. It meant a lot to me.

Laina: I'll say. It meant you were suddenly in the public eye where we hadn't seen a Brattle since your father, right?

Jack: Yes, he enjoyed the attention.

Laina: And you didn't. So how has the fallout been for you?

Jack: At times overwhelming. I thought I was prepared, but you can't really understand what it's like to live under a microscope until you have to do it. I have no idea why anyone would want to do a reality TV show.

Laina: Not lining up for that any time soon, huh?

Jack: Uh, no. I'm living it now, and it's plenty.

Laina: Jack, I know you hid yourself away for a lot of years especially after your father's death. Do you regret that now? Or do you wish you were still in hiding?

Jack: There are moments I wish I could go back to being anonymous. But it was time to own up to who I am and take the responsibilities that came with that. Hiding was safer, but I was living someone else's life. I don't regret the decision to own up to my name. And Hannah has been there for me, so I'm not going it alone.

Laina: Yeah, so what's it been like for you, Hannah, to be a total and complete *star* by association?

Hannah: There are days I really feel for all those celebrities who've ever punched out a paparazzo. But most days I take a deep breath and remind myself that in the big picture, this is what we want, and they can't possibly want to film us walking down the street to buy tissues and dog food forever.

Laina: Now it's everyone's absolute *favorite* part of your story that you two are involved with each other, after the dueling columns in the newspapers, et cetera, et cetera. How do you think your relationship affected the Jack Brattle article, Hannah?

Hannah: I was definitely able to get to know Jack better than if I were just his interviewer. I don't recommend every reporter try to get that close to her subject, but in this case it brought me a truly intimate understanding of what his life had been like as a kid, how that upbringing and his parents' tragedies affected him, then and now, and the struggles he was fighting for so many years. I got to see all that in his decisions and choices as they related to me. I admire him a lot for deciding to take the step of going public.

Laina: Sounds like he's an inspiration.

Hannah: Oh, definitely. At the risk of sounding like a bride-to-be cliché, he's the most amazing man I've ever met.

Laina: Aww. Say it with me, audience. *Aww.* And, Jack, she's inspired you, too, can you tell us how?

Jack: She inspired me to stop hiding from my life.

Laina: Oh, that deserves another very sincere "Aww." Can we get it audience? *Aww.* Good job, thank you. Now, Hannah *what* is your next article on?

Hannah: I'm investigating some promising medications that should be available to the general public—but aren't.

Laina: I'm not allowed to ask more, am I?

Hannah: No, sorry!

Laina: And, of course, what we all want to know is about your wedding plans.

Jack: We're getting married next June. And that's all I'm going to—

Hannah: The Philadelphia Cathedral on June 8. Everyone's invited.

Jack: *Hannah.*

Hannah: What, you can't afford it?

Jack: (Unintelligible mutter.) The reception is private anyway.

Hannah: Yes. Caviar and onion soup-mix dip for a hundred.

Jack: Filet mignon and hot dogs.

Hannah: Chili dogs, mmm.

Laina: It is to die for! Well, Hannah and Jack, I have a million more questions, but we're out of time. We wish you many, many years of happiness together. It's wonderful to have the Brattles as an active part of Philadelphia again.

Jack: Thank you, Laina.

Hannah: Thanks for having us.

Laina: This is *Laina Live*, you all come back after this commercial break 'cuz *I will still be here!*

* * * * *

UNBRIDLED & MIDNIGHT RESOLUTIONS
(2-IN-1 ANTHOLOGY)

BY TORI CARRINGTON & KATHLEEN O'REILLY

Unbridled

Former Marine Carter is staying away from the one thing that's always got him into trouble –women! Unfortunately his sexy new lawyer Laney is making that very difficult.

Midnight Resolutions

A sudden, unexpected kiss between two strangers in Times Square on New Year's Eve turns unforgettable and soon Rose and Ian's sexy affair is red-hot despite the frosty weather...

CHRISTMAS MALE
BY CARA SUMMERS

All policewoman Fiona wants for Christmas is a little excitement. But once she finds herself working a case with gorgeous army captain Campbell she's suddenly aching for a different kind of thrill...

BETTER NAUGHTY THAN NICE
BY VICKI LEWIS THOMPSON, JILL SHALVIS & RHONDA NELSON
(3-IN-1 ANTHOLOGY)

Mischievous Damon Claus is determined to mess things up for his brother Santa. Who'd ever guess that sibling rivalry would result in sensual mistletoe madness for three unsuspecting couples?

**On sale from 19th November 2010
Don't miss out!**

*Available at WHSmith, Tesco, ASDA, Eason
and all good bookshops*

www.millsandboon.co.uk

THE *Balfour* LEGACY

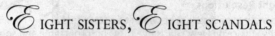

EIGHT SISTERS, EIGHT SCANDALS

VOLUME 5 – OCTOBER 2010
Zoe's Lesson
by Kate Hewitt

VOLUME 6 – NOVEMBER 2010
Annie's Secret
by Carole Mortimer

VOLUME 7 – DECEMBER 2010
Bella's Disgrace
by Sarah Morgan

VOLUME 8 – JANUARY 2011
Olivia's Awakening
by Margaret Way

8 VOLUMES IN ALL TO COLLECT!

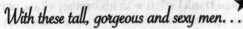

All the magic you'll need this Christmas...

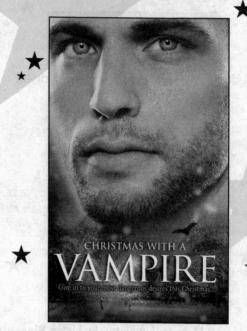

2 FREE BOOKS
AND A SURPRISE GIFT

We would like to take this opportunity to thank you for reading this Mills & Boon® book by offering you the chance to take TWO more specially selected titles from the Blaze® series absolutely FREE! We're also making this offer to introduce you to the benefits of the Mills & Boon® Book Club™—

- **FREE home delivery**
- **FREE gifts and competitions**
- **FREE monthly Newsletter**
- **Exclusive Mills & Boon Book Club offers**
- **Books available before they're in the shops**

Accepting these FREE books and gift places you under no obligation to buy, you may cancel at any time, even after receiving your free books. Simply complete your details below and return the entire page to the address below. You don't even need a stamp!

YES Please send me 2 free Blaze books and a surprise gift. I understand that unless you hear from me, I will receive 3 superb new books every month, including a 2-in-1 book priced at £5.30 and two single books priced at £3.30 each, postage and packing free. I am under no obligation to purchase any books and may cancel my subscription at any time. The free books and gift will be mine to keep in any case.

Ms/Mrs/Miss/Mr_____ Initials _____

Surname _____

Address _____

_____ Postcode _____

E-mail _____

Send this whole page to: Mills & Boon Book Club, Free Book Offer, FREEPOST NAT 10298, Richmond, TW9 1BR